JOHN PENROSE

J. C. TREGARTHEN

JOHN PENROSE

A Romance of the Land's End

CORNWALL EDITIONS LIMITED

FOWEY

CORNWALL EDITIONS LIMITED
8 Langurtho Road
Fowey Cornwall PL23 1EQ UK
Telephone: 01726 832483
email: cornwalleditions@cornishinternet.com
www.cornwalleditions.co.uk
Publisher: Ian Grant

First published in 1923 by John Murray
This edition first published in the United Kingdom in 2004 by
Cornwall Editions Limited

ISBN 1-904880-02-9

Cover photograph: 'His First Catch' by Edwin Harris (1855 - 1906),
Whitford and Hughes, London, UK/www.bridgeman.co.uk

Typeset in Minion MM 367 Regular
Cover and text design by Asterisk Design and Editorial Solutions, Cornwall
Art Director: Roger Bristow
Editorial Director: Yvonne McFarlane

Printed and bound in the United Kingdom by Short Run Press, Exeter
Papers used by Cornwall Editions are natural, recyclable products made from wood grown in
sustainable forests; the manufacturing processes conform to the environmental regulations
of the country of origin

AS A SLIGHT EXPRESSION OF ESTEEM FOR STERLING GOODNESS
OF HEART, OF ADMIRATION FOR PROFOUND INSIGHT
INTO CHARACTER AND DISTINGUISHED LITERARY
SKILL, OF PERSONAL GRATITUDE FOR MANY
ACTS OF KINDNESS, THIS SIMPLE
STORY IS DEDICATED TO
MARIE CORELLI

CONTENTS

INTRODUCTION

by Bert Biscoe

Bert Biscoe is a Cornishman and lives with his family in Truro. He toured widely as a professional musician with a number of bands before being drawn back to Cornwall. A poet, songwriter and Cornish politician, he is a champion of Cornish literature. As a bard of the Cornish Gorsedh with the name Vyager gans Geryow *(Travels with Words), he writes poems, tales and songs about Cornwall, performing regularly at Cornish festivals and other cultural events. Drawn to J.C. Tregarthen's portrayal of the natural world and man's relationship with it, he is eager to promote the rediscovery of 'this tremendous literary treasure'.*

John Coulson Tregarthen was born in 1855 at Penzance. His family had come from the Isles of Scilly where 'Tregarthens' is still a well-known hotel on St Mary's. He gained an honours degree in Mathematics at London University in 1878 and became a maths teacher at Trinity School, Stratford-upon-Avon. Within a few years he had bought the school and made such a success of it that, in his late forties, he was able to sell it to the popular romantic novelist, Marie Corelli, and retire. He returned with his wife to Cornwall, to the Land's End he knew so well and loved so deeply. Over six feet tall, 'upright as a bolt and of a ruddy countenance', he was too youthful and energetic to retire completely. A remarkably gifted field naturalist, he spent his time studying nature, and began writing, encouraged by Miss Corelli who recommended him to her publisher, John Murray. Thus, J.C. Tregarthen's career as an author began, and it is to Marie Corelli, his mentor and close friend, that he dedicated many of his books, including *John Penrose*.

In 1928, the Cornish Gorsedh convened for the first time in the modern era at Boscawen-un in Penwith. An ancient 'college' of bards, revived by a band of scholars, artists, linguists and cultural activists to stimulate and celebrate the Celtic roots and aspirations of a new, emerging post-industrial Cornish identity, the Gorsedh sprang out of the burgeoning 'Old Cornwall' movement, whose aim was to promote the revival of the Cornish language. Amongst the bards who stood in the Circle at Boscawen-un to proclaim their commitment to Cornwall and to celebrate the richness of Cornwall's Celtic character was J.C. Tregarthen.

The establishment of the Gorsedh was a seminal moment in Cornwall's long and admirable struggle to develop a renewed sense of herself which, like the Phoenix, was arising out of the increasingly moribund ashes of the first major socio-economic 'crash' of the Industrial Revolution the previous century. In facing up to this (at that time) incredible phenomenon, the Cornish were characteristically resourceful, worldly and inventive. Economically, in the nineteenth century, the working population of Cornwall transformed itself into a skilled global taskforce.

The strength of cultural bonds meant that, wherever Cornish people went, they formed communities, built societies, used their speech, and shaped institutions. Many Cornish people emigrated to the 'new worlds' in order to escape the organised suppression of religious non-conformity, and in so doing, brought a powerful and well-honed set of liberal, egalitarian values to their quickly emerging, multi-cultural societies. As a result, in the annals of the Americas, the Antipodes and Africa are to be found Cornish names carved into the historical record.

Above all things, Cornish people treasure and refer back to the land that holds their roots. Despite Darwin, genetic modification and the Industrial Revolution, nature remains enigmatic: for all the explaining and dissection, it has at its core an indefinable quality, which might be described by some as 'magic'. It is a fool who challenges this instinctively grounded fact. There is something mesmeric, life-enhancing and beyond reason that instils nature with beauty, making it the reference in our conscious life for a massive metaphor which unlocks our comprehension of the scheme of things. Equally, it is the 'magic' of Cornwall that calls us home, that inspires us, that is, for myriad reasons, a root, a reference, and most of all the 'place' for those who define themselves in their own eyes and hearts as Cornish. This rooting is part of nature; part of the metaphor.

Alongside J.C. Tregarthen, the gathering of talented and forward-looking bards at the inaugural Gorsedh included 'Q', Sir Arthur Quiller Couch, the academic, novelist, poet and educationalist; Henry Jenner, the Father of the Cornish Language Revival, and his mercurial colleague and linguist, Robert Morton Nance; Michael Cardew, the founder of a great Cornish dynasty of craft potters; A.K. Hamilton Jenkin, social historian; and, not least, Charles Henderson – the father of modern Cornish history.

Tregarthen took as his bardic name *Mylgarer* (Lover of Wild Animals). He was by this time an acclaimed author of a number of best-selling books chronicling the life of larger mammals such as the fox, hare and badger. He had been able to transform his careful observations of these creatures in the setting of his native Penwith into narratives that capture the character of the beasts, and portray their lives in emotional terms (that is, in terms of an otter's or fox's life having 'ups and downs', joys and sorrows). Through his understanding of nature and with his narrative skills, he was able to evoke that particular 'magic' and to take his reader into it in an almost real way. In this, as a Cornishman, he offers us an insight into the nineteenth-century world that he was trying to capture before it slipped inexorably away, together with a glimpse of the essential nature of Cornwall which transcends the make-overs of time passing. Tregarthen, at his best, gets to the heart of Cornwall, because he relates the physical world to ethical values.

He is not beguiled by any misplaced sentimentality – his tales invariably involve death, and quite often and unashamedly, death at the hands of a hunt. He is not necessarily an apologist for hunting, but he is, rather, a realist who acknowledges that the hunt represented a major predatorial threat to larger mammals in the late Victorian and Edwardian periods. He acknowledges that the instinct to hunt is one that we, being human animals, have to deal with in ourselves. He understands that, for the hunter to comprehend the consequences of hunting, he (or the otter, or the badger) needs to understand what it is to be hunted.

Tregarthen stood with his worthy contemporaries at Boscawen-un to launch an institution and ritually state a set of values that have come to have a deep effect on how Cornwall is developing today, and how she is perceived by those who care to notice her all around the world. With the advent of the Internet, the recognition that Cornwall is a focal point of identity for millions of descendants of erstwhile emigrants has brought a new and exciting opportunity, as well as a responsibility to ensure that the Cornwall we build remains a cultural and genealogical focus for its evolving global community. Tregarthen captured the landscape, the character, the sounds and the drama of life in Cornwall, whether in his Homeric dramatisation of the life of an otter, or in the romance of John Penrose. This is his gift to our whole community. He knew only too well how many Cornish hearts beat overseas; he offers them the intimate world of the moor, the warm place at the hearth at 'home'. He was one of those who made the Gorsedh emerge as a catalyst for Cornish life and evolution.

Here I must acknowledge my indebtedness to Dr Arnold Derrington of Pendeen, or *Carer Penwyth*, to give him his bardic name. It was through a casual conversation with Dr Derrington during a Gorsedh tea (one of the truly Cornish events of the calendar!) that I discovered Tregarthen's work. I am grateful to Dr Derrington (who has spent many years researching Tregarthen's life and work and has given many lectures and talks about him to audiences all over the country) for directing me towards this tremendous literary treasure. Tregarthen laid the foundations, along with many other strands of Cornish cultural endeavour, for the richness of identity, creativity and cultural flowering that today enriches and distinguishes Cornwall. Dr Derrington shares Tregarthen's love of the undergrowth and the life that lurks there, and the human spirit that endows Penwith, and it is his championship of this overshadowed but most engaging of Cornish writers that is slowly leading to Tregarthen's rediscovery.

John Penrose is Tregarthen's first novel. Written in the form of an autobiography, it shares many characteristics with his other writing – not least a detailed and acutely observed landscape; a finely tuned ear for Cornish dialect; a strong sense of Cornwall as a place in a wider and opportunity-laden world combined with a love of the hearth; a certain element of roguishness bound up in a complex package with high moral values; a commitment to family; a search for a social order in which justice, fairness and merit eclipse privilege and patronage and where equality is paramount.

For many, *John Penrose* will portray a world that their ancestors left to seek their fortunes. It will put flesh on the bones of letters, photographs, lists and leases and provide a picture of the moor, the farmyard, the market, the interior of the cottage, the school-room that is rooted in an unsentimental but nonetheless loving observation. In a sense, Tregarthen brings his powers as a naturalist to bear on the human habitat of Penwith in the nineteenth century, offering us a rare and revealing set of insights.

John Penrose is a well-crafted novel, a product of the same early-twentieth-century period that gave us the 'Penhale' Trilogy of Crosbie Garstin, the works of 'Q' and others. One of the aspects of Cornish cultural development that was to mark this period, as much as the language revival or the academic study of history or the battle to 'gather the fragments lest they be lost', was a flowering of native literature in the adopted English language, a literature that celebrates the diversity of dialect and portrays Cornish heroes in Cornish stories. This was a nationally acknowledged regional genre, which explains why these authors attracted major publishing houses such as John Murray. Tregarthen is a major figure in this and his re-emergence at this time is more than timely.

In another way, Tregarthen's desire to chronicle journeys through life might be taken to be metaphorical, and to draw upon an ancient bardic tradition, with which he clearly sensed some affinity. In this he shared something with the great John Harris, the Dolcoath poet, whose expeditions to Kynance and Land's End inspired major works in the earlier nineteenth century.

I hope that in providing an opportunity for a modern audience to experience *John Penrose*, we can look forward to renewed interest in Tregarthen's other works. Tregarthen was a native of Penwith but a citizen of nature, of the world. He offers a relationship between man and nature in which respect born out of meticulous observation leads to a harmony of coexistence which is profoundly real – it is a relationship to which we can (and ought to) all aspire. In John Penrose he finds a character flawed and noble, roguish and honourable, who is as fascinating as the otter or the badger. He lays out the hard, poor, yet enriching world around Madron and Penzance in a chronicle that contains a series of universal truths. These, above all, make *John Penrose* both an excellently moving read and an intelligent insight into a natural world of which man is but a creature part.

Tregarthen died in 1933; the same year as Charles Henderson. His life and work spanned the era of industrial collapse and the development of the modern economy, with all the concrete, brick, invasive land-management and social change that goes with it. During this period, old certainties died. Henderson battled to capture the human story of Cornwall. Tregarthen fought to secure the dignity and freedom of nature, whether on the moors and clifftops or in the hearts of his people.

Both battles continue.

Bert Biscoe
Truro, 2004

CHAPTER I

JOHN'S PARENTAGE

❧

I
T IS A LITTLE SHORT OF WONDERFUL what a word or two spoken in season may stir even an old man to do, if only they touch his pride. I say
this with meaning, for Parson Boulay chancing to remark last Sunday,
a bit slightingly I thought, "the poor pass away leaving no memorial," I said
to myself, "Passun, you're wrong for once! that is if I live a twelve-month
and the rheumatics keep to my legs," and, then and there, I made up my
mind that I would set-to in real earnest, and jot down my own experiences;
not out of mere contrariness – no, no, not that – but in the hope that they
may raise a smile, perhaps draw a tear when I am dead and gone.

And if any reader of an independent turn think me too much under
pulpit influence to be worth going on with, I beg to tell him the vicar struck
a spark that lit on a place already smouldering, for an inner voice had been
repeating over and over till I was sick to death of hearing it, "John Penrose,
you've time on your hands and a story to tell – put it to paper." Off and on
this has been plaguing me and setting the spirit fretting against idleness,
and it seems likely to drive me out of my senses unless I fall to and lay the
voice by doing what it directs. And, after all, the advice is reasonable
enough up to a certain point. For time on my hands I have, a great deal too
much for one of my active brain and energetic body, and education far
above most in my state of life. As to the story being worth the telling, let
others judge; but whether or no, the putting it to paper is a difficulty, and
that no mean one. I know it well, for five weeks ago come to-morrow, driv-
en almost mazed by the parrot cry, I sat down and tried my hand; but, oh
dear! only to find the task that terrible tough as to make me shy of pen and
paper ever since. But thanks to the vicar and his pointed tongue, here I am
once more in father's chair, with mother's pastry board rigged up for desk,
determined this time to go through with my story and, God giving me the
courage, to make a clean breast of the life I have led. And I beg all and
sundry to judge its crooked ways as tenderly as they can, remembering
always the waywardness of man's nature.

When my lineage is considered, that I should have turned out as I did
will seem almost unaccountable. I come of the best of poor parents, father

1

having been reckoned a steady man as farm labourers go, and never the worse for drink except perhaps on Fair Day, with the hurdy-gurdies going and everybody overstepping the mark a bit, or at "guldice," as we call the harvest supper, and then never so far gone as not to be able to find the farm-yard gate and pick his way over the rough ground to the cottage. These occasions, and one Feast Day when his brother Stephen was home from California, were the only times he forgot himself and, to tell the truth, they were about as much as his pocket could stand. The rest of the year, work and supper over, he sat by his own fireside, chatting with mother or – a thing he dearly loved – listening to her read, and never without a pipe in his mouth, for he liked his smoke.

The only exception was on Friday, when he went to Madron Churchtown for bell-practice, as he had done ever since he came of age. Like his father before him, he rang the tenor bell, and seldom missed practice on weekdays or service on Sunday, he was that regular; not in bell-ringing only, but in everything he set his hand to. For he was dependable man and trustworthy, contented too with his lot, envying no man, regretting nothing except that he could not read or write.

This we knew from a word or two he would let fall on the way home along after service; not every Sunday I do not mean, but once in a while, as when the hymns were all new and he had to stand like one mum because he could not read the words. He used to slip into church after the bell stopped, and sat by mother and me in our seat at the back of the nave, close handy to the belfry. Of course he joined in where he felt he safely could, and he liked to sing the hymns that were familiar to him. The rest of the time he listened to mother, who did her part all the way through, taking verse and verse with the parson in the psalms and speaking the words, so Jim Beare, the sexton, said, as clear as the squire's lady and, if anything, finishing up the long verses a trifle the stronger.

There is no need to say anything more of father for the present, only this, that he was in the Foresters, and one of the two – Josiah Berryman, of Carnequidden, being the other – who carried the big banner through the streets of Penzance on gala days. I thought a deal of father for that, and the very first time I was taken to Penzance was to see him march past at the Fête of the "Queen of the West" Court.

We left home as soon as father had seen to things and given orders to Bill Shellal, the other farm-hand, what to do whilst he was away, and of course after he had changed into his Sunday clothes and black billy-cock hat, taken from the bandbox under the bed. Mother wore her Leghorn bonnet, with white frill and strings to match, tied in a bow under her chin, a small cape and a print dress with little bunches of wild roses all over it. I had a new Scotch cap that day, and a new jacket of mother's knitting, and rode into Penzance on my father's shoulder. And as if the burden of me was not enough, mother has told me that I kept asking questions all the way: as to how a donkey could eat thistles without pricking his mouth, how the capstone was got up on the legs of the Quoit, how much the sea was deeper than our mill-pool, and – when we got into Penzance – why the doors had brass ornaments on them?

Mother and I took our stand close to Branwell's Corner, as was agreed upon with father before we parted company in Alverton Lane, where the procession was being formed up near the "First and Last." We were in the front row of the crowd that filled the street, leaving just room enough for the Foresters to pass; and that passage would have been choked had not the constable come along and cleared it.

Everybody was talking; the buzz of conversation was for all the world like the noise when all the bees are out, only much louder, and, though it was a long wait that we had, the noise never seemed to die down, so that I had to shout in mother's ear every time I asked when the Foresters were coming. At last we heard a band strike up; the music got louder and louder, and presently a tall man standing behind said, "Thank the Lord, they're coming at last." And come they did, in a brave body sure enough; first the band blowing brass trumpets, with the drummer-man beating the big drum, and, close behind him, father, in green sash and white rosette, holding a pole of the Court banner, which was all puffed out with the wind and had gold tassels dangling from the corners. "Now," said mother, who had me in her arms, "Now" – whereupon I, who knew what she meant, waved the paper flag I carried, and cried "Dada" as he was about to go by. Whether he heard me or was attracted by the blue flag, or only remembered we were there and looked for us, I do not know, but his quick eyes picked us out, and instantly he smiled and shouted, "Hallo, Jack boy," and was gone.

I kept looking at the banner until it disappeared round the corner of the market-house, then fell to watching the procession. All the men had sashes and rosettes like father, and white gloves besides, and walked two and two, keeping step like preventive men. Now and again one went by whom I had seen in church or Churchtown. Johnny Dale, of Kerrow, who helped father to ring the pigs was there too; but neither he nor any of the others took any notice, though I waved to every one of them. Besides these, there were many that I got to know later when I was at school, and afterwards when I was working on the farm; but of them all not one is left alive except Reuben Ladner, of Sancreed Churchtown, and he can only just hobble to his gate and back. Come to reckon them up, it is a bravish company that has dropped out these seventy years; I do not mean Foresters only, but Madron folk in general, and amongst them notable men whose names are still warm on the lips: Sir Rose Tresillian, our squire, who loved the wild things as much as ever I did; Cousin Hughie, as everybody called him, village carpenter and parish wit; Andrew Stevens, the earthstopper; Billy Brean, the old Peninsula soldier; and Jim Beare, most tender-hearted of sextons, who sprinkled the dust lightly on mother's coffin, and when all was over took me into the church and spoke words of comfort, and that at a time when there was hue and cry, and pains and penalties threatened all who harboured me.

I can hardly bring myself to tell about mother, after the life I led her; but I must and will, if only to call up her sweet face and do justice to her memory. For noble woman though she was, and a mother amongst a thousand, there were one or two who found fault with all she did, and, as if that was not enough, with what she left undone, especially as concerned myself. They blamed her for sending me to school, for keeping me there until I was past thirteen, above all for letting me go my own way without let or hindrance. They did not know what went on indoors – her entreaties, her tears, her prayers. If only the kitchen walls could have spoken, and men heard, they would perhaps have held their peace.

My mother was the elder daughter of William Pender, of Rosigran, in the parish of Buryan, yeoman; a man pretty well-to-do and uncommonly proud of his daughters, expecting them to marry well. So that when my mother took up with a farm-hand, he threatened to turn her to doors and cut her off with a penny. This, and a few particulars of mother's courtship and wedding, I learnt, not from her or father, but from Jim Beare in the church after mother's funeral. For seeing it was all unknown to me, Jim, after making sure that the door was fastened, began from the beginning. And so it was I learned that mother fell in love with father through chancing to see him pass Mrs. Paynter's Seminary in New Road, where she was a

4

pupil, his looks took her fancy that strong. How she managed to bring about a meeting and make her feelings known he never heard. He did know this, however, that she and father, after they had come to an understanding, used to meet on market days when he was in town, in the little lane between Castle Horneck and Rosehill. And later on, after she had been found out and taken away from school, in Trevider Valley, Trevelloe Carn, and Lamorna Cove – all lonesome, out-of-the-way places, yet come-at-able as being at no great distance from her home. They were driven from pillar to post, and seem to have had as rough a keeping-company time as any young couple ever heard of.

Of the wedding ceremony he spoke as an eye-witness. It took place in Morvah church – the very church where we were – before an overflowing congregation, though Morvah Churchtown is out amongst the moors and miles from everywhere. "You see, Jack," he went on excitedly, "the match was the talk of the West Country, and people took sides. One side condemned your mother for flying in the face of her family and throwing herself away upon a man who, they said, would soon tire of her; the others stood by her, maintaining she was right in her determination to have the man she loved, and that Richard was worthy of her. Of course 'twas a very unequal match; we all owned that much."

"Why didn't her father forbid the banns?" I remember saying, not knowing more of the law than that part that related to game and trespass.

"Forbid the banns, eh! 'Twas more than his life was worth, and he knowed it. They burnt his hayrick as it was; they'd have burnt his house down, and he along with it, if he dared rise up in church; for, after all, he had no just cause, and what impediment was there but poisonous pride? And 'twasn't as if Richard was in any way loose in his habits, a carouser in kid-dlewinks and the like. There wasn't a higher charactered man in the four parishes, nor one better able to hold his own; and then he was only just come five and twenty, in the hey-day of his youth you may call it, and a regular church-goer. I began on a cool axle, Jack, but you see I'm getting a bit heated, and to save my soul I cannot help it –and what's more, I don't want to. However, let me get on and tell thee about the wedding. Mary Pender – your mother, I mean – looked very sweet in her white dress, plain, and in keeping, mind – no falderols about it, or feathers in her bonnet. I say she looked very sweet, her really did, as she walked up this aisle to where your father stood waiting, with a bit of heather pinned to the lapel of his coat, for it was just after corn harvest, when he could be spared a day, or that."

"Who gave her away?" said I.

"Never mind that, Jack, so long as she was joined in lawful wedlock; but this I may as well tell thee, that not one of her family was in church, for I looked round purpose to see, nor any friends, of her own standing I mean, except the schoolmistress, and she was in the front pew there and, like most of the thoughtful ones, crying her eyes out; we were that touched. You never saw in your born days such feeling as was shown; every face was wet over it, especially outside the church door before man and wife – as handsome a couple as God ever joined together – drove away across the downses. And after they passed from sight, some women went back to pray for a blessing on the young pair; that they might cling the one to the other through fair and through foul, at least so I took it, for that was the thought uppermost in all our minds, and what else could they be praying that earnestly for?"

Now to all this I shall add nothing by way of comment, for fear of hurting the feelings of somebody or other, only this, that mother's falling in love with father at sight was, as I see it, in the way of nature, for he was no cripple or weakling, but a fine upstanding man with brown eyes set wide apart in a healthy complexioned face, and with curly hair yellow as the sun: it made quite a light when he took his hat off. Mother looked a little thing beside him, though she was a good height for a woman, and made the most of it, not by the help of high-heeled boots I do not mean, but by the way she held herself and the proud lift of her head. It is not for me to say she was a lovely woman, whatever I thought, nor is there any need when there is outside opinion to go by; she was known as the Beauty of Buryan, and had poetry made about her by different ones of her admirers. She had abundance of chestnut hair, fine curving brows, a straight nose, small ears, a short upper lip and dark blue eyes, with a sparkle of light in them like the sapphire gem stones in Mr. Vibart's shop window. And then her skin was fair as the white heath blowth upon Bartinney, with no blemish, neither mole nor even freckles to take away from its clear smoothness, nothing but two dimples which showed when she smiled.

But though she was so beautiful in feature, and in shape too for that matter, and to boarding-school till close on her eighteenth birthday, far back as I can go and almost to the end, she slaved like any other labourer's wife, and more often than not she sang as she worked. I can see her now with sleeves and dress pinned back, leaning over and scrubbing the kitchen table, which she kept as spotless as the wooden basins and platters we ate from, and not the table only but the stairs, the planchen in both bedrooms, the window-seat I sat in, father's chair, the form and the settle that the schoolmistress had given her. And her work was always done and she tidied and looking like a queen by the time father came in to supper. And after the things were cleared away we sat round the fire, as I have said, at least till I was well in my teens and took to going out. Talking or reading, mother's voice was a sweet thing to listen to, that low and rich it was and never meant for scolding. Nevertheless she could speak out when moved, with a force and animation surprising to witness. At such moments she was like a woman transfigured, and her tongue like the tongue of an angel, she could plead that strong and tenderly.

CHAPTER II

EARLY MEMORIES

I WAS BORN ON THE SEVENTH OF MAY, 1829, at Lanyon farm, in the parish of Madron, where father was chief hand. When a little over a year old I was, so mother often said in my hearing, taken from the cradle to look at the bonfire lighted on Carn Galver in honour of King William coming to the throne. She did not mean that she carried me across the moor and close up to the blaze, of course, but only to the back of the cottage below this window, where the outlook is free away to the north and the Carn looms bold against the sky. Mother went to this trouble, I suppose, for the saying of the thing, and perhaps – or she always looked on ahead – that I might be able to make a boast of it in years to come, as I am doing now.

She also loved to tell – her eyes lit up with fun as she related it – how nicely I behaved at my own christening till Parson Pomeroy said that I must be brought to hear sermons, whereupon I fell to crying as if my heart would break, and spoilt the end of the service. It may be so: if I had understood I certainly should have cried; but the first thing I remember understanding I have told already, how I went to Penzance and saw my father in the procession.

Then comes the recollection of my first fairing brought by father from Corpus Christi Fair, and very clear it stands out in my mind on account, as I believe, of the suspense I suffered in waiting for it. For father, to keep our hearts up whilst he was to fair, had told mother and me when he kissed us good-bye, that he would bring back fairings for us on his return, never dreaming that his words, spoken as he turned to go, would so unsettle me that I should know no rest until he came back. But so it proved.

To tell the truth, he had scarcely waved his hand at the bend of the road before I began to be all excited with expectation, wondering what the present would be and how soon I should get it. I imagined he would go to Penzance, buy the fairing, and come straight home again. As he started off soon after turning the horses to grass, I felt sure he would be back by dark at the latest; but he was not, so I got very fidgetty and a handful for mother to manage. Of course she did everything she could to quiet me. She showed me her beautiful work-box, inlaid with mother-of-pearl, the skeins of silk it contained, the silver thimble and the lovely beads that filled the space beneath the tray. Amongst them was a large yellow bead which picked up small bits of paper after she had rubbed it against her sleeve. Next she drew a picture of the sedan chair we had seen in Penzance; then she took me to the door and pointed out the new hayrick, the barn, the stables, the cowhouses, the corral, and the moon and stars above. Later, when she put me to bed, she told fairy stories one after the other, in the hope of sending me off but all to no purpose; she was only wasting her breath. I could not or would not sleep till I had got my fairing; and at last mother took me on to her lap, folded the old Paisley shawl about me, and, drawing the chair close up to the open window, sat listening in the moonlight for father's footfall.

It was a still, warm night, the air sweet with the scent of the hay, and every sound near and far more distinct than usual; the churring of a nightjar on the moor, the hoot of an owl towards Boswarva Carn, the squeaking of the airymice flitting to and fro – but there was no sound that meant father's return. The pain of waiting was dreadful, though mother kept cuddling me and saying, "Father cannot be long now, it's past midnight."

We might have been harking an hour when I heard, or thought I heard, him coming; then mother heard and, holding our breath, we listened with all our might. It was the sound of footsteps; we felt sure they must be father's, and father's they were, as we knew by the tread, before he undid the fastening of the gate and crossed the yard. "Dada! dada!" I cried out. "Coming fast as I can Jack," and the next minute he entered the kitchen, came straight upstairs and sat on the edge of the bed with his face to the light.

Then, wild with excitement, I leant forward and thrusting my hand into the big side-pocket drew out what I found there, paper and all. It proved to be a little serpentine brooch, which a glance informed me was mother's fairing. But what about mine? Could he by any chance have forgotten it? I looked at him ready to cry my eyes out if I saw that he had. But the smile on his face told me that all was well and, quick as thought, my hand was in the other pocket, and there, as I expected, was my fairing. It was in a paper bag; and at this I tugged and tugged until I got it out. It was full, full, of gingerbread nuts! At the discovery I was overjoyed. How fragrant they smelt! how delicious they tasted! My fairing more than made up for all the waiting. Father watched me feast, I cannot say how long, but most likely until I fell asleep, and mother put me back to bed. The Corpus Christi fairing really was a great event for a child, to whom a stick of barley sugar, a few broad-figs, or an Abernethy biscuit, came but seldom in a twelve-month; and the incident was the more important because the fairing was brought from Penzance.

Penzance! no tongue can tell the impression our market-town had made on me the day father carried the banner. With its shop windows full of lovely things, its big harbour, its new market-house, above all, its hundreds of lamps and candles and the lights of the pilchard boats in the bay, the town was for me a city of enchantment, a sort of fairyland. Often as I sat out in the sun with nothing but my own thoughts for company, and maybe nothing more than a wren about the furze-rick to distract them, the scenes of that day would come before me, stirring the imagination till I was lost to all around. And sometimes I would brood over what mother had said as she held me on the wall of the quay, "The sea stretches far, far away to foreign countries round the world," but all I could make of it was to dot it with the coral islands and palm-trees of my picture-book.

The narrow space before the cottage was where I used to dream and play, but as I grew stronger mother allowed me to wander about the farm-yard. I could not bear to be indoors because there the hours dragged so, and even out-of-doors they dragged too sometimes. But Shep's bark, which told that he and Mr. Pearce were on the way in with the cows, was always a welcome sound; it meant a little life, and bustle and company. On hearing it, I ran to the jut of the wall where, leaning over, I could see the cows come round the bend, led most days by the old billy-goat, their companion, sometimes by a heifer belving for her calf. To me it was wonderful to see our big herd of Guernseys come walking down the road with soft and stately tread and troop through the gateway into the yard. There, after horning one another playfully, they stood ready for the milkers.

Nor had they long to wait. In a minute or two mother would appear, bucket in one hand, stool in the other, and as a rule make a beginning on Ruby. Then Bill Shellal and his wife Betty would arrive – their cottage was behind the big house – then father, and last the three kitchen-maids. Whilst they milked I moved round from one to the other and watched the milk shower into the pail. Betty always had a kiss and a kind word for me; but Bill was a tease, and would ask when I was going to have my curls cut off, get breeched, and lend a hand with the milking. And mother would answer, "Time enough to think of that, Mr. Shellal"; and Mr. Pearce, standing by the stable door, with his thumbs stuck in the arms of his waistcoat, would echo, "Yes, to be sure."

Shellal had a beard like the billy-goat, only jet black; but Mr. Pearce was clean-shaven and looked to be always smiling, as became the cheerful, warm-hearted master he was. Everybody liked him, especially children, and no wonder, considering the trouble he took to amuse them.

He used to hold me on the goat's back and lead him round the yard; he would lay his watch to my ear, so that I might hear it ticking; he would even go to the trouble of taking off the outer case and show me the workings, and sometimes he would strike sparks from the flint and light the tinder he carried in a box in his pocket; Feasten Monday he gave me a new penny.

And these little attentions were really events in my day, perhaps because I had no one to play with, no children I mean, nor brother nor sister. Mother used to fret about this and make up for it as well as she could by giving me every minute she could spare from her work. But she was too busy to give me many. Besides the house and the mending, she saw to the dairying of our four cows – Gentle, Rosebud, Buttercup, and Ruby – whose produce father had in place of money wages. She scalded the milk, reamed the cream, made the butter, and, if no one was going that way, carried it herself to Mrs. Trudgen, the Churchtown grocer, who took it of her. Yet with all these things to occupy her, she always had me in her thoughts, as her actions showed. For she would come to the door perhaps a dozen times during the day and call, "Jack," till I answered back; or if she failed to make me hear, she would come and look for me.

One morning she could neither make me hear nor find me, though she searched the cattle-houses, the mowhay, the pigs' craws, and the stable; in fact, every possible place except the place where I was – the barn. This big chamber over the stable, usually kept locked, had been left open by Bill, and this afforded me the opportunity I had often longed for to enter and explore it. So I climbed the steps, made my way in and examined, as well as the half-light allowed, the various objects kept there: the cayers used for winnowing, a hand plough, the threshels and scythes hanging from the crossbeams, the coils of straw rope, the mongers, as we call the home-made horse collars, hanging on pegs in the wall, and, at the far end, beyond the threshing-floor, a huge iron trap with its jaws clenched home!

Here was a discovery indeed, something that excited my curiosity to the full. I had seen gins, small and big, and knew their use, but nothing half the size of this. What was it for? What animal was it meant to catch? Not badgers or otters, I was sure of that. What then?

I was still wondering, when suddenly the light was still further obscured, and, turning to learn the cause, I saw a figure standing in the doorway: it was mother. "My child, there you are! Why ever did you not answer me? Oh, Jack, how you have frightened me. I made sure you had been spirited away." The rush of her words so dumbfounded me that I could not reply, could only point to the object at my feet. The gesture served. She came forward at once, but not to dwell. On sighting the trap she shrank back like one skeared, and, saying "The horrid thing," hurried me away as from a plague spot. And it was long before I learned that the gin, with its heavy chain and long staples, was a man-trap, a devil's tool which in after years was to prove a terror to my steps. So I was at a loss to know why the trap frightened her as it did.

But I knew what she meant by my being spirited away, for she always used the phrase in expressing her fears to father, when lawless characters were about. Because of them she never went to the well without taking me with her, nor to the fields, where at times she worked.

Sometimes the weather was wet and cold, and then she had to leave me to myself. On these occasions she was all anxiety, and before leaving would beg and entreat me not to touch the fire, not to go near the bull's house, above all to be sure and run in and bar the door if I saw gipsies or old soldiers come down the road. And I was wilful and loved doing what was forbidden. I spent hours in the bull's house, I ran to the gate to see a wooden-legged man go by, and one afternoon I piled the furze on the fire till the flames shot out of the chimney and brought master's sister, Miss Jenifer, breathless to the cottage. "I thought the house was on fire!" she gasped, at sight of me enjoying the blaze, then sank down on the form, panting in a way that frightened me. The fire had nearly died down before she recovered sufficiently to beckon me to her and whisper, "Jack, my boy, if you go on in this way, you will be the death of your sweet mother." Whereupon I fell to crying bitterly, for mother was all the world to me; yet even in my trouble I could not help thinking how cold Miss Jenifer's hand was when at last she led me away.

"You must never be left alone again," she said two or three times, as we crossed the road to the big house. Nor was I. For ever after, as often as mother went to hoe or lop turnips or dig potatoes, Miss Jenifer came and took possession of me for the rest of the day, unless, as happened now and again, she was laid up with asthma or tic, and then I was handed over to Mrs. Pearce and roped to the leg of the kitchen table.

Miss Jenifer's ways were always the same, she was that methodical. First she made the round of the yard and mowhay, collecting the eggs from the regular laying places and such stray nests as she knew of. I used to wish it would take all day, for no sooner had we picked up the last egg than Miss Jenifer led me to her own room where, except for dinner and a walk to the Quoit and back, I spent the hours till milking time. Nor were these hours spent in turning over picture-books or gazing through the window. Miss Jenifer took advantage of the golden opportunity, as she called it, to teach me my letters.

I should say she was meant for a schoolmistress; she had the look for it, and was that firm and patient. I sat in awe of her quick black eyes, strong upper lip, and big chin, and did what I was told. "You are a good boy," she would often say; and sometimes, "You're a bright child, and getting on nicely."

She taught me my A B C; she showed me how to hold a slate pencil and to form the letters – how patient she was over this! – and also taught me the clock. This last I turned to account at once. For the moment the minute hand passed the half-hour between three and four I became all ears for Shep, and on hearing his bark would look up at Miss Jenifer as much as to say, "Milking time's come." But she was mortal quick, and my eyes nearly always met hers regarding me smilingly over the gold-rimmed spectacles. She understood right enough. She would drop her knitting or carding, put the spectacles in the case, take the pink sun-bonnet from the peg, and, saying "School's dismissed," lead me down the long staircase to the garden and to the yard across the road where mother usually was waiting for me at the gate.

Looking back, I see the pains and trouble Miss Jenifer took as one of the prettiest things in my life; but I set no store by it at the time. After the freedom I had enjoyed, her room, cosy as it was with drugget, table-cloth, pictures, looking-glass, horsehair chairs and sofa, curtains and flower-pots in the window, full of red and white geraniums, was little other than a clink, especially when the sky was blue and the sun shining.

More than once I opened my heart to mother, but, to my surprise, without getting a word of consolation: she always stood up for Miss Jenifer. She told me that I was too young to understand, that I should be thankful some day, and that, instead of complaining of Miss Jenifer, who was goodness itself, I ought to say "God bless Miss Jenifer" in my prayers. And so her name found a place there next to mother and father, and there remained long after I gave up kneeling at mother's knee.

More deserving of mention perhaps than acts of disobedience and complaints against Miss Jenifer was the interest I took in wild creatures almost from the first. I cannot tell whether the taste was born in me or came from my surroundings, but there it was before I could shape a ramrod for an elder gun or make a straight shot with a taw. I never tired of watching the cliff hawks that came after our chicks; I would drop hoop or marble to look up at curlew or raven as it flew by; and in bed I loved to listen to the sedgewarblers and screech owls; and, what was more, I longed to be abroad with them.

For, as I say, even when a child, the calls and the ways of the birds were a delight to me, and scarcely less the habits of foxes, badgers, and otters, about which the old earthstopper used to speak whenever he dropped in. I never tired of gazing at the eels and trout that father caught on night-lines. Trout I look on not only as amongst the most beautiful of created things, but amongst the most interesting, and well do I recollect my excitement the first time I saw them rising. I was with father, who was on his way to the mill, and showed my tantrums because he would not let me stay and watch them. But I was determined to see them, and three days later, when mother was spreading the clothes, I slid down the bank behind the cottage to make my way to the pool alone.

It was a lovely sunny morning. King Crowners, as we call admiral and peacock butterflies, were busy on the heads of the hemp-agrimony; everything promised well. I hurried to the water's edge – and what a blow it was! – there was not a trout rising. It was a bitter disappointment; but there was no help for it, so I turned to go back. When I got as far as the bridge, something possessed me to stop and look beneath it. I lay on the camomile growing there, and, leaning over as far as I dared, peeped through the ferns at the stream beneath. I shall never forget the sight that met my eye. There, above the golden gravel, lay in the crystal-clear water the largest trout I had seen; he was longer, I believe he was fatter, than a pilchard – in fact, he was a whopper. He might have been asleep for the little movement he made; but presently, when an insect came floating by, he rose and took it, settling down into the old spot on the edge of the current. The sight of this grand fish held me spellbound, and I could have watched him for hours; indeed, I might have done, had I not heard mother calling me. At the sound of her voice, I backed out of my awkward, rather dangerous position, and made my way up the hill.

I felt guilty as I had never felt before. For this was the first time I had dared to leave the yard. Oh, how angry mother looked! "You may well look ashamed, you naughty, disobedient boy. How many, many times have I warned you never to go outside, and yet you have done it as if I had never spoken. You do not love your poor mother, or you would heed what she said."

"I only went to see the trout, mother," I replied, as well as I could for my sobs, but she would listen to nothing; strange to say, she had become as hard as Miss Jenifer, and for the rest of the day I was not allowed to cross the doorstep.

But I had tasted the joys of the world outside the farm-yard, and yielded at once to the next temptation to leave it. One morning, soon after my visit to the millpool, I climbed the wall of the mowhay to get at some blackberries in Nearer Jets, and was just reaching up to pick them when a rabbit darted from the brambles at my feet. I watched the pretty creature scamper over the turf towards a solitary furze-bush, and, on seeing it enter, determined to secure it for a pet. So I ran to the bush and looked into the creep. As there was not a sign of a rabbit, I was about to pull the sprays aside to see into the bush, when Bill Shellal, who had been watching me from the top of the hayrick, cried out –

"Hallo, Jack, what are 'ee doin' theere?"

"Trying to catch a little bunny rabbit," I cried.

"A bunny rabbot; a cheeld of seven tryin' to catch a bunny rabbot! Well! well! Thee'rt beginning early, Maister Jack; thee'rt a born poacher, I reckon. Be off home, theere's a good boy, or mawther will be missin' 'ee again."

At that I scrambled over the wall, ran round the big corn-rick, and right into the arms of mother, who had come to look for me.

"Jack's been rabbottin', Mrs. Penrose; startin' eearly, edna you?"

"I'm afraid he is; he's mad after the wild things; he turns after his Uncle Jim."

"Uncle Jim? I never heeard that Rechard had any brother besides Stephen."

15

But mother took no further notice, except to bite her lip, as if to punish it for letting out more than it ought.

I told mother all about the bunny rabbit, and that night, when sitting by my bed, she made up a story about him; how he lived happily sometimes under the brambles in Nearer Jets, sometimes in the furze brake by the Quoit, sometimes in the deep earth in Spar Croft with the badgers and foxes.

After that, seeing how I enjoyed the story of the bunny, mother told me stories of the birds and beasts; of the jackdaw of Madron Tower, the king-fisher of Pleasant Streams, the heron of Lanyon reed-bed, the white badger of Carn Kenidzhek, the grey fox of Chapel Carn Brea, and the seal of Lamorna Cove.

She nearly always brought the fairies into them – she brought them even into the seal story – saying that they descended to the caves at night with their reeds and flutes and played to the baby seals whilst their mothers were away fishing.

Mother was a lovely story-teller, and father liked listening to her as much as I did; I am sure of what I say because the moment she began he would open the door at the foot of the stairs and never move his feet or as much as tap his pipe, except in the palm of his hand, for fear of missing something. Once, in the midst of the story of grey fox, a fox began squalling on the moor so loudly that mother had to stop and listen.

"That's a vixen singing out," father called up, " 'Tis a wisht old noise."

At last the cry died away and mother finished her story, but not before she had worked the vixen into it.

If an owl hooted she would bring in the owl; if the wind whistled you might be sure the wind would whistle in her story; indeed it did come into most of her stories.

For Lanyon stands exposed as few places are, and many a time I have found it that biting that I was glad to get into the barn out of the teeth of it and warm myself whilst I drowned the screech and howl with the thud of the flail.

But if I shrank at times from the wind, I never shrank from the dark, not even as a child, rather was I happy in it. Before I was put into breeches I used to creep out of bed and peep through these very panes in the hope of catching sight of the fairies that lived on the moor. Sometimes it was so dark that I could hardly make out the big house; sometimes the moon lit up the moor, silvering the stream and the mill pool; sometimes the sky was bright with stars. The stars! They have been like friends to me. I loved them as a child, as a boy coming home from school; I love them to this day.

And I never look at them without thinking of mother, for it was she who taught me to love them. On a clear night, after helping me with my lessons, she would take me out by turf-trick and tell me their names. How they seemed to take her out of herself!

CHAPTER III

LOST IN THE
REED-BED

❧

W HEN I WAS WELL TURNED NINE I met with an adventure that caused mother and father anxiety to the point of distraction and was nearly bringing my life to an early end. It was of my own seeking and came about through the habit that had grown upon me of looking out of the window when the rest of Lanyon was in bed asleep.

The night was wild, even for December, with evil-looking clouds driving across the moon and casting great blots of shadow across the moor. Black and forbidding though they were, they had an attraction for me on account of the variety and grimness of their shape. Some resembled islands with weird and jagged coast-lines, others forlorn mountain ranges, others again strange beasts. Presently came one in the likeness of a horned monster with a horde of pursuers at his heels; and this so fascinated me that I watched the exciting chase as far as the pane allowed.

Then, as I turned my eyes away, they fell on a light which struck me, the instant I saw it, as something out of the common. I felt sure it was neither the lantern of the earth-stopper nor – though it was near the edge of the reed-bed – a Will o' the Wisp. It was for all the world as if some one with a light were searching for something; but then, as I asked myself, what being could be out on the moor in the dead of night, unless it was the Little Folk mother had told me of? – and I did not for the moment doubt that such they were.

I was bitterly cold, but so excited that I never as much as thought of getting back to bed. The light shone bravely when the moon was hidden; it was visible when the orb, then nearly at the full, rode free, revealing the features of the moor. But of the fairies themselves, though I strained my eyes as never before, I know that I did not get a glimpse, seeing them only in imagination, tricked out in green coat and cocked hat, tripping after the leader as he paced to and fro.

I was all eagerness to call mother, but could not tear myself away for some minutes; and then, just as I turned to go, the beat of approaching hoofs fell on my ears and held me, till I could learn what horseman was abroad at such an hour. Louder and louder grew the sounds, and, as I listened, my thought was that the doctor had been summoned to Mrs. Pearce, then abed with heart trouble. But in this I was wrong, for though the pace of the horse slackened as it drew near the big house, the rider did not bring the animal to a standstill until abreast of my window, and then only with difficulty, judging from the manner in which he lay back and pulled on the reins. He stood up in the stirrups, and so remained motionless with his face to the moor.

"Then you, too, are after the fairies," thought I, "but you know little if you expect to see them after such a rattle-come-chase with your horse."

He might have gazed for half a minute when, to my astonishment, he suddenly slewed round and, after a glance at the dairy window, looked up at mine, and not with his naked eyes but through a spy glass, which I now saw that he was holding. I waved my hand to him, but of that he took no notice, only kept looking at me as though he would, so to speak, stare me out of countenance. Then he dashed off at the same mad pace at which he had come. His path was lit by sparks, and when these disappeared, as the fairy light had done, I crept back to bed and lay wondering who the stranger was, how he knew that the fairies were abroad, and why he, any more than the man in the moon, should trouble his head about them. But I could make nothing of it; least of all could I understand why he should have eyed me in the way he did. The more I thought the more addled my brain became, till only one thing stood out clear – my resolve to visit the moor the moment Miss Jenifer let me out of school next day, and, now that I knew where to find them, surprise the Little Folk in their secret couching places.

It seemed hours before I fell asleep, but I must have dropped off before five, as I did not hear father go downstairs, nor, for that matter, any of the usual morning sounds, nor even the cackling of the geese when they were let out of the craw.

When at last I awoke, mother was standing by the bed looking down at me, and I said, "Mother, I have seen the Fairies!"

"Not seen them, my dear, only dreamt about them, that is all."

"But, mother, I saw their light on the moor, till a man came galloping down the road and made them put it out."

"My dear child, you must have been dreaming; the Small Folk never hold their revels in the depth of winter or in a gale of wind ; why, they would be blown away if they did, lantern and all."

"But, mother," I said, sitting up in bed and pointing to the spot, "I am sure I did see the light, there anist the reeds."

"Come, come, dear, get up and dress, or father will be wondering where his big boy is."

So out I got and into my clothes, just in time for mother to wash my face and brush my hair. Indeed, we were yet standing outside the cottage, where father and I always washed, when he arrived. The moment I set eyes on him I saw by the look on his face that he was very much excited. Soon I gathered that Shellal had told him of some happening in the night; but what I could not learn, for as we went indoors mother put her finger to her lip as much as to say, "Be careful what you say before Jack." A moment later, as we were about to take our places, she said, "Sh! Sh!" to something else, and all break-fast time she kept a close watch on father's tongue and smothered every word that might give me an inkling of what was afoot.

But she need not have been so very anxious, as I was too busy with my own thoughts to trouble much about anything else. I did not want to go on the moor in such wild weather on a fool's errand; so I kept questioning whether I really had seen the fairies or, after all, had only dreamt of them.

I was soon certain sure that I had not been dreaming. I remembered little things that left no room for doubt: the waving of the horse's mane, the quick movement of the horseman as he shut the glass home; I recollected how my teeth chattered with the cold and the excitement, above all how violently I had struck my knee on getting back to bed, and the pain it gave me. As this last came into my mind, I dropped my spoon, and felt the place through my corduroys; it was sore and very tender to the touch. I had not been dreaming. Yet I said nothing, and should have said nothing even had father and mother not been talking so eagerly that I could not. A word about my plans would have put an end to my expedition, and that would pretty well have broken my heart; I was so set upon going through with it.

So I sat with my thoughts to myself, impatiently waiting for mother to say grace. The word "thankful" had scarcely left her lips before I was out of the door and round by the furze-rick for a peep at the moor. There was nothing unusual to be seen, nothing but the wintry-looking browse, the swollen stream, and the great reed-bed tossing and swaying like a thing in agony.

Whilst I watched it, I heard a window open, and, putting my head round the corner of the rick, I saw Miss Jenifer waving the red tablecloth as a sign that I was late and keeping her waiting. So, leaving my shelter, I slid down the bank and crossed the road as quickly as the violence of the wind would let me.

Now whether Miss Jenifer noticed that I walked lame as I crossed the road, or only heard me limping up the stairs, or both, I do not know; but, on my entering the room, she greeted me with the words – "You are very lame; what have you been up to now?" She did not question me further, owing, I think, to her desire to get to work and give me another lesson in Long Division, in which, to tell the truth, I had shown myself a dunce.

Oh, the trouble this rule gave me! How difficult I found it to reckon the number of times the divisor would go! Now I made it out one too many, now one too few; only by chance did I light on the right number. It was so in my lesson of the day before; this morning I could get nowhere near the mark.

For a time Miss Jenifer bore with me, but at last, on my saying nine when it should have been six times, she dropped the pencil on the slate, and in a voice sharper than I had heard her use, she said, "What in the world ails you this morning? Have you taken leave of your seven senses to answer me as you have been doing? Now, sir, I warn you that unless you give your mind to your work, I shall detain you for the rest of the day."

The threat of detention worked wonders; my answers were now the best I had ever given. And this despite the fact that for the life of me I could not resist raising my eyes every time Miss Jenifer's head was down. But nothing escaped her – indeed, I had even come to look upon the big blue bead in the back of her cap as a sort of tell-tale – and presently she jumped to her feet, took the antimacassar from the sofa and spread it carefully over the face of the clock.

"Is there any other temptation I can remove out of your way, sir?" she asked.

She quite recovered herself as the morning wore away, so that when the clock had struck twelve, she said, "School's dismissed, Jack," in her pleasantest voice, and added, "Wait whilst I fetch the hartshorn oil and rub your knee; it may do it good."

But the moor was calling to me with overpowering voice; I could not wait, and the moment I heard the door of her bedroom creak I slipped

21

noiselessly out of the room, and, before she could discover my absence, was through the gate and on my way to the moor.

No one was in the farm-yard: there was no sign of mother as I stole past the cottage; there was no one to see me at all, except the geese in the millpool, opposite which I turned into the track worn by the carts when bringing in turf and furze. But I found that the track soon lost itself upon the moor, which was much rougher than I thought it, and pathless except for the runs made by the moorland cattle.

In the absence of yearling or colt, or other living thing, I was from the first conscious of a feeling of loneliness, which deepened the farther I got. Yet so alluring was the prospect of seeing the fairies that I held on through brakes that, with a gale in my teeth, were almost too much for my childish strength. Had the furze been tall, I might have crawled between the stems, but it was stunted and close, and made a toil of every step. Again and again I beat a retreat and tried to find a way round, but without success. I was only wasting my time in doing so; there was nothing for it but to fight my way through or give up and go back home. But somehow I could not; something within prevented me.

At last, after what seemed hours and hours, I got through the brakes – there were three of them – but in so exhausted a state that I had to stop and rest under shelter of some bushes that circled a hollow rank with rush and heather. This moorland pound was like mother's description of a fairies' parlour, and, as it was near the reed-bed, and apparently the very spot where I had seen the light, I was eager to explore it. The briefest of rests was all I allowed myself before passing between two tall bushes which formed a sort of entrance. That the fairies were hiding within, I had not the least doubt; what was more, I had not taken a dozen steps before I felt that they were watching me. That was why I kept turning suddenly, for thus I hoped to surprise them before they could duck down out of sight. But never a fairy did I see; nothing but rushes, ling, and a stunted alder where a pool of water was.

In spite of failure in the part I had explored, I still looked for success in the part that remained, for it lay dry, was better sheltered, above all, the heather was more luxuriant and afforded better cover. My hopes rose high as my feet sank in the thick herbage. I trod lightly so as to break no bones, and had nearly reached the spot where I felt sure the Small Folk were hiding when up jumped, not a fairy, but a great red fox. I started, but looked

22

him straight in the eyes. To my surprise he glared back, and seemed to say, "What is a boy like you doing out here?" Then he slunk away, his lovely coat slightly aripple as he went. He was a grand fox, his brush-tip white as snow, and every hair in its place as if he had just finished grooming himself. Yet, much as I admired him, I was glad when he was gone, for, to tell the truth, I felt afraid of him in that lonely place, with no one within call and the storm worse than ever. The loud rustling of the reeds helped further to frighten me, and now my only thought was to get back to mother as quickly as I could.

There were two ways home: the long roundabout way I had come, and the short cut across the reed-bed. I know now that I should have returned as I came, that it was the only way for me; but I can hardly be blamed for taking to the reed-bed. I was a child, knowing nothing of its treacherous traps, only aware of this one danger, that I might lose myself and wander there like the men in the forest. It was to guard against this that I climbed the only rock near and crouched on the top of it to take my bearings. There was the big house and the cottage, both showing very grey against the driving wrack, but not a soul in sight. I wondered where father was working and, thinking he might be in Further North Field, which was the nearest, I rose and tried to stand on the rock in order to see him over the top of the reeds, and wave my cap to him if he were there. But the wind was too violent for me to stand up against, and I fell clumsily to the ground, wrenching my bad knee so that I screamed for agony. In my pain and fright I cried, "Mother!" The reed-tops hissed, and that was the only reply. Would that I had taken it as a warning to turn my back on the wicked old place!

I was soon up to my ankles in black mud; in quaggy spots I sank deeper still, and the pain as I withdrew my foot was almost more than I could bear. It is true that the reeds, which rose high above my head, screened me from the wind, but then they shut out the sight of everything and cast a gloom that stirred ugly thoughts in me. I imagined an uncouth being in the form of a strong, shaggy-haired dwarf living in this untrodden retreat, and, fearing to come upon him, I avoided the spots where the reeds grew closest and were most likely to harbour him.

In avoiding them I came on two pools. From the middle of the larger pool rose a big bird of dark plumage, unknown to me then, though I have since thought that it must have been a cormorant, for when I first caught sight of him he was standing with outstretched wings, nibbing his breast, as cormorants often do.

Awed though I was by its forbidding appearance and bright green eyes, there was something which impressed me still more because of the strangeness of it. The creature seemed to be standing on the surface of the pool. The water near the edge was two feet or more in depth and appeared to be at least as deep in the middle. Then, with a settling of the ripple, I saw and understood. Where the bird had been, the top of a small barrel showed. A score or more lay on the bottom of the pool.

It has often struck me since how little the extraordinary discovery excited me. I know not how to explain that, unless it was due to my exhausted state. However, I gave little more heed to the kegs than to the springs bubbling up amongst them, and held on aimlessly along the leat that drained the pool, striving to quiet the voice which now spoke up in me with the words, "You are lost."

Nor was this the worst. Dark thoughts of what might happen began to present themselves. Yet when things seemed blackest a ray of hope appeared. There was a leaf –a long, narrow, yellow leaf – on the seemingly still surface of the leat, and, whilst I watched, it moved slowly, so slowly that its motion was scarcely noticeable, but it did move, and so served as a friendly sign indicating the way I should go.

With the return of hope I grew strong, and, brushing aside the stems, I crept along, as best I could, fully expecting to reach running water. For the leaf was moving towards the stream, and the stream would lead me home.

But I was to meet with disappointment. I came, not to the stream, but to the fork of the junction with another leat, where a single wide channel formed by the two stretched so straight before me that I could look along the water lying between walls of tossing reeds. I was in danger, but things were not hopeless, for I might succeed in fording one of the narrow channels. I never hesitated, except to make choice, and my choice fell on the leat I had been following. Grasping the stems, I let myself over the edge of the bank, bit by bit, hoping every moment to feel bottom. Soon the water was above my belt and my arms nearly at full stretch, but without my feet getting in touch with anything except a bed of mud that offered no support. I might have been within an inch, or even less, of the solid bottom underlying the mud if such there were, but I dared not lower myself any further; as it was, I feared I should be unable to regain the bank even if the stems stood the strain I must put on them. In my dread lest they should give way, I felt about with my feet for a ledge, a hole in the bank, or a projecting root, anything that would furnish foothold, but had soon to give over because my arms were tiring. The thought of losing my life roused me to a big effort, and trusting that the stems might hold, I put my remaining strength upon them, and, digging my toes into the bank, was just able, by the slight support thus obtained, to lift myself to safety.

Wet and miserable as I was, it was good to feel the firm ground beneath me once more. For a moment I forgot my plight – but only for a moment. Then all my fear came back. Strangely enough, it was not the fear of death that troubled me most, but the thought that my body would never be found. In my anguish I cried aloud to my strong, brave father to come and help me. My screeches pierced the storm till I could scream no more. In the calm that came of exhaustion, I imagined him and Bill and Mr. Pearce and Shep looking for me everywhere but where I was. At the thought that they would never dream of searching the reeds, despair seized and nearly drove me beside myself, till all at once I heard the clang of the alarm bell! Oh, the relief it brought! the hopes it raised! Moreover, it set me consulting with myself as to what I could do towards my own rescue, for I realised now that not Lanyon only, but all the countryside would be searching for me and no corner be left unexplored.

There was no time to be lost for the short day was closing in; already a flock of starlings had come to the reeds to roost. In my desperation I rose and tried to retrace my steps, but staggered and fell. Yet my spirit was not utterly broken: I would not give in as long as I could think, and presently, as I lay there, the thought came to me to break off a handful of reeds and hold them above my head as a signal of my whereabouts. Clang! clang! rang out the bell, heartening me as I bent the stems to and fro to break them off near the root. They proved to be very tough and, despite my frantic efforts, it was some time before I succeeded in getting three. These I held up at arm's length. No need was there to wave them, the gale did that; and, indeed, made it difficult for me to keep them above the top of the reed-bed. I listened in the hope of hearing a shout which would tell me they had been seen; but I listened in vain. It was not till dusk, when all hope seemed gone, that I heard voices, then a shout, then another, and presently a third that sounded quite close. Whereupon, gripping the reeds that I had let fall, I raised my arms to the full stretch and waved, screaming out at the top of my voice as I waved.

I don't know whether it was my piercing cry or the signal which attracted attention; but soon I heard a splashing noise and, looking along the lane of water, saw father, but father no longer, so distracted were his looks. Nearer and nearer he drew, and at last he sighted me. Gasping out the words "Thank God," he caught me up and hurried back as fast as the water and reeds would let him. As soon as we emerged from the reed-bed, some boys spied us and rushed shouting to the cottage.

Father ran rather than walked up the hill, and I can see now the sweat upon his face, and his hair blowing about as he strode across the yard to the cottage, where he brushed aside the women in the doorway and laid me in mother's arms.

She looked dreadful, her face like marble for whiteness, and as cold when she pressed her cheek against mine. Presently, as she hugged me to her, she cried and sobbed as if her heart would break. Overcome by her distress, Mrs. Shellal and Mrs. Hicks came forward for the purpose of comforting her, and would have made her worse but for Miss Jenifer, who said, " Let her be, the flow of tears will ease her feelings. But we need not stand like ninnies with the child there wringing wet and famished with hunger. You, Betty, get some dry clothes. I'll see to the fire and the supper."

So, whilst Miss Jenifer pulled the furze out of the wood-cupboard and made a good blaze, Mrs. Shellal ran upstairs and fetched my dry clothes. Then she and Mrs. Hicks changed me, and by the time father came in for the milk pails, I was sitting at the table, comfortable as could be, eating bread and cream and blackberry jam, with mother and little Loveday Rosewarne in a red cloak on the other side of me, and seven Churchtown boys, whom the hue and cry had brought to Lanyon, watching me with noses flat against the window panes.

Later, these same boys began playing hide-and-seek around our ricks and craws, and making such a noise that Bill stopped milking and came and ordered them off. But they took no notice of Bill, so Mr. Pearce had to speak to them.

"Boys," said he, after gathering them around him, "your mothers will be wondering where you are; it's time you were off home. But wait a second, I'll give a fourpenny bit to the first one who tells Parson Veale that our Jack is found and none the worse. Say he was found, like Moses, in the bulrushes."

With that he lined them up, their backs against the big turkey house, every boy with his cap in his hand and hair flying, as I could just make out through the window. At the word "Go" they were off; and a few minutes later, when Miss Jenifer, Mrs. Shellal, and Mrs. Hicks had kissed me and taken their departure, mother and I were left to ourselves.

"Now," thought I," I shall get a bit of scolding."

But no, she went about her duties as if nothing had happened; she brushed the cloth, moved the barley loaf to father's end of the table, set the milk to warm for his supper, hung my clothes to dry, put the tinder-box back in its place, and not until everything was straight and she came and sat by me on the settle did she speak: even then not till she had had another good cry and nearly squeezed my life out.

"Oh, Jack, how could you go away, without a word to anybody or even waiting for Miss Jenifer to rub your knee?"

"I wanted to see the fairies, mother."

"But, my dear boy, a child like you is not fit to adventure out on the moor and into those reeds at any time, much less on such a day as this. It's terrible to think of your being out there alone all those hours; and there you would be still if your father had not noticed the stream was puddled. And who knows if you would ever" – here she broke down, but presently, hearing father coming, stifled her sobs and brushed away her tears. Her distress, however, would out, and whilst father was eating his bread and milk she rushed upstairs and had her cry so that we could hear her through the planchen.

"Bear up, Mary dear, Jack is safe and sound," father called up. "Come now, sweetheart, I've a nice little bit of news for you."

Still she kept on crying, and in the end he went and fetched her.

Later, as we sat by the fire and mother had quite come round, she turned to father and said in her playful way, "Well, Richard, you are a very long time telling me your nice little bit of news."

"I was only waiting for the word, my dear, 'tis about the smugglers."

"Hush! hush!" said mother.

"No, dear, I'm not going to hold my tongue; I've had next to nothing to do with them since Jack was born, and I don't know that I should be so very ashamed of it if I had. Jack will never take any wrong from what he hears me say. Well, the riding officer pulled up at the gate just now and told the master that not a keg had been found, though his men had scoured and searched the country for miles around."

"What is a keg?" I asked.

"A dinky barrel, Jack."

"Then, father, I know where there is a passel of them."

"Where?"

"In a big pool in amongst the reeds."

Whereupon, father looked at mother, and mother at father, as if they had heard the most astonishing news of their life. But they must have been thinking whilst they looked; for, instantly, shifting his eyes to mine, father said, "Now, Jack, don't breathe a word of this to any one outside – not to Bill, nor even to Miss Jenifer."

"And," added mother, "nor even think of it again."

CHAPTER IV

SENT TO SCHOOL

❧

I PAID DEARLY FOR MY ADVENTURE, as it ended in my being sent to school. It was not mother's doing; it was all through Miss Jenifer, who came across next morning and persuaded her that it was for my good. Drawing mother to the form on which she sat, she said, "Mary, I have been awake half the night thinking about Jack, and I am here to beg and entreat you to send him to Daniel's School after Christmas. What do you say?"

"Why, that I am all for his going, Miss Jenifer, if it were not for the lonely, dreary road, and his sometimes having to sit for hours in wet clothes and perhaps catch his death of cold."

"These, my dear, are trifles that can be provided against; and think of the gain. He will have play-fellows; he will be subject to discipline, and over and above these things he will enjoy the advantages of the teaching of Mr. Tasker. You may possibly wonder that I should bother my head about Jack. I do so because I love the boy, because I would see him grow up a fine, manly fellow, confident of his powers and able to hold his own in any company."

Mother gave way after that, but got Miss Jenifer to agree to my having no more lessons between then and my going to school, which was to be in a few days.

Next morning, Miss Jenifer rode away to Penzance, in the teeth of the keen east wind. I watched all the afternoon from the top of the barn steps for her return, and between three and four sighted her velvet bonnet and veiled face nodding to the movements of Snowball.

On dismounting at the heaping-stock, she stood awhile to blow on her fingers, perhaps also to get the use of her legs before descending the steps, which she did slowly after handing me the parcel she carried. Not thinking but that she was going indoors, I ran forward and pushed open the iron gate, that had been kept strictly closed since the pigs got in and upset two of the bee-hives. However, on looking round, I saw she was crossing the road to the yard and, as it proved, to our cottage, to which, after putting Snowball in the stable, I followed her. Laying the parcel down, she said, "Put on a screech of furze, Mary, I am perished with the cold."

29

A good faggot soon blazed up, and Miss Jenifer stood by it with mittened hands outspread to catch the warmth.

"Better here, Mary," she said, "than on Forest Carn in this wind; but I must not indulge, for Jack, as I can see, is all agog to know what is in the parcel."

Whereupon, she went to the table, undid the string, and opened it. It contained an oilskin jacket, oilskin leggings, a sou'-wester, a satchel, and in the satchel a bag of marbles.

"These things are for you, Jack; they will keep you warm and dry in the worst of weathers."

Mother, who had been looking on like one mazed, exclaimed, "Surely you do not intend all these things as a gift?

"Indeed I do; why not? My dear Mary, bear with me this once. I know your independent spirit, and, to tell the truth, I have been dreading this scene all the way up Madron Hill. But, believe me, the obligation is all on my side. These few things are an old spinster's send-off gift to her pupil, and I consider it a privilege to be allowed to make it. I beg, therefore – I implore you not by another word to mar the pleasure it gives me."

At this mother fell upon her neck, kissing her through veil and all, till I longed for a place to hide away out of it.

We were a very happy family that evening as we sat round the fire, though nothing much was said. My mind was constantly on Miss Jenifer's goodness to me, until the thought of going to school and facing forty boys came to trouble me. I was unhappy about it, too, in church on Sunday, and later in the day, when I was sitting alone with mother, she asked me twice what I was brooding over; but I replied, "Nothing, mother." I had not the courage to tell.

That night she came and prayed at my bedside, holding my hand as she prayed. I have never forgotten it, but what perhaps dwells with me more is father's advice next morning. Beckoning me to him, he laid his big palm on my shoulder, and said, "Jack, my son, a father's word: thee'rt go'in forth to stand amongst strangers. Now lad, mind what I'm going to say. Always speak the truth and to once, and try to keep from what's wrong."

With that he brushed my curls back, kissed my forehead, rose and went off to his work, no doubt choking the tears back for, strong man though father was, he was tender-hearted as a girl.

I started a few minutes later, getting quite a send-off so to speak. Bill came to the stable door and called out, "Good luck, Jack, keep clear of the strap." Miss Jenifer waved from the window till I rounded the bend beyond the pound, and here mother, who had come thus far, sped me on my way with her blessing.

It was a lovely morning, the east all rose and pearl, the vault blue like a grey-bird's egg. But lovely though the morning was, it meant little in the state I was in, with mind fidgetting over the life ahead till I made of it a thing to shrink from. Indeed, I worked myself into such a fever of shyness at having to face so many strange boys that I thought of turning back and might have done so had not shame prevented me. However, I got the mastery of myself before reaching Paunshallow Bridge, and began to feel the pasty inside my jacket; then fell to rattling the marbles in my breeches pocket, and presently longed for a game. On the level ground on the top of the hill, I actually made a ring and started to play, knuckling down as well as I could for the grit in the growan and doing my best for both sides.

The chatter of a magpie calling my thoughts off the marbles, I gathered up the two blood-alleys and the four clayers and held on my way, whistling as I went to keep up my courage, for it was the first time I had been by myself on that bit of lonesome road. And so I came to the ridge of the upland where I could see all around for miles: Godolphin Hill to my left; Buryan Tower to the right; Mount's Bay in front, with a fleet of wind-bound vessels making for the Lizard, over which the sun had risen for the space of a good hand's breadth. With their canvas spread, the vessels made a brave sight; but what drew my eyes before all else was the wooded valley at my feet, where game of all kinds harboured in the squire's preserves. The better to see, I climbed the bank, from which I looked straight down upon the spread of tree-tops.

A wood-pigeon flew out, circled round, and resettled in the pine it had started from, and a hern came sailing down the valley and dropped in the upper pond while I watched; but I moved away at last, the fear of being late urging me so that I did not cast even a glance at the warning-board with its notice, "Beware of spring-guns and man-traps," as I went by.

I need not have hurried as I did, for, by the clock above the canisters in Mrs. Trudgen's shop, it wanted twenty-two minutes to nine when I reached the village green, where most – perhaps all – of the boys were already assembled. It would have been no easy matter to have counted them with any niceness, inasmuch as they were gathered round two chaps who were fighting. At the sight, the shyness, which had returned, fled again, so that instead of holding off as I had intended, I joined the ring and watched the fight over the shoulders of those in front.

It was a good stand-up affair, though at first I thought the two unfairly matched. One was a raw-boned boy, with a long reach, the other delicate-looking, with freckles showing on his white face. Frail as he seemed, he stood his ground well, giving as good, or nearly as good, as he got.

I was soon all of a tremble with excitement, and joined in the shouting. My sympathy was all for the smaller chap: so strong was it that whenever he got a clout I felt, or fancied I felt, my right arm swell in response to a long-ing to go to his aid. His hard breathing made me fear he would be beaten: I should have felt certain of it except for the look on his face. But I need not have been afraid, for presently, after a clinch, he caught the big fellow a blow on the chin, bewildering him so much that he reeled and threw up his hands in token of defeat.

The sudden ending surprised me; for I had seen two gipsies fight for half an hour after knocking one another down again and again; yet what surprised me even more was the way the boys who had been looking on dispersed to play, leaving only one other boy besides myself to help the fighters to wash the blood off their faces and put their jackets on.

As we were on the way back from the pump, the bell began to ring, and kept on ringing till we were inside the schoolroom.

I found that the freckled boy's name was Dickie Felton, and that he was a new boy, like myself. We stood by the door, which was in the left-hand corner of the building, till presently Mr. Tasker directed us and three others to a bench at the back, where we sat, quiet as mice, taking in our surroundings.

The room was about as long again as it was wide, with two rows of benches running from near the door to the far end, with a gangway in the middle. Between the front row and the wall stood the blackboard and Mr. Tasker's desk and stool. The rough walls and raftered ceiling reminded me of our barn; but the schoolroom, instead of being dark, was flooded with light from the three windows at my back. So strong was the light that I could read the small print on the map of Europe over against me, and the middle-sized print of the map of Cornwall on the other side of the chimney-piece, where the hour-glass rested beneath a likeness of George Daniel, the Founder.

Madron folk, the parish over, hold the name of George Daniel in honour; and his foundation is the pride of Churchtown.

By his will, dated 1739, he left £16 a year for the support of a school-master, with a house for him to live in; he bequeathed a further sum to provide boots and bread for needy scholars, and, to crown all, a special fund, that every scholar might receive a big saffron bun on Christmas Day.

The light that lit the picture fell also on the strong but gentle face of Mr. Simon Tasker, where he stood beside his desk ready to begin the quarter's work. Mr. Tasker was no ordinary man; he had been the pick of fully a score applicants for the post. He could write in two hands, copperplate and ornamental, in a manner few could equal; his downstrokes, his upstrokes, above all his flourishes, were the admiration of the lawyers' clerks of Penzance, amongst whom was not his match for cutting and splitting a goose-quill. Nor had the parish his fellow as a ready reckoner. No matter what the weight of a pig or the price per pound, the particulars had only to be stated for the answer to roll from his tongue like a thing prepared; he was that instantaneous in his calculations.

Yet these gifts were as trifles in the sum total of his accomplishments, for he was learned in the mathematics, skilled in the use of the celestial globe and Dunn's planisphere, and so great a master of the science of navigation that, had he been put to it, he could have steered a vessel to any port in the world.

At a sign of his left hand, we stood up and sang the Morning Hymn, which he pitched by the help of a tuning-fork that also served to beat the time. After the hymn came work, for which everything – pencil, slate, book – lay on the benches ready for use.

He said, "Form 1 will work the sums on the blackboard; Form 2 study in Guy's *Geography*; Form 3 in Goldsmith's *History of England*; Form 4 will learn words of one syllable."

He waited till the school had settled to the task, then came down between the desks to us. Without asking what ciphering I had done, he set me a sum in Long Division, and later, finding I had worked it right, he gave me a word of praise which, coming from him, pleased me more than I could tell, and made mother's eyes sparkle with pride when I told her. In spelling I made two mistakes, writing "waggon" for "wagon," and "troff" for "trough," though Miss Jenifer had corrected me about them; but I did worse in reading, for I jumped the commas, and counted three instead of four at the full-stops, in my hurry to get it over, partly through fright at the sound of my own voice, partly because the boys in front kept turning round and looking at me.

Dickie Felton and I were put in the Third Form, our places being at the end of the front bench, close by the door, facing the map of Cornwall, where we sat through three quarters before being moved up. Whether slowness of promotion was due more to stupidity than to inattention I cannot say, but this I know, that the least thing served to call my thoughts from off my lessons: the school mouse, whose hole was right below the Land's End, the cries of the daws about the church tower, the whetting of Jim Beare's scythe when he was tidying the churchyard – which was not often; sometimes my attention was distracted with more reason, as once by two Frenchies with a brown bear, once by a Punch and Judy show, and another time by the cry of hounds as the pack swept across the green. Then in summer, the swallows which built their nests in the angles between the rafters and the beams kept flying through the open window or open door to feed their young, and took my mind off my work.

I got, of course, a full share of the strap; though not more than I deserved, for Mr. Tasker, if severe, was just, never losing his temper except over something mean or cruel, or when some trick was played on him. When thus put out, he would pace between the desk and the door, running his thin hands through his black hair till it was ruffled beyond all sign of a parting. He was like this one morning after a boy had been cruel to a donkey, at another time when a boy, lately come from the dame's school at Crowz-an-Wra, put a bit of cobbler's wax on the stool and spoilt the seat of his duck trousers. On that occasion he forget to turn the glass, so that it was well after noon, as the dial above the church porch told us, when at last we were let out.

The dinner-hour, which lasted till half-past one, was a time of great freedom. We were at liberty to eat our pasties where fancy led us, and there is hardly a place between the roof of the church tower and Cousin Hughie's sawpit where Dickie and I have not eaten them.

Here I will touch on the earlier – the earlier by far – of the two most exciting events of my Daniel days, when I had not been more than a week

34

at school. At the time – it was in the dinner-hour – Dickie and I, who by this were sworn friends, were on our way to the kennels. On coming to the smithy we found well-nigh half the village gathered in the roadway with their faces turned up along as if in expectation of a funeral from the direction of Lanyon.

There was no funeral, but something which, when I saw it, made a cold shiver run through me. Behind the riding officer and between eight sailormen, four to either side, with cutlasses on their shoulders, came rumbling our three carts – Snowball, Hector, and Madam in the shafts, and Mr. Pearce, father, and Bill driving.

My first thought was that father and the others had been made prisoners; but the moment I saw the carts were loaded with kegs, and those all wet and muddy, I guessed what had happened – that the preventive men had come on the kegs in the pool and commandeered master to transport the goods to the Custom House.

I was all agog to tell Dickie about the kegs and the man I had seen under my window, but I could not; mother's admonition, never to speak of what I had seen, restrained me.

The onlookers watched the carts and escort go by in silence, but the moment they had disappeared round the bend by the old sycamore, Black Jim, whose head and shoulders were out at the open window of the King's Arms, shouted, as he pointed straight at me, "That boy is the one that gave us away." The man's face was dreadful in his anger, and had I understood his meaning I should certainly have been more frightened than I was. Nevertheless, his face so haunted me that I only half enjoyed the sight of what had drawn us to the kennels, namely, the huntsman's tame fox, which we found curled up asleep on his doorstep.

On my way home that evening, Black Jim cursed me as I passed his door, and next morning Andrew, the earth-stopper, was waiting at his gate to tell me that effigies of father and myself had been burnt on the village green during the night, and to warn me to keep close to the school in the dinner-hour.

"But, Andrew," I replied, "I've never breathed a word about the kegs to any one, and I'm sure father never did."

"I believe you, Jack, but nawthin' would persuade them that you did not. However, put on a bold front and walk down along just as if nothin' had happened."

I didn't half like going, and on coming in sight of the first of the cottages I was on the point of turning back when I saw Dickie hieing to meet me. The moment I did so, I took heart and held on.

Dickie stood by me all day, though the rest of the school kept their distance, and he would have seen me well on the road home had not Mr. Pearce been waiting at the school door.

Father fetched me the next day, Bill the day after, and by that the danger had really passed; but for days afterwards mother came all the way to the rab-pit to meet me, though it threw her out terribly with the milking.

Once a quarter, we had to sit at the table of Mr. Tasker, who ate with a fork like mother, and like her talked all through the meal. One dinner-hour he talked of birds and flowers, another of King Charles's letter, another of the old fogous and cliff castles where the ancient Britons, who raised the Quoit and other memorials, used to flee in troublous times. I enjoyed listening to him except once, after a strapping, when I was sore in mind as well as in body.

This severe strapping came about through five of us scholars wishing to become bell-ringers, as indeed four of us afterwards did. Our plan, which succeeded wonderfully well until we were found out, was to go up into the bellchamber, tie up the clappers, come down into the belfry and ring till we were tired. One day, after ringing, we found that somebody had locked both the belfry and the church door, and that within a few minutes of school. In the difficulty, Dick suggested that we should pull one of the bell ropes through the guides, drop it over the parapet of the tower, and slide down the rope to the roof; and this we did. Four got down without being seen, but when I was half-way Mr. Tasker espied me, with the result that I caught it after the rest of the school had been dismissed. To make matters worse, I had to walk home in a tremendous downpour.

People have wondered at Mr. Tasker having the boys to meals with him, as if he did not get enough of them in school. The truth is, he never tired of their company. After the meal, when the fruit was ripe, he took us into the garden to eat gooseberries or windfalls whilst, pipe in mouth, he sat under the medlar tree and read the *Gazette*. And then on Saturdays, in the midsummer quarter, he took the First Form for outings in the squire's one-horse wain – that is, when he could get it – and when not, on foot, and always to the westward. In these excursions he was as light-hearted as the youngest of us, and as full of the spirit of adventure. Pleasant were the hours we spent with him on the wild hills between Sancreed Beacon and Chapel Carn Brea, especially on Bartinney, which was his favourite; delightful, too, the hours spent in exploring Lamorna Caves; yet of them all none had the thrill of the other dinner-hour incident, now to be told, as it deserves, in a chapter all to itself.

CHAPTER V

A GREAT ADVENTURE

❦

T HIS INCIDENT OR – as it perhaps deserves to be called – event was a visit to the squire's preserves when I was nearly twelve and more than ever fond of wild creatures. I had longed and longed to see them, without dreaming aught would come of it, till Dickie's tales of the valley fevered me to such a pitch that I determined to go there whatever the consequences; and go there I did, though not until the third attempt.

Dickie was innocent; it never entered his head that I could not withstand the temptation, and was as like as not to fall into the clutches of his surly father, the squire's gamekeeper. It was because I loved to hear, he to tell, that he brought me news of the covers and talked of the game, of the birds of prey, of the chance comers, like the hoopoe and the golden oriole, and one morning – it was in the bitter February of '41, when a long icicle hung from the lip of the Churchtown pump – of three wild swans that had taken possession of the middle pond and driven the duck away.

This was more than I could stand. Before he had got out all he had to say, my mind was made up to have a sight of these great birds on the way to school next morning. The Carn brake had always seemed to me the least dangerous line of approach, and, leaving home earlier than usual, I made for it as fast as my legs could carry me.

Alas for a boy's resolve when left to himself, without a comrade to keep him to it! Not that I backed out altogether; it was not quite so bad as that. I did get as far as the Carn, but no farther. There my courage failed me, partly through the cold, chiefly through dread of the man-traps which I felt sure lay cunningly set in the furze and ferns between me and the pond. Yet, though I shrank from going forward, my pride held me from beating a retreat, at least until only just time enough remained to get to school; then I crept back as I had come, on all fours like a newt, and almost as slowly on account of the numbness of my hands.

I reached the track without being hailed, but with feelings very much changed from the high spirits that possessed me when starting out. I felt humbled in my own eyes, and for a day or two the memory of having played the coward kept coming to me on the way home, and especially in bed, where I never could make head against trouble of any kind. I was pun-ished in another way, too, for Dickie's daily report of the swans, which stayed on till the frost yielded, always made me wince.

With the departure of the birds, I was again able to listen to Dickie with-out shrinking, and even to wonder, as I listened, in what shape the next temptation would present itself, and when. Nor, as it chanced, was it later than the middle of April.

This time it was news of a kingfisher's nest, which I was at once all eagerness to see, because I had read that these birds built their nests, not of twigs, grass, moss, feathers, or horse-hair, but – of all things in the world – of fishbones! Dickie had tried to get at it and failed; but this did not discourage me, since, instead of working at the mouth of the hole as he had done, I intended to sink down upon the nest as a badger does upon a stop of rabbits.

In my excitement, I all but let out that I meant to go and try my hand, which would have been a great pity, for, though it might not have cost me his friendship, it would certainly have led to a certain coolness and made him mum as to the valley ever afterwards.

As at my first venture, I decided to go by way of the Carn, and left Lanyon betimes, armed with Bill's thistlespud for the work before me. Again I started in high spirits, determined this time to go through with the enterprise. And through with it I verily believe I should have gone, but for being forestalled and thwarted in a way no one will blame me for not having foreseen.

On climbing the bank opposite Forest Carn, to look round before committing myself, whom should I see seated on the top of the Carn but Mr. Felton himself, with his fierce-whiskered face set in my direction, as if he knew of my coming, and was on the look-out for me! I ducked at once – whether in time to prevent his ferret eyes detecting me, I much doubted. Be that as it might, I was careful not to give him a second chance, for I hugged the wall all the way to Churchtown fields, keeping well below the capping-stones and crouching down at the gaps.

Being thus twice crossed in my purpose, I was beginning to be recon-ciled to never seeing the Bottoms, as we call the valley, when one May morning Dickie came with news of a discovery which inflamed me afresh and to a greater degree than ever before.

I recall the day as if it were yesterday. Dickie was late that morning, so late that I gave him up and joined a score or more chaps who were marching round the Green blowing mayhorns. I had made the circuit a time or two when I espied him coming across Landithy fields as hard as he could tear. He leapt the stile, stood still on alighting to look for me, and, the moment he caught sight of me, beckoned, and kept beckoning till I left the others and joined him.

"I've got news this morning, Jack," he said; and, putting his arm through mine, he led away from the noise.

"Well, was it made of fish-bones?" I asked, thinking he had got at the kingfisher's nest.

"Oh ! it's not that at all."

"Then what is it? Why do you keep it from me?"

"Jack, I have found what I have been searching for since father came to Trengwainton – a spy tower. It's a tree, a hollow tree, with a woodpecker's hole for look-out. It stands near the end of the upper pond. I was there yesterday at dusk, and what do you think I saw?"

"The kingfisher?"

"No, but I saw a fox come and roll on the turf, and an otter with three cubs fish in the pond! I would give anything to take you there if I could, but I dare not; it might cost father his place if I did."

If Dickie was excited by the discovery, I was doubly so. Ever since mother had read "Robinson Crusoe" to me, look-outs, peep-holes, even our barn steps, had become things of delight. And then the hollow tree looked out on the valley that had been calling to me, and on the part of it I longed most to visit. It was all I could do to prevent myself going off there and then; and off I should have gone but for mother's continual warnings against minching, as we call playing truant. So I followed the others in when the bell rang, and during class did my best to appear attentive, so as to escape being put down in the detention book. Through my fingers I watched the last grains run down, and the moment Mr. Tasker uttered the words, "You may go," I put away my slate, rushed through the doorway, up along through Churchtown, and never stopped to draw breath till I reached the Carn. Even then I dwelt but a few seconds before stealing down the rocks to the fox brake, through which I crept on all fours, trying with a stick each suspicious spot I came to. I sprang no man-trap, I set off no spring-gun, I came on nothing more dangerous than an adder, which rustled away into the browse out of my path.

40

Half-way down, I took off my cap, raised my head till my eyes were on a level with the furze blowth, and looked round. As I saw no one, I resumed my crawl, and I continued it to the lower edge of the brake. From there I could see right into the wood, which called to mind our church by the aisles among the tree trunks and the gloom cast by the leaves. The sight of this wood, the first I had ever seen close, filled me with awe, so solemn it looked and so still. But I had no time to lose. I rose, entered, and stole along between the stems and noiselessly as ever Jim Beare tiptoed down the nave in the middle of a sermon. I was making for the spot where I expected to find the hollow tree, for I had plied Dickie with so many questions as to its exact whereabouts that I never doubted of reaching it. At last I sighted it. There was the woodpecker's hole, and there the open space where Dickie had seen the fox roll, but unlike what I had imagined it, for instead of being smooth like the grassy margin of the pond, it was all hummocky with anthills. In my haste, I fell over one of them, knocking out what little breath remained to me.

This misadventure befell me when I had come close to the tree and was beginning to feel disheartened at seeing no sign of a hole to enter it by. Yet I was sure there must be a way in, for I had never found Dickie out in a lie; and a way in there was, as I discovered the moment I peeped through the brambles round the foot of it. Then I lay flat, wriggled along a sort of creep till my head and shoulders were through the hole, and, turning on my side, managed, by pressing my left hand against the inside, to get into a sitting posture and draw the rest of my body in.

I cannot describe the delight I felt, a delight in which fear and joy were strangely mingled. After a short rest, I got up on my feet, ran my hands over the walls to find what they were like, and then looked up. It was like looking up a chimney in the dead of night, so black it was, and a star shone in a bit of sky at the top. This may excite comment, but I believe to this day I did see a star. Diggory Angwin, the well-sinker, told me afterwards there was nothing strange in that – he, himself, having seen stars in broad daylight from the bottom of a peeth and, as a lad, when climbing the ladders of Balleswidden mine shaft.

There was something that puzzled me a good deal more than the star; a strange beating noise, which I presently discovered to be nothing more mysterious than the thumping of my own heart.

But I had not a minute to lose if I was to be back for afternoon school;

so I started climbing forthwith, making good speed till about eight feet up. As above that my hobnails could get no grip, without further loss of time, I dropped to the ground, or rather to the touchwood which lay thick there, took off my boots, and made a fresh start in my stockings. This made a great difference. With the hold I now got, I was able to pass the bad place to the nubbly part above, where, however, on account of the lie of the knots, I had to keep turning round and round as I mounted.

Once on a level with the woodpecker's hole, I made a seat of the bulge that lay handiest, held myself there by pressing my feet against the opposite wall, and peeped out.

What a picture! The beeches and birches in the freshness of new leaf, the pond reflecting them, the islet tufted with ferns and – like the slope below the Carn – the slope of the Great Downs opposite, a sheet of golden furze blowth. Everything was very still. What little wind there was came in puffs, ruffling the water only to leave it smooth as glass, except for the rings made by the rising trout. Presently a cock pheasant came to drink, later an owl with white in its wing flew across a glade, and then from a tall pine out flew a sparrow hawk. I felt so sure the hawk had a nest there that I decided to climb the tree and get the eggs. So down I came, crept out through the hole, and ran to the pine. On reaching it, I was disappointed to find that its girth was altogether beyond my span, and that only by the greatest good fortune could I hope to reach the place where the branches began. But I tried. Twice I nearly fell, once when a piece of bark came away in my hand, and again because a branch – it was the lowest – snapped off as I tried my weight on it; and in each case I was saved by the firm grip of my knees, got from riding bareback. Afterwards it was easy, and up and up I went till I got to the nest.

To my joy it contained four eggs, all so beautifully marked that I wasted time choosing the three I at last settled to take. These I put in my cap, which I gripped in my teeth so as to have my hands free in the descent. All went well till I got to the main stem below the lowest branch, where, do what I could, I kept slipping and tearing my hands till they became so tender that presently I let go and dropped. How far I fell I can hardly say, but it was far enough to give me a nasty jar, and leave me all dazed and foolish.

I was brought to suddenly by the sound of footsteps, which sent me skeared to my hiding-place. Once inside the tree I climbed to the look-out, which I reached just as Mr. Felton came rushing out of the wood. He had caught sight of me and was completely at a loss to know where I had gone. I have seldom seen a more puzzled look on a man's face, but what struck me even more was the way his fishing-rod shook. If he had seen a real ghost, it could not have shook more. I felt quite sorry at seeing him so, and was on the point of calling out, "Don't be skeared, Mr. Felton, it's only me," when he turned and walked towards the pond, untying the rod-case as he went. Again and again I came near calling to him, on account of the way he kept looking over his shoulder, and should have done so, but for the ashy whiteness of his face, which frightened me so much that I kept silent and watched him whip the pieces of rod together with bits of string, fix the reel, run the line through the rings, attach the flies, and cast them on the water.

Suddenly he threw down the rod and the creel, and – grown man and gamekeeper though he was, and a terror to the parish – took to his heels as if Dick Hal's ghost were after him. He did not retreat by the way he had come, but made off athirt the Great Downs along the earthstopper's track, and was soon lost to view.

Then I heard the Trengwainton clock strike, warning me to be off.

Meanwhile a fish had taken one of the flies and was making the reel sing. Down I came, landed the trout, left it kicking on the bank, and in a twinkling was back in the tree doing up my boots as fast as I could for the darkness. I had just finished tying the second lace when I distinctly heard some one sneeze. My first thought was that I was done for, that nothing could now save me from being late; and then I began to wonder who the new-corner might be

I do not know how I managed to climb in my boots, but I did; and, on looking through the peep-hole, saw the squire standing gazing down at the trout with much the same look on his face as I had seen on the keeper's.

"That's never Felton's doing, and the rod couldn't land a fish of itself. Who the devil, then?"

As he uttered the last sentence, he looked about him, and particularly up along the valley past the tree where Dick Hal was known to walk. I thought that he was dismissing the matter, for he began casting, letting out more and more line to reach a rising fish. I was wrong, however. The thought of the ghost was still in his head, for all to once he began looking over his shoulder as if afraid of being pounced upon from behind.

Interested as I was, I was most unhappy at heart; bitterly did I chide myself for not going off when the coast was clear. I feared Mr. Tasker's anger and the fuss he would make, mother's trouble, and Miss Jenifer's sharp tongue. I was all anxiety to be gone, but dared not run the risk whilst the squire kept turning round as he did. In my anxiety, I decided to try the sound of a voice; he might take it in the way I wanted.

"Tee-hee! Tee-hee!"

The effect was instantaneous. He leapt from the ground like a shot rabbit, and tore through the wood at a speed I should not have thought possible for a man always in the saddle. Then down I came again, picked up my cap and eggs, bundled through the hole, and raced up the slope reckless of trap and gun.

All Churchtown seemed to be at their doors to see me go by. That was painful enough, but nothing to the feeling I had when I reached the school door. I do not know whether I should have had the courage to lift the latch and go in, had it not been for the advice of Jim Beare. Leaning over the churchyard wall, and stroking his white beard, he said in a low voice, "I can see how 'tes with 'ee; now take an old man's advice and go in." So I opened the door, shut it behind me, and walked across the floor to my place.

Mr. Tasker, whom my entry had interrupted, resumed with the geography lesson without a sign in his voice that he was put out, though what his face was like I dared not raise my eyes to see. However, he looked so bright and nice during second lesson that I began to hope he had forgotten all about me. He had not. At the close he said, in his severe voice, "Penrose, I wish to speak to you." Whereupon every boy looked at me; and I noticed the reproachful eye of Dickie, who guessed where I had been. That was bad, but it was worse when the door was closed, leaving me all alone with Mr. Tasker.

Whilst he was putting chalk and duster away and the globe back, there came to my mind father's advice: "Speak the truth and to once."

It came in the nick of time to save me from telling a lie.

"What made you nearly three-quarters of an hour late?"

"I wanted to see the hollow tree, sir."

" Where is it?"

"By the upper pond, sir."

"Do you mean to tell me that you have dared to trespass on the squire's sanctuary?"

"I did, sir, and skeared Mr. Felton and Sir Rose out of their lives!"

"Explain yourself, boy."

44

So I told him the story, looking straight in his face, and never taking my eyes off, till he slewed round towards the map so that I should not see he was laughing, which was foolish because his sides were shaking with laughter.

When at last he turned, as serious as Judge Bevan, he said solemnly, "Penrose, I will let you off this time."

CHAPTER VI

CHRISTMAS MARKET
୨ୣୢ

A WORD OR TWO should, perhaps, be said to explain why I was kept at school past the age of boys of my standing. It was not that I showed a particular turn for lessons, or that I was undersized, it was simply that mother was determined I should have a good education.

Firm as she was about it, ready also to make any sacrifice, circumstances presently proved almost too strong for her, for the one and only thing we had to look to for a living – I mean the butter from our own little dairy – dropped from 7d. to 5d., and could not be disposed of even at that.

Mother did her best to find a market. Whilst the glut lasted, she carried the week's making to Penzance, in the hope of getting rid of it there. The first time, to our great rejoicing, she met with good speed; then market-day followed market-day without an offer, so that she had to bring the butter back home, and salt it in; what else could she do? Money had to be taken from the savings to buy salt and – what was more serious – bussas, the price of which had been clapped up by Mr. Sloman, the potter, in consequence of the heavy demand. Mother said again and again, that it was like parting with her life to touch the nest egg; but then she could not help herself, the few pounds in the chest-of-drawers being all she had to turn to.

Those were hard days; we lived on skimmed milk and barley bread – sky blue and sinker we called it – with salt pilchards and taties on Sundays. Father smoked herbs and gave up his glass of beer on practice nights. Everything was cut down except the bit of fat in my pasty, father's Foresters' money, and granny's weekly allowance.

Through the distress, mother bore up better than father, who paced the kitchen long after mother and I had gone upstairs.

On midsummer eve, as we sat before the door watching the glare from the bonfires, mother said, "Richard, I'm troubled to know what to do for the best, whether to keep Jack at school or put him to service."

"Why, I thought we'd settled that months ago."

"We did, but times were different."

"True, times are bad, bad as I mind them, but they will mend; and if they don't, I am still for the lad staying on as long as we can last out."

46

"You are?"

"I am; no one knows the value of education like the man who can neither read nor write. You'll never know what I've suffered, what agony it was to me to make my cross on my wedding-day, and the old school-mistress looking on."

He spoke with a strength of feeling that upset mother, so foreseeing the scene that would follow, I edged off the seat and slipped round by the turf-rick to be out of sight and hearing. Poverty, that made father and mother so tender to one another, had a sobering effect upon me. Whilst it lasted, I kept out of mischief; I went straight home from school, so as to lend a hand, seeing to the geese, fetching turf and water, as I did again next morning before starting out.

After corn harvest, butter rose; the worried look left father's face, and mother went about her work again as light-heartedly as ever. The harvest was heavy, especially for oats, with abundance of straw filling the mowhay to overflowing, so that it was hard for anybody but me to squeeze between the rick and the walls. But every bit of fodder was needed, for winter set in early and the cattle were housed weeks before the usual time. It was very cold for us. I remember the havoc caused amongst the daddy-longlegs by two nights' frost late in September, better still the early coming of the woodcock in October, above all the November frosts which made the road ring underfoot till the wind shifted from north-east to north-west, with gales that lasted off and on till close on Christmas.

Of all people, except thatchers and coast-watchers, I perhaps have most reason to remember the gales, on account of the difficulty I had in making head against them on my way home from school. The most violent was the one on the last day of the quarter. It came on to blow in the afternoon, and the wind rose higher and higher till the rattling of the windows and the roar in the elms were too much for Mr. Tasker, who at last gave over further attempts to make himself heard, and fell to rolling up the maps for the holidays. Whilst watching him I listened to the gale, and as I listened, wondered whether I could reach Lanyon, and what mother would do if I could not. For once I felt sorry when school was over; for once the boys, when let out, followed Mr. Tasker's advice and went straight home. By the time I was abreast of the King's Arms, whose signboard was creaking badly, Jesse Thomas was the only boy to be seen, and when he dropped into the house next Mrs. Trudgen's and slammed the door behind him, I was alone with the empty street and the storm.

The wind was even worse than I had feared; I had difficulty in forcing my way, though I bent half double to make myself as small as I could. It was minutes before I got to Billy Brean's, and minutes more before I passed the end cottage, where a light was burning in the upstairs window. But it was when I reached the high ground that the real battle began. I got some protection from the rhododendrons on the Forest Carn; but beyond, the storm had me at its mercy: there was no shelter till I should reach the rab-pit. What a struggle I had as I rose the hill – the wind made a toil of every step. On the ridge I was almost brought to a standstill. In my difficulty I went on all fours, dropping flat when the gusts came, crawling in between times. And so after what seemed hours I reached the cave in the rab-pit, glad to be sheltered from the gale that howled, as I thought, like a pack of wolves. On leaving the cave, I kept close under the hedge, which protected me as far as Paunshallow Bridge. There, hoping to get some protection from the furze, I forsook the road for the croft, where the salt foam-flakes kept striking my face as I fought my way through the pitchy darkness. I was close upon the Quoit before I was aware, and never, I think, were the old stones more welcome. Whilst I crouched at the foot of the broadest of the uprights, I heard the deep-sounding roar of the sea calling from the Morvah cliffs.

"You'll not frighten me," I said within myself. "I shall be indoors in a minute or two."

Though Miss Jenifer had put two candles in the window to light me by, it was hard to find the farm-yard gate, and harder still to close it.

"I'm thankful you've come, Jack," mother called out from the dairy. "Are you all right?"

"Yes, mother; and what little dog is this before the fire?"

"Dog, did, you say?"

"Yes."

"I don't know; it wasn't there five minutes ago; it must have come in with you."

"Mother!"

"Yes."

"It has got a bladder about its neck."

"I'm coming."

With that, mother came out of the dairy, patted the dog, removed the

48

bladder, and read aloud the script which she found inside, and which is before me as I write: "Ce chien s'appelle Victor; Dieu bénisse qui le protège. L. T., Concarneau."

"What does it mean, mother?"

"Why, that the dog is called Victor, and – I think – that God will protect it."

"Protect what?" asked father, coming in.

"Why this little waif of a dog, Richard; see, it is licking my hand with joy at hearing its name."

When father had heard the tale, he examined the bladder and the tarred rope that had bound it, and said, "This is a shipwrecked dog; the bladder was to keep its head above water."

"And the script dry," added mother.

"Just so, and the script may carry a deal of meanin'. Anyways, there is only one thing to do – to take paper and all to the Custom House, which you can do on Saturday, Mary, when you go into market."

It was now Wednesday, and between that and Christmas market Victor and I became good friends. He was out and about with me from morning till evening, much of the time with his muzzle deep in some rabbit-hole. He slept on my bed, licked my face to wake me in the morning, and could be trusted in the dairy, which Shep never could.

On the Saturday morning, mother and I started soon after eight, she carrying the basket, I leading Victor. At Paunshallow we changed about, but at Churchtown mother took the basket again, and would carry it, heavy as it was, the rest of the way.

It wanted a quarter of an hour to ten as we rounded Branwell's Corner, for mother had timed it so as to be at the Custom House the moment it opened, get first hearing, and be back at the butter-market amongst the earliest comers. Victor made us laugh twice on the way: first, by barking at a road-sweeper in Chapel Street, then by sitting and howling at a German band in Quay Street.

On reaching the harbour, I stood watching the sailors push long balks of timber through a hole in the bow of a ship into the water, where two men collected them into a raft. I could have stayed there all day; as it was, I remained until mother had reached the flight of steps leading to the Custom House, and I had all I could do to overtake her before she passed in.

The room was a good size, with green walls and a whitewashed ceiling, from which a lamp hung to within a foot or two of a sort of counter, behind which sat the officer we had come to see. He was a jolly-faced old gentleman, and so spick and span in his blue cloth coat, clean collar and shirt front with gold button in it, that he might have just stepped out of a bandbox.

He was very nice to mother, at least from the moment she spoke, begging her twice, while she was telling her story, to be seated on the cane chair on our side of the counter. When she had done, she handed over the script, which he laid on the sloping desk before him and examined though a burning-glass.

"It is as I feared," he said, leaning back in his chair. "The message, as the initials and handwriting tell me, is from Captain Louis Trefarreg, of Concarneau, who for many years traded with rock-salt between Noirmoutier and Mount's Bay or St. Ives. This is not the first intimation of the foundering of the vessel, for word reached us early this morning that a board with *Marie-Rose* – the name of the smack – had been washed up at Gurnard's Head. But where is the dog?"

"Here, sir," I said.

"And a very pretty little dog, too," he said, leaning forward and looking at it over the counter.

"May we keep it, sir?" I asked in fear and trembling.

"Well, yes; at least I think so – that is, of course, unless it is claimed."

"May I ask what the message says?"

"Certainly, madam; it says, 'This dog is called Victor: God bless the man or woman who gives it a home.'"

"Then we will give it a home, sir, as long as we may."

"That is very good of you. And now may I ask your name and address?"

"I am Mary Penrose, wife of Richard Penrose, farm-hand at Lanyon."

At the mention of Lanyon, he sat bolt upright, dropped the quill he had picked up, fixed his grey eyes upon me, and said –

"Have you seen any kegs in the pool lately, Jack?"

"No, sir," I replied, as soon as I could find breath to answer such a dumb-founding question. "I haven't been anist the pool since the day I was lost; but please tell me how you know I was there at all."

"That's telling, Jack," he replied, throwing himself back in the chair and roaring with laughter till his bald head was flushed and his upper teeth moved up and down for all the world like a thing on hinges.

Then he suddenly sobered down, and addressing mother, said, "Mrs Penrose, if you know of any one you care for being mixed up with smugglers, and especially with the Prussia Cove gang – "

"My man has nothing to do with them, if that is what you mean, sir."

"That is what I did mean, Mrs. Penrose, and I am glad to hear what you say."

Then he rose and stepped to the door, which he opened and held open for mother and me to pass out.

"What a gentleman!" said mother, as we hurried up Dock Lane towards the market, where most of the seats were already taken. Mother, however, got the end place of the bench under the toll-board, close to a stall where a man was selling all manner of tin things from a milk-pan to a farthing whistle.

Whilst I looked about me, mother turned back the white cloth from the things she had to sell: two geese, six pounds and three half-pounds of butter, printed with the wheatsheaf, and a brace of snipe father had caught in the mill-leat.

Now, lovely as these things had looked in the dairy when mother took father and me in to see them, they looked mean and poor in the market. It was partly on account of the basket, which looked shabby compared with the baskets of the farmers' wives, partly because the cloths were darned all over. And then mother was poorly dressed.

We sat there quietly, like people apart from the rest: nobody spoke to us, nobody as much as asked the price, though buyers were in plenty, and our neighbours doing a brisk trade.

I wonder now that I should have been so pained at the slight, but, to tell the truth, I felt it so that I could hardly keep back my tears.

"Take a round of the market," said mother, some time between twelve and one; and so Victor and I went past the vegetable stalls, the sweet stalls, the toy stall, with its big Christmas tree full of lovely things, and the man dressed up like Father Christmas; past a gypsy woman telling fortunes, past a cheapjack, past Henry Quick selling his poems, past a man taking in stockings to dye and badger skins to cure, till I had seen pretty well everything, and worked my way back to mother.

To my joy, I thought she had got a customer, but I was wrong; the man she was talking to was only the toll collector. One by one the farmers' wives left, as they sold out; by three o'clock the great market was nearly empty, and buyers few and far between. Presently a dealer offered mother 7*d*. a pound for the butter, though others had got 8 1/2 *d*. She accepted the price rather than run the risk of taking it back home; but she refused 5*d*. a pound for the geese. Half an hour later, the dealer repeated his offer, which mother rejected with a show of indignation that drove him off for good.

Between four and five, when we were almost the only ones left, a nudge from mother awoke me – for I had fallen asleep – and, looking up, I saw a nicely-dressed lady, whom I had once seen at Lanyon, come through the middle gate straight towards us. It was mother's old schoolmistress, with a maid in attendance, carrying a basket.

"My dear Mary," said she, shaking hands affectionately with mother, "I am glad to see you and John; what a fine boy he has grown. And now let us come to business. These geese are just the thing I am in search of, neither too gross nor too lean. What are you asking?"

"Sevenpence a pound."

"I shall not think of paying less than eightpence for such splendid birds," and eightpence she paid in spite of mother's protests.

"Then you must let me throw in the brace of snipe?"

"Very well, Mary, you always would have your own way, and shall now," she said, smiling.

After settling for the geese and begging mother in vain to go to the schoolhouse, she took us to the toy stall, and to my delight bought me a lancewood bow as tall as myself, and a bundle of arrows. It was from Father Christmas himself that she bought them; it was from his hands that I took them.

There the schoolmistress left us, she going one way, we the other, towards the eating-house in Market Jew Street, where mother always went. On going in, mother asked for three pieces of saffron cake – one for herself, two for me – and a piece of barley bread for Victor. As we ate, mother busied herself looking at the list of things she was going to buy, while I watched the emigrants thronging the brightly-lighted office on the Terrace opposite.

The moment I had finished eating the second piece of cake, we left to do our shopping, and though mother only wanted a yard of ribbon, a pipe for father, a few oranges, a pound of wheaten flour, and a bottle of harts-horn oil, it was nearly seven o'clock before we started off home, on account of having to wait our turn in the crowded shops.

By then I was very tired, and longed for a lift, but though cart after cart passed, no one offered, perhaps because of mother's sunbonnet, which showed we were poor. Between Heamoor and Churchtown, after a cart with only a woman in it had passed us, she suddenly broke out, "Never mind, we'll drive home in our own trap some day, Jack, my dear. I'm saving every penny I can scrape to stock the little place I've got my eye on. Your father's son, God willing, shall be a rich farmer some day."

"You mean me, mother?"

"Yes, you, my dear, who else," she said, kissing me.

Christmas Eve was being kept in Churchtown; the carol singers were singing, "While shepherds watched," at the Vicarage, the church tower had a lighted lantern at each pinnacle, men were carousing at the King's Arms, and every cottage up along had a light in the window, the last of the row, indeed, had two. And so we came to Forest Carn and to the ridge beyond, and oh! how friendly the stars looked!

Father met us at Paunshallow, all anxiety to hear how we had prospered; and he danced, making the frosted ground ring, when mother told him she had sold out, and got 8d. a pound for the geese.

We sang the rest of the way, and that night I had lovely dreams. I dreamed of the Christmas tree, lighted up as I had seen it, of the grocer's shop smelling of dates and spices, of the timber ships of the old gentleman of the Custom House, not, however, in his armchair there, but on the moor across which Victor and I were leading him to Smuggler's Pool.

CHAPTER VII

A YOUNG EMIGRANT
❦

ALL THROUGH CHRISTMAS the talk indoors and out was of little else but emigration. The reports of nuggets to be had for the search, and of fortunes made in no time, lured everybody's thoughts to the goldfields. Many had already sailed. The St. Just miners led the rush; one batch in October, another early in December, and now not miners only, but quarrymen and farm labourers had caught the yellow fever, as some called it, and were all agog for the New World.

Half the berths had been taken in the brig *Triton*, then being fitted up alongside Penzance Quay, though she was not due to sail under a week. Willie Thomas, a crofter from Kerrow, was to start in her, and his excitement about it so worked upon our Bill that on the Monday forenoon he suddenly threw down the threshel, fetched eight golden guineas out of his thatch, and started off to secure berths for Betty and himself. The terrible thing was that Betty was against leaving, and as he went strothing off, kept calling after him, "Now mind, Bill, I won't go." But he kept on as if he had not heard her.

Mother ran across two, if not three, times during the day to try to comfort her, and we all waited up to see Bill on his return, when he would come across for a last look at the horses.

The moment the gate clicked, father went to the door and called out, "That thee, Bill?"

"Iss, Richard, 'tes me, or all that's left of me; what with fightin' to keep my standin' in that old office, what with Betty since I comed back, I feel less than nawthin'."

"Sit down and rest yourself," said mother, as he came in.

"Thank 'ee, Mrs. Penrose, I cain't stay only just to tell 'ee, we're sailin' Thursday."

"Betty too?" exclaimed mother.

"Iss, Betty too: she was in some tear when I showed her the passage papers, and what do 'ee think she did?"

"What?" asked mother.

"Why, she flinged herself upon the floor and wrastled in prayer till she heard the Lord say, 'Go.' Then she rose to her feet a changed woman, and now not all the King's hosses should turn her. goodnight all."

With that he was gone, leaving father and mother sitting there looking before them, and never a word did they speak till I went to bed. But after I had gone upstairs I heard them praying, not under their breath like church-folk, but fervently with all their souls like Methodists: they quite frightened me. Whether the Lord answered as he did Betty, mother never said; any-way nothing came of it. But though they were content to stay on at Lanyon, I was all for going; I was all eagerness to see the New World.

In the day or two that remained, we could not do enough for Bill and Betty. Next morning I cleaned Bill's boots, and very nice they looked on the tailboard of the trap when, after breakfast, he and Betty were driven off to Penzance, back to back with Mr. and Mrs. Pearce. They returned in the evening with a brand new carpet-bag packed as full as it could hold, a pick, a shovel, and two shallow milk pans for washing the gold in.

The day before sailing, Bill spent in Spar Croft with Henry Warren, a Levant miner, who learnt him to bore, tamp and blast, in case he had to work on a lode, and in the evening he and Betty were treated to a farewell supper in the kitchen of the big house, with their friends for company. Father, mother and I sat together, with Dickie next to me. After we had done eating, master and missus came in, and master said, "Fill your mugs, friends, I'm going to ask you to drink to the guests of the evening, Bill and Betty. Bill, lad, I am sorry to lose you for, boy and man, you have served me well, and a better hand with horses I never wish to see. Mind, I don't blame you for trying to better yourself, not a bit. You and Betty are going to a land full of promise for labouring men. They tell me that here and there along the creeks and gullies you can see the gold showing colour amongst the gravel and – mark this – to be had for the getting, without fear of spring-guns or man-traps. (Great laughter.) Hardships you will encounter, no doubt, but then you've got Cornish hearts to meet and overcome them with. And if you strike it rich, Bill, gold won't be good enough for thee to eat."

"And if poor," put in Betty, "sky blue and sinker will be too good." (Great laughter.)

"I wish you both, and all Lanyon wishes you, the best of luck."

Then master raised his mug and said, "Friends, here's to Bill and Betty." At that the company rose, looked towards Bill and Betty, called out "God bless 'ee," and drank. When they sat down, Henry Warren, who had a nice tenor voice, sang "Sweet Nightingale," father keeping time on the flute he had brought.

In the silence that followed, Bill got on his feet, tossed back his forelock, and said: "Maister Pearce, I thank thee and Missus for your goodness to me and Betty. This night puts the crown on all thee'st done these sixteen years past. I ax your pardon if I speak a bit freely. Thee'st bin a man to us men, big-hearted and never a black look, no not when butter was so to say being given away. Do'ee remember, Richard, how we used to talk it over in the barn?"

"I do, Bill."

"Well, that chapter is closed, and now Betty and me, of all people in the world, are off to the Diggings. It's neck or nawthin' with us. There's an old saying that distant fields look green, but when you come up to them they are barren. What if we meet with poor speed? Au! my dear life, don't 'ee speak of it! But theere, I don't believe the All-Merciful God would 'tice us across the waste of waters to our ruin. It edn as if it were just the gold we were after. No 'tedn't that. I'll tell 'ee what it es. 'Tes a little holdin' of a few quillets here touching Lanyon, where Betty and me could tend a little dairy of our own and end our days in peace. That's our dream. So now you know what's drawin' us to Californie; tedn't the gold, but the bit of land that only gold can buy. One word more, and only one to ask a laist favour. Please don't any of 'ee come to see us off, we caan't abeer it. Maister and Missus, may God make it up to 'ee, for we never can."

But we had made up our minds to see them off; we had already arranged to be abroad early so as to have the work well forward and be able to get away. And abroad betimes we were. To my astonishment, Bill was out and about as usual, fetched in hay and turnips for the bullocks, and then for the last time went to see to the horses.

Hector and Madam had been to him almost in the place of children; he had seen to them when foaled, when colts on the moor, had broken them in, worked them, fed them, stood listening to them munch the corn, bedded them and looked in upon them last thing at night before turning in. And now it was touching to watch him. He patted their necks, he smoothed their manes, tidied their forelocks, held their muzzles in his hands; he did this over and over till I thought he would never have done. At last he tore himself away, but faced round at the door. Better if he had not, for their great soft eyes were following him as if they knew they would never see him again. As he crossed the yard, he took no notice of Betty, who was taking to mother the cradle she had never wanted.

Father and I started off for Penzance in the middle of the forenoon, stepping out briskly along the road fresh-rutted by the wheels of the trap which had taken Bill, Betty, and mother.

We kept our thoughts to ourselves; mine were all on the New World. I had got scarcely any sleep for thinking of it, and as we walked down Causeway Head I began to wonder whether I could find a hiding-place in the *Triton* and get away to sea without being discovered. On reaching the Quay, we found the deck of the brig black as an emmet bank with the emigrants and their friends. Such sobbing and weeping as was there I shall never witness again.

We crossed the planchen to the vessel and stood at the hatch looking down upon the lower deck. The women were on one side, the men on the other, with a deal partition between. Presently father went down the ladder to the men's side, I to the women's, where Betty and mother were. The berths took my fancy at sight. Each had two bunks, one above the other, and each bunk had a palliasse and two blankets with "Triton" on them in red worsted. All the woodwork, except the side of the ship, was freshly planed and roughly put together. In the chinks of the floor I could see the China clay that served for ballast.

All these things interested me till I happened to notice there was just room enough under the lower bunk to admit me. Then my one thought was for an opportunity to gain this hiding-place unobserved. That offered when the bell summoned the emigrants to the upper deck for prayer; and whilst the last of them was yet on the ladder, I raised the bit of hessian that draped the bunk and crept in under. Lying there, I heard Parson Veale read the prayers; I heard Mr. Tasker start the hymn, "Oh God, our help in ages past," and the people join in; I heard the friends of the emigrants go ashore; and when at last I heard the captain shout, "Cast her off" I prayed that I might not be discovered till we were so far from land that I could not be put ashore.

It seemed to me hours before Betty and her berthmate came down to bed. The stranger, a stout woman from Brahan, had the lower bunk, and law! how it creaked under her! I thought every minute she would break through and come down on me. And though I fell asleep, I must have been haunted by the dread of it, for I dreamt that our threshing-floor was being lowered slowly till it threatened to crush me; then I screamed out, "Mother!"

In a jiffy the fat woman flopped out on to the planchen, screeching like a whitneck.

"Whatever in the world is the matter?" exclaimed Betty.

" Matter, indeed! Why, there's a man under my bunk!"

"Nonsense, thee're edn room. However, I'll soon see."

With that, Betty jumped down, kindled the tinder and, kneeling down, blew upon it as she looked in under the bunk. The faint glow fell on me. I was discovered.

"It's only me, Betty."

"What! our Jack! then the Lord help us! Whatever art 'ee 'doin' here?"

"Oh, Betty! I want to see the New World."

"That's all very well, but what of mother? 'Twill be the death of her; come out to once, we must go straightaway and see the capun."

So I edged out, and followed her up the ladder to the deck. The sea was all around, the sails ghastly against the stars, but what comes back plainest is Betty's tall figure as she led aft between the rigging and the water-casks, with the ends of her shawl and the strings of her milking bonnet flying in the wind. A few steps brought us to the sailorman at the helm.

"What's wrong?" he asked, but the moment he saw me he understood, and before Betty could reply, he called down the cabin, "Capun Wakeham! Capun Wakeham!"

"What ho!"

"There's a stowaway here to see you."

I was more glad than I can tell of the grip of Betty's warm hand.

"Now, sir," Betty began, the moment the captain's head showed, "thee'rt the faither of cheldren yourself, and a good Christian man, and won't judge harshly.

Jack here has done wrong, but hear why. The cheeld's head is turned with the talk about the New World, and the dear of 'un wants to see it for hisself."

"Who is he?"

"He's the only cheeld of as sweet a woman as ever drawed breath, and unless he's put ashore, 'twill be the death of her. Caan't 'ee land un some-wheere, capun?"

"Come here, boy, and let me look at you."

So I stepped right up to him, and stood still whilst he held a lantern to my face.

"Well, you're a nice-looking boy, but you have done very wrong. Don't cry, I'm not going to have you punished, but I fear there is little hope of your seeing Cornwall again for some months."

"Capun, dear, think of his mawther, as lovin' and beautiful a crittur as ever stepped, and he an only cheeld; au, capun!"

"I can't help it, my woman; unless we fall in with a fishing-boat, and that's hardly likely, I hold out no hope. Now go below; I'll see to the boy."

With that he took me to his cabin, gave me a ship's biscuit, a blanket to wrap myself up in, and told me to lie down upon the floor. As soon as I had done so, he went up on deck again. I soon dropped off, dreaming this time of the hollow tree and the star shining out at the top. When I awoke it was still dark, but a grey light came creeping through the little round pane, up against which a wave washed every now and then. Day was breaking. The light grew; the sun rose. I heard the captain hail somebody, and then a distant shout. A voice replied, and a short talk followed. Whilst I wondered what it all meant, the captain came to the head of the stairs and called to me to come up. On reaching the deck, I saw a boat being rowed towards us. It had a crew of seven men, one at the tiller, six at the oars; and it was a marvel to me that she managed to live in such a sea. As she drew near, the captain fastened a rope under my arms, and the moment the boat came alongside he lowered me into it. Two of the men slipped off the rope and lifted me to a place beside the man in the stern.

"See that the boy is restored to his parents, Matthey – the sooner the better," shouted the captain, throwing a cake of tobacco into the gig.

"Aye, aye, sir," the man by my side called back; "we shall be in Sennen tomorrow night; I'll see to him."

By this the *Triton* had sailed away, leaving us on the tossing waters.

"Well," said the coxswain, turning to me, "I don't know now who you are or where you come from."

"I come from Lanyon, sir; my father, Richard Penrose, is chief hand to Mr. Henry Pearce."

"What! never a son to Dick Penrose and Mary Pender! Do 'ee hear that, mates? And to think we should come across their cheeld out here on the Powhll! But how came 'ee to run away from home? – unhappy were 'ee?"

Without waiting for my answer, he shouted, "Out killick," whereupon the man in the bow threw overboard an anchor with rope attached. I thought the rope would never stop running, so deep was the sea under us. When it did, the men got in their oars, put out their long lines and, holding them between their fingers, sat feeling for a bite. Nor had they long to wait. First one, then another, felt a tug and stood up to haul. I was greatly excited, because I guessed from the tautness of the lines and the efforts of the men that the fish were big ones. Closer up, and still closer up, they were brought, till at last I could see them sheering about in the greeny water. The first to be brought to the surface was a great codfish, the next a pollack, the next – on the other side of the boat –an enormous skate, nearly as big over as our kitchen table. All were gaffed and lifted into the boat by Matthey, whose job it was. He was kept quite busy going from one to the other. And so the sport went on till the bottom boards were covered with big fish – turbot, conger, ling, pollack, and cod.

The bed of the sea must have been alive with these monsters, and the only thing that put a stop to the sport was the tide, which after a time ran so strong as to lift the sinker and bait right off the bottom out of sight of the fish, so that no paying out of the lines was of any use.

"May as well wind up," said Matthey; "we shan't do any more good, and, after all, we've got as much as we can safely carry."

So the lines were wound on the wooden frames, and the oars got out to keep the boat from drifting whilst the killick was being got up. The moment it had been lifted aboard, all six started pulling, keeping good time as they rowed the boat towards the bits of land that hove in sight above the top of the biggest waves.

The bits of land were the Scilly Isles, on which we were to spend the night before crossing to the mainland. Rows of shags stood like images on the rocks and ledges, their heads turned one way like those of grazing cattle. Nor were they the only living things in that lonesome place. Matthey pointed to a seal lying on a reef, to another in the water, and soon I could find them for myself. I counted eleven in all, the last being on the outermost of a chain of rocks called the Haycocks. Then Matthey pointed out the chief islands, but except Sampson, Tresco, and St. Mary's, where we were to lodge, I have forgotten their names.

We landed at some steps, and walked up the quay and along a street till we came to a great open place. There, after agreeing upon the time to leave in the morning, we separated, Matthey taking me with him to Porth Cressa, to the house of a Mr. Trevellick, where quite a fuss was made of me.

After a good meal of fried pollack, I started out by myself to see what there was to be seen. In my wandering I came to a great fortress called Star Castle, and, passing under the lofty archway, presently reached the batteries that guard the approach to the anchorage. From there I went to Buzza Hill, attracted by a windmill at work. It was the first "I had ever seen, and I stayed to watch the sails before making my way to a small village called Old Town. There, close to the sea, I found an ancient church and a scattering of housen; but the thing which took my fancy most was the parish brine-trough. Such a trough I have never seen since. I should say it would hold a dozen ten-score pigs and more. It was not for salting pork, however, but fish, such as we had in the boat. Two men were there salting them, whom I stood and watched till it was dark, noticing that the stones used for keeping the fish under were stones with rope-holes through them that had been used for sinking kegs. It was quite late by the time I got back to Porth Cressa, so late that Matthey was quite anxious about me.

"That boy's a handful," I overheard him say to Mrs. Trevellick, whose round eyes, as they looked at me over her spectacles, expressed the won-derment I had aroused in her. But she said nothing till we were alone – nothing, indeed, till she showed me up to my room, and then only, "I hope you will be a good boy after this, and never run away again."

I slept in a three-cornered attic that had a tiny window high up above the foot of the bed. Through it, as I lay, I could see Charles's Wain just as I had seen it hundreds of times above the Galver. That so set me thinking of home and mother that I broke down and sobbed myself to sleep.

It was still pitch dark when Matthey woke me. We had breakfast by candle-light. At parting, Mrs. Trevellick kissed me affectionately, and gave me her son's oiler. We found the crew aboard, and started at once. The stars were bright as we rowed through Crow Sound, nor showed sign of paling till we were well out in the open sea. There the waves ran high, breaking clean over the boat every few minutes; so that every now and then two of the crew stopped rowing to bale, and I was glad of the oiler, the collar of which I turned up to keep my neck dry. In the grey dawn we passed some wicked-looking rocks, called the Seven Stones; they were in a smother of foam. I was glad when the sun rose, angry though it looked. It tipped the waves with crimson, set the sou'westers of the men all agleam, and lit up

Matthey's anxious face.

Matthey kept his weather eye open; when he saw a big sea coming, he shouted, "Look out, boys!" Thereupon, the men clenched their teeth, and laid an extra grip upon their oars. But none of them spoke except once, when the man in the bow talked of throwing the fish overboard, and found nobody to answer him. Soon after this, a school of porpoises came playing around us. Then a bird like a small pigeon made as if it would settle on the water; but never did, and in the end was lost to view.

Judging by the sun, it was well after noon when Matthey, who had been straining his eyes, shouted, "Land ahead, boys!"

As the boat rose again, I saw it, too, and shouted, "The Galver!"

"No, no, not the Galver; 'tis Chapel Carn Brea."

Bit by bit all the end of the land came into view, with it the Longships and the sea breaking over it; but a head-tide joined with the head-wind made us late, and the Longships had been lit an hour or two when we got to the Cove. As we approached the slip, Matthey shouted, "Get the line ready!" then "Pull for dear life!" while the men bent to their oars and urged the boat forward on the heave of the wave, till a score hands on the slip grasped the line thrown to them, and hauled the boat up, high and dry.

Great was the delight at the catch, especially amongst the women.

When Matthey had divided up the fish, I went to him and said, "Mr. Matthey, I thank you for bringing me across; I'm going home to mother now."

"Thee'st better wait till mornin'."

"No, Mr. Matthey; mother will be fretting herself to death."

"Can you find your way?"

"Yes; thank you."

" Well, shake hands, and be a good boy in future." With that, I shook hands and started off.

I passed the Quakers' burying ground, the Round House at Crowz-an-Wra, Tregonebris Farm House, Sancreed Churchtown, where the owls were hooting, and New Bridge. At New Bridge I was in two minds whether to go by the road or up along the river. After a minute's hesitation, I chose the river, following along the left bank till I came to Boundary Pool, where I crossed by the earthstoppers' stepping-stones. Then I made up across Great Voorns, Deep Field, Further Jets, Nearer Jets, Mill Pool Field, leapt the wall by the goose craw, opened the door, and walked in.

Father and mother, who were in the settle, looked at me all skeared as though at one risen from the dead. Then mother gave a loud screech and fell back in a faint.

CHAPTER VIII

THE PRIZE
DISTRIBUTION
❧

Thas year 'forty three stands out in my memory, because it marked the end of my Daniel days and the beginning of my workaday life. Eager as I am to come to that, I must, in justice to myself, deal with the closing quarter at school; for then at last I turned to with a will, in the hope of carrying off the class prize at the Lady Day distribution. Mother was quick to note the change. Indeed, she could hardly help it: the moment supper was over I sat to my lessons without once looking up till I asked to be heard. The sparkle in her eyes told how pleased she was, yet she spoke never a word of praise, probably for fear my zeal would prove but a nine days' wonder, and die away as suddenly as it arose. However that may have been, she heard me with the greatest care, never once failing to repeat a question I had been unable to answer the first time of asking.

Nor was mother's the only help I got. Miss Jenifer, hearing of the turn things had taken, insisted on my going across to her three nights a week, to be primed in spelling, ready-reckoning, and the "Elements of Universal History." I expected sharpish handling, but nothing like what I got. I am not thinking of the number of questions she asked me, but the to-do she made whenever I tripped. I remember very well when I spelt "accommodation" with one "m," she stormed up and down the room in a manner I had seldom seen equalled, even by Mr. Tasker. Daniel's scholar of five years' standing that I was, and big for my age – facts which Miss Jenifer did not omit to remind me of – I don't think I could have put up with such severe treatment from anybody else. And yet the moment she had done catechising, she was an altered woman – she was kindness itself. I can't recollect ever being allowed to go away without an orange, a couple of broadfigs, or an Abernethy biscuit. Then she always stood on the landing to light me down. Sometimes she descended the long stairs, and would stand, handkerchief to mouth, at the open door, listening till I was well across the yard.

This went on through January, February, and the greater part of March, indeed until the Thursday before the examination. That evening, just as I was about to go across, Miss Jenifer walked in to say there would be no lesson that night nor on the Saturday.

"Let me explain, Mary," said she, seeing how mother was taken aback; "Jack's brain is full of a hundred and one things that need time to settle if they are to be used to advantage. It is because I want him to be clear-headed during the examination, able to make the best use of his knowledge, that I think it well to do no more learning: I am sure it is for the best. Now promise me, Jack, that you will not look at any lesson-book between now and Monday." Of course I promised her; what else could I do? Yet scarcely had Miss Jenifer turned her back before a passel of things kept plaguing me to look them up.

To take my mind off them, mother read aloud the place in "Robinson Crusoe" where Crusoe comes on the footprint in the sand; on the Saturday, from the "Vicar of Wakefield," where Moses goes to the Fair and comes back home with the green spectacles.

Though I slept well, I was as fidgetty as possible the next morning, thinking of the examination. In church I could not keep my thoughts on the service. For pastime, I read over and over the list of charities on the north wall and King Charles's letter on the south, till in the middle of the sermon, mother fearing Jim Beare would be sent down to caution me, gave me a sharp nudge to call me to attention. Thereupon, I left off turning my head from left to right, and stared straight up at Parson Veale in his three-decker, wondering as I did so what sort of sums would be set next morning.

Monday came at last, and, after a slight breakfast, I started off with three goosequills, cut and tested by Miss Jenifer, in my breastpocket, and mother's words of encouragement ringing in my ears.

On reaching the green, I was surprised to see only half a dozen boys at tig, and those the cleverest in the school; the rest, I soon discovered, were gathered before the school door with heads buried in their books, and touchy as could be when you spoke to them. At the stroke of the bell we trooped through the door to our places, and whilst the sand was running down watched Mr. Tasker as he paced to and fro, hands behind his back and fingers all of a twitch. As the last grain slid into the lower bulb, he turned the blackboard, exposing the questions written in his best copperplate. We read them down excitedly; then with a sigh from one here and there fell to with the quill, mine running as smooth as oil.

I kept pretty cool until about half-time, then a bit of a fever seized me, through my discovering a bad mistake in multiplication. But by dint of will, I steadied myself and finished middling well, at least so I thought. I took care, however, not to write down the answers, in case Miss Jenifer should get a copy of the questions and see whether they were right. Nor would I tell her the answer I gave in the oral examination to a question that went and still goes the round of the parish. It was this: "A ha'penny a tail and a farthing an eye, how many fish will a shilling buy?" I dreaded Miss Jenifer much more now than during the priming, especially after the examination in the "Celestial Globe" and in the "Elements of Universal History." I did tell her the questions, but when she tried to draw out the answers, I said, "Miss Jenifer, why should I make you miserable by telling you the mistakes I have made? You will know everything on Thursday. Pray let me be." And she did.

The questions were set by a great scholar – no less a person than Dr. Fynes-Clinton, the headmaster of the Penzance Grammar School, to whom the answers were delivered over in Parson Veale's sermon bag by Mr. Tasker himself.

Three full days we boys of the First Form were kept close at it, the examination ending at four o'clock on the Wednesday, in time for the last papers to be looked through and marked before the distribution.

On Thursday morning, with a pasty in my pocket, I went tickling for trout, though without much speed, owing to the rise of the river after the night's rain. I ate my dinner on the rail of the flushet, and had just finished when "Toot! toot!" went the mayhorn, summoning me home to be tidied up for the prize-giving. Mother was waiting by the tub with soap and flannel, with which she washed my neck and face before beginning on my ears, which she scrubbed till they burned. Then I went upstairs, changed into my Sunday best, and for once brushed my hair to mother's satisfaction.

I started in advance of the others, mother calling to me from the bedroom window, "Now, Jack, whatever you do, don't rumple your collar or soil your hands, and remember to bow nicely if you get the prize." At the word "prize", which had never before been breathed between us, I coloured up to the roots of my hair, and ran off, reaching Churchtown in good time without having as much as thrown a stone at a yellow-hammer by the way, or even at the squire's caution-board.

On the road in along, I had tried to think what the room would look like, but the picture I called up fell short of the display that met my eyes when, at three o'clock, we boys were let in to take our places. Never had Mr. Tasker gone to such pains before. The wall facing the door was hung with flags which covered all but a narrow strip where, in gold letters upon a blue ground, shone the Daniel motto, "Nothing without work." The portrait of the founder was done round with sprigs of myrtle; so, too, the likenesses of the masters dead and gone: Thomas Cox, Tobias Read, and Uther Penkivell, that always stood on the mantelpiece close to the old hour-glass.

Mr. Tasker, looking his best, was as busy as a bee, putting the finishing touches to the decorations, and seeing that every boy's hands were clean and his hair brushed back off the forehead.

The eight of us who were leaving he put three forms in front of the others, almost forward enough to read the names on the back of the prizes on the table. The four books had the green cloth all to themselves, except for a jug of lent-lilies, a decanter of water, and a tumbler. Between the table and the wall stood five chairs, the centre one an arm-chair, right under the middle of the gold lettering.

Soon the mothers and friends began to troop in, filling form after form till the room was full, even to the raised bench at the back, where the old men of the village, themselves once Daniel boys, always sat on Prize Day.

Presently voices were heard from the direction of the schoolhouse, and the next minute in came Mr. Tasker, side by side with the examiner, Lady Tresillian with Parson Veale, and, a few paces behind, the tall, slim figure of Sir Rose, swinging his white hat as he strode.

I like to remember the squire as he was that day, for, to my thinking, he never looked better, not even in the hunting-field. He wore a full-tail coat, a high linen collar that showed white as snow against his black hair, close-fitting drab trousers, and shiny boots. I noticed all this, and the big buttons at the waist, whilst he stood to look at the likenesses; and when, on reaching the table, he turned to take the chair, I saw that he had on a frilled shirt, black neckcloth, and a buff-coloured, waist-coat fastened with gold buttons, bright as the seals which dangled from his fob. That he was in a good humour you could tell by the smile that crinkled his face as his eyes wandered over the crowded room.

Lady Tresillian, looking handsome in her Tuscan bonnet, velvet mantle, and ermine boa, sat to his left, the examiner to his right, with Mr. Tasker outside, the counterpart to Parson Veale. The parson kept talking to her ladyship till the squire rose, then he clasped his knees, tilted his double chin, and beamed through his tortoiseshell spectacles up at the rafters.

"I call on Dr. Fynes-Clinton to read his report."

A hush fell on the room as the doctor began reading. After a few general remarks, he came to the result of the examination, but – a thing he had never done before – began at the lowest class, simply, I thought, to tantalise me, mother, and Miss Jenifer.

"Get on, get on," I said under my breath. When at last he reached the first class, you might, as the saying goes, have heard a pin drop. Even then he tried me almost beyond endurance; for instead of saying who was top, he read – very slowly, too – the names in each subject in order of merit, though giving no marks. He finally announced the totals –

Oliver Gendall 135,
Edwin Jenkin 131,
John Penrose ... ... 128.

To say I was disappointed, bitterly disappointed, is to say almost nothing of what I felt. And the worst was to see how sadly mother and Miss Jenifer took it; their heads, that had been held higher and higher as the lists were read, were bent as though in shame. Though last in Scripture and – a thing I could never understand – last but one in geography, I was second in composition, first in orthography, first in mental arithmetic, and first in the elements of universal history. To be third, after all, was gall and wormwood. My interest in squire, lady, and all the colour and glitter was gone; my one wish during the reading of the prize essay was to get away out of it, and hide in the Quoit brake.

Yet, as has more than once happened with me, in that dark moment a surprise was in store which did more than set everything right. And it came of a word idly dropped by the examiner, who chanced to say, as he laid Gendall's essay down, that it had taxed him to decide between it and the second. The squire seized on his words, and, in his quick commanding way, ordered the second best to be read. Up jumped Mr. Tasker, all of a flurry, and, thinking that the squire wanted me to read it, called out, "John Penrose, come up."

Before I knew where I was, Dickie and the others pushed me into the gangway, along which I made for the table with my brain all in a whirl. I took the foolscap from the examiner, pulled my wits together, and faced the company, ready to make a start the moment they had done clapping. My voice, which quavered at first, gathered strength as I read, as follows: –

"LANYON FARM.

"Ours is a bra big farm of well over a hundred customary acres, not reckoning the outs. It lies right away by itself in the High Country, with furze brakes all around. Every lace is in tilth or pasture except Spar Croft, which is choked full of rocks and brembles. The badgers have a big set there with loads of room for the foxes. Badgers, foxes, and rabbits live comfortably together, like the Happy Family I once followed about the streets of Penzance. Winter nights, I see the earthstopper crossing the moor for the Galver; I know it's him by his lantern. Badgers plague the life out of the earthstopper. For why? Because they scratch out the stopping and let in the foxes. It makes Sir Rose vexed as fire when a fox gets to ground, for I've seen him – what's more, I've heard him! (Loud laughter, in which the squire joined.) Badgers live on beetles, dumble-dores, apple-bees' nests, and spring chicks, but the worst damage they do is to the standing corn. They beat roads athirt it, and wallow, making the work toilsome for the reapers. Harvest is a grand time, with all hands busy outdoors and in, not forgetting Miss Jenifer, who keeps the key of the stillroom and gives out the beer and the sweet drinks. My job is to carry out croust and afternoon crib, bring back the empties, and gleany in between whiles. 'Tis a sight to see Bedny Kervis or Peake's Croft with the mows set up and the sun upon them last thing before setting, and later under the red moon. Father cries the neck, sings the 'Barley Mow' at guldice, and puts up his wedding-scarf Thanksgiving Sunday.

"Like father, and grandfather before him, I'm going to work upon the land; to plough, harve, sow, reap, thresh, winnowy, cut furze and turf, meat the calves, help see to the lambs, and have an eye to the young stuff upon the moor. Thousands upon thousands of stares come to roost in our reeds in winter-time. I lie behind the hedger of Further North field, and fire up at them with my bow and arrow as they come flying in over. Our fields, of which there are forty-five all told, have got names every one of them. This is all I can think to say in the time, except that the grey goose is sitting on thirteen eggs, and that mother has saved a bravish bundle of quills for Mr. Tasker."

Amidst laughter and hand-clapping, I ran back to my place.

Then Lady Tresillian handed the prizes, and when Oliver Gendall, who was the last to be called up, had been given his, Mr. Tasker got up and said –

"Sir Rose, Lady Clarice, and all present: I have every reason to feel gratified at the examiner's report. One remark there was that especially pleased me. Dr. Fynes-Clinton said that the older boys showed a knowledge of where they stood in time and place. That is one object I have always in view. Education, as I understand it, does not consist in merely learning to spell and cipher; it should enable a boy to realise his place in the universe, and where he comes in in the history of the world. Not content with that, I would have his mind so trained that he should be able to appreciate the beauties of nature, which are nowhere more lavishly displayed than in this West Cornwall of ours. I beg of you boys who are about to pass out of my hands, who have been my companions in the Saturday excursions, to keep up your observation of the birds and the flowers, and to maintain your interest in the quoits, stone circles, and other monuments of the Old People. You will, I know, have to earn your bread by the sweat of your brow, but that need not dull your senses to the glories of the hedgerows, or blind you to the splendour of the heavens. Remember that Robert Burns was a ploughboy; John Clare a peasant lad. I am pleased by the large attendance. It is evidence to me that the interest taken in the education given here is as strong as ever. One thing, one favour I would ask of you parents: I beg you not to keep the boys at home more than one afternoon during blackberry-picking, and none at all during the whortleberry season – you've no idea how irregularity of attendance throws the work out. There has been complaint about the currants, or rather want of currants, in the Christmas buns. I have only to say that the fault did not lie with the trustees or the baker. The vessel that brought the fruit was beating about in the Channel when she should have been in Falmouth harbour, and Mr. Toman's wagon broke down the other side of Helston two days before Christmas, and did not reach Penzance till Christmas Eve.

"And now my last words to you who are leaving for good. Boys of the First Form, you are going forth into the world. Whatever your work, do it in such a way that men shall be compelled to own you are capable of doing something better: that way advancement lies. One word more: spend your time in such a way that the world shall be the better for your having lived in

70

it. And may my blessing go with you."

Then, turning to Sir Rose, he said, "I cannot sit down without thanking you, Sir Rose, and you, Lady Clarice, for the interest you show in the school on every occasion, and for your presence here today." (Applause.)

It was a good minute before Sir Rose got on his feet to reply.

"My friends, it is with much pleasure that my wife and I have come here to show the interest we take in the Daniel School. We are proud of this foundation, which now for over a century has been doing valuable work in our midst. George Daniel, sagacious man though he was, could hardly have foreseen the good that has come of his charity, a result almost wholly due to the accomplished and painstaking teachers who in their day occupied the post now so ably and so worthily filled by my friend Mr. Tasker. (Cheers.) I was particularly pleased to hear Dr. Fynes-Clinton say in his report that the reputation of the school for reading, writing, spelling, and ciphering had been fully maintained. I have one disagreeable thing to say: full use is not being made of the school library. I want you all to read, especially the old boys. You would find many a winter's evening pass pleasantly in reading aloud the stories with which the great writers have endowed us. The library shelves are full of the best literature, and I would draw your attention to three recent publications to be found there, in the hope that my words may induce you to take them out and read them: Macaulay's *Lays of Ancient Rome*, Lever's *Charles O'Malley*, and Dickens' *A Christmas Carol*.

"And now a word to the boys who are leaving." Here, at a sign from Mr. Tasker, the eight of us stood up. "Boys, prove yourselves worthy of your school, and live up to your motto. Remember that labour is dignified, and is lightened by pride in the achievement. Above all, lead clean, manly lives, fear God, honour the Queen, be respectful to your betters, and never lose your tempers, as you have been told I sometimes do. (Laughter.) In conclusion, I wish, on behalf of the trustees, to thank Mr. Tasker for the conscientious manner in which he discharges his duties." (Applause.)

He was about to sit down, when Lady Tresillian nudged him. As he leant towards her, she whispered in his ear. The moment he caught her meaning, he handed her something out of his waistcoat pocket, and turning to the audience, said –

"There is one other matter which, as my wife reminds me, I should have mentioned; I mean the description of Lanyon Farm, and the spirited way in which the composition was read. I agree with her that a breezy bit of writing like that should not go unrewarded. I have not a book to give, but if the boy will come up, my wife will be able to make good the deficiency."

At an encouraging nod from Mr. Tasker, I walked up to where her ladyship stood.

"I have," she said, in her sweet, gracious voice, "much pleasure in handing you Sir Rose's pocket-knife, and I hope you will enjoy working on the farm which you have so charmingly described."

I bowed low, as mother had told me, and went to my place, scarcely feeling the planchen under my feet.

Thus ended what I have always looked back upon as one of the great occasions of my life. I felt uplifted, and mother and Miss Jenifer seemed as proud as Lucifer. They did not say much as we drove up along, but once clear of Churchtown, and out of hearing, they broke forth. I still hear their exultant voices, still see their beaming faces, the pines afire from the sun, and Snowball going proudly.

CHAPTER IX

GOES TO WORK

🙰

I BEGAN WORK ON MONDAY, going straight away with Hector and
Madam to harve Further North. Father came along to put me in the
way of it, perhaps to prevent me from spoiling the look of the field, as
a raw hand is well nigh sure to do, for the chances are he will harve in the
line of the ploughing or right across, rucking up the sods that should be left
to rot. But father showed me how to drag the harrow athirt the combs,
breaking up the soil about the roots whilst leaving the turf undisturbed.
When we had gone to the further hedge and back again, he handed me the
reins, walked alongside till satisfied that I could manage without him, and
then went off to his own work. It felt ever so strange, to be left there in the
great ten-acre field all by myself. The loneliness of it was almost more than
I could bear. But as on the day I went to school, so now, I called upon myself
and faced the situation as I should.

It was a bright spring day, with the larks singing up in the blue and the
moorhens calling from the reeds. Forth and back across the field I trudged,
behind the pair of great upstanding horses, guiding them as best I could
neither to miss ground nor overlap more than need be; and so the hours
passed till croust time. Then, as our custom is, I sat in the lewth of the
hedge to eat my morsel of barley bread, and there – a thing I have not dared
tell till now – fell sound asleep. I was awoke by the ringing of the Daniel bell,
which sounded as plain in my dreams as it used to do in reality, and came
to myself with a shock – for I had been playing tig on the village green – to
find the larks still singing, the moorhens calling, Hector and Madam still
nibbling the browse.

I jumped up and went at my task again, nor once stopped till the
shadow of the rubbing-post in the middle of the field had crept so close
to the foot of the stone as to tell me it was dinner-time. Then, unhitching
the horses, I rode back to table, gave them a feed, and ran in to have my
own dinner. As soon as I had done, I went back to field for the rest of
the day, and again on the morrow, staying well past milking time so as to
make a finish of it.

The ten acres fresh from the harrow made a brave show. I felt so proud when riding through the gate that I slewed round on Hector and let my eyes dwell. A pleasing sight it was, with the great spread of rich dark soil, especially the part on the higher side beyond the rubbing-post, where the heave of the ground caught the sun without a tab to mar the comeliness; and all my work, except the two turns father had done.

As I rode up the hill, father drove into the yard with a load of seed barley, and whilst I was in the stable taking the gear off the horses, Mr. Pearce, who had come across, called me to him. He wanted to learn me sample the barley. "See Jack," said he, shifting it from one hand to the other; "the shell is smooth, the grain bright, clean and well matured," and putting it to his nose, he added, "And it is free from the musty smell that comes of heating in the mow. If seed can do it, we shall have no occasion to complain of the crop. But there, 'tis early days to talk about the crop with the ground not yet ready for sowing."

"I've harved it brave, master."

"Yes, Jack, and a very good job you've made of it; but that is only a beginning; you must harve and roll, roll and harve, till the growan is worked to a powder. Why? Because a light soil, as ours is, burns up in a dry summer unless pulverised, and you haven't got it to that stage yet."

So I harved and rolled till Further North was as smooth and fine as an onion bed and, to my thinking, in perfect tilth. But I was overruled, for master would have it harved and rolled again.

"No need, sir," I replied, "'tis as fine as March dust; 'twill only be a waste of time."

"Do what I tell you, Jack."

I did not answer, but I did the next worse thing, I went and sulked in the barn, till mother found out where I was, and reasoned with me.

"Obey your master's orders: harve and roll till he says stop, and always, my son, with your eyes on the sheaves of harvest."

Then I went to field and carried out master's orders, and at last all was ready for the sowing.

It was the eighth of May, and burning hot as it should be for barley, when father and I went forth to sow. Father, of course, did the actual sowing, dipping his hand into the seed-lap and broadcasting as he strode. A prettier sower could not be, so evenly did he scatter, never missing a foot of ground.

My job was to replenish the seed-lap, which I did from the bags of barley I had laid at intervals along the lower hedge. At the finish father let me sow the wet piece in the lower corner, where the ground had been crimsoned with sour sops before Bill ploughed it, and where a bit of faulty work did not make much odds. He said that I did it middlin' well for a beginner; which was a long speech for father.

Next morning, as soon as it was light enough to see, I was at work with the tormentor burying the seed to a depth of three inches or so: then I harved and rolled again.

With the planting of the field, my troubles began. The first plague was the crows which came after the grain. They must have come from miles round, there were such flocks of them. They were as bold as brass too, taking next to no notice of tin-can-beating, or of the buccaboos which I set up upon the far side beyond the rubbing-post. They kept me going forth and back all the time, from sunrise till sunset.

The second day, I took my sling and pebbles from the stream, and slung away at the rogues till my arm ached, without really scaring a crow. That night I begged to be allowed the use of the blunderbuss, but master would not hear of it.

On the fifth day, as the barley, which had begun to sprout, was no longer to their liking, the torments took themselves off with a loud jeering caw that vexed the heart out of me, and a week later Further North, as seen from our rick-yard, was tinged with green.

"Your work, my dear, is beginning to show," said mother.

The next trouble was the rabbits; they nibbled the springing blades all along by the hedges. One evening, whilst bringing in a load of turf, I counted the best part of a score, out feeding, and three hares to the far side of the rubbing-post. "This will never do," I said to myself, though puzzled to know how to alter it, for neither Miss Jenifer nor master would countenance the use of gins – the one on the ground of its cruelty, the other for fear of trapping the foxes.

After lying awake half the night cudgelling my brain, I decided to try and stop the rabbits in. I spent evening upon evening at the task, only to find my labour wasted, for, as I came to learn, the tunnels in the earth between the stone facings, ran the length of the hedges, so that if but a single hole was overlooked, every rabbit could find its way out. The evening after completing the work, I counted in the teens along three of the hedges, and seven by the gate hedge. It was hard to have to own myself outwitted by a passel of rabbits. In spite of them, however, the barley continued to thrive, and by the end of the month stood to a height of three or four inches, was vigorous in stalk and blade, and full of promise. There was no crop on the farm that interested me like that.

My next task was to build up the wall – hedge we call it – between Nearer Jets and Bedny Kervis, in order to keep the sheep out of the dredge corn; but high as I built it they continued to get over, and so master ordered them to be spanned. Next morning, on my way to cut rushes for the spans, I saw a sight which to my thinking is the grandest a farm can show. Master's fancy was a herd of bullocks at summer feed, with the grass up to their gambrels; he could lean on the gate and watch them by the hour; he loved also to watch the wind playing over a hayfield ready for the scythe; father's fancy was a flock of newly shorn sheep just turned to pasture; but surely both must give way to the barley in Further North as I saw it that fresh dewy morning. Every baby ear held as in a cup a crystal dewdrop, and the sight was enough to take the breath away, for these dinky drops, reflecting the rays of the rising sun, changed the field into a glittering fairyland.

Though the crows and the rabbits proved too many for me, I succeeded with the sheep, though that in a way is nothing to boast of.

Next, as my work was on the south side of the farm, and my spare time taken up with odd chores, amongst them the writing of master's letters till the whitlow on Miss Jenifer's forefinger had healed. With one thing and another, weeks passed without my going near my favourite field, and when at last I did go, I found something seriously amiss.

Two beaten tracks ran athirt the field, one to either side of the rubbing-post; and going along them I came on places – parlours we call them – which looked as though the pigs had wallowed there. Of course it was not the pigs, it was the doing of the badgers in their traffickings between Spar Croft and the Trucks. But why make two tracks where one would have done? Why choose a valuable crop to roll and play in, with reeds and rushes in plenty around them? The wanton damage vexed me beyond endurance, and straight away I ran to Spar Croft, determined to stop the badgers in.

Yet, on reaching the earths, I was nearly turned aside from my purpose, for the ground about the sett was covered thick with foxgloves, then in their full glory; and the paths of the badgers ran amidst this spread of purple loveliness. Eyes never looked on prettier avenues. Whilst I held my hand, a voice whispered–

"The paths across the barley have been badger trails from long before the Quoit was raised. It is man that has interfered with the badgers, not the badgers with man."

"True," I replied, "but man must have the dominion."

So I fetched stones from the ragel and jammed them into the holes.

"Get out if you can," I shouted as I left.

This was on the Tuesday; Thursday dinner-time I went to look to the stoppings. To my amazement the badgers had dug themselves out. There were three fresh holes, and before each were at least two barrow-loads of soil. In my vexation I thought of the man-trap, but refrained from using it for fear of getting master into the squire's black books. I decided, instead, to lie in ambush on Saturday at the place where the badgers broke the hedge of Further North, and turn them when they came.

I fixed on the Saturday, partly because I could lie abed a bit longer next morning, but chiefly because the moon was then at the full; and when the great silver light – parish lantern we call it – had risen clear of the Forest Carn, I started out for my hiding-place, fetching round, on father's advice, by Fraland and the moor, so as not to taint the track by the well where the badgers' trail ran.

My heart was beating hard when at last I crouched beside the trail, in a silence broken only by the whisperings of the barley as the night wind stirred it. I had a clear view of the badgers' line of approach, which lay between the hedge and a long rushy pool; but while the moon climbed higher and higher there was not a sign of a living thing except some glow-worms, till at last I began to fear that the badgers had gone off on some other beat, and that I might as well be in bed.

All at once a note of alarm from a moorhen set me on the alert, and, peering along the trail, I saw a badger coming. His body looked very silvery, but it was the white face-markings that struck me most. Lost as I was in observation, I forgot to turn him; indeed, he had nearly gained the top of the hedge when I jumped forth, seized his tail and swung him off his feet. Then I realised that I had got into a situation I did not know how to get out of. Law! how he snapped and snarled! To escape being bitten, I held the heavy beast at arm's length, and continued to hold him till my arm ached. I might have dropped him – I should have dropped him, but that I felt sure he would turn on me. Suddenly, when I was on the point of letting go, the thought flashed upon me to throw him into the pool and run for it. Planting my feet on two clumps of rushes, I swung him forth and back, till at the end of the fourth swing I let go. He made a tremendous splash, which I heard but did not see, as I was in full retreat before he struck the water. On reaching the bridge I stood to listen, though only a second or two, for thinking I heard him coming, I tore up the hill and rushed indoors. The instant I had got my boots off, I hurried up to my room and put my head out of the window in full expectation of seeing him. The road, however, was empty, the stillness profound, and after waiting awhile to no purpose I undressed and got into bed.

In spite of the badgers and the rabbits, and a sea-fog that made us fear an attack of rust, the barley throve, and made me feel proud of having had a hand in its cultivation.

One morning, as master stood gazing out of the barn window, I said, "Further North is looking well, sir."

"Yes, Jack, very well, to all appearances; I must go and inspect it shortly."

That was on the Monday, but it was not till the following Sunday afternoon that he went, taking me with him. The sun, I remember, was blazing hot, the reed-bed lay like a thing in swoon, and over Further North the heated air danced as it dances above the Barbican lime-kiln. To get a good view, master climbed the hedge, where he stood looking and looking over the ten acres of corn, then yellowing slightly to harvest. No wonder his face beamed, for, as the drooping bearded heads showed, the grain had kerned well, whilst the straw was unusually long for the High Country.

"I don't know," he said presently, "when I've set eyes on a prettier field of barley; you see now, Jack, what comes of good tillage."

It was the third week in August, the wheat and the oats being then secure in arish mows, that all hands turned into Further North to reapy. The sun was strong, but the heat was tempered by the breeze that came in from over the moor. Father was leading scythe, Mary Carn followed, then Jim, the pedlar, Andrew the earth-stopper, Tom Bennetts, John Curnow, and myself last of all. Except for me, you could not have found a smarter lot of hands in the parish. We began at the corner beyond where I had waited for the badgers, father starting off, the others falling in behind like half a skein of wildfowl; and by the time we had got to the further hedge, what had been standing corn, lay in seven swathes the full length of the field. Back we strolled, whetted scythes, the men wetted their whistles, and we began afresh; going forth and back till croust-time, and then again at father's call, till dinner-time, and again through the long afternoon till evening, when all was levelled except a handful or so in the sour-sop corner, left purposely for the neck.

Then, the rest looking on, father stepped forth, cut and gathered it, and, jumping on the hedge, shouted as he held up the little sheaf –

"I haben, I haben, I haben!"

"What have 'ee, what have 'ee, what have 'ee?" we asked in chorus.

"Ah neck, ah neck, ah neck!"

"Hurrah! hurrah! hurrah!" we all shouted, frightening the very rabbits in their burrows, and startling every fox, hare, and otter within hearing.

Five days later, when the barley was ready, we bound it into sheaves, which we built into mows, so that by set of sun there stretched ten lines of golden cones across the arish. This was followed by the ingathering into the mowhay of all the harvest, the produce of nine-and-thirty customary acres; three big ricks, well thatched against winter storms, testifying that the work had been nobly done, and food and fodder provided for man and beast till harvest should come again.

That night, as our custom is at guldice, the firstling of the flock was served for supper with fresh-cut vegetables, and baked figgy pudding to follow. Supper over, Miss Jenifer took down last year's neck from near the blunderbuss and hung in its place the new neck, bedizened with pink ribbons, whilst we harvesters upstanding sang, "The Barley Mow." It was the end and crown to all our efforts, putting master and man on right terms, and sending us home contented.

As father, mother, and I were crossing the yard, father suddenly stopped to listen.

"Do 'ee hear 'em, Jack?"

"Yes, father, I hear them."

The partridges were calling from the barley arish.

CHAPTER X

THE FISHERMAN CAUGHT

🌿

KINDLY AS I TOOK TO WORK, a day's sport was the thing most to my liking. Nor could I have got along without it. For with nothing to break the daily round, work would have become drudgery and life been little above the beasts. Not that I got, nor for that matter needed, much, as the afternoon's rabbiting on Feasten Monday set me up till Christmas, whilst a day on the moors with Mr. Coulson, the timber merchant, kept me going till trouting time.

Mr. Coulson always came on New Year's Day, unless it fell on a Sunday, and the night before I got little or no sleep, so great was my excitement, though my duty was the modest one of carrying the game bag, and marking in the woodcock. He came not only to the day, but to the hour, driving into the yard just as day was breaking, so as to be ready to start off the moment the light was strong enough to shoot by. He used to wear a dove-coloured top hat, with a mallard's tail-feather stuck in the band, a tweed coat, all pockets, cord breeches, stout boots, and leggins to the thighs. Though well past middle age, he could stand a long day; and we worked miles upon miles of moor, nor thought of stopping till dark. By that time, the setters he shot over were glad to have done, and the bag seldom held less than two brace of woodcock, three or four of snipe, a leash of golden plover, and a couple or so of duck, widgeon, or teal, as the case may be.

Mr. Coulson was a dead shot: what the first barrel did not bring down, the second generally did. I have heard moormen – men who should have known better – say that it was the gun that did it. With such idle prate I have no patience. For what is the best gun in the world unless held straight, whether a Joe Manton, as Mr. Coulson's was, or another? I am the first to own that good results can be got out of a second-rate weapon, but there again the credit is the man's, only more so. And this is true, not only of a gun, it is true also of a fishing-rod, as I shall hope to show.

Here let me say that dearly as I came to love a gun, I loved a rod no whit the less. Of the two, the rod perhaps brought me the greater moments.

No tongue can tell the pleasure I found wandering beside our stream. There is no prettier anywhere. From moorland to cove it is a chain of crystal pools. Come on it where you may, it is a thing of beauty; and nowhere more than up along with us, where it rises. It bubbles to the light on the moor beyond the reed-bed in a scattering of springs, whose waters, like veins on a leaf, join up soon as may be to form a rivulet with stickles and falls, loops and bends quite after the fashion of a full-grown stream. And there are trout nearly all the way up. Less than a bow-shot from the springs, where in summer the banks are white with nodding cotton grass, you may espy fingerlings, whose shadowy forms scarce show against the gravel. In the pool, where the feeder from Ding Dong adit comes rushing in, you are always sure of a trout of two or three ounces; once, when the heather was in blowth, I whizzed out a quarter-of-a-pounder there. Between clumps of rush and camomile greens, under arching sprays beloved of the kingfisher, the water winds and falls, chiming over the pebbly shallows, adding music to its delights. So it reaches its first bridge with sheltering ferns, whence it sallies with a brave swirl before sobering down and coming to rest in the millpool. And, as I say, there are fish every-where. Many are the fish I've pulled out from under the bridge, many have I caught in the mill-pool, though the master-fish of our waters, and the most. knowing, was the trout of the pulrose, as we called the deep pit beneath the mill-wheel.

Beyond the mill the land dips, and adown the foothill the stream leaps by half a score falls to the lower moor below Spar Croft and Great Voorns, where lies our boundary pool. You may tell it by the king ferns, more sure-ly still by the spar stepping-stones used by Andrew when stopping the Kenidzhek country.

For fishing-rod I had a nine-foot stick from a pollard ash; for gear, a yard of whipcord and a strand of gut, with a little bluey-steel hook bent on to it. I was proud of my tackle, prouder still of the rod, on the butt of which I had cut the letters "J. P." Besides the ash I had a whippy rod for fly-fishing. This I got in Jimmy Roscruge's withy moor, unbeknown to Jimmy, one evening when he was to market. The casting line consisted of strands of hair from Snowball's mane; the flies I made of feathers from the guinea-fowls, peacock, and a yellow-hammer.

The millpool was my fly-water, and thither of a summer's evening mother and Miss Jenifer would come to watch me. They always sat on the same bit of bank, never without a shawl spread under them. They looked comfortable as could be sitting there, side by side, talking and laughing and enjoying the sport; and I have known them stay on till the sun had set and the swifts gone home. Those are happy times to look back on.

But of all the days I spent by the stream the one most deserving of red letters is the day I am coming to. I was then turned seventeen, though it could only have been by a month or two. We were just finishing with the hay; indeed, I was pitching the last load to father, when master came into the mowhay and said, "Jack, I want you to catch me a dish of fish in the morning; I want them for Mr. Coulson." The lowness of the water and the brightness of the sun were dead against sport, but I raised no difficulty; for that matter it would have been a waste of breath, because master, though educated at Helston, where a trout stream runs along by the curb, knew no more about trouting than a Sancreed man about rock-fishing.

Early as I was out and about, I could not manage to get away till the forenoon, on account of a hundred and one things to be got through before I was free. Then the bluebottles and grammer sows, on which I relied for bait, were as scarce as I have known them. But at last I reached the stream, and tried under the bridge, in the pulrose, and at the head of Boundary Pool, without getting a touch. At Music Waters, where there is a nice stickle, I crawled to the bank and peeped through the meadow-sweet to see what there might be, and there, in the shadow of an overhanging fern, lay a nice fish, seemingly well on the feed. But the moment I lifted the rod, upstream it rushed, raising a wave and spreading suspicion right and left as it went Thinks I, "I might as well have left the frele at home." At my wit's end, I tied a bunch of ferns to the end of the rod, believing it might prevent the fish from being skeared; but it only frightened them the more, as I discovered to my disappointment in the next pool I tried.

By this time the sun was blazing hot. Penhale moor, when I came to it, droned with the hum of insects; dragon-flies darted to and fro between the heads of the figwort, lizards sat like green images on the bremble leaves, and the heated air was laden with the scent of the bracken. I worked pool after pool without as much as a twick. Some fish lay beneath thickets of honeysuckle and wild brier, under which I let the bait travel at the risk of losing my hook, all to no purpose. I was beginning to despair, when from a deep, stillish pool in the moor, below New Bridge, I pulled out a beauty – a short thick fish, all seven ounces in weight. With its bright crimson spots, and golden belly, it was a picture at the bottom of the frele.

The difference that trout made! It put heart into me, just as the cracking of my duck's egg had so often done at a cricket match. And as if fortune could not now do enough for me, lo, and behold, there on the bracken, rested the first ferny-cock of the season. At the sight, I knew that my basket was as good as filled, for of all our baits the ferny-cock is the most deadly; deadlier than tab-beetle, brandling worm, or down-looker fly. I was tremendously excited. After baiting, I wriggled on my stomach to the bank, and, all of a tremble, dropped the ferny-cock on the shadowed water beneath an alder. In a twinkling, a fish grabbed it, and joined the other.

Leaving the rod there, I started searching the bracken and other browse for the little bronzy beetle, feeling sure that if I searched long enough, I should find; and at last, in the corner of the moor, where the brembles ran riot over a sort of ragel, I picked over a dozen. What a find! I reckoned a fish for every bait.

Then came trouble. In a bend of the stream, touching Roskennal Mill, where the current carried the bait under the hollow bank, I lost a whopper, and, oh dear! oh dear! my little bluey-steel hook along with it. For a time I could do nothing but pace up and down, bewailing my fate. Two or three times I was on the point of calling across to the mill-boy, who lay asleep by a bed of foxgloves, but, thinking the better of it, kept my trouble to myself and let him be.

Having bent on my spare hook, I approached the mill, and dropped the bait in the white water at the foot of the wheel. In an instant the line tightened, and I pulled out a nice fish. I caught four there, and, missing a fifth, got hitched up in the overhanging sycamore. I climbed the tree, freed the hook, and within a few minutes pulled out three more; one from between the wheel and the wall, the others from the run between the white water and the mouth of the cundard. With nine fish in the basket, my spirits rose mountain high, and again I wanted to wake the boy, this time to tell him of my good fortune; but again I thought better of it. The last time I looked he had a smile on his face, as if he were dreaming. So leaving him, I held on in the roasting heat, picking a ferny-cock here and there, and catching or missing a fish in almost every pool I tried. By the time I reached the little ash grove above Skimmiel Bridge, I had got fifteen. Then conscience was at me to be off home and give a hand with the work.

At my feet lay a splat of turf, level as a fairies' green. There I tossed up my rod. If the letters came uppermost, I would go on; if otherwise, I would make for home. To my joy, the J. P. came right on top, and, with conscience at rest, I picked up my rod and climbed the high bank into the grove. The light was greeny there, the air cool as a dairy. I took from my pocket a hunk of bread mother had forced upon me, and sat me down by a waterfall to enjoy it. A prince could not have had a prettier spot to eat a bit of crib in. Ferns sprang from the bank, moss covered the boulders, the freshest of turf carpeted the ground between the silver stems and the tumbling water, and roo-hooing wood-doves made sweetest music. If I relished the barley bread, I relished still more the pipe that followed. Thought I, "A gentleman's life is a pleasant life." Then conscience was at me again, and I decided to be off home.

There were two ways: the one I had come by, the other athirt the downses, and this I took. I might have gone a quarter of a mile, when suddenly I came upon the earth-stopper. He was in his shirt sleeves, putting a capping-stone on a fox-drain, built horseshoe shape. On hearing me, he looked round, put up his hand to shade his eyes, and said, "Never you, Jack, out fishin' this time o'day! But theere, thee'rt not the only one takin' a holiday. Look! there's Loveday close behind thee."

As I turned, she rose from under the may tree that shaded her, and came towards me. How lovely she had grown, to be sure! Her beauty took my breath away. In face and form she was the most perfect maid I had set eyes upon.

"You've quite grown up since I saw you last," I said. "Do you remember when that was?"

"Is it likely I should forget?" she replied. "It was that wild day you were lost in the bulrushes."

"Yes, I remember I thought you looked like little Red Riding Hood. When did you come?"

"Only yesterday."

"And how long are you going to stay?"

"A day or two, whilst father's boat is being repaired."

"You will come and see mother?"

"I have just seen her, and she has asked us to tea on Sunday."

"That's splendid."

"Not much of a basket, 'spose?" said Andrew, who had stood listening to the conversation.

"Pretty middling," I replied, removing the ferns that covered the fish.

"Iss, fay! a good catch, and no mistake. However did 'ee manage it in this blaze of sun?"

"Ferny-cocks!"

"Ah! I was thinking as much, though I hadn't set eyes on one yet. A nice level lot," he kept repeating as he turned them over. "There's only one thing wantin' – a whacker to top the basket."

"'Tis my own fault; I had one on, but lost it, hook and all."

"Was it a very big one?" asked Loveday, her large dark-blue eyes wide with interest.

"It was. It had a great golden side that gleamed through the water like the side of Mrs. Pearce's jamming-pan."

She laughed at this, showing her teeth, white as the foam of the waterfall.

"I must go back to my work," said Andrew.

"And I, too," I added. "I've been away since croust-time; so-long, Loveday; so-long, Andrew."

Now, had I gone straight home all would have been well, but I did not. When abreast of the upper pond, I yielded to the temptation to top the basket with one of the squire's trout, and, crossing the field to the Great Downs, looked into the valley to see whether the coast was clear. As I saw no sign of anybody, I made my way down the slope to the pond, threw the line in, and, laying the rod on the bank, hid behind the nearest hydrangey, and waited the result. It was my intention at the first sign of a bite to rush out, seize the rod, fling out the fish, and run. I had not, however, been there many minutes when, to my consternation, the squire suddenly appeared, and sat himself down on the opposite bank. He had come to fish, and was waiting for Felton to bring his rod; at least so I thought on noticing the impatient way he kept turning his head in the direction of Sunny Corner. For the most part, however, his eyes were on the trout, particularly on a big fish that kept rising near my bait, and why they failed to see the rod is beyond me to explain. I was in a serious predicament. It is true that it was open to me to steal away unseen, but that would mean the loss of my little rod, which I could not make up my mind to leave behind; on the other hand, to make a dash for the rod involved the risk of identification and trouble – possibly grave trouble – for Lanyon.

Twice I was on the point of running the risk; and before I could summon up the courage, a fish took the bait, got hooked, and made for the middle of the pond, dragging the rod after it. The commotion in the water brought the squire to his feet, and while he was in two minds what to do, I crawled away, on all fours and escaped. I was very unhappy at the loss of my rod, more unhappy still when I reflected that the lettering on the butt would most likely lead to the poaching being brought home to me.

Master, of course, was delighted with the fish, and rode off to town with them then and there.

When I went indoors, mother exclaimed, "I have interesting news for you, Jack; a very pretty girl is coming to tea on Sunday."

"You mean Loveday Rosewarne; I saw her just now on Tregavara Downs. Isn't she beautiful?"

"Very; I'm afraid you'll be losing your heart to her."

"Mother," I replied, "I've lost it already."

CHAPTER XI

IN TROUBLE

ᶌᶒ

I AWOKE TO THE CONSCIOUSNESS of trouble to come. It seemed as if nothing could save me from being brought before the squire. All through milking-time I expected Felton to come through the gate; later, whilst cutting thistles in Great Fraland, I kept jumping on the hedge to see if he were in sight. The morning, however, dragged to an end without a sign, and at last the horn sounded for dinner. On the way in, I resolved to unburthen myself to mother; and this I did after father had got up from table, for, somehow or other, though he was the best of fathers, I shrank from telling him things I didn't mind telling mother.

On hearing what I had done, she was like a woman beside herself, but understanding that the little bluey hook would, as readily as the lettering, lead to my being traced, she threw the shawl about her, and started off for Penzance in the old sunbonnet just as she was. She went straight to Mr. Cunnack, who had sold her the hooks, told the trouble she was in, and begged him not to give her name, should Mr. Felton come to inquire. She was only just in time, for on the way back, near the prison, she met Felton with my rod on his shoulder and the hook hitched in, half-way down, at the full stretch of the line.

But though, by her prompt action, mother had forestalled Felton in the matter of the hook, she confessed that the lettering was beyond her wits to deal with. She could only suggest that I should go and see Andrew, adding, "If there is anyone who can help you he can." So that evening, after touching myself up a little, I went to Forest Carn to consult the old earth-stopper, and – why should I not say it? – to catch a glimpse of Loveday.

Twice I was on the point of turning back when almost there, because the nearer I got the more I shrank from confessing what a simpleton I had been, before Loveday, too; and as I lifted the latch and walked in, my heart sank.

"Thee'rt the very one I wanted to see," exclaimed Andrew, looking up from the paper flags he was making.

"Oh! how's that?"

"Well, Jack, I was curious to know what happened after you left us yesterday. I've been wonderin' whether you managed to top the basket?"

At this I quizzed the old man, then Loveday, then the old man again, and replied, "I did not, though 'twasn't for want of trying."

"So I understand; and, like the sheep with their tails, left the rod behind thee."

I coloured up fiercely at this, but Loveday, bless her! made a show of tidying the dresser, while Andrew, anointed rogue that he was, gloried in my confusion.

"Mother has been here," I blurted out.

"Iss, mawther dropped in and asked us to tea on Sunday, but that was yesterday mornin'; no, no, 'twadn't mawther as told, if that is what you mean; the news of the rod is all over Churchtown."

"All over Churchtown?"

"It is, Jack," said Loveday, timidly.

"That the rod is mine?"

"No, not as yet," replied Andrew, "and this thee mayest take to thy comfort, they'll hardly suspect that it is."

"How so?"

"Why, who ever heard of a farm-hand trout-fishing in the middle of a July afternoon? I never did; but after that Felton may bring it home to 'ee. Hast 'ee breathed a word to any livin' soul?"

"To nobody, but mother."

"And theere's nobody outside Lanyon can say the rod is yours?"

"There's one."

"Who's that?"

"Dickie Felton."

"Then it's all up; the lad is sure to stand by his father."

"That's right enough; but for all that, I can't believe that Dickie will split upon me."

"Hark!" exclaimed Andrew, excitedly, "that's surely Felton's step! It is! Does he know thee?"

"That's more than I can say."

"Then leave him to me."

A loud rap on the door, a sharp click of the latch, and in strode Felton.

"Who's the stranger, Stevens?" he asked, as he took his stand with his back to the fire.

"A friend."

"Won't you take a chair, Mr. Felton?" said Loveday, handing him one.

"No, thank you, Loveday, I can't stay. Stevens, I've come about the poaching in the pond. You've heard of a rod being found there?"

"Iss, I've heeard what they're sayin' in Churchtown, that the squire saw it being dragged about the pond."

"And you can imagine what the squire's feelings are at this daring act of trespass? Well, he has sent me to ask whom you suspect."

"What is there to go on?"

"The letters J.P. cut on the rod."

"Law bless 'ee, that edn much of a clue in Maddern Parish. Of J.P's there are no end, why the squire himself is one."

"Stevens, you forget yourself. I beg to remind you this is a most serious matter."

"Serious matter? Matters are what they're made. Serious or not, it is no crime. I have no patience with you tryin' to make out it is. Judgin' by your face, you would send man or boy, whichever it is, to Botany Bay for the rest of his days, all for catchin' or tryin' to catch a trout!"

"I would; and you are going to tell me the names that have J.P. for initials. Remember, I am here by the squire's orders."

In the strained silence that followed, Andrew kept puffing out smoke like a dragon, and when at last he spoke, it was in anger.

"Your hard-hearted ways make me mad; it is not the squire that's to blame, but you, who urge and drive him to desperate courses."

"That's how you describe my duty, and you a servant of the squire."

"Iss, a servant of the squire, as of his father and grandfather before him, years and years before thee wust born. I have a right to spake, and I tell thee to thy face, Felton, that thee'rt a curse to the parish."

"Well, now that you have said what you think, perhaps you will tell me the names."

"I don't mind doin' that: John Polsue, Jimmy Penhaligon, Josiah Pender, Johnny Pidwell, Jeremiah Polkinghorne – law, I could tally up a score or more, only give me time to think. Here are two, Job Penberthy and Joey Pentreath. Tell 'ee what, Felton, I'll get Loveday there to write down the list and let 'ee have it tomorrow."

"That will do. Loveday shall bring it to Sunny Corner by three o'clock; Dickie will be home by then, and will like to take her round the ponds."

With that he said, "Goodnight," and took himself off.

"He didn't seem to know thee from Adam, Jack, and he don't know one farm-hand in a dozen. That's wheere he fails as a keeper. Why, he should make a point of knowing the hands in all the farms around, not only their faces, but the prents of their boots, and above all – here he smiled – their Christian and family name."

"You'll not put my name on the list, Andrew?"

"Jack, thee'rt surely triflin'. Dost eh take me for a greenhorn, after a life spend circumventin' varmints?"

"Don't be put out, granfer; Jack did not mean it that way, and besides, he would never have got into this trouble if you hadn't put it into his head to top the basket."

"Thee'rt a clever peacemaker, my dear, but whether I misunderstood Jack or no, I'll do my best to prevent his bein' driven out of the parish, both him and his people, as they will be if the rod is traced home to him."

"They could come over to Prussia Cove then, granfer."

"Yes, my dear, but they must live wherever they are."

"Well, they could take a little place, and Jack could lend father a hand with the smuggling."

"Rechard might; Rechard would do on the land, but as for Jack bein' cut out for a smuggler, well, after yesterday, what is a body to think? Oh, Jack! Jack! what a numskull thee wust to leave thy rod behind thee, with, of all things, thy name upon the butt! Whatever wert 'ee thinkin' about to do such a fool's thing?"

"Don't, Andrew, don't," I exclaimed, rising to go.

"I've done, lad, I've done, and tell mawther I'll screen thee if I can. Thee did well to come and see me or – here the roguish twinkle came into his eyes – was it Loveday who drawed thee? Ah! you sly fox, goodnight."

"Goodnight, Andrew, thank you; goodnight, Loveday – see you all Sunday."

Mother was sitting up for me. On hearing that Andrew had spoken his mind to Felton, she was so delighted that I think she would have clapped her hands but for fear of waking father.

"Ah! Jack, my son, Andrew is a fine character; I rejoice to think that he spoke his mind to him, man to man. But how is it Felton did not know you, and you such friends with Dickie?"

"I can't say, except that he never looks me in the face. And then he

90

makes a boast of it, that yokels and yawbucks are beneath his notice."

"Insolent fellow! But be sure not to tell your father that; he'd go for him if you did."

Mother was all of a tremble when I kissed her goodnight.

Next day, on the way in with the Saturday's butter, I noticed that the board on the Carn had been painted afresh, and I had scarcely set foot in the shop when Aunt Grace, as we called Mrs. Trudgen, told me that Felton, looking very fierce, had spent half the morning walking up and down Churchtown with a brand new man-trap slung over each shoulder. She was terribly put out. If I had not heard her, I should not have thought it possible for so mild-mannered a woman to speak in the bitter tones she used.

"Strothing forth and back with man-traps on his back! What for, but to intimidate the village? And all because some poor little urchin left his fishing-rod in the pond! Things have come to a pretty pass; we shall be sent to jail next for looking over the hedge. No wonder people are up in arms, threatening to pull down the dams and let the water out, trout and all. If I've had one in about it, I've had a dozen. The village is boiling over with the iniquity of it."

Aunt Grace was not the only woman whose feelings had been outraged. On reaching Lanyon, I heard Miss Jenifer speaking in a voice so loud that it seemed to fill the town-place.

"More man-traps, indeed! How can you stand by, Henry, and see these inhuman machines laid down without a protest passes my comprehension – you a Pearce of Lanyon too! The very thought of those cruel jaws lying there ready to close on a man's leg makes my blood boil. Oh! Henry! Henry! If you had but a tithe of my spirit!"

The rest of the sentence was lost through master coming forward and shutting down the window.

"Things have come to a pretty pass," I said to myself as I crossed the yard, and all because of an idle word dropped by Andrew. Not that I wanted to throw the fault upon the old man. Heaven forbid! No; I was alone to blame, not only for the general upset, but – what mattered ten times more to me – for throwing Dickie and Loveday together. For why? Because I felt sure Loveday would take to Dickie; what girl would not? and that Dickie would be over head and ears in love with Loveday. What I suffered from jealousy that afternoon no tongue can tell.

The list of names brought Felton nothing but trouble. Joe Penbale, to whom he went first, put an end to their long talk by threatening him with the pitchfork, and when Joe told how he had been questioned and cross-questioned, the roguish ones amongst the J.P.'s put their heads together and arranged to give Felton a warning he would understand. So a few evenings later they burnt him in effigy on the green. We heard of it the same night from Jim the Pedlar, who sat talking of it for hours. After I had returned from seeing him comfortable in the barn where he slept, mother and I discussed the serious turn things had taken, but came to the conclusion – and, as it proved, the right conclusion – that the squire would now, in the face of the bitter feeling aroused in Churchtown, let the matter drop.

CHAPTER XII

FORGET-ME-NOTS

ALL SUNDAY AFTERNOON, mother was as busy as a bee preparing for our expected visitors. I never saw her go to such trouble before. She got out the best cups, the best plates, the lustre teapot with milk-jug to match, the glass sugar-basin, and – to crown all – her only bits of silver, the sugar-tongs and the five apostle spoons; she provided saffron cake, heavy cake, wheaten bread, a pot of blackberry jam, and a big basin of cream.

The table was laid and mother tidied, when I went running in and exclaimed, "They are all three coming down the road, and Mr. Rosewarne has got a black beard, black whiskers, and a great mark across his cheek."

"Sh! my dear," mother replied, "Mr. Rosewarne is no stranger to me. I have known him these many years."

"How did he come by that scar?"

"From a cutlass, I believe; but that was many years ago; on no account refer to it."

Mother was at the door to welcome them. She kissed Loveday, then, holding out her hand to Mr. Rosewarne, said, "Henry, I am very pleased to see you after all these years; how many is it?"

"I have just been asking myself the selfsame question."

"Well, when was it?"

"Guess."

"At the opening of the Market House?"

"No; not so long ago as that. Try again."

"At the fixing of the pole and cage on the Ryman Reef?"

"No."

"Then, I give it up."

"It was when I broke into the Custom House and recovered the goods the Preventive men stole from me."

Father and Andrew roared with laughter at this, and even mother could not help joining in.

When the tea had stood a minute or two, mother arranged us around the table. She put Loveday and me in the window-seat, Mr. Rosewarne on her right, with Andrew farther along the form close to father. Mother's bright face and merry tongue set everybody at their ease. She talked all the time she was pouring out the tea, first to one, then to the other, while I gave all my attention to Loveday, taking no notice of the winks which mother and Mr. Rosewarne exchanged. Soon Mr. Rosewarne began to speak of old times.

"I remember, Mary, when first I came to this cottage. Jack was a baby in arms, and like a bit of quicksilver."

"No holding him, you mean? I shall never forget the trouble I had with him in church the day you and Honor were married."

"And the cheeld was faither to the man," put in Andrew. "Look where you will, you won't find a more active chap, nor a better looking, not even at Prussia Cove – now will you, Loveday?"

"Steady, An'rew," said father; "if you talk like that you'll spoil Loveday's tea."

"It is too late for that, Mr. Penrose; I've nearly finished."

And so the meal went merrily on.

Later, when mother and Loveday were clearing away the things, father, Mr. Rosewarne, and Andrew sat out on the bench smoking, whilst I stood in the doorway, where I could see Loveday, and watch her father blow rings of tobacco-smoke, at which he was very skilful. He would blow a ring, then another through it, and more often than not a third through the second.

"Thee'rt as good as a showman at that," said father.

"And I ought to be; it was my chief occupation when in the French prison."

"Was that when you got the cut, Mr. Rosewarne?" I asked.

"For shame, Jack," exclaimed mother, coming to the door; "after my warning you as I did."

"Don't let that trouble you, Mary; I don't mind his knowing when and where I got that scar; and perhaps it's as well that he should hear a word or two about the perils and penalties of Free Trading. No, Jack, I did not get the scar in France; I got it in Cornwall, and this is how:

"January month, 1831, I had a freight for Helford, where, being told on arrival that the coast was clear, I brought the lugger to an anchor off the mouth of the river. Then all hands set about loading the boats which had come off to us, and as I watched them go and return in the darkness, I reckoned on a good landing. Yet all the while the Preventive men were closing in upon us.

We had only a score or so of kegs to handle, when sounds of strife on shore told their tale. We had been surprised. My first thought was to save the lugger, but thinking it my duty to stand by my friends, I jumped into a boat, reached the slip, and, seizing a boat-hook, joined in the fray. I do not care to dwell on the fight; we made what resistance we could. But what could be expected from unarmed men opposed to cutlasses? The men had only their fists, but I had the boat-hook, with which I laid about me to such purpose that I drew on myself the attention of the officers, and thus, as I found afterwards, enabled most of my men to get away. Enraged by my defence, the Preventive men used their cutlasses without mercy. I was terribly mauled about the head, got a bad gash on the left shoulder, and a cut on the face, which left the scar you see. So it was not long before I was beaten to the ground, where I lay dazed, and evidently, in the eyes of the officers, dead, for they left me lying there. When I saw them coming back with lanterns, the thought of how they would gloat over my capture nerved me to effort, and, turning over on my stomach, I started creeping away on all fours towards a cottage that loomed against the stars. I could not reach it, my strength failed me, and I sank into a swoon a score yards or so from the door. When I came a little to my senses, I found myself in a boat with two men, whom I took to be officers in charge of me. What a relief when the one who was holding me up whispered in my ear, 'I'm Tom Flinders, the man at the sculls is Bill Munday; you mind me and Bill?' 'Coverack boys?' 'Iss, Coverack boys.' 'Where are we?' 'Drifting with the tide up the river.' Later, we turned into a creek, overhung, I think, with trees, as it got suddenly dark; and there the men lifted me out, and carried me across open country to a hut in a wood. There, again, I became unconscious, and on coming to was surprised to find that it was day, with the sun shining between the stems of the trees. I was still more surprised when Flinders told me that the doctor had been and attended to my wounds. 'How long has he been gone?' I asked. 'He rode off as day was breaking, but left word that he would come again.' And come he did, at dark; not on horseback, however, as before, but in a chaise, in which he drove me miles and miles before we reached our destination. By the time we arrived, I was too exhausted to take note of anything but the cheerful wood fire that lit up the bedroom to which I was taken. I fell asleep at once, and awoke greatly refreshed, to find myself in a comfortable bed with snow-white sheets standing beside a window, through which I could see a dovecote with fantails strutting and cooing on the roof, an old stone gateway with a sundial on it, and two holly trees red with berries. My sanctuary was Godolphin Manor-house, where I remained a day or two over the fortnight. By that time a reward of £300 was offered for my apprehension, and – what was more serious – word had got about that I was hiding in Breage.

"My friends were so much alarmed by this, that the night following the appearance of the advertisement in the papers I was moved to Kenegie, in Gulval, and we did not get there without another fright. Where the track to Prussia Cove branches off from the Falmouth road, two men called upon us to pull up."

"And did you?"

"No fear, Jack, the driver whipped up the horses, and dashed past at a gallop, leaving the men to stare after us. At Kenegie, the squire and his lady were waiting up to receive us, and, after I had had a basin of hot broth and told my story, the squire and the old butler between them helped me up two flights of stairs and down a long corridor in a little-used part of the house, to a room where a fire burned in the grate and a bed had been got ready. But there, I am making my story too long."

"Not a bit," I replied. "What happened next?"

"Well, I was treated as kindly at Kenegie as at Godolphin; the squire came to see me every day, the butler brought me food, and most likely I should have remained there till I had completely recovered and the trouble blown over, had it not been for a woman's curiosity, and, what was worse still, her long tongue. One Thursday evening, about an hour after the squire had left me, and my part of the house was as still as death, I heard, or thought I heard, a noise as of some one moving stealthily in the passage; but as nothing came of it, I gave over listening, relit my pipe, and settled down again in my chair. Somehow I still suspected danger, and kept my eyes on the door. Presently it was quietly opened, and the face of an oldish woman appeared round the edge of it. I said nothing, but the moment her eyes met mine she drew back, and stole away as silently as she had come.

"My visitor, I learned later, was the housekeeper, who, on reaching the ground floor, rushed into the kitchen and screamed out that there was a sailor-man in the haunted room, with his head all bandaged. Fortunately, the squire soon got to know that my hiding place had been discovered. He came to me in a state of great excitement. 'Rosewarne,' he said, 'I'm very sorry, but your presence is known to all the servants, and you must be moved tonight. I'm just off to make arrangements.' With that he was gone. A few minutes later I heard a horse gallop down the drive, and then, except for the wind in the trees, nothing more till the old butler came to fetch me. The clock in the hall was chiming eleven as I followed him to the pony-carriage standing outside the door. He drove, not along the main road, but by the bastion drive to Badgers' Cross, and from there, by lanes and by-ways, to the Eastern Green, and across the beach and the wet sand to the edge of the low tide, where we began to look for a boat that was to take me off. Owing to the darkness, it was some time before we were able to find it; but at last we succeeded, and, to my surprise, the squire was in it, and with him a gentleman who was a stranger to me. On getting aboard I offered to take an oar, but to this they would not listen. So I took the tiller, and being accustomed, like Andrew, to use my eyes at night, managed to avoid the reefs and ledges that lay thick in our course. We passed close to the Ryman, where two shags were roosting in the cage, and soon were off the August rocks on our way to the back of the mount, where we were to land. We had got about a gunshot from the place when, all at once, we heard voices. At this, the squire and his friend ceased rowing, and, resting on their oars, held a whispered consultation. 'They've got wind of our coming,' said the squire. 'They're after that £300,' added his friend. 'And will get it if we are not careful; and what's to be done now I don't know. Can you suggest anything, Rosewarne?' 'What about Marazion, sir; we have friends there?' 'True, but there's too strict a watch there.' 'Acton Castle is empty, sir.' 'I know, but there's the getting there; it's a devil of a way to Perran, and my hands are blistered already.'

"I again offered to take an oar, only to be met with a refusal, and presently the two settled down to the long pull to Perran against the choppy sea. Once or twice it looked as if the task were beyond their powers, but they stuck to it like men, and about three o'clock we landed on the beach. Leaving the boats there, we climbed the cliff and followed the track along its edge, at last reaching the castle. 'Leave me now, gentlemen,' I said; 'look to yourselves.' But no, they insisted on waiting till I succeeded in finding a way in. Door after door we tried, to no purpose; but, as luck would have it, the dairy window had been left unfastened, and through this I managed to clamber. 'I'll see that you are made comfortable as soon as possible,' said the squire, as he turned to go. He was as good as his word. That night two of my men from the cove brought blankets, food, tobacco, and a sack of coal. I remained there eight days, till the smoke from the chimney betrayed me, and forced me to hide in the cliffs. From there, after many hardships, I was at length taken off in a boat and put on board a London trader."

"What then?" I asked.

"Well, Jack, I reached London."

"And then?"

"Why, after a stay of two months, owing to the influence of some Cornish gentlemen who interested themselves on my behalf, I got a free pardon and returned home. So now you know how I came by the scar, and what I went through before I recovered my liberty."

"Thank you," I said, "that's as interesting a story as ever I heard."

"And mind you profit by it," said mother, coming to the door with a troubled face, "and have nothing to do with such a perilous trade. Now what do you say to taking Loveday round?"

"Say, mother? Why that I should like it before everything."

"And I, too," added Loveday, in her bright, sprightly way.

I took her downalong – why, I don't know. Nor does it matter, for all ways are good ways when with the girl you love. We stayed quite a while by the millpool, watching the trout leap and rise. I had difficulty in getting her away; she was so interested. Before leaving, I stepped to the water's edge, and picked a bunch of the forget-me-nots growing there.

"We call them forget-me-nots here with us," I said, softly, as I handed her the flowers.

"So do we," she replied coyly, turning her face away.

On the way to the mill, I told her of the trout in the pulrose, and when I had done she said, "Promise me that you will not try to catch it."

"I'll promise you anything," I replied; "but why the trout?"

"Because, if you promise, I shall know it is there, and – "

"And what?"

"How impatient you are, Jack! I was going to say I shall think of it some-times."

"And of nothing, of nobody else; never of mother or of – ?"

"I shall certainly think of your mother."

"And of nobody else?"

To this she gave no reply, but seeming to me, her brown cheek looked a shade the warmer.

Then, along the turfy path between the bracken, we made for Boundary Pool.

"What a fine fern!" she exclaimed, at sight of the tall kingfern in the shallows there.

"It was that I brought you to see."

"And not granfer's stepping-stones? May I cross?" she asked, as she started tripping from one to the other, light as a fairy.

"You have the freedom of Lanyon to do as you will, and I am content to stand and watch you cross and re-cross, till you tire."

And so I could, for never had maiden a more bewitching foot and ankle than Loveday Rosewarne.

"Come, Jack," said she presently, "let us be moving, or father will be wondering what has become of me."

I took her to the old tumbled-down Quoit in Deep Field, thence to Further Jets, where our milch cows were grazing, and casting their shadows to the farther hedge.

"What a sweet sight! how lovely the setting sun makes everything!"

"It is shedding its blessing on the earth."

"What a pretty thought; wherever did you hear that?"

"It is only a saying we have."

On reaching the Quoit, she said, "If only the stones could speak, Jack!"

"They do whisper to me at times."

"Do you really mean it? What do they say?"

"They say, 'We are very old; you are very young.'"

"Is that all?"

"Yes; like the mill, they have only one thing to say."

"And what is that the mill says?"

"'Master, he do make it; and Missus, she do waste it.'"

"Oh! that is too bad. Cornish women are very saving; their only extravagance is bonnets."

Then we crept along a gully to where we could overlook the Trucks, and see the young foxes, if they were sunning themselves. As luck would have it, there they were, in charge of the vixen. What antics to be sure! Now jumping over one another's backs, now rolling on the turf, and – a thing which caused Loveday to draw in her breath – every few minutes going and licking their mother with their little crimson tongues.

As I dared not speak, yet felt that something had to be done to express my feeling, I squeezed Loveday's hand. I hoped, I almost expected, that she would squeeze mine; but no – she drew her hand away. There was nothing forthy about Loveday Rosewarne. A minute later, we crept away as quietly as we had come.

On reaching Trucks Lane, Loveday suddenly stopped, and said, "Listen! the sea!"

"Yes; it is calling to you."

"And when I am not here?"

"Then it calls to the heath."

"You are a poet, Jack."

"No, I am no poet; I am only repeating a saying of the old people."

Then for a while we went on in silence.

Said Loveday, as I let her through the gate of Barn Field, "Yours must be a nice life, Jack."

"It would be if it were all like the last hour, or if I had somebody I loved to care for me."

"Dear me; how ungrateful you are. You have the best of mothers, and nothing in the world to wish for."

"Ah! Loveday, you little witch; you are clever at turning things off."

"I am no witch, I am only a smuggler's daughter; as to turning things off, that is a girl's only defence against her tormentors."

"I give in; I am no match – in mouth-speech, I mean – for you."

Lanyon looked a picture, with the smoke curling up from the chimneys to where the swifts were enjoying their evening flight, and the scene – the mowhay, the stable, craws, yard, and cottage – often comes back to me, with Mr. Rosewarne, Andrew, father and mother, seated on the bench beside the door.

I felt a bit shy as we approached, for mother and – as I thought – Mr. Rosewarne looked quizzingly at us as if to learn how we had got on together. But neither they nor Andrew, whose tongue I dreaded, said anything.

Father and I saw our visitors home. On leaving her, I whispered to Loveday, "I will do my best to see you off in the morning."

"Then I will look out for you," she said.

In the morning, with a deal of persuading, I got master to let me go to Penzance for a load of lime, which we did not really want. Early as I set out, I reached the pier-head only in the nick of time. To my astonishment, Dickie was there at the foot of the steps talking as freely as you please to Loveday. At the sight, my jealousy blazed up like a beacon fire, and had I not noticed the forget-me-nots pinned to Loveday's dress, I hardly know what I should have done. But the sight of the flowers gave me courage, and, brushing past Dickie, I stepped aboard and sat beside Loveday, with only the tiller separating us.

"I'm miserable at your going," I whispered; "and how I shall be able to get along without sight of you, I don't know."

"You'll soon forget me, Jack."

"Never, so long as I draw breath."

"Well, now, my young friends," said Mr. Rosewarne, as he hoisted the blue flag with the word *Kittiwake* in white on it, "'tis no use offering you a passage, I suppose?"

"No, sir, worse luck," I replied, rising to my feet "but come back soon, and be sure to bring Loveday with you."

He laughed at this, and pushed off, whilst Dickie and I raced up the steps to the pier-head. There we waved and waved, and Loveday waved back.

We remained till the *Kittiwake* had passed the Cressers and put about, then walked back along the quay together. Not a word did we exchange till we reached the Barbican lime-kiln, and then it was I who broke the painful silence.

"Dickie," I said, feelingly, "let there be no misunderstanding. I mean to marry Loveday, if I've got to go through flood and fire to get her."

"So do I," he replied, not in his usual quiet manner, however, but with a show of spirit that surprised me.

CHAPTER XIII

A HEAVY
RESPONSIBILTY

❧

THE FALL OF THAT YEAR remains clear in my memory for the good fortune it brought me. Michaelmas Day in the morning the head kitchen-maid came running to the mowhay with word that Miss Jenifer wanted to see me at once. So after binding the truss I had cut, I slipped on my jacket and went across, wondering what I could be wanted for. I found Miss Jenifer seated in the high-backed chair with her papers and keys on the table.

"John," said she, looking up at me, "I have been talking the matter over with your master and I have decided, now that you have nearly reached man's estate, to entrust you with the care of the poultry."

"Yes, Miss Jenifer."

"I am afraid from your tone that you do not fully appreciate the responsibility of your new charge."

"You mean on account of the varmin, miss?"

"I mean on account of the foxes and the vermin. Foxes, remember, are not vermin, to be classed with badgers, fitchers, stoats, and whitnecks; they are beasts of the chase to be carefully preserved as such, but none the less destructive to poultry and to be guarded against. Now listen: there are the keys; the moment the sun sets you are to lock the houses and make all secure for the night. Fail of that and we shall awake to havoc, for not a night passes but some marauder comes prowling around ready to take advantage of any oversight."

"I will do my best, miss."

"That is better, you cannot say more. Now, here is a list of the birds; keep it by you and understand that from this moment the poultry are under your sole charge. Have I made myself clear?"

"Yes, miss."

"Now, you are quite sure?"

"Yes, miss."

"Very well, you may go back to your work."

Before returning to the mowhay, I went indoors, hung the keys to the window side of the chimney where they would catch my eye, and, after giving the nail a tap or two with the jennyquick iron dropped into father's chair, and ran my eyes down the list.

It read as follows: hens, cockerels, mabyers, chicks, and roosters 137, turkeys 48, geese 19, guinea-fowl 13. That included everything except the peacock, which roosted with the guinea-fowl in the sycamore before Miss Jenifer's window and which, besides being an ornament to the townplace, was worth its keep for warning us of the approach of dirty weather. Law! how he would squall whenever the wind got back in the rainy quarter after a spell of drieth; he could be heard all over the farm, and even on the moor.

Then, reckoned with the poultry, though not one of them, there was the grey shrike, whose home was a wicker cage on a pole by the stable and whose duty it was to warn the poultry of the approach of birds of prey. The eyesight of the little sentinel, who was hardly as big as a cock blackbird, passed all belief. He would suddenly start screeching – and couldn't he holloa! – at what you would take for an empty sky; but, as you looked, there would come into view a hawk, buzzard or raven, making, more likely than not, straight for Lanyon. At his cry the chicks would take refuge in one or other of the open sheds, or seek cover under the blackthorns which I had cut and set for them, alongside the farm dairy. Master saw to the feeding of Watch, as we called the shrike, and at milking-time his favourite leaning place was the pole that supported the cage.

My new duty brought me a rise of one shilling a week, with promise of a present at Christmas, if prices warranted it. We reckoned this handsome consideration because, as father said, the work was trifling and the responsibility nothing to lose flesh over. I was in high jubilation at the increase of wage, for it brought my earnings up to nine shillings a week, and within three shillings of the sum that most Madron men married on; aye, and in many cases, reared long families on, too.

I took kindly to my new duties, locking up regularly within a few minutes of the sun sinking below the hills. If foxes and other varmin did come prowling round, as father, mother and Miss Jenifer all maintained, it was only to find every bird under lock and key, or out of reach in the branches of the sycamore.

But did they come? I misdoubted it, for, like most youngsters I thought I knew better than my elders, and had nothing to learn by experience. I reasoned thus with myself. Was it likely that shrewd creatures like foxes and varmin, which lived by their wits and had only the hours of darkness to pick up a living in, would waste their time coming night after night to closed craws when there were pertridges, rabbits and hares to be had for the catching? Why no. Nevertheless I held my peace till I should have put the matter to the proof, for which three different plans came to my mind. I first thought of watching from the kitchen window, then of setting up a hand-mow near the craws and peeping out between the sheaves, but gave up both ideas in favour of a scheme by which I could learn what I wanted by means of the footprints left.

To this end I spread a barrow-load of riddled earth before the doors, patted it smooth, and left it to do its work. The night was dry, with a fresh northerly wind and the moon shining from time to time through the clouds. On going upstairs, I stood awhile by the open window watching our own little rick-yard below but, as I expected, saw no sign of a marauder. Then I undressed, tumbled into bed and slept like a top. I was awoke by the clock striking five, and before father was stirring I had dressed and was out examining the tell-tale earth by lantern-light. My word! It was pitted with footprints! In front of the fowls'-house I made out the tracks of fox, fitcher and of another creature, unbeknown to me at the time but which I know now was a marten-cat. One of the foxes – for the different size of the pad-marks told me there had been two – must have paced forth and back like a wild beast in a cage for ever so long, to leave the beaten track he did. What a lesson to me! I was glad that I had kept my own counsel; but it left me with a slight opinion of the brains of foxes and varmin.

Of course I became more particular than ever about locking up, and by way of additional reminder, I tied a bit of red flannel to the bunch of keys.

Though Miss Jenifer never came across at lock-up, she now and again put in an appearance at feeding time. I had every reason to welcome her coming, for the poultry, especially the turkeys, did me credit and made a brave show. There were many birds that we judged at twenty pounds, and as prices promised well, I had hopes of a record market and a substantial Christmas-box.

But in spite of all my precautions, the chief turkey-house was broken into during the great December gale, and every bird within the marauder's reach wantonly slaughtered. Never shall I forget the sight that met my eyes that morning as I forced open the door against the howling wind. The dead lay on the floor anyhow, the survivors – the three turkey-cocks being amongst them – sat close huddled together on the upper perch, whilst in the dark corner, away from the freshly made hole in the thatch, glowed the bluey-green eyes of a great dog-fox. He had scratted his way in, had his fill of murder and been unable to get out.

Flustered though I was, I did what was right: I fastened the door, stopped the hole, and ran across to tell master. It was with a heavy heart and an unwilling tongue that I entered the kitchen, for I feared the bad news would send Miss Jenifer into 'sterics.

Nothing of the kind! Master went on buttoning his leggings, just as if I had not spoken! Miss Jenifer, to whom word was taken by one of the maids, uttered neither scream nor cry.

"Now, Jack," said master, when he had done up the other leg, "I am at your service."

"But," said I, casting my eyes up at the flint locks, "aren't you going to take...?"

"No! no! no! none of that! I should as soon think of shooting a man as a fox."

On reaching the craw he motioned to me to throw abroad the door, and stand to one side. This I did as quietly as the creaking hinge would let me. For a good two minutes there was no sign – nothing but the stamping of the turkeys; then, with just a faint rustling of the straw, out bolted the fox. He came with such a rush that he looked a mere blur until abreast of the barn-steps, where he stopped and looked back at us over his shoulder.

He was a magnificent fellow, in full pride of pelt, with no trace of murder upon him except a feather on his upper lip and a daub of blood on the tip of his great brush. The next moment he slipped over the mowhay wall, leaving me standing there dumbfounded at master's forbearance. For master did not as much as shout at the rascal as he rushed past. Indeed, he never opened his mouth at all except to say, "Bury the birds out of sight."

I buried them a good two feet deep in the corner of Nearer Jets, and stamped the earth well down to prevent the foxes and badgers from digging them up. It was a melancholy business that took me all two hours to get through. When I had done, I hurried across to Miss Jenifer, and told her everything. Why not? I had nothing to hide. Unfortunately I wound up by saying, "And master let the varmint go scot free." How she flared up!

"What else would you have a Pearce of Lanyon do? Surely not kill the fox?"

There she paused, ready to fly at me, if I went against her.

"Well, Miss Jenifer," I replied in my soberest voice, "If you are satisfied, I am more so, for I am glad to think that grand old fox is curled up safe and sound in the Trucks, and not lying like carrion on the midden heap."

She clapped her hands at this, and before dismissing me said, "I am rejoiced to know that no blame whatever attaches to you."

"Thank you, Miss; ever since I took the poultry off your hands, I've tried to be as good as my word."

"Never fail of that," she added, as I turned to go.

On leaving the big house, I fetched Tom Tregoning, the thatcher, who made good the damaged craw, and then saw to two riffles in the cattle-shed, finishing up by lantern-light so as to get the work out of hand while he was on the spot.

Such was the tragedy of the turkeys, which I have related chiefly to show my old master's loyalty to the squire and his sport.

If old Moore himself had said that worse was to befall Lanyon before Christmas, I should have laughed in his face, yet, as things turned out, I should have lived to regret it.

CHAPTER XIV

THE DEAD FOX

❧

I T WAS A MERCY that on the very morning of the trouble I am now to relate, it should have fallen to me to take the cows to field in place of master, inasmuch as it spared him a sight that he would never have forgotten. For there, in Trucks Lane, lay a dying fox, with Jethro Felton stooping over it. At a glance I saw the gun-shot wound in the throat and the steel-trap on the fore-leg, and as I raised my eyes, met Felton's malicious smile.

"This means trouble for Lanyon," he snarled out.

"Yes," I replied, not grasping his meaning, "Master will be greatly put out."

"You look very innocent!"

"I look as I feel," I said, now alive to what he was driving at.

"Well, here it is almost at your door, and no other farm near!"

"Do you mean that I or master killed this fox?"

"I do."

"I know nothing about it, and any one who insinuates that my master killed the fox deserves to be burnt in effigy."

"You dare insult me, you contemptible muckworm," he hissed out, rising to his full height.

"I do!" I shouted, throwing up my arms in case he let out at me. But he drew back and seemingly fearing to trust himself longer in my company, snatched up the fox, and started off in the direction of Trengwainton.

The moment his back was turned, I ran to the big house, and rushed into the parlour. My sudden entry startled master and Miss Jenifer who were busy with the accounts.

"What in the world has happened?"exclaimed Miss Jenifer. "Has the bull broken loose?"

" 'Tes ten thousand times worse than that, Miss. Felton has come on a fox with a trap on its leg and a gash in its throat, and gone off with it to the Squire!"

"Where?"

"In Trucks Lane."

"How dreadful!"

"Dreadful isn't the word, Jenifer; it's horrible! Did Felton say anything?"

"He said it meant trouble for Lanyon."

"And what did you say?"

"Nothing at all, master, until he insulted you; then my blood was up and I told him he ought to be burnt in effigy."

"You did?"

"I did, right to his ugly face."

"Sh!"

"Henry, you must go and see Sir Rose this instant, before the matter is misrepresented; you really must."

"I can't face it, Jenifer; I'm worse than useless."

"Then I must go myself."

"You are not fit, Miss Jenifer!" I exclaimed, as she moved towards the door. "What's more, you'd never reach the mansion in time. I'll go."

"Now, Jack," shouted master, as I was at the door, "keep a watch on your tongue or you'll do more harm than good; and remember Sir Rose is Sir Rose."

Without saddle or bridle, I galloped off on Snowball, who went as if he knew the best was required of him. Near Forest Carn I broke in over the hedge of the preserves, and held on past the warning-board and the Round Plantation, wondering by then where Felton could be. At the pace we had come I never dreamt he could have been in front; but so he proved to be, for on topping the rise beyond Rocky Hollow, I sighted him two score yards ahead, running at full speed. As I flew by, he shook his great bony fist at me, and poisoned the air with his curses.

A mile or so on, a high bank rose between me and the mansion wood. I did a rash thing, after the long gallop, in setting Snowball at it; but in a bound he was on the top, and gathering his hoofs under him, took off splendidly and landed light as a feather on the other side. Ah! Snowball was a grand horse. As we threaded the trees I managed to steady him, and it was at a walk that we passed through the big gates into the yard.

"'I want to see the Squire,'" I said, addressing a groom who came running out of the stable. For answer he pointed to the bell-handle, which I pulled till the mansion rang with the ding-dong.

Almost at once old Mr. Tripconey appeared with a look that said, "How dare you ring like that?" But my stern face, possibly the tone of my voice, as

I said, "Take me to the Squire, and at once," silenced him; and he went trotting back without a word.

Seizing the opportunity, I picked up a wad of straw lying there and started rubbing Snowball down. Before I had finished, Mr. Tim returned with the message, "The Squire wishes to know your business."

"My business is for the Squire's ears, and his only."

So he went off again and, returning, motioned me to follow.

The long corridor and the lofty hall, with their array of red-coated soldiers gazing down upon me from their gold frames, would have impressed me at any other time. But not then. Indignation at the slur cast on master gave me courage, and I passed through the door which Tim held wide open, primed for the trial before me.

The Squire, who was writing at a table littered with papers, did not so much as look up; and as I waited, eager to give my explanation, I began for the first time to feel the influence of my surroundings.

Suddenly he dropped the quill, leant back in his chair, and said, "Well, my man, what brings you here at this early hour?"

"Please, Squire, my master, Mr. Henry Pearce of Lanyon, has sent me about a fox found this morning in Trucks Lane. I'm to tell you that it did not come by its death at our hands."

"Were there any signs of foul play?"

"Yes, Squire, it had a gunshot wound in the neck, and a gin on its foreleg."

At this he sat bolt upright, and said angrily, "Why didn't your master come himself? The matter is serious enough in all conscience."

"Master didn't come because he can't face trouble; he owned as much just now, in the parlour. Miss Jenifer wanted to come, but she is touched in the wind, and I wouldn't let her."

"You wouldn't let her! You wouldn't let Miss Jenifer come, did you say?"

"I did, Squire."

"Dear me; you make yourself out to be a very masterful person. You work on the farm, I suppose?"

"I do, Squire, and look to the poultry."

"Why did you emphasize 'and look to the poultry'?"

"I will tell you, Squire, and then you can judge for yourself whether master was likely to have had a hand in the death of this fox. You remember the great storm?"

"Yes."

"Well, Squire, that night a fox scratted his way in through the thatch of the big turkey-house, and killed seventeen out of the seven-and-twenty birds ready fatted for Christmas market. But he couldn't get out; and when I opened the door next morning, there he was up in the corner with eyes glowing like living coals. I ran across for master, and after he got his leggings up, master came back with me. 'Throw abroad the door,' he said, and I threw abroad the door."

"And then?"

"Why, my shaver came out with a rush, and looked back at us in wonderment before slipping over the mowhay wall."

"You mean that your master never touched him?"

"Never touched him? Why he didn't as much as mob him, and yet Mr. Felton said to me just now, as we stood by the fox, 'This means trouble for your master.' I tell you, Squire, knowing what I did, I could hardly keep my hands off him."

He laughed aloud at this, but in a mocking way.

"I take it you would have killed the fox?"

"Most likely I should but, asking your pardon, Squire. . ."

"Well, what is it?"

"I'd rather not, because master said, last thing as I was coming away, 'Remember, Sir Rose is Sir Rose.'"

"Never mind me; out with what you were going to say."

"I could never dig out a fresh fox and fling it to the hounds, as I have seen you do."

I expected he would fly out at this, but he did not; just the opposite. He sat for a minute: or more like a man lost in thought.

"You say that there was a trap on the fox? Have you many traps at Lanyon?"

"None whatever, Squire, though the rabbits do a lot of damage and the badgers too. Now I remember, we have one trap but I would rather not say anything about it."

"Say what you have to say; let us have no mysteries."

"Well, Squire, it's a man-trap with two tongues, seven teeth two inches long on each side and a double spring; but then it is never used, and I've heard master say he'd rather give up farming than use such a brutal engine."

He blazed up at this till his face was the colour of the leather chair he sat in; and before he could speak, Felton, who had been knocking at the door walked in, carrying the dead fox.

"Shut the door," bawled the Squire, "And now, Felton, let me hear your story."

"I was on my way to unstop the trucks, Sir Rose, when I came on this vixen, just as you see her."

"Where exactly was she lying?"

"At the head of the lane leading to the earths, and bleeding so freely that she could not have come any distance."

"Have you any fowling-pieces at Lanyon?" asked the Squire, his suspicion rekindled.

"Three flint locks, a yeomanry musket, two horse-pistols and a blunderbuss; but never once has any one of them been used against a fox."

"The fellow is outspoken, Felton, and has an honest look."

"A deal too outspoken for a farm-hand, Sir Rose; and as to the looks, the less said the better, for of all born actors, commend me to Madron men, as I found to my cost when I was trying to trace the owner of the fishing-rod."

"Have you anything against this man?"

"Yes, Sir; only a fortnight ago I saw him in a place and at an hour which excited my suspicion. He was close to Boswarva Downs, and what he could be doing there at midnight with a lighted lantern, I can't imagine."

"He's telling the truth, Squire; I was there."

"What in the world for?"

"I was there by my master's orders, to keep the badgers off a bosom of vears."

"Do you mean to tell me that badgers eat sucking-pigs?"

"When they can get at them, Squire; nothing better. We've lost two litters since I can mind."

"Then why, in the name of goodness, don't you keep the sows in?"

"It's not for want of trying. They lift the doors off the hinges, and the gates too, all to get to Skilly Quillet."

" Skilly Quillet?"

"Yes, Squire, they're Skilly Quillet mad when their time is up, and no holding them; but why, I don't know more than the man in the moon."

"An extraordinary explanation, Felton; but I suppose we must accept it, and, after all, the man was in Lanyon rights."

"As you will, Sir."

" 'Tis true as I'm standing here, Squire, every word of it."

"I have a much more serious charge, Sir."

"What is that?"

"I have good reason to believe that he was the owner of the rod found in the pond. His name, John Penrose, agrees with the letters on the butt; he is, I learn, a keen trout fisher, and was seen crossing the St. Just road straight for the pond on the afternoon of the trespass."

"Is not this the first time you have brought this to my notice?"

"It is, Sir; I've had my suspicions, but it's only quite lately I have come by the evidence."

"Well, Penrose; what have you to say?"

"I own that the rod is mine, Squire; I cut the letters with a knife you gave me."

"Then you admit to poaching in the pond?"

"Squire, I admit that the rod is mine, nothing more."

"You are a shrewd fellow, but I warn you here and now that if you are caught in my preserves, nothing can save you, Daniel prize-boy or Daniel dunce, from jail, or worse. Now go and tell your master that I regret he did not come himself, and that I am greatly put out by the murder of this fox."

Whereupon I touched my forelock, found my way to the yard, mounted Snowball and rode away home at a hard gallop.

I was eager as could be to tell what had passed, yet not a whit more so than master and Miss Jenifer to hear. As Snowball and I came clattering down into the town-place, both jumped forth to the window, and beckoned to me to go to them, then and there. Before doing so, however, I led Snowball into the stable and threw a cloth over his cheens. It would have been the horse's death to have left him at the gate in his heated state, and with such a cold wind blowing.

Master and Miss Jenifer listened to my story without a single interruption. By the time I had done, Miss Jenifer was beaming up at me through her spectacles, but master was pacing up and down between the fire and the door with a face as white as goat's milk.

"Do you mean to say you told the Squire that I, your master, could not face trouble?"

"I did, Sir, and that you owned as much before I started."

"Terrible, terrible! and did you really say I would rather renounce farming than set such a devil's engine as a man-trap?"

"I did, master, using the very words I heard you use in the barn."

"And how dared you taunt Sir Rose with flinging a fox to the hounds?"

"He would have it, master; he made me speak out, though I tried to keep it back."

"And what did he say?"

"Why nothing, only sat looking before him."

"Terrible, terrible! I'm ruined! I can never face him again!"

"Fiddlesticks, Henry, if I should say so before the lad! Would you have the Squire insinuate that we, Pearces of Lanyon, trapped and shot foxes, and no word of rejoinder? For my part I am delighted to learn that Jack gave him a Roland for his Oliver, and I don't care who knows it. What a spirit the lad must have to speak up as he did in the midst of all that grandeur! Didn't you feel at all abashed?"

"Not a bit, Miss; I wasn't thinking of Squire at all, I was thinking of you two."

"Heaven bless . . ."

It was not want of breath, it was her tears that prevented her finishing.

CHAPTER XV

MYSTERIOUS
HAPPENINGS

HE YEAR '48 stands head and shoulders above most of the years of my life, because of a memorable journey taken in company with my master. In my eagerness to tell of it, however, I must be careful not to pass over one or two strange things – visitations Miss Jenifer called them – that caused such an upset as has seldom been seen in our neighbourhood.

The New Year was barely a fortnight old when Churchtown, of all places, became the scene of a most mysterious happening. It fell on a Monday in the dinner-hour after the washing had been spread to dry in an atmosphere that, as many remarked, was unnaturally calm and sultry. All of a sudden a noise, like the roar of a high wind in the pine-tops was heard, causing the people to hurry to their doors to learn the meaning of it; and whilst they stood looking up and wondering, there came flash after flash of lightning, followed by a rush of air which drew the washing off the bushes as if by suction and carried it up and up clean out of sight, never to be seen again.

For a time people were too dumbfounded to speak but the moment they found their tongues they began casting about for the reason of Churchtown being singled out for punishment; and for days without result. But murder will out; and when on the fifth day it became known that Parson Veale's surplice was the first thing to be carried up, and the second, the roof of the Squire's gamecock craw, every Methodist in Churchtown, and not a few of the churchpeople, set down the visitation to sin in high places.

The whirlwind was still the subject of conversation when suddenly there appeared in the heavens a body the like of which no one in the High Country had ever seen. It had a long, fiery tail, that was terrible to behold. Mother was the first to see it and give the alarm, which brought all Lanyon out into the town-place. To us it appeared to be right above Chun Castle where, except for a solitary star, it had a bravish bit of sky to itself. Miss

Jenifer, round whom we mustered, expressed her belief that the end of the world was at hand, and the heavenly body a messenger sent to warn us to repentance. How it was with the others I cannot say; I only know that I went to bed that night in fear and trembling, after saying much longer prayers than usual. At this time of day some may find occasion for laughter in all this; but if such there be, I can assure them that they would not have laughed at the time.

Nor must they think I took it lighter than would appear when I say that I sent Loveday a valentine; for, in my darkest despair, I clung to the belief that the world was too lovely a thing to be destroyed, and that Loveday and I would yet come together. The valentine I chose was a pretty and a delicate thing. It had a filigree border round a good-sized heart, garlanded with the bluest of forget-me-nots. As there was no letter-print, I wrote below, in my best copperplate, "With Jack Penrose's love and affection till the crack of doom" and inside, three stanzas from mother's album with Loveday in place of Mary.

> "When Loveday on the plain appears,
> Aw'd by a thousand tender fears
> I would approach, but dare not move; –
> Tell me, my heart, if this be love.
>
> "Whene'er she speaks, my ravished ear
> No other voice than hers can hear,
> No other wit but hers approve; –
> Tell me, my heart, if this be love.
>
> "If she some other swain commend,
> Though I was once his fondest friend,
> His instant enemy I prove; –
> Tell me, my heart, if this be love."

I posted the valentine at Aunt Grace's, though not till after dark, for fear of being seen putting it into the box; and on the way home along and day after day at my work, pictured Loveday breaking the seal and reading the words. Then I would fall to wondering whether mine was the only valentine she received; and at the thought that Dickie might also have sent her one, I became jealous as fire, and – a senseless thing to do – cracked the whip viciously at the unoffending horses.

At the earliest possible day for a reply, I was back in Churchtown for the return valentine. I did not go straight up to the window but walked slowly past, casting a sly eye as I went, so that the fellows standing there should not have the laugh of me; but amongst the valentines behind the panes there was none for me. Evening after evening I was back there to no purpose, till I was sick at heart and cared for nothing and nobody. I had come to a dark pass with myself, the black east wind was in keeping with my feelings, and my life was a burden to me.

Whilst I was at this low ebb, there came another visitation; this time not in the skies or in Churchtown, but under the very cottage itself. One night towards the close of March we were frightened by a dull, rumbling noise seemingly under the dairy.

"Whatever in the world is that, Richard?" exclaimed mother, looking up from her knitting.

"I'm sure I can't say; I only know that the cottage stands upon the solid rock."

The noise died away as suddenly as it came, but mother was so disturbed that she could not go on with her knitting.

The next night about the same time, we heard it again, and then mother became seriously alarmed; she would have it that the rumbling was the forerunner of an earthquake that would swallow us all up. Father tried to laugh it off, but mother kept to her idea, and in the end declared that continue to live there she could not. So in the morning father went to look at an empty cottage at Lower Bosullow.

When news of this reached the big house, Miss Jenifer sent word that she was coming to hear for herself, and at eight, by the clock, in she walked.

"Good evening, all; I hope I am not late," she said jokingly.

"We have heard nothing yet," mother replied, making room for her on the settle. "And you will not, Mary."

Sitting there Miss Jenifer at first poked fun at our fears; but the moment the rumbling began she turned pale, and if mother had not held the spirits of hartshorn to her nose, I believe she would have gone off in a faint. She left as soon as she felt able, and I still can recall the grip she laid on my arm as we crossed the yard, and the violence with which she slammed the door behind her.

After that, Miss Jenifer raised no further objection; and if the owner of the cottage had not haggled over repairing the thatch, we should most likely have quitted the old home for good.

It was well that the owner did haggle, for before father and he could come to terms I had cleared up the mystery and done away with the necessity for moving. I discovered the cause of the trouble by the merest chance. I had been tealing some early kidneys in the Bartons, as we call our potato-ground near the millpool, and stayed late so as to use up the seed in the second basket. The moon was up before I had done and I recollect how it shone on the blade of the shovel I was using. Now if, after putting on my jacket, I had gone straight away home, the mystery might never have been solved, but I did not. Instead I leaned on the hedge watching a pair of stoats at play on the farther side of the millpool. Once they came and sat on the top of the flushet; twice they ran full tilt along the road to the bridge, and back as if showing off before me. I might have watched their antics for perhaps ten minutes when, to my horror, I heard the rumbling noise again.

Some men – Parson Coker, the spirit-queller, amongst them – say that they do not know what fear is. If so, they are differently framed from me. As that wisht sound grew louder and louder, I went all cold. To tell the truth, I could not have been more skeared if I knew that Old Nick himself had been approaching. The rumbling was followed by a rustling in the thicket in the corner, and the appearance of an object, white as a ghost. Whatever it was it climbed the hedge and kept along the foot between me and the pool. Urged by a curiosity stronger than my fear, I craned my neck and saw it go by and as it did, I caught the scent, the unmistakeable scent, of a badger.

"You git stink," I said, "so it's you that's at the bottom of all this upset."

In my excitement, I left shovel and basket, ran home and burst into the kitchen.

"Whatever is the matter now?" exclaimed mother; "the way you come tearing in is enough to drive me into my grave; do try and come in quietly."

"Sorry, mother, but I've found out what the noise is."

"You have?"

"Yes."

"Well, what is it?"

"Why, a badger!"

"What! A badger under the dairy?"

"Yes, and a white one!"

"Thee'rt never makin' fun of our trouble," said father angrily, taking the pipe out of his mouth.

"No, father, I'm in sober earnest."

Then I up and told the story, but without convincing them.

" 'Twon't do, Jack; the cottage stands on sound granite that no badger could drive through, and then look at the distance from the cottage to the Bartons."

"I know, father, it's a long way, but I believe I'm right."

Father was for going to the Bartons then and there, and would have gone had not mother protested and said she must not be left alone. So he reluctantly put it off till the morning.

It was on the stroke of five when father and I set out with a lantern and furze-hook to see whether I was right or wrong. The first thing father did on getting to the place was to search for tracks; and there they were along by the hedge, plain as the sow's tracks in the gateway of Skilly Quillet. I held the light whilst father cut away the thickets, exposing the hole the badger had come through. It was big enough to allow of a man going in on all fours. When father took the lantern I could see he was greatly excited, and ready for anything, but I never imagined what he had in his mind. Pushing the light before him he entered the passage and soon he was out of sight. After what seemed a long while I heard him coming back.

"Foul air, father?" I asked, when he had backed out.

"No, not that; I got to a place where the roof has caved in so that I could not pass, but I think you could perhaps just squeeze through."

So in I went and after a time came to the low place.

"Much as ever," I thought as I looked, at it. However by twisting and turning I managed at last to get past and, as luck would have it, without bringing down two big stones that threatened to fall.

After that I got along as fast as I could crawl, till at length I came to a sort of steps up which I clambered; to find myself in a cave with three pillars, much the same as the pillars that prop up the Quoit, only shorter and part of the solid rock.

"What labour," I thought, "to mine the granite! What toil to remove the broken stone!"

Roomy as was the cave, the air was just as close as in the tunnel and smelt quite as strongly of badger. Holding up the light, and looking round,

I saw a great heap of grass and fern in the farther corner. All excitement I tiptoed to within a couple of yards and, with the lantern held at arm's length, looked for a sign of the creature itself. And there, where the grass was a little thin, I saw distinctly a bit of its white coat. I was in two minds about rousing him, and it was well that I did not, for more likely than not he would have turned on me, and perhaps have got the best of it. So, keeping an eye on him, I set about exploring the rest of the cave. I soon learnt the use to which it had been put; for I came on a heap of keg-slings, and near them three kegs set on end like the legs of a brandis, whilst on the floor between lay a broken pipe, the bowl and stem coloured quite black, lying close together.

"Here they sat and smoked," I said to myself. And not in the dark either, as was plain from the gutterings of many candles on the lumps of clay against the pillars.

Just beyond the biggest pillar was a step in the wall of rock, and looking up, I made out the round of a stone, which I took to be a trap-stone. Whilst I stood wondering where I could be, I heard father's step, and knew I was under the cottage. The moment I tapped he stood stock still, evidently locating the sound; for then I heard him move till he was overhead.

"That thee, Jack?" I heard indistinctly.

"Yes, father; where am I?"

"Under the wood cupboard."

"There's a trap-hatch above my head."

"Then wait a minute till I've shifted the furze."

"'Tes all clear?"

With that I put the flat of my hand under the middle of the stone, heaved, and felt it give way. The next minute I had scrambled through into the kitchen.

"Where's mother?" I asked excitedly, in my eagerness to let her know.

"In the milkin' shed; break it quietly, we don't want all the world to know."

So to mother I ran and whispered the good news to her.

"I feel as glad as if master had given me the fee of the cottage," she whispered back. "It would have broken my heart to leave."

The discovery was kept from everybody except master and Miss Jenifer, for fear that people should talk and Lanyon get a bad name; but the effect upon me was to make me like the cottage ten times as much as ever before.

I used to lie awake conjuring up the scenes the cave had witnessed, and imagining the face of the smuggler who had coloured the clay pipe. But in all my romancings I never dreamt that I should put the cave to any use; any more than I dreamt of the trials I was to be called upon to endure.

CHAPTER XVI

A MEMORABLE
JOURNEY

W ITH THE INGATHERING OF THE HAY the time had come for
master to start on the journey which he was in the habit of
taking as regularly as the year came round. What his business was I never knew exactly; I only know that it had to do with farm
property of which he was trustee, and that he always took maps and papers
with him. Till now he had always gone on horseback, but this time he was
to drive, as I learnt when taking up my wages on the Saturday afternoon.

"Overhaul the trap and harness, Jack, and have all ready by Tuesday."

But when Tuesday came he put off starting till Wednesday, and so day
after day, until at last we began to talk, to wonder at the cause of the delay,
and to ask ourselves whether master's visit to the Quoit every afternoon
could possibly have anything to do with it. What added to the mystery was
that master, who was generally as open as the day, let drop not a word of
explanation.

In spite of his secrecy, however, I got to learn something. The next
Tuesday afternoon, when seeing to the sheep, I heard the neigh of a strange
horse answering a little roan pony master had bought at Marazion Fair, and
locating the sound in the Quoit croft, made home-along that way instead of
back across the fields, in order to find out whose the stray animal was.
There was the strange horse, and I wish that had been all. But there by the
Quoit, talking excitedly to each other over the back of a grey pony, were
master and as rough a looking sailor-man as I ever set eyes on. That was
bad enough; but my suspicions were still stronger when master ceased talking the moment he saw me, and looked as if he did not know what to do
with himself.

"Dear! oh, dear!" I said to myself, "that man is what master has been
waiting for; there is something dark afoot – whatever can it be?"

That evening master put his head in at the door – he generally came
right in – and said, "Jack, have the horse and trap at the iron gate by
two o'clock."

121

"Do you mean in the small hours, master, or tomorrow afternoon?"

"Afternoon, Jack."

"All right, master."

I was terribly disappointed that that was all he had come to say. I had been hoping from the moment he told me he was going to drive that he would take me with him, if only to see to Snowball.

"Ah!" I said to myself, as I lay in bed, "it's the business with that sailor-man which prevents him taking me."

But, in the morning, mother burst into the turnip-house, exclaiming, "Jack, you are to go with master."

"Do you really mean it?"

"Mean it? Have I ever fooled you, my son?"

"No, mother; but the news seems too good to be true."

"You may well think so when I tell you – what I had not dared tell you before – that he is going to spend a night at Acton Castle this time; and that Acton Castle is only a couple of miles from Prussia Cove."

"Never, mother!"

"Yes, my dear; you are in luck this time. I think I see the hand of Providence in it. Now, before I forget, be sure and make yourself agreeable to Mrs. Rosewarne, as well as to Loveday; for, of all women, she dearly loves a little attention."

"I'll try to remember that," I replied.

After seeing to the hundred and one things that needed doing, I changed into my best clothes, and had the trap round to the front gate by the time appointed. The big house gave no indication of the preparations that had been, and were, going on inside. But I knew, as well as if I had seen it done, that master had had his head and face washed with flannel and soap, and his ears well scrubbed in two waters; that Mrs. Pearce had been busy packing his bag, and Miss Jenifer seeing to his maps and papers, and filling his blue silk purse with gold and small change.

At half-past two the kitchen-maids appeared carrying home-cured hams, one for each of the three houses we were to stop at. These I laid carefully in the well, which reached pretty nigh as near the ground as the belly of a laying goose. Father was the next to turn up; then mother came running with the collars and handkerchiefs she had washed and ironed. "Be sure to put on a clean collar every other day," she whispered, handing me the cardboard box that contained them. Three o'clock came without a sign of master; and then Snowball got so fidgetty that father had to go to his head. Scarcely had he done so, when Martha Angwin, the head maid, came out with master's bag, followed by Mrs. Pearce with master's bed-stockings and night-cap done up in whitey-brown paper.

"See that your master puts these on every night," said she, handing them to me, "or the damp sheets and the mouldy pillow-cases will be the death of him. In the right-hand corner of the bag you will find a bottle of camomile syrup, in case he gets the stitch, and a bottle of mother-of-thyme, in case he's taken with a nightmare. Be careful not to give him the wrong remedy."

"You may depend upon me, Missus," I replied; "I'll see to him."

It was all half-past three when at last master came out with Miss Jenifer and the rest of the household at his heels. He was in his market best; but instead of the half-farmer he generally wore, he had on a broad-brimmed straw hat, fully big in the head, with a white elastic band under the chin.

"Be sure and see to Watch, Richard," said he, before jumping up; and the moment he said, "Give him his head," off we went. Shep followed till whistled back, leaving us quite to ourselves. At the bend of the road past the millpool, master stood up, faced about, waved his green bandanna, fetched his pipe out of his coat-tail pocket, and settled himself for the journey.

It was as fine a day as heart could desire, with great rounded white clouds – woolpacks we call them – in a pure sky, and a breeze from the nor'-west to temper the sun. The heath to either hand was sober-coloured as yet, but the sea, as we saw it from the comb of the High Country, was as blue as a corncockle, and lovely enough to stir a man to speech for the sheer beauty of it. Whatever master may have thought, he said nothing. He only puffed at his pipe. Indeed, I do not recollect that he opened his mouth till we were leaving Zennor Churchtown, when he said,

"Jack, don't forget that we're out to enjoy ourselves; be sure and make the most of it, boy."

"I'll do my best, master; I feel as if I were sucking pear-drops already."

What with master's comfortable company, Snowball's easy paces, fresh scenes at every turn of the road, and the consciousness that minute by minute we were getting nearer and nearer to the tantalizing little witch who had not answered my valentine, my cup was full. I wondered, as we passed along the winding lanes, whether master knew my secret, whether the smile that every now and then played over his clean-shaven face had to do with me or some memory of his own. However that might be, I rejoiced to see no sign of shadow, except the shadow of his hat; nothing to tell me that trouble lay ahead, or that master feared I had surprised his secret.

Furze-chats and yellow-hammers on the low bushes, magpies on the windclipt thorns, farm-hands in field and mowhay, watched us go by. The high lands were gay with furze blowth to our right, whilst on our left rich pastures dotted with milch kine ran down to the cliff.

"Where do we sleep tonight, master?" I asked, as I walked Snowball up a stiff rise.

"At St. Ives, Jack; we are nearly there."

And so it was, for when we reached the top of the hill, the town, its bay and its beaches, lay like a picture below us. Lovelier sands I never saw, nor a lovelier sea. The water, shot with blue and green, recalled the spring plumage of the old peacock, and the dazzling white of the breaking waves, the drifted snow.

"Drive on, Jack, or we shall never get there."

"But, master, what are those headlands away there?"

"Why, the north coast of Cornwall, to be sure."

"Are there no towns?"

"No, nothing but fishing hamlets, and only a few of them. Come, drive on, I want my tea."

We put up at the Sloop Inn, overlooking the harbour, where the fishing-boats were being got ready for sea. When I had put Snowball to rights, I joined master in the upstairs parlour. He was seated at a round table in a big bay window, in the act of pouring tea out of a silver teapot.

"Sit you down, lad, and make yourself at home."

"I'll try, master, but it is all strange and grand to me."

As I sat drinking sweet tea and eating new plum cake, I tried to forget I was only a farm-hand, and master did what he could to draw my attention off myself by his remarks: "That's a big brown sail being hoisted," "Those men going off in the punt have a retriever dog with them," "She'll never clear the pier-head," and such like.

Ah! my dear master, failings you may have had, but in matters of feeling you were a great gentleman.

After tea I set out, at his suggestion, to see the town. I looked in at the haberdasher's window in search of a present for Loveday, but saw nothing to my fancy; I stayed ever so long outside the druggist's gazing at the great bottles full of red, green, and blue stuff; I watched the gulls on the rocks behind the church, and then, noticing that the boats were still going out, I hurried to the end of the pier and stood there while they passed, every boat with a boy on board, and every boat with the name on the stern. Nor was that the last I saw of them, for, after wandering about the back streets, I made my way to the top of the Island, as the headland is called, and, standing near a little ruin, beheld the fleet against a sunset sky, for all the world like a forest afire. It was a wondrous sight, yet to me not more pleasing than the sandhills across the bay bathed in the rich light of the afterglow.

"But what," I asked myself, without finding an answer, "can be the meaning of that wide belt of crimson water at their feet?"

On my way back, chancing to meet the parish constable in Norway Square, I made bold to ask an explanation.

"There's nawthin' strange about that, young man; the sea along the Gwithian shore is made red by the iron water coming down from the mines. No, there's nawthin' strange about the colour, but why the soyles should fancy it as they do is a thing I've puzzled my brains again and again to discover, without being any the wiser."

"By soyles you mean seals?"

"Iss, saals, if you like it better, though we St. Ives people call them soyles, like our fathers before us. But the name does not matter. What I wanted to impress on you is that the soyles are to be seen at most times in the red water, as if they preferred it to the blue, but, for the life of me, I can't tell 'ee why."

"Thank you," I said; "for years I've longed to see a seal, and now is my chance. First thing in the morning I shall be there."

"Young man, on no account go tomorrow morning; there is a good reason why you should not."

"Oh!" thought I, as I made my way back to the Sloop, "I wonder if this is the business the sailor came about. But whether or no, it will not prevent my going."

It was just ten by the clock on the landing when, after knocking at master's door and asking whether he had forgotten his bed-stockings and night-cap, I went up to my room. As I felt no inclination for sleep, I threw open the window, leant on the sill, and looked out upon the harbour, all silvery in the moonlight. The lantern at the pier-head burned steadily; here and there a light twinkled in the houses. I stayed till every window was dark, until the last footfall had died away, and the only sounds were the swish of the waves and the whistling of the curlews on the sand-hills. Then I lay down in my clothes, so as to be ready to start without loss of time, and slept till I was awakened by the cry of the watchmen: " 'Tis two of the clock, and a fine night."

The thought of the seals was in my mind as I rubbed my eyes, and, fearing to oversleep myself if I dozed again, I jumped out, stole past the room where master was snoring, tiptoed down the lowest flight of stairs to the front door, opened it noiselessly, and passed into the empty street.

Once clear of the town, I followed a cliff track till I came to an estuary, where, as I was wondering how to cross, I made out a man standing by a boat at the edge of the tide. On reaching him, I said, "Will you be so kind as to take me across?"

"Young man, I'm the ferryman, and will take you; but, if you will listen to my advice, you'll stay this side Hayle river, and keep out of trouble."

"Trouble! what do you mean? I'm on my way to see the seals."

"Well, that's the best I've heard this long time; jump aboard."

On taking my penny, he said, "If it's soyles thee'rt really after, keep along the beach, and shun the Towans as you would shun the devil."

By this, the night was greying to the dawn, and as I trudged along, a faint blush tinged the sky, and was reflected in the wet sand. I kept close to the foot of the cliffs that served as buttresses to the dunes, and the farther I went along the lonely beach, the surer I felt that both the constable and ferryman had been hoaxing me; yet every step was bringing me nearer and nearer to the danger against which they had warned me. I had covered, perhaps, a couple of miles when I espied a bare-headed man half-way up the cliff, beckoning with gestures of a violence I had never before witnessed. Had his life been in danger, he could not have signalled more excitedly for help. Without thinking twice about it, I started to reach him, and after a stiff climb, got to the ledge where he stood. To my astonishment, it was my friend of the previous evening, the constable of Norway Square.

"Well," I said, "what in the world is the matter?"

"Sh! sh! Spaake low, or you'll spoil everything. We've got them surrounded."

"Got who?"

"Never mind; you'll know in good time. The thing is, I've sprained my ankle, and can't clemb a foot higher; and the others are waiting for me to give the signal."

"What's that noise?" I asked, on hearing a sort of subdued cheering.

"Can't 'ee wait a minit? You'll know in good time."

"Now on with my toggery; I want you to take my place."

With that he slipped off his swallow-tailed coat, which he made me put on, together with his shiny hat.

"Mind what I am goin' to tell you," he said excitedly, whilst fastening the belt. "Once you reach the top, stand to your full height; and then, when I call out, start running towards them like a ball of fire."

With curiosity roused to the highest pitch, I started climbing the upper cliff. The higher I got, the more plainly I could hear the voices. Within a few feet of the top, I took the hat off and peeped between the sea-pinks.

There, in a hollow of the sand-hills, stood all the young squires of the West Country, amongst them Sir Rose, with – by my life! – a pair of false ginger whiskers! Apparently they were at something wrong, for one after the other kept looking over his shoulder, like a fox I once saw drinking at a pool. And so it proved, for presently, between their legs, I caught sight of two gamecocks fighting furiously. In my excitement I forgot all about the constable until I felt something strike me, and looked down. He was urging me by his gestures to show myself; and as I had no wish to vex him, I put the hat on straight-away, climbed up to the top, and stood on the edge of the cliff.

As I did so he bellowed like a bull, causing every face to be turned on me. For a moment the cock-fighters were rooted to the spot; but, as soon as I started running, they took to their heels, making in the direction of the Red River. I chased the Squire but, hampered as I was by the long coat, I had no chance; and it was just as well, for what should I have done if I had caught him? So they all got away, and the last I saw of them was their heads moving rapidly along a gully, towards which a whole posse of constables was rushing to stop them.

In the pit I found a gamecock lying dead, and near it a velvet bag, with a coat-of-arms in gold upon it. I did not know which to admire most, the bag or the bird, as handsome a rooster as I ever saw. He was pheasant-breasted, with a high rose comb, wings long and wide, tail high and strong, clear-cut yellow legs, and – by all that's good! – with a silver spur to each leg! To leave the spurs would have been wicked waste; so I unstrapped them and put them into my trousers-pocket with the velvet bag, into which I had stuffed the ginger whiskers that I found blowing about on the turf. There was the gamecock too; and rather than abandon it to the ravens already croaking overhead, I decided to take that too. Then, the risen sun reminding me that I had no time to lose, I hurried across the sand-hills to the ferry. On reaching the spot where the beach lay open to view, I again heard the fearful bellowing, looked round, and saw the constable coming painfully towards me over the sand.

"What do you mean, running off like that?" he roared on overtaking me. "What do you think the St. Ives people would have thought, had they seen you tearing along the street in my toggery, and me, bare-headed and in my shirt-sleeves, toiling after you?"

"You are a most ungrateful fellow," I replied, with indignation. "I've risked my neck climbing the cliff. I ran the risk of being fallen upon by a score of desperate men; and, for all this, not a word of thanks. Here are your things; I am glad to be shot of them."

"Hand here that gamecock."

"Not if I know it; findings is keepings in our part."

"Let un keep it, William Rechard," said the ferry-man, who had come across; "gamecocks are dry eating."

I left him at the landing-place, and ran all the way back to the Sloop. Master, who was in the middle of his breakfast, looked as if he would have chided me. But if so, the sight of the gamecock, which I held up, stopped his tongue. Before he could recover from his surprise, I handed him the velvet bag.

"Where did you get this?" he asked, excitedly. "These are the Tresillian Arms."

"And inside," I added, "are the Tresillian whiskers."

Then master dropped knife and fork and wanted to hear everything. So I told my adventure, and kept him laughing till the tears streamed down and he owned it was as good as a play. And when we were on the road – we were crossing Hayle Causeway at the time – he broke out again.

"We must have that cock stuffed," he kept saying.

On inquiry, we found a bird-stuffer at the farther end of Hayle, that part which is called Copperhouse. The man undertook the stuffing for fifteen shillings, including the glass case; but master gave him a sovereign, and arranged to call for the bird in a month's time.

As we drove through Gwithian, we met a man with carroty hair and whiskers, and this set master off again.

He was as merry as a cricket, and presently started singing, "Ride a cock hoss to Banbury Cross," and, "Stick a feather in his cap and call him macaroni." He wasn't a bit homesick – not the least in the world.

And so we came to the Red River, and, as will be seen, the bridge across it led to further adventure.

CHAPTER XVII

THE GIPSY QUEEN

A S WE ROSE the track beyond the bridge, where the stained sea-water came into view, I kept a sharp look out for the seals, but to no purpose; not a head was to be seen. Master found a reason for this in the very low state of the tide, which was so far out as to leave quite a desert of beach, across which the river wound like a great red snake.

Desolate as was the scene it presented, the country was in keeping, the fields being half covered with blown sand, the bushes haggard as can be imagined, and not a soul in sight. Master must have thought I found the prospect depressing, for presently he said, "Cheer up, Jack, Gwithian is a wisht place, but remember it leads to Perran and to a pretty little spot called Prussia Cove; you must, I should think, have heard tell of it?"

With mounting colour I replied, "Yes, master, I've heard tell of Prussia Cove; to me it's the sweetest place on earth."

"Ah! Ah! I was thinking as much."

"Yes, master, the girl I love lives there."

"Ah! and does she love you?"

"That's a question, master, and how to answer it I don't know."

"Like that, is it? Persevere, lad, persevere, and good luck to 'ee."

This he said feelingly; then looked away, and fell to puffing his pipe. As for myself I had as much as I could do to keep the well of the trap clear of the outcropping rocks.

When we had got a mile or more from the bridge and over the brow of the rise, we espied three men drop over a hedge and come hurrying towards us, across a field of clover.

"Pull up, Jack, 'tes the young master of Reskageage, where we are going to stay."

"Which one of the three?"

"The one with a coil of rope over his shoulder."

"And the man with the sack?"

"That's Tom Penberthy, the shepherd; but the wizened-faced gentlemen between them I don't know."

"What can they be at, master?"

"A sheep overcliff, or maybe a cask of wine or other flotsam washed ashore."

"Good morning, Willie."

"Good morning, Mr. Henry, glad to see you; father is on the look out for you."

"What's up?"

"I'm taking this gentleman to the seal cave. What do you say? Will you join us?"

"No, thank you; but I feel sure my man will, if you care to take him."

"Certainly, but he must come right away; 'tes close on low water, and not a minute to spare."

So I handed master the reins, jumped down, and, as the party moved off, sidled up to the shepherd, who was a step or two behind the others.

I was greatly excited at the prospect of seeing a seal, so much so indeed, that when my companion told me under his breath that the strange gentleman was no less a person than the judge down for the Lammas Assizes, I felt no astonishment. I gathered from the look he gave me that my indifference surprised him; but then he did not know – as how could he? – that a seal meant ten times more to me than a judge. Nevertheless, I did not fail to notice that, old as the judge looked in the face, he seemed very young as seen from behind, having the figure and nimble step of a man of forty.

Little was said on the way to the cliffs, less still when we got there; the fearful precipices and sullen booms from the caves hushing us to silence. Following in the steps of Mr. Willie, who made the best of guides, we made our way down the steep cliff face to an adit that brought to my mind Aladdin's Cave in the *Arabian Nights*. Even from there the rollers looked a dreadful way down, and, what struck me even more, the shags oddly small.

The moment our guide had kindled a torch, he led along the adit for some thirty paces to a hole in the roof of the cave. There I found the noise from below deafening, and even terrifying. Nor was I the only skeared one of the party, for I noticed that the judge had turned ghastly white. Mr. Willie, handing the torch to the shepherd, took from the sack a rope ladder, one end of which he set about securing to a stout iron rod that projected upwards from the wall of the cave. When he had made it fast, he pushed into the abyss the part of the ladder lying on the floor of the adit, and I can yet hear the faint tinklings of the steel rungs against the face of the rock before the ladder came to rest. Next came the roping of the judge as a precaution in case he lost his hold in the descent. This the guide did, quickly passing the noose over the judge's head, and securing it under the armpits by means of a running knot, as was done to me when lowered from the brig *Triton*.

The preparations being completed, the guide stepped on to the ladder and, ordering me to pay out the judge's rope, disappeared from view. When, with the steadying of the ladder which told that the guide had reached the cave, the judge's turn came, he shouted in my ear, "Pay out slowly, my man, and hold on."

"Like grim death, my lord."

This reply seemed to hearten him, for a smile puckered his face, and after a nip from a silver flask, he leaned over the chasm, gripped the sides of the narrow ladder, stepped on to it, and, turning an appealing face on me, began the descent. He went down very, very slowly; three times he seemed stuck, but in the end he reached the bottom.

I stepped on next, and made my way down without much trouble, till I got to a place where the ladder lay close against the sheer rock, and my clumsy boots time after time failed to grip the rungs. Luckily I thought of going down hand under hand, and in this way reached the cave without further mishap.

The judge, for all he looked so dried up, was mopping his head when I stepped down near him. And no wonder, for what with the roar of the surf at the narrow slit of a mouth, the intense gloom, and the feeling that a mere thread of a ladder was our main, indeed our only means of escape, there was enough to unnerve the strongest.

As soon as the guide had handed me one of the two torches he had kindled, we advanced with the judge between us. The floor and sides, polished by storms, gleamed in the bluey light, by which, high up, I caught sight of projections of rock looking like angry faces gazing down upon us as if in protest at our intrusion. A little farther on, the guide pointed overhead to the yard of a ship that had got wedged in like a crossbeam, and to the cliff owl perched upon it, and shortly after to the glowing eyes of a seal that swayed to and fro over a pallid patch of sand, the further side of a pool.

"Like to wade across and see the seal at close quarters?" he shouted.

"No need in the world," shouted the judge; "I have an admirable view."

I was surprised at the guide's suggestion, and still more so when he took my torch and commanded us to stay where we were till he returned. The instant his lights disappeared, the judge edged up to me and slipped his arm through mine. To tell the truth, I was as glad of the feel of it, bony though it was, as he was of mine. What we should have done had the creature plunged into the water and come at us, I dread to think; and I was thankful that it was content to wallow on the sand, belving like a bull.

When at last the guide returned, he beckoned to the judge to follow – impatiently, I thought, as though we had kept him waiting and not he us – and led to where a baby seal lay on a little beach all by itself. With its cream-coloured coat and full eyes, that pleaded as pitifully as ever a motherless calf's, it made just such a picture as I had called up when listening to Andrew's story about the baby seals and the fairies. Like my mother, he used to tell how, to amuse them whilst the mothers are away fishing, the cliff fairies descend to the nurseries with their reeds and flutes and soothe the little creatures with their sweetest music.

After a moment or so, the guide took us back along a passage where the black rock was beautifully marbled with spar. Though there was barely room for two abreast, the judge kept his hold on me, nor did he let go until we reached the foot of the ladder and the re-roping began. Then I understood the guide's impatience, for all at once, following a loud roar, a big sea forced its way into the cave and swirled about our legs.

"Quick, man," shouted the judge, "or I shall be drowned."

For answer, Mr. Nicholas smiled as he went on coolly with his work; and when the next sea broke, the judge had set foot on the ladder and was making his way up towards the shepherd's torch flickering far above, I following.

The moment we reached the top, our guide coiled up the rope, put the ladder in the sack, and led along the adit to the open. The blazing sunlight, the wealth of sea-pinks and birdsfoot trefoil were doubly welcome after the gloomy magnificence of the great bare sea-hall. Yet the spell which the seals' retreat had cast over us was not broken till we had set foot on the fields, where the judge jokingly remarked that he had the rope dangerously near his neck.

"May you never have it nearer, my lord!" said Mr. Nicholas.

"I hope not," answered his lordship.

On reaching Reskageage, he thanked Mr. Nicholas for his care of him, and, turning to me as he stepped into the chaise, said – what I have always thought handsome of him – that if ever he visited the cave again, he hoped I should be one of the party. Old Mr. Nicholas and master came to the gate to see him start, and raised their hats as he was driven off.

"You are having a great time, Jack," said master, as I passed him on the way to the stables.

"I am so, master, and the day is young yet."

As soon as I set foot in the yard, Snowball whinnied, and when I entered the loose box he was so delighted that I stayed with him until dinner-time.

At table, the talk was all about the woods, and particularly the Tehidy Woods, which old Mr. Nicholas maintained were finer than those of Trelowarren. How the argument ended I cannot tell, as I slipped away before it was finished, in my eagerness for a sight of the trees which Mr. Nicholas had so eloquently championed.

Crossing three fields and threading a belt of pines, I entered a plantation of beech. "If," I said to myself, "the beeches of Trelowarren are finer than these, they must be fine, sure enough." I had seen nothing like them either at Trengwainton, Trevaylor, or Rosmorran, and for a while I wandered from one to another, looking up in admiration at the towering shafts and lofty canopy of leaves, and listening to the fairy bells sounded by the wood wrens in the tops. Then, the softened light and cool fragrant air tempting me, I sat down and leant against one of the smooth grey stems, where I had a view of the lowland and the sea beyond. But beautiful as was the outlook, I had no eyes for it, nor thought of anything in the world but Loveday Rosewarne. And a lovely waking-dream I had of her till Dickie broke in and shattered it. Then I left the plantation; though not before I had cut LOVEDAY on the most graceful of all those graceful trees.

From the beeches I passed to a plantation of larch, from that to one of spruce, and so came to a furze-covered hill with a carn at the top. On reaching it and looking over the precipice beyond, I saw a tree that pleased me more than any I had seen – a gaunt and weather-beaten pine, that half-way down sprang from a fissure of the rocks, where a bird or the wind had carried the seed. As I was thinking what a safe nesting-place its crown would make for a hawk, out shot a peregrine, whose flight I was able to follow as far as some birches, and even beyond to a pool, where at last it passed from view. The picture dwells with me, and as I sit smoking of an evening, I often recall the grey cliff, the red stem, and deep green top of the pine, the falcon, the silver birches, the light blue pool, and the deep sapphire sea beyond. And from this the mind passes to some venerable oaks I chanced on in my wandering. They looked to me like the survivors of an ancient forest. Every one was hollow-trunked, every one extended bleached branches to the sky, yet, as the leaves showed, all lived and drew support through the gnarled roots that in places all but met across the glades.

Whilst I was measuring the girth of the biggest of them, I heard the sound of cheering, and hurrying towards it, found myself presently face to face with as bright and pleasing a spectacle as the eye could wish for. There, in the broad sunlight, lay a park, mown smooth, like the squire's archery lawn, with cricketers in white flannels and black top-hats, at play in the midst of it. I had not looked on for more than two minutes, when one of the batsmen – a tall man with a long reach and free action – drove the ball over the heads of the bowler and the man in the deep field, into the plantation, and almost to my feet. The fielder called to me to shy it to him, but instead, I threw it back to the bowler, and indeed a little beyond, for it fell between the wickets. For an instant all eyes were upon me, as if I had done something wonderful. The next ball sent the tall man's middle stump flying, amidst rousing cheers and the wild waving of parasols. I stayed there watching quite a while, and would have seen the game out, but for two of the players who never once moved their bats out of the block hole, and, to my way of thinking, spoiled the sport. I allowed them three overs a-piece, then walked away in search of something interesting.

Farther on I came to a narrow winding valley with a stream in it, and then, instead of making for home, as I thought of doing, I was lured to go as far as the bend, just to see what lay beyond.

Ah me! the price I had to pay for my curiosity!

I had scarcely gained the spot I made for, when my eyes lighted on a gipsy, who, the moment he saw me, started beckoning, and, oddly enough, with his left hand. He was near the stream, but partly hidden by a wall against which he seemed to be pinned. I thought he was held fast by a man-trap. On reaching him, however, I found that he had thrust his arm right up to the shoulder into a rabbit hole, and been unable to withdraw it. "Water! water!" he kept crying. So I made a cup of my hands, filled it from the stream, and held it to his mouth. Five times I had to do this before he would allow me to set about liberating him. With proper tools I could have done it in less than half the time it took me. On removing the stones, I found that he was held prisoner through having forced his hand into a small opening between two boulders, and even now that I had laid the place bare, I had but wasted my time, unless I could force the boulders apart. But how?

"You'll never do it without a crowbar," he said, with a moan.

"Leave it to me," I replied.

Whereupon I placed a wedge-shaped stone – it was a bit of blue elvan – in the cleft, and started driving it home with a lump of spar.

"It's giving," he said at about the tenth blow, and after two more I succeeded in freeing him.

"Feringey," said he, in a grateful voice, "you have been to me like a brother."

Then, after drinking at the stream till I thought he would never have done, he picked up some rabbit nets and a white ferret lying asleep on its bag, and walked away.

Now, had I let him go alone, no harm would have come of my meeting with him; but I could not do that, for the simple reason that he looked ready to drop. So I ran to him, took him by the arm, and led him to his encampment. It consisted of three tents, a light cart, and a bright yellow caravan, on the bottom step of which a gipsy woman was sitting with a panther stretched at full length at her feet. She was young, and very handsome, but her good looks were forgotten in a sort of vague fear when she rose and came towards us, with just the same stealthy action as the beast beside her.

"Geordie," said she, "what makes you so late? I was afraid you were taken."

He answered in a tongue I did not understand; but the moment he had done, she turned to me with a smile, and speaking quickly, said –

"I thank you for your kindness to one of my tribe and I will do what is in my power to return it; have you had your fortune told?"

"No," I replied, "the chance has never come my way."

"It has come now," she exclaimed, as she started to return to the cavern, saying as she went, "I must fetch the cards."

"That is Zillah, queen of the gipsies," whispered Geordie, excitedly; "she is skilled beyond all in reading the future; but hush, here she comes."

She led me to one of the tents, and motioned me to sit by her on the side away from the panther. Then, without as much as "By your leave," she took my hands one after the other, and examined the creases of the palms.

"You are in love with a girl of great beauty; many seek her in wedlock; you will drink the cup of jealousy to the dregs."

"But shall I marry her?" I asked, looking straight into her black eyes, "for that is what I want to know."

"And that is what I will not tell."

"Because you cannot, and are above pretending that you can."

"I have said," was her brief but firm reply.

After smoothing the head of the panther, she took the cards and cut them, more than once, I think. Presently, she uttered a little cry of distress, and exclaimed –

"Trouble is coming upon you."

"In what shape or form?" I asked.

"That the future will tell."

Then she arose, and as she left the tent, she said,

"This is only a poor return for your kindness."

"'Tis a bad look out," I replied, "if what you say comes true."

"If! Have you any doubt?" she hissed.

"None in the world," I replied, double quick, on seeing what a devil's temper she had.

By this we had passed the caravan and a fire, over which a kettle was steaming; and as she showed no sign of returning, I began to wonder whether she and the panther intended to see me home, and what master would think of me in such outlandish company.

To my relief, she came to a standstill where the track met a lane, and there she asked my name and place of abode.

"I'm John Penrose, and live touching Lanyon Quoit. The gipsies camp on our moors, and sometimes by the millpool."

"And I may camp there myself some day; who knows? Who knows?"

With that she turned, and made back along the sun-lit ridge, and as I watched her and the beast, I felt my blood run cold.

CHAPTER XVIII

AMONG SMUGGLERS
❧

THAT NIGHT I SLEPT lost to the world till awakened by the bleating of sheep under my window. Rubbing my eyes, I got up, looked out, and counted them as they crowded into the shearing-pens: wethers, ewes and lambs, they numbered ninety-three all told, and most of them carried good fleeces.

A grey pony, tethered to the mowhay gate, arrested my notice. "Surely I have seen that pony before," I was saying to myself, when I caught sight of a man in a knitted guernsey by the hayrick, and at once recognised him as the sailor I had seen at Lanyon. He was talking to somebody whom I could not see, till presently the brim of master's hat showed, and roused my worst suspicions. Then, fearing that master might catch sight of me and perhaps think I was spying upon him, I drew back into the room. As I put on my clothes, I kept asking myself, "What mischief is afoot?" but without finding an answer.

At breakfast master ate heartily, talked freely and afterwards settled down comfortably to his papers in the parlour with old Mr. Nicholas. In no way that I could detect did he betray the slightest uneasiness. Nor later, when, as I passed the window, he called out to me to have the trap ready by noon, was there anything the least peculiar in his voice or manner. But I was not deceived, and his subsequent behaviour showed me to be in the right.

From the time we left Reskageage, master was not himself; he was more than usually silent, and what little he said told me that his mind was elsewhere. Once he seemed to be on the point of letting me into his secret, but he checked himself, gave a nervous cough, and held his peace. So that I was glad when at last we reached Helston and put up at a good-looking inn called "The Angel".

After I had seen to Snowball, master, who stood waiting for me in the archway, said, "Now, Jack, you are free to go and look round, and here's a trifle to spend."

"Thank you," I replied, closing my fingers on the florin he had placed in my hand; "and please what time must I have the trap ready?"

"Four o'clock sharp"; and with that he entered the inn.

In addition to the florin, I had a crownpiece, a four-penny bit, and five pennies – in all, seven shillings and ninepence. It was by far the largest sum of money I had ever had to spend, and as I came out upon the pavement, I felt rich enough to buy up the street. The first thing I did was to go the round of the haberdashers' windows in search of a natty necktie, and in the third I came to I saw the very article ticketed up at sevenpence half-penny. After passing before the door a time or two, and peeping in, I took courage; walked boldly into the shop, and asked the serving-woman to be allowed to see it.

"That's the latest from London," she said, as she handed it to me across the counter. "It's known as the Union Jack."

"I'll have it," I replied, and scarcely were the words out of my mouth when she asked, "And the next article?"

"I want a lady's tie with forget-me-nots on the ends, like I've seen in Penzance."

She stooped, fetched up a long, thin cardboard box, full of ties, and, lifting one after the other, near the bottom came to the very thing I needed.

"That's it," I exclaimed.

Whereupon she drew it out, tied it round her own neck, looked at herself in the glass, faced round so that I could see it, and said, smilingly, "She will be sure to like it."

"Who do you mean?" I asked in surprise.

"You know very well whom I mean," she replied, with an arch look.

This second tie cost me a shilling and a farthing; so that I left one shilling and sevenpence three-farthings behind in that one shop; but, then, I had got what I wanted, and – to my thinking – good value for my money. From there I went to a respectable cook-shop in Meneage Street and had dinner, for which I was charged ninepence. Then, after a look at the crown-piece, the groat, and a farthing that remained, I buttoned up my pocket and started to see the town.

Of all the streets I ever saw, Coinage Hall Street is the widest; but, to my thinking, the beauty of it lies less in its width than in its little stream of clear water; and the special beauty of the stream is the trout. I counted three in the pits between the Angel and Grylls' Green.

Here I stood and watched six gentlemen playing at bowls. Each player had two "woods," and the game was to get them as near as possible to a little whitey clome ball, called the Jack. They were old hands, I should say, judging from their skill; and to this day it puzzles me to know how they managed to get the twist they did on the woods, delivered as they were from the open hand, with no screw put on that I could detect. I stayed till one of the gentlemen, whom I asked the time, told me it wanted twenty minutes to four, then I ran back to the stable, got Snowball harnessed, and had the trap waiting outside the inn as the town clock chimed the hour.

As I stood at Snowball's head, master, with three friends, rounded the corner of Meneage Street and came to a standstill in the middle of the road, where they remained in close talk for some minutes before they separated. Master walked a bit unsteady, I thought, as he came towards me, and when he got up in the trap, he settled himself in my seat and took the reins.

Seeing that he had had a glass too much, I begged him to change places, but, oh, no! drive he would, with the result that opposite Penaluna's bun-shop he nearly knocked the wheel off the Lizard bus. The driver shouted to him to stop, but master did not, or would not, hear, and so we got away. As soon as we were clear of the town, master's tongue began to wag.

"How long does it seem to you since we left home Jack?"

"Ages, master."

"Forgotten what Lanyon is like, I expect."

"Pretty nigh. Last night, before dropping off, I tried to see my way from the big house to the winnowing stock; but, for the life of me, I could not – 'twas all so hazy."

"Do you think you would be able to find your way to Prussia Cove?"

"I shouldn't wonder; though they say love is blind."

"Nice little maid, is she?"

"Aw! master, how can 'ee ask?"

Farther on, he said, "I wonder how father's getting along without us? Busy as a bee, I warrant."

Such were his remarks, without ever a word to make me suppose that a dangerous business was afoot, and now and again he fell to humming odds and ends of song. In time we turned from the Mullion road into an avenue of small-leafed elms, leading to a length of open road and another avenue of pollard ash, which presently showed us as pretty a picture as heart of man could desire. For at our feet lay the Looe Pool, stretching a full mile to the Looe Bar, shining under the sunlight like gold between the blue inland and the deeper blue of the sea.

We were near our journey's end. On rounding a clump of holly bushes, we came suddenly upon a farmhouse, at which master had no sooner pulled up than Mr. and Mrs. John Oliver came running out to bid him welcome. It did me good to see the love shown to him wherever we went.

For quite a while after he had gone indoors, I stood leaning against the shaft, watching the trout that kept rising in the openings amongst the weeds; then, as Snowball began to paw the ground, I led him round to the stables, and after rubbing him down and making him all snug for the night, I set about cleaning the harness.

Whilst so engaged, I caught the sound of voices from the barn opposite. Though they were pitched in a low key, my suspicion was not aroused till, having finished and hung up the harness, I went to the door. The sudden silence set me scenting trouble, and I determined to learn what was in the wind. I crossed the yard to the barn steps, but before I could set foot on the lowest of them, the door, which had been slightly ajar, was quickly closed and – as I found on trying it – bolted. That, however, did not prevent me from peeping through the latch-hole; and this is what I saw: Mr. Oliver wrapping the blade of an oar in hessian, and, by all that's good, master picking oakum!

Master's guilty eyes were fixed upon the door, but Mr. Oliver went on unconcernedly with his wrapping. Three other oars, already wrapped and tied, lay on the barn boards with their leathers coated thick with tallow. I had seen enough to understand, and stole away to the back of the cattle-shed to think things out by myself. "Heaven help me!" I said; "master is come a-smuggling, what am I to do?"

The thing that troubled me was the disgrace to the name he bore, and the grief in the big house if he were caught; and then, too, if it leaked out that I knew, and never raised a finger of warning, what sort of a defence could I put up when confronted by Missus and Miss Jenifer? Yet, though I knew I could never brook their injured looks, I hadn't the heart to face master and beg him to desist; for the reason that if he withdrew at the last moment, after weeks of preparation, he would be for ever shamed in the eyes of Mr. John Oliver and others, and never able to show himself again in the South Country. No, I could not do that. The only course open to me was to stand by him and act as circumstances dictated.

But, as I was soon to learn, plans were being made to thwart me even in this. About an hour after tea, Mr. Oliver came to me, and said – "Penrose, I hear you are handy with the fishing-rod; now, here is a rod, tackle, and basket; what do you say to catching a dish of trout for breakfast?"

"'I'll do my best, sir." What else could I say?

"Very well, if you will come with me, I'll take you to the best of the water." With that, he led along the open shore to a wood, through which we passed to another stretch of open shore, where he recommended me to begin.

"You'll get fish of half a pound here, but the biggest fish are farther up the pool, and take best by moonlight. There is no need to hurry back, we shall not expect you till midnight, or even later."

He spoke as if his one anxiety was that I should have good sport, whilst all the time, as I could see, his object was to get and keep me out of the way.

"How far is it round the pool?" I asked.

"A good seven miles; but on no account cross to the other side. The old squire's ghost walks this month, and people have disappeared and never been heard of again."

He was about to leave me, when the canvas of a cutter showed over the bar, and held him at gaze. He watched till the Western Cliff shut her from view, then turned on his heel, and made back along, muttering as he went.

"What a fool he must think me," I said aloud, when he had passed out of hearing; "neither trout nor ghost shall prevent me being in the thick of it."

Of course he had been put up to it by master, and against master I felt very, very sore till, thinking it over, I came to the conclusion that he meant well, and that his one and only object was to keep me out of trouble. Even then master's silence rankled, till it flashed across my mind that he might be under oath of secrecy.

I put the rod together and started throwing the fly. At the third cast I rose, and hooked a good trout, which, after playing, I led into a little bay, and landed. It was a handsome fish of nearly a pound weight, and at any other time I should have been excited over my capture. But the thought of the smuggling was so over-powering as to take away all zest, and though I continued to fish, my heart was not in it.

In skirting a creek, I came suddenly upon a man at work, and, checking myself in my stride, stood and watched him. He was engaged in greasing the leather between the tholls of a boat, and the tholls themselves were bound with oakum. Presently he started singing:

"When I am dead, borne to my grave,
A gallant funeral may I have;
Six highwaymen to carry me,
With good broadswords and sweet liberty.

"Six blooming maidens shall bear my pall,
Give them white gloves, and pink ribbons all;
And when I'm dead, they'll tell the truth,
I was a wild and wicked youth."

It struck me that I had seen him before; and when, hearing me move, he started, and faced round, I immediately recognised the sailor I had seen at the Quoit and in Reskageage mowhay. He looked as black as thunder, and I passed by him without a word being exchanged.

Near the head of the creek, I saw four other boats lying under the withy bushes, and though they had no oars aboard, all but one had oakum round the tholls, and all had grease on the leather between.

The plans of the smugglers were clear to me now; they were to land the cargo on the bar, carry it across to the boats, and get it dispersed and hidden before daybreak.

The thing that amazed me was that they should have fixed on a summer's night, with the moon nearly, if not quite, at the full. But there, who was I to find fault with their plans?

I gave over fishing, and sat by the pool with my back to a bed of bulrushes, to await the closing in of night. Whilst there, I heard the tread of men; but how many they were, and whether master was amongst them, I could not see for the rushes. I was all ears to their movements, but, with the dying away of their footfall, a silence fell, which was only broken by the roar of the sea and the wing-beats of passing wildfowl. I sat on till the afterglow had paled and the pool grown grey and sombre under the beclouding sky, and it must have been well past ten o'clock when I set out to gain the opposite shore. What with the leats, and what with reed-beds and swamps in my way, it was no easy task; but at last I reached the head of the pool, only to find myself face to face with a stream that looked beyond my powers to leap. The take-off, too, was but poor, but I managed to get across with nothing worse than a wet foot.

Once I was on the farther bank, however, my troubles were over, for, threading a long withy bed and climbing a high bank, I found myself on a sort of track, which I took to be the haunted path. And surely no more suitable walk for a ghost could be found, lying as it did beneath overhanging oaks, dark as dark, even with the moonlight. I had not followed it more than a score paces, when I heard a sneeze, and in my terror fell down flat. A tall white figure appeared round a bend, and glided by within three feet of me, as I lay shivering with fright. It was foolish of me to be skeared by a ghost that had sneezed, but I was; and minutes passed before I felt able to crawl away to a spot opposite the place where I judged the boats to be lying. Meanwhile the clouds had gathered and gathered until the moon was nearly obscured, and only a patch or two of light to be seen on the pool, and that, I thought, would favour the smugglers; but for an hour or more I lay there without sound or sight of anything. Was I mistaken after all?

I was on the point of making for the bar, when I saw a boat silently cross one of the splats of moonlight, and head straight for me, until it gained the shadow of the trees, when it swerved and came to rest, with its bow towards the sea. Deep as were the shadows, I could make out the rowers leaning on their oars, and the man in the stern, sitting bolt upright. Soon there came three other boats, which took up their stations behind the first, still so noiselessly that phantom craft could hardly have disturbed the silence less. So impressive was the sight, so oppressive the thought of the manifold risk, that for a while I could scarcely breathe. Then another side of the adventure struck my mind, and I could hardly keep from jumping to my feet, and shouting, "Here they are!" Fortunately, fear of master restrained me; he would certainly have recognised my voice, and perhaps never have forgiven me. But it would have served them right, after the manner I had been treated. I have often regretted that I let the opportunity slip, and as often been glad that I did; for I should have missed the landing, and the adventures that followed.

It must have been about midnight when I stole away to the bar, and crept over it to a spot where I could command both the pool and the sea. Before I had been there long, I noticed a light away on the Lizard coast, and as I watched, it grew and grew, until great flames shot up into the sky. At sight of it, I said to myself, "The smugglers have fired the beacon." Now, knowing there was a Preventive Station at Porthleven, I guessed that the fire was to lure the watch away from the bar; and so it proved, for in a short time two mounted men, whom I took to be riding-officers, galloped past, followed by a straggling lot of men on foot, all heavily armed. Then, for a while, the bar was again as empty as a desert.

Presently looking seaward, I made out two big boats approaching the bar. To judge from their depth in the water, they were fully laden; and they presented the appearance of seine-boats – not only from their size but from their having four if not five rowers on each side of them, as I gathered from the glints of moonlight on the oar-blades that came and went in such a way as to give the impression that the boats were racing. The sight so held my attention that I forgot the smugglers under the trees until I heard a grating sound which made me turn my attention to the pool whence it came. I was just in time to see the crews of the four boats leap ashore and come hurrying up the bar, like men on a desperate errand. They passed within a few yards of me, and I recollect wondering, as I lay flat to escape their eyes, how they had managed to time their movements to fit so exactly with the arrival of the landing party. They made for the boats, apparently an equal number to each, and soon man after man came running back with a keg slung over each shoulder; twenty at least were engaged in transferring the cargo, noiselessly except for the sound of their feet on the pebbles, and their laboured breathing.

On the third journey, one man, and that the hindmost, was so exhausted by his efforts, that he sank to his knees and fell over on his side like one dead. Seeing his plight, I ran to him, reckless of all consequences; and ever thankful I have felt that I did, for, despite his disguise, I saw it was my master.

"What! you, master?" said I.

"Yes, Jack," he gasped out; "save yourself, lad."

For answer, I freed him from the kegs, raised him to his feet, and almost carried him to the boats. There I found the crews busy stowing the kegs; and when they had got all of them aboard, it was a sight to see them push the boats over the shallows, leap on to the gunwales, get out the oars and row away – all without a word said. Never have I seen men exert themselves as they did.

145

Master and I were in the last boat, which did not gain a foot on the boat in front despite the exertions of the crew.

At the creek, the busy scene of the beach was repeated, when the kegs were removed to the backs of the mules standing there; and so quick was the despatch that, within a quarter of an hour, not a keg was to be seen – nor was there anything to tell of their disposal, except the clatter of hoofs as the mules were goaded up the hillside.

Meanwhile the preventive men had learnt of our whereabouts; and when Mr. Oliver and I, with master between us, were half-way through Degibna Wood, we heard the officers, as they galloped along the haunted track, shouting to inform their men of the road to be taken. Some minutes later a rocket shot up into the sky, quite unnerving master, for I could feel him trembling, as I helped him through the back-door. It was all I could do to hoist him up the stairs to his room; and never shall I forget the trouble I had to get his boots off, or for that matter the Guernsey frock, which fitted him tight as wax. Master's impatience added to the difficulty; he kept on saying, "Look alive, Jack!" and each time a rocket went up, "For God's sake, hurry, boy!"

When at last I had got him stripped of his outer garments, he was all for getting into bed as he was; but I insisted on his undressing properly and putting on his night gear – bed-stockings, flannel shirt, and lambswool night-cap; and after a deal of fuss I got my way.

"Take and hide the things – wet boots, stockings, and all; for they are sure to be here. Look alive!"

So I gathered them up, ran to my room, and stuffed them up the chimney out of sight. Then I opened the window quietly and looked out. Away to the south-east the sky was still lurid with the glow of the burning beacon; but the pool and sea, now silvered by moonlight, looked all innocent of the landing that had taken place, and the forces of the law at work. Presently, however, the silence was broken by the neigh of a horse, and, looking towards the place whence it came, I saw three horsemen coming along the shore of Carminowe Creek, straight for the house. At the sight, I ran down to warn master.

I found he had locked the door; but on my saying, "It's only me, master," he jumped out and let me in. To my surprise, I found that he had arranged his better clothes on the chair, and laid his leather leggings and boots on the floor beside them.

"I see that you are ready to receive them, master; and I've come to tell you they are here."

The words were scarcely out, when we heard the jingle of the horses' bits; then a bang on the door from what – I feel sure – was the butt-end of a horse pistol.

"Who's there, at this unearthly hour, when honest folk are abed!" Mr. John called down from the window of the next room.

"I understand you have strangers in the house; let us in, and no further nonsense."

"Walk in; the door is unfastened."

"Stay by me," said master, as he heard the officers dismount; "but, no, you had better not be found here – begone and get your clothes off."

So out I stole; and before I closed the door, master started snoring fit to wake the dead. I could hear him from the top landing, and even from my room, whilst I was undressing.

And this was my master, Mr. Henry Pearce, of Lanyon, leader of the yeomen in the Prince's procession, Muster Master for the High Country, and the very soul of respectability!

I listened at the door as the officers came upstairs and, without as much as a rap of the knuckles on the panel, walked straight into master's room. Still the snoring went on.

"Wake up! wake up!" I heard them call out, followed by a sort of scream from master. A lucky thought struck me. I rushed down and into his room. Two officers were standing by the bed looking down at master, who, to all appearances, was struggling with a nightmare.

"Who are you?" asked the taller of the two, as he turned the dark lantern on me.

"Mr. Pearce's servant. I've come down to give master his medicine."

I went to his bag and fetched out the mother-of-thyme. With the bottle in one hand, I raised the night-cap from the ear that was next me, and putting my mouth close as I could get it for his writhing, I called out, "Wake up, master, and take your medicine; it will do you good." At the second time of calling he sat up, sucked and sucked the bottle till it was half empty, then looked up at the officers with eyes as innocent as an unweaned calf's.

"There's nothing to be done here," said one of the officers, and they left the room. But we soon learnt they had not done with us, for presently Mr.

John came in and told us that they were returning in the morning to take our depositions.

"Then," said master, sitting up in the bed, with a smile on his face, "they'll find the birds flown."

CHAPTER XIX

THE HONOUR OF LANYON

❧

W E LEFT CARMINOWE early, so as to be well on the road by the time the officers called. Now, there were two roads to Acton Castle, our next destination; one by way of Helston, the other along the cliff track beyond the bar, to Porthleven; and, to my astonishment, master chose this, though warned of the bad state of the road, and reminded again and again that the chief riding-officer was stationed there.

We held along the shore of the creek to the bar, where, to ease the horse, master and I both got down. But if the sands were heavy for Snowball, the ruts along the track proved worse than had been described, with the result that the things in the well kept bumping against the side with a violence that threatened a smash. This led to a discovery that caused master no little anxiety. We had just passed some fishermen spreading their nets, and were about to enter the village, when, after a severe jolt, master said, "Whatever can it be, banging like that?"

"'Tes only the big ham got loose, sir," I replied.

"Never a ham making all that clatter. Jump down and see."

"You are right, master," I said, after looking into the well, "'Tesn't the ham, 'tes a four-gallon keg!"

"A keg, did you say?"

"Yes, master, with the slings on it," I replied, looking up into his horrified face.

"Then we are lost! Oh, that rogue of a John Oliver, and he knowing me as he does! Whatever is to be done? If we attempt to hide the keg, the fishermen will inform; see, they are watching us now; and if we stick to it, where shall we be if challenged and searched? Have you nothing to say?" he added, with a show of irritation.

"Why, say 'twas a gift."

"And if they question it?"

"Say it again, master, for the truth will stand telling twice."

"Then you are for sticking to it?"

"I am, and trusting to Providence."

"Jump up, we'll run the gauntlet."

Except for a woman at an upstairs window, we saw no one till, on turning a corner, we came to the Preventive Station. There a score or more fishermen were watching two preventive men at a game of marbles. In a moment all eyes were upon us, and it looked to me as if we were lost. And lost, I verily believe we should have been, but for master's presence of mind. Abreast of the players, he jumped down, seized one of the taws – it was a glassen alley – knuckled down, fired kibby at the clayers in the ring, and was back in his seat before you could cry "Jack Robinson". His quick movements, his odd way of firing, above all, the bad shot he made, caused a roar of laughter, amidst which we drove off with the keg rattling as loud as ever.

"Bravo, master!" I exclaimed, "I should never have thought you had it in you."

"Ah, Jack, you never know; the man himself never knows what is in him till he is put to it. But I do not feel that we are out of the wood yet. Did you notice that grey mare at the station door?"

"I did, master, saddled and bridled too, and a handful for the man holding her."

"Give the horse his head, Hue!"

So we sped at a spanking pace along the narrow winding way, till after plashing through a stream in a deep valley, and coming to a stiffish rise, I threw the reins on Snowball's back and let him take his time.

Then master got out his cherrywood and puffed away in silence. Near the top he said, "I wonder they let us go by without question or search."

A minute or two later there came a faint rat-tat of hoofs, and, looking back, we saw a man come galloping down the hill behind us.

"Heaven help us!" exclaimed master. "It's the riding-officer!"

Then, for the first time in his life, master used the whip upon Snowball. Feeling the lash, the startled horse nearly leapt out of the traces, and, but for the gear being as good as new, he would have torn it to ribbons. The speed at which he went I have seldom witnessed even in any runaway horse. Our pursuer was soon left behind, for master, who kept looking back, saw nothing of him from the moment we topped the hill to the moment we turned into a lane, where the furze bushes growing on the hedge shut out the view. We passed through Tregear townplace at the same fearful speed, scattering fowls and pigs and donkeys, till coming out beyond the farm to the downses we managed at last to pull Snowball up amongst the burrows of Old Wheal Rib.

"Remember, Jack," said master, excitedly, "that whatever happens, I did my best to keep you out of it."

"You did; but never mind me, master, it's you, it's Lanyon that matters."

"Yes, Jack, it will be a terrible blow to the family."

"I wasn't thinking of the family, master, I was thinking of you as leader of the yeomen in the Prince's procession, and the come-down it will be if you are caught and sent to prison."

"Yes, Jack, yes; and not only the leading yeoman, but Muster Master for the High Country in the third generation. Terrible! terrible! The disgrace would mean the downfall of an honoured family and be the death of Miss Jenifer."

"Cheer up, sir," I said, "you are going too far; time enough to talk like that when we are nabbed."

"What was that? Listen!"

"Nothing, master, 'tes only your fancy."

"Climb the big heap and see whether he is coming."

Thereupon I jumped down, scrambled up the highest of the burrows, and, lying on my stomach, looked back over the way we had come. There was at first no sign of any one except a man hoeing turnips. But whilst I looked I caught sight of the officer's hat above some bushes. He was moving along the road towards the lane, and I watched eagerly, hoping he would pass the end of it and make for Porthleven. I turned my head with the intention of reporting to master, but seeing that he was patting Snowball's neck and making it up with him, I held my tongue, and directed my mind again to the enemy.

On reaching the lane, the officer pulled up, and sat staring down at the ground as if to discover our tracks. What he saw I cannot say, but he came along the lane at a trot and hailed the man in the turnips, as I concluded from seeing the fellow suddenly run to him. Then I thought it full time to tell master.

"He's inquiring of the man in the turnips."

"The devil he is!" exclaimed master, flinging open the lid of the well. In two minutes he had got the keg out, and was rolling it towards the mouth of the shaft.

"Steady, master, the man hasn't split upon us."

"How can you tell?"

"From the way the officer is shaking his whip at him."

I was right. The talk ended, and the mounted man turned the horse's head and rode back. On reaching the road, however, he did not make for Porthleven, but, to my dismay, held on in the direction in which we were bound. As soon as he disappeared from view, I came down and gave master a full account.

"Shall we be safe on his heels?" he asked, pulling nervously at his Holland waistcoat.

"I doubt it; it's an old trick of Felton to return on his tracks; and most likely the riding-officer will do the same, for he is in the same line of business."

"But how should he know us?"

"What! not know us, with a white horse, a white hat, and white elastic!"

"He never saw us."

"But do you think he was not told?"

"Maybe you are right, but what about the keg? I confess I am loth to drop four gallons of good stuff down the shaft, especially after all we have gone through."

"Well, then, I'll put it aboard again," and with that I fetched it and replaced it in the well.

We made a fresh start, but instead of retracing our steps we followed the overgrown track from the waste heaps. It led to a bremble-choked lane, the lane to a pack track, and that to a road which master recognised by a duck pond.

"We are touching Breage church; see, there is the tower showing above the elms. Push along, and turn in at the green gate."

As we passed up the drive, master inquired of the old man raking the gravel whether Parson Pomeroy was indoors.

"Not indoors, Maister Pearce; I believe you will find him in the greenhouse."

When master had got down, the old man said, "Go along, too, young man, I'll see to Snowball."

"Certainly, Jack," exclaimed master, to whom I had looked for his assent.

We found the vicar – a tall, thin man, with a pleasant face and silvery hair – busy thinning grapes.

"Hullo, Pearce, glad to see you and your friend; on your annual round, I suppose? Dear me, how the time flies. It doesn't seem like twelve months since you were here."

"It's a year almost to the day, vicar."

"Well, now, let me take you and your friend round the garden; but first, what do you think of my grapes? There are two hundred and thirty-seven bunches, eleven more than last year; and, as you see, the black hambros are colouring nicely."

As master made no response, I ventured to put in, "And the house must look very pretty when the fruit is ripe."

"Very, it was a fancy of mine when I came here from Madron to plant the white muscats and black hambros alternately."

I expected master to say something, but he spoke never a word; and the look in his eyes told me that his thoughts were still on the riding-officer.

We followed the vicar along a gravel path, with a neatly-trimmed box border, to where the apple-trees were trained against wooden uprights provided with cross pieces, along which the branches stretched thick with fruit.

"I am very proud of my apples this year, Pearce; I have never known the shy bearers so heavily laden. Look at the crop on this gilliflower and on the golden pippin. Did you ever see such a crop on a Sops in Wine?"

I gave master time to answer, but seeing no sign of speech, I said, "They are traced as thick as onions, sir, and if I may make so bold, they would be all the better for a little thinning."

"You are right, but they must wait; their turn will come after I have finished with the peaches and nectarines."

But still the master was silent. I felt vexed with him. Here were we in a place of tranquillity and safety, with every attention shown us; and yet he was content to leave it to me, his servant, to help keep the conversation going. At the forking of the path, where the vicar ran off to fetch the key of the summer-house, it was as much as I could do to hold my tongue, and presently, as we were preceding the vicar through a little green door in the wall, I whispered in master's ear, "Why not make a clean breast of it? Anything rather than go on as you are."

That seemed to bring him back to himself, and hoping that he would act on my advice, I purposely lagged behind. The turf path led to a thatched summer-house, and when, as soon as they had entered, master closed the door behind the vicar, I said to myself, "It's all right now," and made for a pond that showed between the shrubs.

I was surprised to find what a big sheet of water it was, and greatly delighted to discover that a bridge led to an island in the middle of it. This I crossed, and from a bench watched a moorhen and her chicks as they cruised about amongst the waterlilies. Looking up at the summer-house from time to time, I saw master and the vicar standing by the window, and master doing all the talking. I thought he would never finish, or the vicar cease stroking his chin; but in half an hour the confession came to an end, and the vicar fell to patting master's back, and was still at it when they came out.

As they were making for the pond, I slipped across the bridge and went into the summer-house, for I was all curiosity to see what it was like. It was a dear little place, with shelves full of books, an old scarlet leather chair, and a round table on which lay a copy of the Sherborne Mercury, a jar of French tobacco, an inkstand made out of a pony's hoof, a basin of fine sand, and a sheet of paper with writing on it. I suppose that I ought not to have read the writing, but I did, and it was this –

"And I went out by night by the gate of the valley and viewed the walls of Jerusalem which were broken down."

Then, as I caught sight of master and the vicar passing through the green doorway, I hurried away and joined them. They were on the way to the church to see the tomb of Lady Margaret Godolphin.

"This lady, like Lady Grace Grenville, has left a memory whose fragrance will never perish," said the vicar, in a low and reverent voice.

Master being as absent-minded as ever, I replied, "Then this is the lady whose body was brought all the way from London Churchtown by road?"

"You are quite right; wherever did you learn that?"

"From Mr. Tasker, sir, who told us that it was at harvest time and men busy in the cornfields."

"I should like to congratulate your master on his pupil; excellent teacher, Simon Tasker."

Leaving the Godolphin Chapel, we noticed that master had gone off somewhere; so the vicar took me to the tower for a view of the country round. On the way up, I kept wondering what had become of master, and great was my surprise, when I lifted the trap-door, to find him on the roof, hat in hand, peeping out between the battlements.

"Clucky down," said he to me, rather sharply too, the moment I set foot on the leads; "'twill never do for you or me to be seen up here."

I never doubted, from the nervous way in which he spoke, that he had sighted the officer; but I was soon undeceived, for, turning to the vicar, he said, "As the road seems clear, Jack and I had better be moving."

"Don't go; dinner is about to be served. Cannot I induce you to stay? There is a fine cockerel, pickled pork, apple tart and cream, a ripe cheddar and a bottle of Madeira."

"Very tempting, vicar, but you know the predicament we are in."

"Well, I don't feel that I ought to press you, if you must go."

On the way down – master and the vicar having preceded me – I opened the door of the bell-loft and had a good look at the famous tenor bell. It is a monster, and, except the trees, was the only thing I had so far seen that we could not match at home. I would have given anything to have rung it, but when I got down I found that master had had Snowball put in the shafts, and was so impatient to start that I had to forego the opportunity. Then master and I shook hands with the vicar and got into our places.

"Good-bye, Pearce, please remember me to your wife and to Miss Jenifer. Good-bye, lad," and off we drove, without sip or sop, or even a pull at the bell. Thought I, as we passed out of the gates, "Smuggling, like poaching, has its drawbacks."

Perhaps not the least of these was the necessity of keeping to the by-ways and farm lanes. No one who knows the state of the tracks leading to Trewoofe, Trevarrian, and Rinsey in the 'forties, will believe it possible for a welled trap to traverse them without having its bottom smashed in; yet, by dint of manoeuvring, we accomplished the journey without serious mishap. The going across Pra Sands was delightful after the jolting we had had; so, too, was the travelling along the Falmouth Road to the Packet Inn, where we turned off for Acton Castle.

On sighting the keep, master said, "I hope he is not waiting for us."

"I hope not," I replied, "if it means my not going to Prussia Cove this afternoon."

"Thinking of her still, are thee, lad?" he asked, in a voice that was ever so tender.

"Yes, master, I can no more get her out of my head than you can get the riding-officer."

And so we came to the castle.

We – master, I mean – got a right royal welcome, Mr. and Mrs. George Pearce, their three daughters and two sons, all trooping to the entrance with faces full of greeting. Uncle Henry, as they called him, was all but lifted out of the trap in their eagerness to get him indoors. Nor could any one be nicer to me than Jim, the elder boy. He not only showed me the way to the stables, he stayed whilst I saw to Snowball, and afterwards took me to my room at the top of the keep. Nor would he hear of my taking my boots off before going upstairs, as I always did at home. We ascended by a winding stair with ever so many more steps than in Breage Tower, and at last we reached the room, but not to dwell, for Jim, after telling me that Mr. Rosewarne had hidden in this room, climbed the ladder in the corner, and I followed him to the leads.

It was a beautiful scene we looked down upon; Mount's Bay in the full glory of its summer colouring, and a brig with sails all set, and a boat in tow, making for St. Michael's Mount. But what were these to the sight which met my eyes when I turned? – for there, a mile or so away, lay Prussia Cove, with the boats, and on the brink of the cliff the home of her I loved. I gazed so long that at length Jim asked what interested me.

"I was hoping to get a sight of Mr. Rosewarne, but perhaps he is away at sea."

"I cannot say whether he is at home; I only know that his daughter Loveday is, for I saw her this morning."

CHAPTER XX

THE OLD STORY

I T WAS CLOSE UPON FOUR O'CLOCK before I was ready to start, minutes later than I should have been, but for the life of me I could not tie the new necktie into a bow. I was quite in a fever when I gave over trying and sought the assistance of the dairywoman, who helped me willingly, her tongue going all the time.

"Theee'rt some prinked out, thee art, what with the stand-up collar and flam new neckerchief. Why, to see you, one would think you were off to the Flora. I'm wonderin' what it all means, and you a stranger in these parts. Goin' to see her, are 'ee? Ah! that's it, I'll be bound. Like the rest of the world, thee'rt over head and ears with Lovey Rosewarne!"

"Who's Lovey Rosewarne?" I asked.

"What! never heerd tell of Lovey? My dear young man, Lovey's the idol of Perran and all the parishes round! Never heerd tell of Lovey, when there edn standin' room in Rinsey Chapel for the men that flock for a sight of her? Ah! thee'st heerd of her, I can see; thee cusn't deceive me; no, no, not for all thy simple questions and innocent looks. It's to find favour in her sparklin' eyes, thee'st tricked thyself up like this. But mark my words that, good-looking tho' thee art, thee'st got thy work cut out to win her. Lovey's heart is like this castle, built to stand a siege. Iss, fay it is. But I wish 'ee well," adding, as I moved away, "Go slowly; win her inch by inch – 'tes your only chance."

Master was waiting for me at the gate, and – will it be believed? – with a big bag of fairings.

"Never any harm to take your welcome with you," said he, handing it to me. "God speed thee, lad."

Master's kindness took me in the throat so badly that I could hardly get out a word of thanks; but I saw that he understood.

My way led between hedges of honeysuckle and brier to the cliffs where the bell-heather was in blowth, and the air sweet with wild thyme. As I went along, a voice within whispered, "John Penrose, you are only a labouring man: no right to look so high."

157

At this, I nearly let go the bag of fairings, so unnerving were the cruel words.

"Rubbish," I replied; "catch the maid's fancy, and all will be well."

So I plucked up courage, and held bravely on.

Yet my heart beat wildly as I walked up the garden path and knocked at the door. It was opened at once by a pleasant-faced woman, who, as her eyes met mine, exclaimed –

"What! Never John Penrose?"

"It is, Mrs. Rosewarne; but however did you know?"

"Why, from the likeness to thy mother. Thee'st got thy father's hair and build; otherwise, thee'rt her living image. Well! well! I'm proud to see 'ee. Walk in, my dear, and welcome. Take father's chair – that one there at the head of the table. I'll sit here, on the end of the form. Now, make yourself at home. Why, thee'rt a grown man," she went on. "Not married, of course, or I should have heard of it from father."

"No, Mrs. Rosewarne, nor tokened."

"Nor walking out?"

I shook my head.

"Well, then, thee'rt like Loveday, with your troubles all to come. Not that she has lacked for offers. No, my dear life! 'Tedn't that. Look at that big box on the shelf: it is full of valentines. The men are like bees about her; and some from a distance. There's young Felton; you must know him – he's the son of the keeper at Tregwainton."

I nodded.

"Well, hardly a Sunday has come and gone since Loveday returned from Forest Carn but what he has sailed over here. No weather keeps him away; and he has started off back in a sea that has kept me awake half the night, wondering whether he has got across. His daring is enough to make any girl love him; but I don't know. Then there is Willie Thomas, a young farmer, milking eighteen cows, and nobody dependent upon him. He thinks the world of her. Whether it is because he's a bit in-kneed, I can't say, but there it is, Loveday won't look at him, any more than she will look at Reuben Lewarne, who has got a slight impediment in his speech. And when she says 'No,' nothing shall move her. Well, the trouble is, she's afeard of her soul that somebody will marry her for her looks, and then get tired of her. But tell me about yourself, and how you came to be at Prussia Cove."

"On purpose to see you and Loveday."

"Never come from Lanyon to see me and Loveday?"

"I did and I didn't. It's like this. Master took me with him on his round, and I've just come from Acton Castle, where we are staying over Sunday. But I have been looking forward to seeing you ever since I left home."

"When was that?"

"Wednesday."

"Then you must have come by a roundabout way?"

"We did; we came by St. Ives, Gwithian, Helston, Carminowe, and Breage, and met with adventures all along the road."

"Adventures, eh!"

"Yes, adventures; and, if you like, I'll tell you all about them."

"If I like, did you say? The longer your story, my dear, the better. Any news from the outside world is welcome in this quiet spot, especially when told by a nice young fellow like yourself."

"I'm glad if I'm making myself agreeable, Mrs. Rosewarne, because mother told me to do so. She also said that you dearly loved a little attention."

She laughed at this, but returned to the subject of my adventures, and begged me to tell everything from the moment master and I set out.

"But where is Loveday?" I asked, unable to keep the question back any longer.

"I'm wondering myself; I've kept looking for her all the time we've been talking, and here, at last, she comes."

I looked through the window, but too late to catch sight of her; and the next minute she entered the kitchen, and transformed it into fairyland.

I jumped forward and shook hands.

"Well, whoever would have expected to see you, John! When and how did you come?"

"That's exactly what John is on the point of telling," said Mrs. Rosewarne, "so come and sit by me and listen. I'm dying to hear."

I began at the beginning, with all Lanyon out in the townplace to see us off, and told them of the journey to St. Ives. Then I described the cockfight on the towans. Law, how they laughed over the squire and the constable, and again over the judge! That brought me to the visit to the woods, and, taking my courage in both hands, I told them of the cutting of Loveday's name on the most graceful tree I could find. Then I paused, hoping that Loveday, or, if not Loveday, her mother, would ask why I cut it. But they read 'my mind, and said never a word. At great moments, women can hold their tongues. You smile perhaps, but it was a great moment to me, for a word would have brought the confession of my love. Then I related the telling of my fortune by the gipsy queen. Twice I repeated the gipsy's statement, "You are in love with a beautiful girl," but without a word from my listeners. So I was forced to go on. I came to the smuggling. Then there was such a silence that the very walls, the walls that had heard more of smuggling than any along the coast, seemed to be listening. How the women hung on my words as I told of the visits of the sailor, the preparations, the landing, the hurry and scurry that followed, and master's play-acting in the bedroom. But the kitchen rang with their laughter when I told them of master's taking the medicine, and again and again as I recounted the incidents of our escape.

"Thank 'ee, John," said Mrs. Rosewarne, when I had done, "twas as good as listening to a play. Thee would make thy fortune as a droll-teller."

"That he would," added Loveday, "I enjoyed every word, and was sorry when he came to an end."

"Well, now, to show your gratitude, take John down to the Cove – that is, after we have had a dish of tea – and show him what there is to be seen, for there is no knowing whether he will ever be this way again."

That struck cold to my heart, for it showed that all my little attentions to Loveday that Sunday at Lanyon, my farewells at the pier, and my valentine, instead of being taken seriously, as God knows I meant them, had been treated as if I were nobody. For a moment I could not help showing that I was hurt, and a silence followed, during which I was thinking, "This comes of looking above your station." Ah me! the injustice of it! Here was I, a good-looking, upstanding chap in the pride of life, to school till I was fourteen, able to do anything in farm work, an honest and straightforward fellow, who had never kissed a maid, and not for want of chances, neither, and yet I was not to be thought of as a match for Loveday, and for why? Because I was only a farm servant. As if it were right and just that a man should be appraised by the value of his worldly goods and not by his personal worth. However, I put on the best face I could, and whilst Mrs. Rosewarne busied herself about the tea I handed Loveday the necktie and the fairings.

"The tie is my own little gift; but the bag of fairings was paid for by master, who said, 'Nothing like taking your welcome with you.'"

At this they burst out laughing, though what they saw to laugh at I cannot understand to this day. They ceased to laugh, however, on opening the bag, for besides gingerbread-nuts, it contained a dozen macaroons and half a pound of sugared almonds.

"What a grand fairing!" exclaimed Loveday, "and how your master must value you to think of such a thing!"

"Then he knew you were coming here?" said Mrs. Rosewarne.

"Yes," I replied. "He knew that I am in love with Loveday."

The effect of these words was extraordinary. Loveday flew upstairs like a skeared bird, whilst Mrs. Rosewarne made for the dresser, and stayed there with her back to me, for no reason that I could see, as the tea-things were all on the table. There she stood, handling plates and jugs, and putting them back in the places she had taken them from, whilst I stood looking at her, lost in wonderment. But the painful situation ended well, for presently Loveday came downstairs again, and, lo and behold! with the forget-me-not tie around her beautiful neck.

"That is very sweet of you," I said, "to put it on so soon."

She blushed slightly at this, making my heart leap with joy, for I interpreted the blush as the dawn of love.

We did not sit long over tea, and then Loveday showed me the garden, the flowers, the tamarisks, the fuchsia bush which she was very proud of, and told me the story of the old figurehead by the summer-house. As I turned to latch the gate when we passed out, I caught sight of Mrs. Rosewarne looking eagerly at us through the window. It was only a glance I got, but it enabled me to read her thoughts. I would have laid my crown piece against a brass token that what was passing through her mind was something like this: "What a nice couple they would make: what a pity it could never be!" And why could it never be? I asked myself, when she was willing, as I gathered, to favour the suit of Dickie Felton. Was a boat-builder, the son of a gamekeeper, to be preferred to a farm-hand, and the son of a farm-hand whom master always spoke of as his hind?

On the way to the Cove, Loveday told me all about her grandfather, the king of the smugglers, his sloops and the guns they carried, and took me to the spot where the battery was mounted which beat off King George's cutter.

"We are being watched," I said quietly, seeing a Preventive man suddenly duck his head behind a rock.

"We think nothing of that after a landing," she replied. "Come, let us go as far as Cuddan – that is, unless you are afraid of trusting yourself to me."

"Afraid! I would trust myself with you anywhere."

"Then jump aboard and take charge of the tiller."

So we pushed off.

"What's this little tassel of rope?" I asked, as we passed the rock at the mouth of the cove.

"Why, a fender, of course; it's to prevent the boat being injured."

"Ah, Loveday, if only you would let me be your fender through life!"

"But a boat wears out half a dozen fenders."

"No matter; rather one year of life with you than a score without you."

"Oh, what a pretty speech! John, I fear you have broken many a girl's heart."

"Not one; on the contrary, a girl has nearly broken mine – a girl to whom I sent a valentine."

"Poor fellow! How sad! Well, now, pay out that fishing-line by your side. A good bite from a pollack or a bass will make you forget all your troubles. They pull ever so much harder than trout. By the way, have you caught the pulrose trout?"

"Loveday, how could you put such a question? Did you not beg me never to try for it? Ah! if you only knew how I respect your every wish. I have never tried for that fish, nor never shall."

"That is nice of you, John; I thank you. More than once since I was at Lanyon, I have thought of the big fish under the mill-wheel."

"I am glad to hear that, because you can hardly have thought of the fish without thinking of the person who told you about it."

"Now, silence, John, whilst you admire this stretch of the cliffs."

"It is very grand; and what a magnificent cave that is – I mean the one the chough has just flown out of."

"It is. But remember that you cannot judge the size from the mouth; as a rule, the bigger the cave, the smaller the entrance."

"They make perfect hiding-places for smuggled goods, I should think."

"Hush!" she replied, "I am not allowed to speak about that; the hiding-places are family secrets."

"May I hope to be let into them some day?"

"I cannot tell; I cannot see into the future like the gipsy queen. Besides, if you put me such difficult questions I shall be running into the rocks, and remember there is no fender below the water-line."

It was a delight to see her handle the sculls. Never once – not even when

I spoke of the valentine – did she catch a crab. She was the picture of health and strength, of beauty and grace; and as I sat there watching her, I felt as if I were in dreamland.

She rowed past Cuddan to where the Mount could be seen rising in all its stateliness from the blue waters. There she rested on the oars so that I might admire it; and when she turned the boat, said –

"If ever I leave the Cove, I should like to live at the Mount."

"Or Forest Carn," I ventured to suggest.

"Yes, or Forest Carn, because I always think Red Riding Hood lived there. I am coming to look after granfer some day."

"Never!" I exclaimed.

"I am, whether you like it or not!"

"Like it or not? What do you mean? Don't you know that it is my heaven on earth to be near you?"

"John, you frighten me; you are so passionate. Now, if you value your life or mine, look to the steering, or we shall never reach land."

I was very much agitated; but remembering what the dairywoman had said, I managed to hold my peace, and for the time we said no more. She allowed me to help her out of the boat; I was thankful for that, for it showed that she was not angry with me, and on the way up the cliff I said –

"May I come over tomorrow?"

"Of course we should have been glad to see you; but, unfortunately, we are spending the day at Kenneggy."

"Oh dear! oh dear! I am sorry for that."

"Well, we shall be at Rinsey Chapel in the morning, if it is not too far."

"Too far! I would go to the end of the world to be near you."

At that she ran indoors; and when I entered the kitchen, she was seated in her father's chair, her face all smiles, and more bewitching than I had ever seen it.

"Good-bye till to-morrow," I said. "Good-bye, Mrs. Rosewarne; thank you very much for your kindness."

CHAPTER XXI

LOVE AND DEATH

HAT NIGHT AS I LAY AWAKE, I recalled every look and word of Loveday, in the hope of discovering some signs of love that had escaped me. She had worn the necktie, it is true; and there was the faint blush – but nothing more. Then I brooded over the mother's hard words, which, though they struck cold at the time, now sent me into such a fever that I flung off the clothes, gathered up the blankets, and made my way up on to the roof. It was good to feel the night wind, comforting to be with the stars, soothing to hear the gurgle of the tide; their gentle influences quieted me. I wrapped myself in the blankets, lay down, and, watching Charles's Wain, fell asleep.

But my excited mind was not perfectly at rest; I dreamt of the morning of my going to school of my father's charge, "Always speak the truth and to once," and of the scene at Branwell's Corner, and father in gala dress swinging past with the banner; then he was leading the reapers in Further North; again in the belfry ringing the minute bell. I awoke to find it grey dawn, the airy-mice flitting about the battlements, and the choughs crying piteously on the cliffs below.

At the first sound of stir, I dressed, made my way down the long winding stair to the hall, and passed through a little arched doorway to the open. After seeing to Snowball, I filled the trough in the lower yard, stripped to the waist, had a good wash, and felt fresh as a daisy. I went, jacket on arm, to the harness-room. There, by the help of a bit of looking-glass, with a pair of clipping scissors, I cut away the straggling hairs on my chin and cheeks. I did this because I had noticed, both in the kitchen and the boat, that Loveday's eyes kept returning to them as if they teased her. Then I put on my last clean collar, tied the necktie into quite a neat-looking bow, twisted the ends of my moustache into two little curls like the dandies of Helston town, and to keep them in place, fixed them with a bit of beeswax. I was more than satisfied with my appearance by the time I had done tittivating myself; indeed, to tell the truth, I thought I looked quite fetching.

On the way in to breakfast, I was waylaid by the dairywoman. She looked at the necktie and said, "Thee'st soon learnt to do without me, I see. How did thee speed? Did 'ee make the lovelight come into her eyes? Ah! I can see by thy looks thee did'st not; but don't despair, young man. Press your suit, and keep pressin' it; walk round the walls seventy times seven if need be; Loveday Rosewarne is a jewel above price, and her love worth all it will cost to win."

"Thank you," I said, "you give me fresh heart; but I meant to try again."

During breakfast, master kept casting anxious glances at me, and – just as I was about to start for chapel – beckoned me to him into the room at the foot of the keep.

"Well, lad," said he, the moment he had closed the door, "you are looking a bit down; tell me how you prospered."

"Very slight, master, I am afraid; I don't feel I made any headway to speak of."

"Well, what of that; did you expect the little maid to light up with love at your first approach, and to say, 'I will' at your first appeal? Such are to be found, no doubt; but not the ones to be most prized. Is anything worth the having that you can get for the asking? You know it is not. As to having made no headway, how do you know? How can you tell she wasn't awake half the night thinking of you, that she hasn't told her mother, or, if not her mother, herself, that you are the one man in the world for her? How do you know? I say, answer me; and for Heaven's sake! don't look like that."

"I don't know, master; but if things are as you seem to think, then all I can say is, that a woman's tongue and a woman's face are given her to hide her feelings."

"Did you catch her looking at you on the sly?"

"Never."

"Did you note whether she changed colour?"

"She did once, master; but no more than the blush on a brier rose."

"Quite enough to show the state of her feelings."

"Ah! master, if you only knew all!"

"Well, out with it."

"Why, master, she has got a dozen chaps dangling after her, all better circumstanced than me; and what I feel is this, that if I don't get some sort of a promise out of her today, it's good-bye to Loveday Rosewarne and to the joy of life for Jack Penrose."

165

"Fiddlesticks! I'll wager there isn't another such upstanding chap amongst them, nor one as good-looking; no, nor as good company. It's the man a girl wants, not his money."

"You've a clever tongue, master; but if, when I see her after chapel and ask for my answer, as I mean to, she says, 'John, it can never be,' what then?"

"Why, tell her such language does not become her rosy lips; that you've made up your mind to marry her, and that nothing in this world could stop you. Women like a strong, masterful man. But mind how you deliver yourself. Give it out in a voice firm, yet tender, and full of pleading, and with a face to match."

"And if that fails, master?"

"Why, do what I did myself; drop on your knees and refuse to rise till she gives way."

"Thank you, master; I'll act the part as best I can," and with that I started off.

I was late for service; the congregation was well through the opening hymn when I opened the door and walked in.

I expected to be shown to a seat, but as nobody took any notice, I found a seat for myself between two other farm-hands at the back.

Loveday, who was in the choir, standing sideways to me, was singing as naturally as a thrush upon our scaw-tree, and in her print dress, Leghorn hat, and lace collar, looked a picture. I hadn't a chance of catching her eye, as she never once looked round, nor other than straight in front of her, till the minister mounted the pulpit, then she looked up at him.

He preached from the text, "They were lovely and pleasant in their lives, and in their death they were not divided," and so held the congregation that you might have heard a pin drop. Other than his voice, there was no sound save the sea, at least until towards the close, when the silence was broken by the neigh of a horse.

"Surely, Snowball," I said to myself, "what can it mean? Never master come to drive me back to Acton! It could not be that. What, then?"

Presently the door opened, and to my amazement Andrew looked in, and – God help me! his face was as white as death!

I did not wait until his eyes lighted on me; I knew he wanted me, and, as I tiptoed out, my dream and the gipsy's warning leapt to my mind, in a foreboding of the bad news which I felt sure Andrew had brought.

"Is father badly hurt?" I asked.

"Worse than that!" replied master, who was also there.

"Never dead?"

"Try and bear it, Jack; 'tis God's will."

"Father dead? Father?"

"Yes, he has fallen off the hayrick."

Then I broke down, and, leaning against my master's shoulder, cried like a child. Dear old Andrew kept patting my back to soothe me, saying, "Be brave, Jack," and I tried to be; but it was no use, my grief would out.

Presently I said, "Master, I'm ready," and whispering to Andrew, "Tell Loveday why I've gone," I got up, and we started for home.

The sun shone brightly, but for me everything was black, black as the shadow cast by Snowball on the dusty road. It was close on two o'clock when master drew up at the iron gate. Instantly Mrs. Pearce came out, and said quietly, "Jack, your mother is here; you will find her in the parlour." So I got down and went in. With a heart-rending cry, mother fell into my arms. Her grief was terrible, her words piteous.

"Where is father?" I asked, as soon as we had had our cry out. "I must see him."

"You shall, dear; we shall go together."

Taking my hand in hers, she led me across the yard and into an outhouse. On three planchen, supported by trestles, a sheet covered a motionless form.

"Take off your cap, dear."

I did so. Then mother gently doubled back the covering to where the hands were crossed on his breast. Oh! how pale he was, and – when I kissed him – how cold! But though death had robbed him of warmth and colour, it could not dim the glory of his hair, which, as in life, circled his brow like a halo of gold. At a sign from mother, we knelt, and, after a few moments of silence, said together the Lord's Prayer aloud. I kissed father again, and for the last time, before mother put the sheet back. Then, like a man in a dream, I started out just as I was, in my Sunday best, to see to the hundred and one things that, in the morning's confusion, had had to be left undone. And thus the day passed to its close, with a sunset that gave a wonderful colour to the fields, now ripe to harvest.

I spent the night by my father's side, with Shep for company. It was as still as still until the small hours, when the cocks started crowing. I felt no fear, but I suffered the agonies of remorse. For I reflected that to

167

my shame I had, not once alone, but again and again, thought slight of father for eating with his knife; worse still, I had looked down upon him because he was illiterate. I gazed again in penitence on the marble face with bitter regrets for my heartlessness, and, whether it was fancy or not, I shall always believe I saw a smile that told of forgiveness play about the mouth.

As day was breaking, mother came in. "Are you all right, dear?"

"Yes, mother."

"Have you slept?"

"No." "Then you had better go and lie down."

"I must go to field first."

And I went, but without Shep, who refused to budge.

Everything reminded me of father: the track across Barnfield, the mended gap in the far corner, the partly-hoed turnips; and when, on coming to Long Downs, I saw that the sheep had been shorn, I wept aloud. For it showed the effort he had made single-handed to keep abreast of the work whilst master and I were away; and I shall always believe it was anxiety to get the rick thatched by our return that led to his working then and breaking his neck.

No crowner's quest was held; and for this I was thankful, as it was mother who had found father, and would have had to tell the jury so.

Monday evening, Andrew rode into the yard with a wreath tied to the saddle. On dismounting, he went indoors and handed it to mother, with this letter: –

> "Prussia Cove,
> "Sunday night.

"MY DEAR MARY,

"We are grieved beyond words for you and John. 'Tis dreadful to think that Richard has been cut off in his prime. Loveday, poor child, was distressed to hear John sobbing outside the chapel, and very much disappointed to find him gone. In the afternoon she gathered the heath and tamarisk, and twined them into the wreath which father will bring you with our loving sympathy. Henry would attend the funeral, but he is across to France and cannot be back in time. With my love to you and John, whom we enjoyed having here,

"I am,

"Dear Mary,

"Yours affectionately in your trouble,
"HONOR ROSEWARNE."

Enclosed was the following for me: –

"DEAR JOHN,
"I am very, very sorry for you. To hear such sad news, and so unexpectedly, must have been terrible. What a trying journey home you must have had. I searched Rinsey Cliffs for white heath, and the few sprigs I found you will see in the wreath.
"With my tenderest sympathy to you both, and love to your mother,
"Your true friend,
"LOVEDAY."

Father had once expressed a wish to lie in Morvah Churchyard; and there, to the north side of the church, Jim Beare dug his grave. The funeral was quiet and simple, the only mourner from outside Lanyon being Andrew, who led Shep by a bit of string. We all walked except Miss Jenifer, who came last in the dog-cart. I was too dazed for impressions to get a hold on the memory; but I recollect two things that were said – one by mother, the other by master.

"On another such day," said mother, as we were crossing the moors "I returned along this road a happy bride."

And when we were at the grave, taking our last look at the coffin, master said, "A more faithful servant man never had."

CHAPTER XXII

THE GREAT WINTER

❧

A S MASTER WOULD HAVE IT so, I took father's place in the harvest field, without – as I like to remember – any giggling or grumbling on the part of the old hands. Of the thirty-two acres under corn, the barley alone was badly laid, so that we made tolerably good progress, finishing on the sixth day in Great Fraland, where it fell to me to cry the neck. Mother came to hear me: better if she had not, as my voice brought the memory of father back, and sent her home in tears. To spare my feelings, I shall always think, master called in Johnny Curnow to do the thatching and finish the hayrick, though he was a poor thatcher, and anybody could see where father's work ended and Johnny's began.

From Michaelmas to Martinmas the weather was for the most part fine, with a wealth of sunshine, which crimsoned the haws, sweetened the black-berries, and made ploughing and harving a pleasure. Yet we had scarcely got the fields sown and rolled, when rain set in and fell day by day till the river came down in flood, swamping the valley and converting the marsh into a lake. The amount of wet was a hindrance in more ways than one. There was no working the mill, for the height of the water against the wheel; whilst the sodden state of the land made carting turnips a slow, dragging business for both man and beast.

Our troubles, however, were light to those of the farmers behindhand with their sowing; and if Parson Veale had not put up the prayer against rain, and stopped the downpour, there is no knowing when they would have got it done, or given over growling.

The dry spell which set in on the Monday was attended by a change of wind, which shifted grudgingly from sou'west to nor'east; but once in that quarter it ruled so firm that, as more than one observed, the vane on the shrike's cote seemed nailed to the upright. On the Sunday the weather turned suddenly cold, with a nip in the air which made itself felt as we sat by the fire; and next morning, as I crossed to the stables, the ground under-foot rang like a bell.

"There must be hard weather up along," I said to myself whilst rubbing Snowball down.

Soon birds of different kinds put in an appearance in unusual numbers; winnards, snipe, woodcock, golden plover, lapwing, and then – what I had been eagerly on the look out for – wildfowl. I learned of their arrival by their cries one morning as I was milking. To hear better, I called to the maids to hold their hands, but to no purpose; they kept showering the milk into the pails just as if I had not spoken. It was not that they did not hear – the truth is they were as jealous as fire of Loveday, and as nasty with me as could be, for passing them over.

When dawn came stealing through the cobwebbed pane, I went outside and looked up. Against the fading stars I made out skein after skein of wildfowl, some V-shape, others in line, others higgledy-piggledy, all heading westward, as if to some known gathering-ground beyond the Land's End; and not only those I could see, but, as wild trumpetings told, others higher up out of sight.

These travelling companies of wildfowl greatly excited me, though not a tithe as much as others I saw just before breakfast. Going to fetch in furze from the rick, I beheld on the marsh no less than five bunches of duck – one lot on the edge of the ice, the other four on the water; and as I stood looking, a big skein of widgeon, after circling twice, dropped in amongst the reed by Smuggler's Pool. Such a spectacle had not before been witnessed in my time, nor, I believe, since the great frost Andrew loved to tell of.

What would I have given that day to be a gentleman, free to go forth with a gun! Situated as I was, I should have begged an hour or two off had the work been forward: what is more, I should have got them. But the rains had thrown us all behind, and I had not the heart to ask. There was nothing for it but to wait till night.

In the dinner-hour, however, unable to stand the tantalising sight any longer, I took my walking-stick gun and sallied out. I had no need to go as far as the marsh. When I reached the bridge, a teal rose from the millpool, affording an easy shot. At the pull of the trigger, the bird fell, and was carried by the stream to the hatch, whither I ran and picked it up. From there I hurried to the flooded ground by the mill, where I fired at a mallard. Though I feel sure I held straight, I failed to bring him down. Truth to tell, my little gun – wonderful weapon that it was – did not throw a sufficiently heavy charge for a wild duck. I feared it as I pressed the trigger, and, as I watched the bird fly away towards Music Waters, I thought of the blunderbuss, and resolved to beg the loan of it. This I did later in the turnip shed.

"Certainly," said master, "and you'll find powder and shot in the spence."

I was in high spirits when at night, with the blunderbuss loaded and primed, I set out for the marsh, making for the western side, where a tongue of land jutted out within range of the wildfowl. By crawling under the furze, I succeeded in reaching the very tip of the little promontory without my presence being suspected. There was a mere sickle of a moon; but with the stars that shone like diamonds it furnished what light I needed, showing row upon row of duck on the ice, and – if my eyes did not deceive me – a countless host on the rough water.

The moment I had breathed a little warmth into my fingers, I seized the blunderbuss, which I had laid down, and jumped to my feet. Was there ever such a whirring of wings? For a moment I felt bewildered; but the next I had pulled myself together, shouldered the weapon, and let drive. Though the report set my ears ringing, and the kick nearly knocked me backwards, I lost no time in stepping on to the ice, and, leaning well forward against the wind, made for the spot where I could see some birds lying. After picking up five, I turned my attention to others which had fallen on the water and drifted against the ice. But how was I to get at them? I dare not venture to the edge for fear of the ice snapping and letting me in. So I lay flat on my stomach, stretched my arms to the full, and, seizing bird after bird, flung them behind me. Eleven I recovered in this fashion, and so should have had sixteen in all, but on returning to the birds I had laid down first, I found only four. What became of the fifth is more than I can say. Some prowling fox or otter had probably helped himself to it.

Getting back to the point, I picked up the blunderbuss I had left there, and made for home as fast as the wind and my load would let me. Snow was beginning to fall before I reached the bridge, and was coming down pretty thick as I crossed the yard; nor was there any sign of clearing when I looked out at my window last thing on turning in.

A blood-red sun uprose on a country-side strange and beautiful beyond all telling. The hills and carns seemed as if mantled with goose-down; so too the roofs and ricks, indeed every exposed object even to the bee-skeps and shrike's cote. The snow was to my liking in every way, from the crunch of it underfoot to the patterns graved by the wind on the drifts, and it thrilled me to think that another such fall would cut Lanyon off from the world.

After dinner, Shep and I went at once to moor to fetch in the colts and yearlings. It took quite a while to get them rounded up; and then, as I was about to start for home, I suddenly thought of the little roan mare, that was unfortunately heavy in foal. So leaving Shep in charge, I went to look for her. I sought her in a score likely places, calling as I went; and before giving up searched the wild coombe below Hannibal's Carn, but without finding a trace of her. Longer I dared not stay, as night was closing in, and the snow coming down thicker than ever. Indeed, but for Shep's bark, I doubt if I should have found the herd, for it had strayed wide of the Little Galver, where I had left it. I drove the willing creatures along the foot of the Barrows, out of the teeth of the wind, which had us at its mercy as we crossed the open stretch leading to Trucks Lane, down which we passed to the road.

Master, white as a miller, awaited us at the open gate, and soon we had the herd all secure and snug within the big enclosure we call the corral. A linhay with manger and rack ran down one side; and on the way in along I had been thinking what a business it would be to carry hay and straw for so many heads. But to my amazement every rack was full and bedding spread; I say amazement, because with the mowhay where it was, there would be a great task for one pair of hands.

"Master," I said, "you must be dead beat; leave them to me."

"I'm all right, lad; besides it does me good to see them."

Twice before leaving we walked to the end and back, the lantern I carried lighting up yearling and colt and the breath that hung about them like a fog. I felt a bit done by the time I had made the round of the sheds, yet could not resist the temptation of making a visit to the marsh, whence I again returned towards midnight with as many fowl as I could well carry.

The time of the snow was a heavy one for all hands, and had not Mrs. Pearce, mother, and the three maids turned to and taken all the lighter chores off our hands, master and I could never have kept the stock going. As for Miss Jenifer, though never out of doors except for the purpose of feeding and watering the small birds, she was as busy as a bee in the house and – what all the rest were glad to be rid of – did all the thinking. And her thoughts ranged beyond Lanyon, as I was to learn in the second week of the snow, when she sent for me.

"There are six thousand mouths or more to feed," I heard her say as I came up the stairs, "and all the supplies cut off, except by sea."

On entering the room, I saw she was addressing master, who looked up at me and said, "Do you think you could get through to Penzance with butter and pork?"

"I might with the sley, master."

"Capital," exclaimed Miss Jenifer. "Now, Henry, lose no time." So next morning, which was Wednesday, we killed a six-score pig; and with this, the week's butter and three score wildfowl, we loaded up before going to bed, so as to have all ready for an early start.

The light was barely grey when I stepped into the traces and got the sley under weigh, yet early as it was for Miss Jenifer to be stirring, she was at the window to give me a send-off.

Without a word from me, master came along to lend a hand up Paunshallow, but I was glad of his help long before we got there; for I could hardly have won through the drift by the Quoit or the one by Boswarva Carn Lane, which blocked the road completely. We rested awhile on Paunshallow Bridge to recover our breath; and there my heart almost failed me to see that the snow on the hill was pretty well level with the hedgetops.

"Ready, master?"

"Ready, lad," and with that we fell into our places, I in the traces, he behind, resolved to gain the top if it were humanly possible.

For a time we got along better than I expected, but at the stiffest part of the rise we were brought to a standstill. Determined not to be beaten, I unloaded, shouldered the pig, now stiff as a board, and floundering through the snow carried it to the top of the hill. Leaving it there I returned and fetched the butter, and laid it by the side of the pork. With the sley thus lightened of more than half the load, we succeeded in dragging the rest to the level ground beyond the rab-pit, where, after a breather, we reloaded and went on again.

"Master, I can manage single-handed," I said after a bit; but it was not till we got to the side lane leading down to Billy Hal's Moor and Trevean that I got him to turn back.

I reached Penzance as the clock was striking twelve, my appearance causing no little excitement, especially amongst the Blue Coat School, that is to say the butchers, who came running after me to the Butter Market.

I had resolved to sell by auction, and took up my stand in front of the very seats where mother and I had sat the day we had little Victor with us. But in what different circumstances! Then no one took any notice of us, now all eyes were on me; and as I looked at the eager faces I thought of the time when my wounded feelings drove me from mother's side so that I could have my cry without her seeing me.

"Please have the exact money ready," I shouted. "I can give no change."

Then holding up a pound of butter, I said, "How much for this lot?"

"Eightpence, ninepence, one shilling, one-and-two-pence, one-and-fourpence, one-and-sixpence, two shillings, two-and-sixpence."

"I will take eight pounds," said the highest bidder, handing me a sovereign. I sold all the butter at this price.

Next I offered the wildfowl. For the wild duck I got four shillings, for the widgeon three shillings, for the teal one-and-ninepence.

Were ever such prices heard of?

Next, removing the white cloth, I dealt with the pork.

"This pig is six score lumping weight, and has been fed on home-grown meal and skim milk. How much per pound?"

This brought such a babel of bids that, to end the confusion, I held up my hand for silence. When at last I was able to command it, I said, "Be so good as to nod your bids." But this proved no more satisfactory, for what could I do with thirty heads nodding at the same time? It made me laugh to see them.

"This is no use either," I said presently. "I'll start the bidding myself and come down, and the first to hold up his hand will be declared buyer."

"Going at two-and-six a pound, two-and-threepence, two shillings, one-and-tenpence, one-and-ninepence, one-and-eightpence, one-and-sevenpence, one-and-sixpence," at which Mr. John Laity became the purchaser, and counted me out nine sovereigns. What a handful of gold for a little six-score pig!

Then, while buttoning up my pockets, I looked round upon the crowd, and my eyes lighted on a man with a weather-beaten face and keen black eyes gleaming under his sou'-wester. It was Mr. Rosewarne, who, as my eye caught his, held up his hand and beckoned me to go to him.

"You're a born auctioneer, Jack," said he, gripping my hand. "Never have I seen a better salesman."

"Nor such ready buyers, sir."

"That's true. And now come and have a bit of croust."

With that, he led across to the Temperance Hotel, where, after an excellent meal, we drew our chairs up to the fire for a chat.

"Well, how are you getting on?"

"As well as can be expected, sir, considering I never get a glimpse nor hear a word of Loveday."

"What! like my little maid, do 'ee?"

"Like is no word for what I feel. To me she is the loveliest thing in the world."

"Beauty is only skin deep, Jack."

"Law! sir, that is only a tithe of what I see in her. She has the prettiest ways I ever saw, a tongue that could not scold, and a lovely cool hand for butter-making."

At this he fell to laughing, till I thought he would roll off the chair; and when I asked him what tickled him so, he started laughing again. On recovering himself, he said –

"You are right in looking at the practical side. But, my dear Jack, Loveday is only a slip of a girl."

"But fast growing to a woman, sir; and meant, if ever a woman was, to be the light of a home. Anyway, I hope you will put in a word for me."

"I shall certainly say you made an excellent salesman, and never parted with the goods without first getting the money."

"Can't 'ee go a little bit farther than that? You see, sir, I'm not there to speak for myself; farm work don't permit of my getting away, even of a Sunday, and I live in dread of hearing she has given her hand to some rich farmer or young boat-builder. And, oh! sir, if ever that came to my ears, the sun would be darkened for me, and life not worth living."

"Feel like that, would you?"

"I should, but don't breathe a word of it, sir. Only I want you to understand. Is Loveday coming to Forest Carn for Christmas, as they say?"

"If the frost breaks up; but only for a few days. She would have come this morning if I'd let her."

"You don't say so? How I wish she had!"

"Yes, she is very fond of her grandfather, and of Forest Carn. And now I must settle, and see about getting a few groceries and things, for we are cut off from Helston. Good-bye, lad," and with that we parted.

I reached Lanyon at dusk, and went straight into the big house to hand over the takings. Master and Miss Jenifer were amazed at the prices fetched, and looked at one another in wonderment when I emptied my pockets upon the red table-cloth.

"Let me see," said master, rising from his chair and leaning over the money, "the pork fetched nine pounds, the butter five, so that if I take fourteen pounds the remainder is wildfowl money." Whereupon he picked up gold and silver to that amount, and said, "Jack, the rest is yours, take it across to mother."

"But, sir!"

"Do what I say," he rapped out.

So I picked up what remained, which was all silver and copper, except one half-sovereign; and after thanking master as well as I could, ran across to mother.

Mother was quite overcome when I handed her the money, but recovered after a cup of tea, and was more like her old self than I had yet seen her since our great trouble.

CHAPTER XXIII

LOVEDAY AT FOREST CARN

❧

B Y THE NEXT MARKET DAY the frost had gone, and the wildfowl with it. Then my thoughts turned wholly to Loveday, for whose coming I kept even a sharper look-out than for the widgeon and the teal. As regularly as the dinner-hour came round, I hurried to the high ground above the rab-pit in the hope of sighting the *Kittiwake* till, on the Tuesday before Christmas –which was on the Thursday that year – I beheld, as I watched, the snow-white sails of the little craft heave clear of Cuddan Point.

How much those bits of canvas meant; what a thrill they sent through me! I leapt for joy; and with difficulty restrained myself from rushing off to the pierhead to greet my love. In fact, but for half a score jobs that cried out to be done, I should have gone. Instead of that, I went home with the good news.

Mother said, "We must make much of Loveday the few days she is here. You will be seeing her tonight; now, whatever you do, don't forget to give her my love, and say that I am expecting her here to tea tomorrow, and Christmas Day as well, and Andrew too, of course."

Between seven and eight o'clock, I started for Forest Carn, primed with mother's parting advice: "Now mind and lay yourself out to be very agreeable. I begin to suspect there is some attraction on this side of the Bay."

"May be," I thought, as I went along; "but if so, is it Dickie or is it me? and if it is my rival, if she receives me coldly, what then?"

My reception, however, was anything but cold. Loveday greeted me with a face all smiles.

"Are you not surprised to find me here?" she asked.

"Not at all, I knew you had come, I saw the *Kittiwake* round Cuddan Point."

"But you can't see Cuddan from Lanyon?"

"No, but you can from the top of Paunshallow."

"Surely you did not leave your work!"

"No, only my dinner."

178

"Left your dinner for the sight of a boat!"

"Ah! you know it was not for the Kittiwake, but for the little tease it carried."

"Well, here is the freight come to spend Christmas with granfer."

"And here is John Penrose come to pay his respects the very first minute he could get away."

"Now, lad," said Andrew, his face beaming at the conversation, "try a pipe of the tobacco Loveday has brought."

I took the canister he handed me, loaded my pipe, and after a whiff or two, I said –

" 'Tes rare good stuff, this French tobacco; and all the sweeter for the hand that brought it."

"John, you are quick at compliments," said Loveday.

"Mother shall know that, for, as I was going out of the door, she said, 'Now, whatever you do, mind and lay yourself out to be very agreeable.' But that was not all."

"Then, give us the rest," exclaimed Loveday.

"You are sure you will not be offended?"

"Offended! how can I be?"

"Well, mother said, or rather whispered, 'I begin to think there is some attraction this side the bay.'"

At this, they shrieked with laughter, whilst I sat looking, first at one, then at the other, lost in wonderment. Whatever they saw to laugh at, I don't know.

"Jack," said Andrew, "thee'rt a born actor; and how thee canst say the things thou dost and keep thy face is altogether beyond me. And now I'm goin' to ask 'ee to entertain us further by singin' 'The Farmer's Boy'. I'm expectin' to hear somethin' good, as Jim tells me you brought the house down at the bell-ringers' supper."

Whereupon I laid my pipe on the hearth, stood up, and sang –

"The sun went down beyond yon hill
Across the dreary moor,
When a boy there came, both weary and lame,
Up to a farmer's door.
'Can you tell me if any there be
That can give to me employ?

179

> I can plough and sow, reap and mow,
> And be a farmer's boy."

"First rate, John," said Loveday, clapping her hands. "Go on, please."
"So long as ever you like; you've only to say the word."
"I hardly know where to look, after your pretty speeches."
"Don't turn your face away; I can't see half enough of it as it is."
"Get on with the song, and don't tease."

> "And if that you cannot me employ,
> One favour let me ask,
> Will you shelter me till break of day,
> From this cold winter blast?
> At the break of day I'll trudge away,
> And will try to get employ;
> I can plough and sow, reap and mow,
> And be a farmer's boy."

At this point, Dickie, dressed in brand new clothes which made mine look poor and mean, walked in, and received from Loveday a welcome heartier, if anything, than she had given me.

"Finish your song, Jack," said Andrew, encouragingly, noticing that I was put out; so I continued –

> "The farmer said, 'Let stay the lad,
> No farther let him seek,'
> 'Oh yes, dear father,' the daughter cried,
> While the tears ran down her cheek,
> 'For those that labour, 'tis hard to want,
> If that you can give employ,
> He can plough and sow, reap and mow,
> And be a farmer's boy.'

> "At length of time he grew a man,
> The good old farmer died,
> He left the lad the farm he had,
> And the daughter for his bride;
> So the lad that was, now a farmer is,
> Often smiles and thinks with joy

Of the lucky, lucky day he came that way,
To be a farmer's boy."

"Thank you ever so much, John; you sang splendidly."

"So he did, my dear – the music suits a tenor voice; but 'twas the feeling he threw into the words that made it go so well."

"Now, Dickie," said Loveday. "Sing your song; I'm never tired of hearing it."

Whereupon Dickie sang, "Come Live with Me and be My Love."

"Come live with me and be my love,
And we will all the pleasures prove
That grove and valley, hill or field,
Or wood and steepy mountain yield.

"And I will make thee beds of roses,
And then a thousand fragrant posies;
A cap of flowers, and rural kirtle,
Embroidered all with wreaths of myrtle.

"A jaunty gown of finest wool,
Which from some pretty lamb we'll pull,
And shoes, lined choicely for the cold,
With buckles of the purest gold.

"A belt of straw and ivy buds,
With coral clasps and amber studs,
And if these pleasures may thee move,
Come live with me and be my love."

He sang with such a pleasing and refined voice that in the silence which followed I felt as if I should sink through the floor.

"Now boys, sit round; and you, Jack, put on a good big faggot in honour of Loveday."

"At your service, Andrew; but, to do justice to the occasion, we ought to fire the beacon!"

"Sh! sh! Jack, to give breath to such a thing! Here, fill up, and hand the canister to Dickie."

"Thank you, Andrew, I don't smoke."

"Dickie," I said, "is too good for this world. He don't smoke, he don't drink, he has never been heard to swear, and I should think never kissed a girl in his life. Though, for that matter, I never did but once, and she was old enough to be my mother."

"What, Jack?" said Andrew, looking me straight in the face. "Can you say that you never kissed a girl but once in your life?"

"I can."

"And that, I suppose, was Betty, aboard the *Triton*?"

"Who?" asked Loveday, as curious as could be. "Who was Betty?"

"What, my dear, never heard of Jack running off in the *Triton* with Betty?"

"Never a word!"

"Then, thee'st yet to hear the greatest adventure of his life. Now is your chance, Jack."

After a few words by way of preliminary, I began with Bill throwing down the threshel and starting off to take passages for himself and Betty. Then I came to Bill's return home, the answering of. Betty's prayer, the day of sailing, and my stowing myself away under the bunk. From that moment, or rather from the moment the *Triton* got under weigh, Loveday's eyes – how beautiful they looked in the firelight! – never left mine till I had finished my story. After touching on the thoughts that passed through my mind whilst Betty remained up on deck, I described hearing the women come down the ladder, the fat woman getting into the bunk, my dream, the calling out in my sleep, the hubbub and my discovery.

"Please go on," said Loveday, when I paused, "I am anxious to hear what came next."

Then I related how I followed Betty as she led up the ladder and along between the bulwarks and the water-casks on the way to see the captain; and how, despite my fears, I noticed the ghostly look of the sails against the starry sky, which like a great blue down-turned bowl reached all the way round to the dark plain of the waters.

"Go on," said Loveday, rather impatiently, for I had stopped again to collect my thoughts. So, imitating Betty's voice as closely as I could, I repeated almost word for word her appeal to the captain, and told how it moved him – for so I shall always think – to go out of his course in the hope of meeting with a fishing-boat. This brought me to the point where the captain called down to me in the grey of the morning to come on deck, and I found the six-oared gig heading for us in the rough sea. I described how I was let down into the boat without saying good-bye to Betty.

"Dear! oh dear!" exclaimed Loveday, "what the poor soul's feelings must have been when she learnt that you had gone!"

"And what a relief!" added Andrew.

"True, granfer. And what happened in the boat?"

Then I gave a description of the fishing, of the row to St. Mary's, of Mrs. Trevellick's kindness. But it seemed to me that no part of the story gripped Loveday like the incidents of the crossing. The smother of foam on the Seven Stones, the sun's uprising, the porpoises, the bird which she said was a Mother Cary's chick, the Longships and the landing at the slip.

"Well, John, I don't think I ever heard a more interesting story. You were a naughty boy, a very naughty boy, but you had a grand adventure, and thank you very much for relating it."

"One more favour, Jack, by way of finishing up the evening," said Andrew. "Give us the last verse of 'The Farmer's Boy.'"

And this I did, the other three joining in the chorus.

When Dickie left, I gave mother's message.

"Thank your mother, John, but we've promised to go to Sunny Corner."

"Then you'll come on Christmas Day?"

"We're engaged to go there on that day also."

"You are?" I said, in a voice which showed how hurt I was.

"Don't blame me or Loveday, Jack; it was all fixed up by Honor more than a week ago. The truth of the matter is that Mrs. Felton wishes to make some return for the kindness showed to Dickie."

"Then you will come to us the day after Christmas Day?"

"We shall be delighted, shall we not, granfer?"

"Iss, my dear, I'm always ready to go to Jack's."

"And now, Loveday," I said, "I want to ask another favour. May I bring the handbell ringers here tomorrow after leaving the mansion?"

"Do, I should love to be serenaded like the princess in the fairy story; I will be sure to be awake if you come before midnight."

"We will be here before then."

And as the mansion clock was striking eleven, we ringers, to the number of sixteen, passed the Carn on the way to Forest Carn, where we formed up round Oliver Gendall, who held the lantern and beat the time as we rang, "I saw Three Ships come sailing by," "The Farmer's Boy," "Good King Wenceslas," "Noel," "God rest you, Merry Gentlemen."

Then, as at the mansion, we sang, "Hark, the herald angels sing."

In the silence that followed, Loveday came to the window, and said, "One and all, I thank you."

CHAPTER XXIV

FOUL PLAY

❦

O N CHRISTMAS DAY, the knowledge that Dickie had Loveday all to
himself drove me wild with jealousy. I could settle to nothing;
and when, at night, I went to Forest Carn, expecting that
Loveday had returned, I found the cottage in darkness. But I waited; and to
pass the time till she came, kept strolling between the cottage and the Carn,
stopping, however, every few steps to try and catch the sound of her voice.
The wind soughed in the pines, the mansion clock struck nine, ten, and, at
last, eleven. Then I concluded that Andrew was out earthstopping and that
Loveday was spending the night at Sunny Corner.

In desperation, I set out for the Galver, in the hope of finding Andrew.
What urged me to do that I can hardly say, unless it was that he was so
near and dear to Loveday. But the earth had been stopped, and the old
man gone on, seemingly, some little time, as I could see no sign of a
lantern on the moor beyond. Thus thwarted at every turn, I made
homealong, feeling as miserable as a fellow could feel. Yet my troubles
were not at an end. In Trucks Lane I all but ran up against Felton,
who, the moment he recognised me, snarled out, "You, is it? and up to no
good, I'll warrant!" I was too wretched to answer him, but I said within
myself, "Sure as there is a God in heaven, a day of reckoning will come
for you and me."

The big house, like Andrew's cottage, was in darkness; but, to my
surprise, a light burned in mother's room. "She has dropped off and
forgotten the candle," I thought, as I crept up the stairs.

"That you, Jack?"

"Yes, mother; you're not asleep?"

"No, dear, I'm going over the preparations for our little tea-party, and
thinking what I can do for Loveday's entertainment. For one thing, I am
going to show her my workbox with its little treasures; and then there is my
album with its pretty pictures and love poetry."

"I fear it is all no use, mother; Sunny Corner is going to prove too
much for us."

"Never in the world! you may trust a mother's perception in a matter of this kind, and if Loveday's choice lies between you and Dickie, you will be the one she will take. Now go and dream of wedding bells."

These words, and the conviction with which they were uttered, did me good; and I fell asleep at once.

Next morning I went to the Quoit to see the hounds cast off, and, scrambling up the nearest pillar, gained the table-stone as Sir Rose, with his cry of "Wind him, my lads," cheered the pack into cover. Instantly my troubles lifted like mist before the sun; and no wonder, for the sight of fox-hounds drawing a brake is a sure remedy for the megrims.

From my high station I could follow the working of every hound, not only of those whose sterns waved above the dwarf bushes, but those hidden from view, yet traceable by the shaking of the furze as they forced a way along the creeps. Sir Rose sat his grey like a statue, with eyes fixed on the cover, nor stirred when presently Cunavol's bell-like voice broke the silence, putting new life into hound and man and horse. Soon every hound joined in the cry, "Fox afoot!" What music! what lashing of sterns! what dash and bustle! what eagerness to oust the midnight prowler from his retreat! Twice, as the movements of the pack showed, he threaded the brake from end to end before he could make up his mind to quit; and when he did, he cleared the wall like a greyhound, and took to the moor with his mask set straight for the cliffs.

It was pretty to watch him as, with wondrous suppleness, he twisted in and out the little paths amidst the heath, getting less and less distinct, till presently the eye lost touch and shifted to Andrew, standing on the Barrows with cap hoisted on the top of his stick, as a sign that reynard was gone clean away. No tally-hoing was needed, nor toot of horn, for the pack, led by Cunavol, streamed over the wall to the moor, where, after feathering, they hit the line and went away with a crash of music that must have shaken the heart of the fugitive.

I waited till the last of the riders had passed over the skyline, then went back to my threshing. I might have beaten out a score of sheaves when Andrew came in. The moment I looked up at his face, I saw that something was wrong.

"Did the fox get to ground?" I asked.

"No, no, it edn't that; I'm wretched because of what I saw yesterday; Felton and his missus are all agog that Dickie and Loveday should

186

make a match of it. You never saw anythin' like the fuss they made of the cheeld. And Felton talked as if Dickie and Loveday were as good as tokened a'ready."

"You can hardly wonder at it, after the way Mrs. Rosewarne has encouraged him to the house."

"Stuff and nonsense; the cheeld is not of an age to marry."

"But she soon will be."

"Ah, well! I s'pose so. Now, 'tes a delicate thing to speak of, but all along I've been looking for you and Loveday to make a match of it; the cheeld is happy in your company, she glories in your adventures, she was mighty pleased with the Christmas carols. Felton seems to know the cheeld's leaning, for from somethin' he said, he looks on you as the obstacle in Dickie's path."

"That is good hearing, Andrew; now tell me, did Loveday sleep at Sunny Corner?"

"Indeed, she did not; she went the round with me."

"You don't say so?"

"She did, and wasn't a bit tired."

"Nor frightened?"

"Well, she was a bit; the sailors were hailin' laast night; but, mind you don't speak of it before her, or of anythin' else I've said, unless you want me to look a fool."

With that he went away, leaving me to my work and my reflections, reflections that grew brighter and brighter as the passing of the hours brought Loveday's arrival nearer. Everything promised well; and when, after milking, master ordered me to Boswednan to secure some seed oats, I raised no difficulty, knowing that by taking the short cut I could get there and back and have time to change before Andrew and Loveday were due. But I never reckoned on the devilish trick that was to be played me.

I started off at once, making a bee-line across the farm and the preserves. On reaching Boswednan I saw Mr. Hicks, bought the oats and set off homealong by the track I had come, singing as I ran, for I was in high spirits.

Then came the blow.

At the far side of the Great Downs, on dropping from the hedge, I landed in a man-trap. It clashed on my right leg with such violence as to drive the teeth nearly to the bone. When I tried to force the jaws apart, the

187

double spring resisted all my efforts. The only course open to me was to withdraw the staples, and hobble home as best I could; but so deep in the ground had the pegs been driven that it took me what seemed hours to extract them. At last I moved away, my foot squelching in the blood that had run down into the boot; and as I struggled on, there came over me the fear that I might bleed to death, and with it – as in the reeds – the dread that my body might never be found. I even pictured Felton tracking me by the blood, and coming upon me in the grey of the morning, exhausted and at his mercy.

The pain was hard to bear, but harder still the knowledge that the trap had been set since I had passed; and no doubt with the object of preventing me from spending any time with Loveday.

On reaching Billy Hal's Moor I was so far gone as to be on the point of giving up; but at the thought of Loveday and mother, I laboured on with the accursed trap now grown twice as heavy as at starting. Yard by yard I gained, and after hours of agony came to our boundary hedge. For a while, so great was my weakness that I despaired of getting any farther; but after a long rest, I called upon myself, and not in vain; for I succeeded in crossing the farm to the townplace, where I leant against the gate-post and shouted up to master. The third time he heard me, put his head out and, on learning my plight, came down just as he was. Without a word he knelt on the ground, gripped the jaws of the trap, one in each hand, forced them apart and set me free. Then he helped me indoors, gave me brandy, and by the light of a candle bandaged the leg with strips of linen. As soon as I felt able to move, he threw the table-cloth over his shoulders and took me across.

Mother was sitting up. "Don't be alarmed, Mary," said master, opening the door; "Jack has been caught in a man-trap; but with rest and treatment he will soon be all right."

"No need to ask who set the cruel thing," exclaimed mother in her distress. "And how such a man is allowed to live I don't know."

Then she took off my boots, bathed my foot, washed and re-bandaged the wound, and with master's help got me upstairs and put me to bed.

"Tell me about Loveday," I said, when master had gone.

"Well, my dear, what can I say except that she kept wondering till wonder changed to anxiety and then to distress as the hours went by without a sign of you? She has not been gone very long, not until master and Andrew returned from Boswednan, where they went to inquire for you. She did not want to go then; but as she has to leave first thing in the morning, I would not hear of her staying. Had I only known your terrible situation I would have flown to you, and Loveday too!"

The night was turning grey and the cocks crowing before mother left me to snatch an hour's sleep. I lay in bed all day and the better part of the next; and for a whole week had to stay indoors owing to the inflammation which could not be got under earlier, in spite of Miss Jenifer's cold water bandages and pennywort poultices.

Then, having cured my leg, Miss Jenifer and mother, who read in my looks or gathered from my fevered dreams the resolve I had formed to punish Felton, begged and prayed me to put away all thought of revenge.

But in my state of mind their advice, kindly meant though it was, might as well have been addressed to the Galver.

CHAPTER XXV

REVENGE

❧

A S SOON AS I WAS ABOUT AGAIN, I lost no time in putting into exe-
cution the vengeance I had planned. It was Felton's practice of a
Thursday – that is, when the hounds met near by on the Friday –
to call at Forest Carn and arrange with Andrew for the stopping of the
"home" earths.

His way from Sunny Corner led past the Carn. That gave me the opportunity I wanted. Where the track bent sharply round the Devil's Caldron I
would set the self-same trap he had set for me. I felt no qualms. I acted on
the principle of a tooth for a tooth. Nor did the penalty of transportation if
I should be caught red-handed weigh with me in the least; I had too bitter
memories to trouble about consequences.

So on the Wednesday, under cover of darkness, I set the trap; and
leaving it to its fiendish work crept back along the little-used path by which
I had gone.

I did not lack the stern reproof of conscience. Indeed, the meanness
of what I had done so smote me in the night that I was more than once on
the point of leaving my bed to set the diabolical engine off; but the
recollection of what I had endured mastered my better feelings; with
the morning I was as relentless as ever. My face must have told tales, for
twice I caught master looking at me from the corner of his eye; at meals
mother's face was full of trouble, I was myself very unhappy; but I carried
my evil thought all through the day, and the sun had not long set when I
stole away to the Carn. There I lay up in a patch of furze which commanded Felton's line of approach, for I wanted to see him walk into the trap, to
hear the clash as the jaws sprang home; above all, I looked forward to
witnessing his antics.

The suspense of waiting was trying enough; yet that was as nothing to
the agitation I felt on seeing my enemy emerge from Sanctuary Wood and
come along the track. That it was Felton I never for one moment doubted
till he was half-way up the slope, when to my dismay I saw it was the Squire.

Never was anybody in such a quandary. I would have warned him if I
could without inculpating myself and – what was present to my mind –

running the risk, if not of imprisonment or worse, at least of banishment from Madron. I found it hard to restrain myself from going forth and trusting to his mercy; but I let him come jauntily on, swinging his ivory-handled stick. Within a score paces of the Carn he stopped and looked back, as if attracted by the cry of a pheasant, which something had startled. I hoped, I prayed that he might retrace his steps; but no, on he came, if anything more briskly than before, as if to make up for lost time. Now he skirted the rocks, now he rounded the Devil's Caldron, now the trap had him. Lor' a mercy, how he squailed! I felt quite ashamed, I really did, that a seasoned soldier with a great hooked nose and fierce hawk eyes should cut so poor a figure.

Like me, he made a frantic effort to unlock the jaws; like me, he wasted his time. The deeper the teeth bit, the more he screeched, and soon so pitifully that I could hardly bear to hear him; and at last, his cries being more than flesh and blood could stand, I went forth to let him out. The sight of me was like a red rag to a bull. He bellowed out –

"You infernal scoundrel! you, was it?"

"I've come to let you out, Squire."

"Curse you; look sharp about it – look sharp, I say; this infernal engine is torturing me."

Only he used much stronger language; indeed, I never heard a sailor swear worse; and seeing that I could expect no mercy, I decided to extract a promise before releasing him.

"Squire," I said, "I won't let you out now unless you give me your word that you won't prosecute."

"Dare you make terms with me? Let me out at once, you miscreant."

"Not before you give your word. I didn't set the trap for you; I set it for Felton, because he set it for me. Look at this leg," I said, turning down my stocking and going close up to him; "have you ever seen such wounds as these? I dragged that very trap from the Great Downs to Lanyon; for seven hours I suffered the tortures of hell. Now promise, or I leave you."

He did not speak, he looked towards the woods.

"You refuse, then I go."

"I give you my word," he hissed.

Having let him out, I asked, "Shall I help you home, Squire?"

"Then take your stick," I said, handing it to him. But he seemed not to hear me.

191

At this moment Felton came running up, and seeing the man-trap and the blood on the Squire's breeches, looked ready to kill me.

"Felton, you can do nothing. The fellow has done this for revenge. Tell me, did you set the trap for him?"

"I did, Sir Rose."

And in spite of this confession, the Squire took Felton's arm and hobbled away.

I breathed not a word to mother, or indeed to anybody except Andrew; and never shall I forget the look on the old man's face when I told him.

"Do you mean to say that you caught the Squire and refused to let him out till he had given his word?"

"I do."

"You do? And you there face to face with him, and he in the trap?"

"I do; that was my only chance to get fair play."

"I see; you were thinkin' of your own skin?"

"Well, why not, when a word from him was all I asked?"

"You had faith in that?"

"I had and have."

"So have I; but see to it that you do not give Felton a chance; for as sure as you do, he'll make you suffer."

CHAPTER XXVI

FELTON OUTWITTED

ᴥᶋ

NDREW'S WARNING WAS STILL FRESH in my mind when I narrowly
escaped falling into Felton's clutches. Yet I would not have missed
the adventure for gold. It came about through my being sent by
master to get a brace of birds. I went to Little Pokess, then in turnips,
attracted by a covey I had seen drop in just before dinner; and before I had
beaten many rows I flushed and shot a pertridge. Whether this was a solitary bird or one of the covey, I cannot tell; anyway I did not set eyes on
another until near the far corner, when, from under the boundary edge, up
rose seven birds which flew away over the Squire's land. They were no
longer ours, but to stay my hand was more than I could do; so I fired,
knocking a cloud of feathers out of the bird on the right, and when it fell,
which it did a couple of gunshots off, I leapt the hedge and made across the
preserves to pick it up.

I had scarcely reached the spot where I had marked it drop when I
heard shouts, and, looking in the direction whence they came, beheld to my
dismay Felton and the under-keeper making for me at full tilt up the slope.
But I meant having my bird, and after a frantic search espied it where it lay
on a lichen-covered boulder. Felton shouted as I stooped to pick it up, and
again when I put it in my pocket; and as I took to my heels, I heard him say
to his mate, "Run and watch the cottage; we've got him at last."

And in the eye of the law he had got me, for – to say nothing of the trespass – I was liable to a penalty of £5 for having no gun certificate, and to a
further penalty of £5 for each of the brace of birds, besides the forfeiture of
my little gun.

The thought seemed to give wings to my heels. I flew like the wind past
Boswarva Carn and up the lane leading to the Quoit Croft, where, like
many a hunted fox, I hoped to elude pursuit. As the first brake was stunted
and thin, it was useless for my purpose, and I held along the turfy border to
within a furlong of the Quoit. The furze there was tall and close; so after a
hurried glance to see that Felton was not in sight, I plunged into the bushes, wormed my way along between the stems until I heard him coming, and
then lay still as death. Suddenly, whilst I listened, the beat of his footfall

ceased, and in the silence I pictured him erect on rock or bank watching with his steely eyes for some sign that should betray my whereabouts. For a half hour or more neither of us stirred. Then I heard the sound of iron against stone, and said to myself, "He's climbing the Quoit."

This move of his challenged my spirit of adventure, and instead of keeping close till night should conceal my movements, as I had thought of doing, I considered the possibility of trying to effect my escape under his very eyes. If I could thread the brake, gain our northern boundary wall, and under its cover fetch round by Further North to the tatie garden, I should be able to reach the cottage by the secret passage.

I imagined with a quiet chuckle the astonished face of the under-keeper on seeing me come out of the cottage, and that inclined me to make the attempt; but what finally decided me to brave the peril was the out-witting and discomfiture of Felton. I say peril, because between the cover and the boundary wall lay a strip of turf where a rabbit could hardly escape the eyes of a watcher on the Quoit, and it had to be crossed. Yet, as I said to myself, where there is no danger there is no adventure; and I determined to run the risk, be the outcome what it might.

I moved with the utmost caution so as not to rustle the furze, or stir the dust, which is like pepper for making you sneeze. My real fear, however, was not that I should sneeze, but that I should startle a woodcock or a pheasant, and so disclose my position. As good fortune would have it, I disturbed no living creature but a fox; and this did not trouble me, as I knew he would not expose so much as a hair of his brush. On past his warm, round kennel I crept till I lost my bearings, and had to try to ascertain my whereabouts.

So, removing my cap, I raised my head till it was flush with the blowth, and peeped through the stems of the taller bush in front. As I live, I was quite near the Quoit, right under Felton's eyes. How he failed to see me I don't know, unless it was that my hair, like the pertridge with the lichen, matched tolerably with the furze blossom. Fortunately I had enough pres-ence of mind not to duck my head, but lowered it as slowly as I had raised it, and altering my course held on towards the Trucks.

In time I came to the gully along which Loveday and I had once crept, and wormed myself on my stomach to where it ended and the naked turf began.

I felt very much excited. Now that I was face to face with the peril, it seemed madness to make the attempt. Peeping over the bank, I saw that

Felton was as vigilant as ever. That he was completely in the dark as to my whereabouts, however, was plain from the manner his eyes kept wandering over the brake; and as the sudden shifting of his glance showed, his fear that I should escape him even now.

Seizing the moment when his head was turned the other way, I dashed across the sward and flung myself on my face under Further North wall. The actual crossing was without hitch or stumble, but marred to my betrayal by the gun-barrel striking a stone as I fell. So loud was the noise, so sure did I feel that Felton had heard it, that I was on the point of making off before he should be upon me, when all at once I remembered a hole in the wall a few yards on through which I had once seen a coursed hare pass and escape the greyhounds. I hoped it would befriend me now.

On hands and knees I gained it and, leaning on my side, just managed to squeeze through to the other side, where I found shelter in a furze bush. It was so small that I had to lie doubled up with my knees against my chin, and even then I was not quite sure that some part of me was not exposed. But I had made my choice and must abide by it. I heard him run up immediately, and come to a standstill on the other side of the wall at the spot – so near as I could judge – where I had struck the stone. I cannot say whether he looked over the wall; I only know that my agony was as acute as if he did. Whether or no, he was at a complete loss; for I overheard him say to himself, "Well, that's very strange; I couldn't be mistaken." The next instant he was gone, tearing through the furze in his eagerness to regain the Quoit.

When the noise ceased, I crept back through the hole and retreated under cover of the boundary wall, till at length I came to the well, where I stayed to quench my thirst. From there I espied the under-keeper going like a sentry to and fro along the end of the cottage, so as to keep both front and back under observation. The moment his face was from me, I slipped across the road, leapt the stream and the hedge of the tatie garden and, after resting a moment to catch my breath, entered the secret passage. It was blindman's work to crawl along in the dark and feel my way with the gun-barrel; but I succeeded in reaching the cave, where I groped from pillar to pillar till I found the corner beneath the trap-stone.

On hearing mother overhead, I tapped and lifted the stone.

"That you, Jack?"

"Yes, mother."

"Felton and another man are outside; what's wrong?"

"Nothing to trouble about; I'll tell you all by'm bye."

With that I squeezed through the opening to the kitchen, and after putting the birds in the dairy and the gun on its rests, and brushing the furze-prickles and burrs from my cap, jacket and breeches, I opened the door and walked out. The look of astonishment on Felton's face when he saw it was me I shall never forget. He stared as if he could not believe his eyes. What was more, he was so tongue-tied that he let me pass unchallenged.

On reaching the stable, I stood in the doorway to see what he would do. Three ways of getting to the road were open to him: the bank at the back of the cottage, the lower gate, or the main gate. If he chose the last, he would have to pass me; and I somehow fancied that after being fooled and knowing I knew it, he would shrink from doing so. But in this I underrated his power of outfacing an awkward situation. Instead of slinking round the end of the cottage, or going down at the back of the big dairy, he came striding along the yard, with no hang-dog look either, but with his chin up, and an insolent air that drove me wild.

I managed to hold my tongue till he slammed the gate; then, unable to brook this insult to Lanyon, I jeered at him to my heart's content. Infuriated as an old dog-fox by a mobbing magpie, he stopped dead and turned on me a face livid with rage. I expected he would come back and have it out, but he got the mastery of himself and marched off with the under-keeper.

When I took the birds across and told master all that had happened, he lost his temper, not with me, but at the indignities I had suffered, and rounded on the game laws in language of a violence that surprised me. Never had I heard him break out so, no never, not even on the afternoon when yeoman Blee burst into the barn with word of the Repeal of the Corn Laws.

CHAPTER XXVII

THE PEDLAR'S STORY

❧

A N INCIDENT OF THIS TIME that must not be passed over was the homecoming, when all hopes seemed gone, of the little roan mare. She arrived in the early morning soon after I had gone to stable. Indeed I had only just lit the lantern, when I heard her whinney; and, running to the door, saw her come trotting through the gateway and, by my life! attended by the sweetest little foal I ever set eyes on.

As if skeared by the light, she suddenly stopped, but on my saying in a coaxing voice, "Good mare," she came boldly forward with a look in her beautiful full eyes that seemed to say – that did, I believe, say – "Well, here I am alive and well; and see what a dear little stranger I have brought with me." So I made much of her, patting her neck and smoothing her face and muzzle, whilst the foal frisked about, or stood stock still with out-stretched neck and nostrils as near to the lantern as he dared. The wee fellow was the image of his mother, with a blaze on the forehead and a stocking on the near hind foot. I soon had them comfortable in the corral, where I stayed a minute or two watching the mare munch the corn which she must have found appetising after the hard fare of the moor.

As it never rains but it pours, who should come along next week but Jim the Pedlar, whose visits were generally as regular as Parson Veale's at tithing time.

"We heard you had gone round land, Jim," I said, as he came in at the gate.

"I have been hearing that all along the road, Jack."

"Who started the report?" I asked.

"No knowing, unless it was the people at Treen. After I left there the snow fell heavy; and it was all I could do to battle through to Sennen, where I was weather-bound for a fortnight."

Jim was in a chatty mood, and after supper, told us what mother had often tried in vain to get out of him – the story of his life.

He began, "I have no recollection of father or mother, or of any home other than Wendron Poorhouse. There the matron was very good to me whilst a broken-down schoolmaster taught me to read and write. At ten I went to work at Clahar Garden, a farm in Mullion parish, where I remained till my fourteenth birthday. Whilst there I used to go a-fishing at night on Polurrian beach, and I have fished ever since when opportunity offered, and always at night. Then, from seeing ships come and go in Mount's Bay, I decided to go to sea, and got a berth as cabin-boy in the schooner *Grace*, trading between Penzance pier and Carpenter Smith's wharf, within a stone's throw of London Bridge."

"Then you've been to London Churchtown," I exclaimed.

"If I've been once, I've been a couple of score times, and should have been oftener still but for head winds that drove us into Falmouth, or kept us anchored in the Downs, sometimes for a week or more at a stretch."

"You've seen St. Paul's Cathedral?"

"Aye, and I never see the dome of Penzance market-house without thinking of it, nor for that matter the Longship's Lighthouse or Ding Dong engine-house without thinking of the monument by Billingsgate. Seen? I could keep you all night telling of the sights these eyes of mine have witnessed. I have seen a Lord Mayor's Show; I've seen the Lifeguards march through the city; I was in the crowd that watched the burning of the Royal Exchange. And the funny thing was that in spite of these grand sights, I was never weaned of my love for Cornwall or ceased in my longing to return to it. This hankering after home where oddly enough no home was – nor friends except the matron, the old school-master and a farm boy at Bonython – used to come over me in all sorts of places. It used to come when as the *Grace* lay alongside the wharf and I was in my bunk, with the ebb or flow of the tide in my ears and the clocks striking the hours; above all perhaps in the Downs with the east wind whistling in the rigging. The mention of the Downs reminds me of one of the grandest sights I ever saw – the Fleet going down Channel under full sail. Mark that I said one of the grandest, because a fleet of full-rigged ships in Falmouth Roads with the light of the rising sun upon their yards and topmasts as I saw them more than once, is a sight second to none.

But, as I said, Wendron and West Cornwall were calling to me, and when I had saved money enough to stock a pack and keep me in bread whilst working up a connection, I gave up the sea for the road, and there I've been for fifteen years or more."

"Why not settle down here at Lanyon? Master has been looking for a man this long time, and would, I know, be glad of you."

"Settle down, Jack?" he replied; "as soon expect a bird of passage caught in the frost to be content with its cage when the frost had gone, as Jim the Pedlar to settle down after the free roving life of the road. I know how it would be; I should in a manner of speaking be like the bird beating my wings against the bars, I should be longing all the time to be on the tramp. No, Jack; I shall keep to my beat between the Land's End and. Wendron so long as I can put one foot before the other and people don't turn me from their doors."

"No fear of that," said mother, "you are too good company to have the door shut in your face."

I was at him again in the morning to stay; but seeing it was of no use, I said, "Well, Jim, if you won't stay, will you undertake to deliver a letter?"

"Tell me where, and I'll give you an answer."

"At Prussia Cove."

"Certainly, with pleasure."

This was my letter: –

"13th Jan., 1848.

"DEAR LOVEDAY,

"I am sending you these few lines by Jim the Pedlar, who is waiting whilst I write. It was a bitter disappointment not to spend that last evening with you. The fault did not lie with me, as I daresay you have heard.

"Loveday, not a day breaks but I think of you. Everything that is beautiful, everything that is sweet, calls up a memory of you; the stars, the sky at rise and set of sun, the twittering of the birds at dawn, the grey bird's evening song, the chiming of the stream. This is not much of what I wanted to say, but Jim is fidgeting with his feet and anxious to be gone, so I must close. Mother sends her love, and I look forward to the time when you will let me send mine. Meanwhile I sign myself your loving friend,

"JOHN PENROSE."

"Jim," I said, as I handed it, "let me hear you read the address, as I wish to make sure that it is plain."

"Plain? Plain as a pikestaff! 'Miss Loveday Rosewarne, Prussia Cove.'"

"Do you know the house?"

"Bless the lad! Do I know the house? This is not the first love-letter by many I've had to deliver to her."

With that he put the letter in behind the tapes and reels of cotton, swung the box on to his back with the fishing-line attached, and with a "So-long", started off on his journey.

"I wonder," said mother that night, as the rain came pelting down, "where Jim has found a lodging."

Once or twice in the next week or two the same thought came to me, as February proved very wet. March, however, was very dry, with dust blowing on the Morvah Road, and a black east wind affording no promise of the genial weather ahead. For April came in with kindly showers and generous sunshine, which between them spanned the heavens with bows of such brilliant colours that more than once I was forced to stand and behold them.

Soon the wheatear appeared in its old haunts by the Quoit and the Trucks and the sedgewarbler in the reed-beds, whilst the cuckoo could be heard telling its name to the crafts and carns. All birds, indeed every living creature, seemed to rejoice at the return of the love season; all save the peacock, the shrike, and myself. One evening towards the end of the month, however, when I was sad at heart, Andrew came with a letter from his daughter Honor, from which, after putting on his spectacles, he read, "Tell Jack Penrose that we were all very sorry to hear of his terrible sufferings, and that we shall be glad to see him at Prussia Cove whenever he can come."

I could hardly believe my ears. If a lawyer's clerk had driven up and said I had been left a fortune, I could not have been more delighted. And to think that Honor of all persons had sent the invitation, and in her own handwriting!

"Thank Mrs. Rosewarne," I replied as soon as I could collect my thoughts, "and tell her I will come the very first minute I can get away."

CHAPTER XXVIII

AT THE FLORA

"I TOLD YOU MY SON," said mother, when Andrew had left, "that there was an attraction this side of the bay." "You did, mother; but then I never expected a special invitation like this. It isn't sent out of pity for my sufferings in the man-trap, I suppose?"

"What, after all these months? No, no."

"What then?"

"Why, Loveday is pining for a sight of Jack Penrose, and has got her mother to write and ask you over. And I am glad she has, for it is the wish nearest my heart that you and Loveday should come together."

"But I've nothing to go in except my old corduroys, and it will take three or four pounds from the savings for a cloth suit."

"My dear, this is not an occasion for pinching and squeezing; you must have whatever money you need, for you must go looking nice."

But after all, not a penny had to be taken from upstairs though how mother managed to give things the turn they took is more than I know. Anyhow, one day soon after, Martha Angwin came to the winnowing stock to say that Miss Jenifer wished to see me at once. Whereupon I dropped the cayer I had been using, and followed Martha to the big house, wondering what I could be wanted for.

As soon as I entered the room Miss Jenifer began, "I am sorry to call you away from your work, but I could not rest till the question was settled."

"What question, Miss?"

I'm just coming to it; your master and I have been having quite a heated argument as to whether you or he is the bigger man. I maintain that, excepting the size of your head, there isn't a pin to choose between you. Now off with your jacket and slip on this," she proceeded, holding up the green coat with its array of gold buttons, in which master had ridden before Prince Albert.

"I was right, I knew I was," exclaimed Miss Jenifer, "it fits like a glove. But, dear me! you look so well in it that I should like to see you in the complete suit. Now, to please me, take the rest of the things across, jack boots, beaver and all, put them on, and come back and show yourself."

Nothing loth, I gathered up the breeches, waistcoat, frilled shirt and other things and hurried across.

"Don't be long," Miss Jenifer called through the window, "I shall be waiting in the parlour."

Mother was out, but returned whilst I was up in my room changing.

"What are you doing upstairs this time of day and without taking your boots off?" she called up angrily.

"You'll soon see, mother."

"My dear Jack," she exclaimed as I came down the stairs, "you've most taken my breath away."

The next moment she flung her arms about my neck, and kissed me on both cheeks. There were tears in her eyes when she let me go and, standing back, looked me up and down.

"I'm proud of my son; you look splendid: the hat is a bit big, but I'll soon put that right."

Whereupon she folded a half sheet of the *Penzance Gazette* and put it inside the lining.

"Capital," I remarked, putting the hat on, "it fits as if it grew there; now I must go across and show myself."

My grand dress did not disguise me from the poultry: they followed to the gate as usual. Miss Jenifer was in the parlour, with her were Mrs. Pearce and master. As I walked into the room their eyes became round like marbles, and speech was at first confined to exclamations. "Well, well, my gracious! gracious me! gracious, goodness me!"

"On with the beaver," said master.

I did so, tilting it after the manner of Urban Gard, the Penzance dandy.

"He is the image of somebody I've seen, Henry; but who, I cannot recall."

"I can tell you, Jenifer; young Squire Caerthillian."

"Yes, to be sure; as he stood on the steps listening to the address of the tenantry."

"Now Jack," said master, "You look your best, and if by any chance" – this he said with a knowing smile – "there's a young woman you would like to show yourself to, you are free for a couple of days and Snowball to carry you, that is, after the barley is in."

"Thank you, master," I replied, "that's the very favour I was going to ask. But do you think I've face enough to go forth in this gala dress?"

"Think? I don't think about it after the way you faced the blue-coat school in the market and the squires on the Towans."

"Well, master, after that comforting speech, I'm game to go as I stand, and as you very well know, my destination is Prussia Cove."

Working early and late, I got the barley in within a week; what was more, I managed to clip the horses, and to get the work generally advanced so far as was possible for one pair of hands. And master not only saw what I had done, but recognised it. In the evening he came to me in the stable, and said –

"I'm very pleased with what you've done, here's a sovereign to spend, and a letter to my brother, who I know will be pleased to put you up."

"Thank you," I replied, "man never had a more considerate master."

Next morning, all Lanyon gathered in the townplace to see me start. Twice they made me ride to the pound and back for nothing else but to feast their eyes upon me; and when at last they let me go, Miss Jenifer called out, "There goes the pride of Lanyon."

It was a lovely May morning; the furze blowth, the blue sky, the songs of the birds, all were in keeping with my mood.

Andrew, quick of eye though he was, did not recognise me at first glance.

"Well, well," he exclaimed, raising his hands from the gate, "thee art Jack, I can see that now; but I declare I shouldn't have knowed 'ee but for Snowball. Why these fine feathers, though? Goin' guise dancing are 'ee?"

"I'm on my way to Prussia Cove."

"Ah! that's it, I understand now. Thee'rt like the cock birds, in courting plumage. Good luck to thee! one word, lad: put on a bold face, for a fool in borrowed plumes looks ten times worse than a fool in fustian. But there," he added, as I moved away, "I've faith you'll carry it off all right."

At the bend of the road I swung round in the saddle, and looked back. As I expected, he was watching, and the dear old man raised his badger-skin cap with as grand an air as though he had been saluting a duke.

I walked Snowball through Churchtown where Felton, who was standing in the smithy, touched his hat as I passed.

"Ah!" thought I, "it's not the man, it's the rig that compels respect."

It was the same in Penzance, where the people are reckoned sharp-witted considering the distance from London town: Wingy Pascoe, the one-armed constable, who never took notice of anybody less than the

Mayor or a Justice, saluted; Miss Peggy Tremenheere bowed behind the window of her sedan chair, whilst Mr. Bolitho stood still at the bank door and looked and looked as if he felt he must know me, but could not be quite sure. It was as good as a play, and I could not help feeling as I moved towards Chyandour, that I acted my part pretty well for a yokel.

I met the coach, Firefly, on Ponsandane Bridge and then, the turf inviting me, I crossed the Eastern Green at a hand gallop. In Market Jew I caused quite a stir, people running to the doors to see me ride by. One boy shouted, "There's a circus coming," whilst a woman waiting her turn at the shute said to another filling her pitcher, "He's on the way to the Flora; I'll be bound he is."

My own love did not recognise me at first sight; and when she did, she dropped the wallflowers she had been picking, ran to the door and called out, "Jack's at the gate." Both Mr. and Mrs. Rosewarne, who came running out, roared with laughter on recovering from their amazement.

"I took you for young Squire Erisey," said Mrs. Rosewarne, "when I saw you through the window. But jump down and come indoors; you must be famished after your ride. You, Henry, take the horse; and don't be long, for dinner is ready."

The conversation – after I had told how I came to be dressed up – was about the Helston Flora, for which great event, Mrs. Rosewarne, like the other woman at the shute, felt sure I had come. When I protested and asked when it was, Mrs. Rosewarne exclaimed, "Why you great ninny, tomorrow of course. The eighth of May is Flora Day as everybody knows. We are all going, and will take you with us; that is, if you would care to come."

"Care to come? I shall be delighted."

"But can you dance?" asked Mr. Rosewarne, who had now returned.

"Dance, sir, I can do anything except sail a sloop."

"Good, I'll put you to the proof when your dinner has had time to settle."

So an hour later he took down the fiddle, and saying, "Now Jack and Loveday," started playing the Flora tune for us young people to dance to.

"Law! what a pleasure to have such a partner! Light on her feet, does anybody ask? I reply, no fairy could be lighter."

"You'll do," said Mr. Rosewarne, after we had been round the kitchen five or six times: and now I must try and borrow a horse for Loveday to ride. She's a capital horsewoman you will find."

"No difficulty about that, sir. Mr. George Pearce will lend me one, and Loveday can ride Snowball."

Mr. Pearce said at once when I asked him, "You can ride Nubian," and no sooner were the words out of his mouth than Mrs. Pearce, who was standing by, added, "And I shall be pleased to lend Loveday my new side-saddle."

The world was at my feet that day; it seemed to me I could have anything for the asking, and that night as I lay abed in the little room at the top of the keep, I almost blamed myself for not asking Loveday for her hand, when parting at the gate. Whilst we were dancing together I had determined to do so, but changed my mind as I cooled down, the look on Mrs. Rosewarne's face helping me to a decision.

At ten o'clock next morning Loveday and I rode away to the Flora. In her pretty print gown, little blue cape and simple bonnet with a fillet of red roses and white satin lining, she looked like a May Queen; and to my thinking, Snowball never stepped more proudly. Our way led along cliffs gay with sea-pinks, over downs fragrant from the furze blowth and never out of sight of the sea, till having crossed the Looe Bar and left Carminowe Creek behind, we passed into the avenue leading to the Helston Road. There we overtook Mr. and Mrs. Oliver in their trap, and as we went by I heard Mrs. Oliver say, "There goes Loveday, how sweet she is looking! and what a handsome young squire she has got with her! My good Lor'! never Bevil Erisey is it?"

It was not; it was only me; and as soon as we had got out of hearing, Loveday and I had a real good laugh. I never knew anybody who could enjoy a joke more than she, and told her so.

"'Tis well," she replied, "that one of us should be able to see the funny side of things."

"Then you do not think I can?"

"Not always; I've heard you say things that you were never meant to repeat, and look puzzled at the laughter you've excited. But let that pass; you've got all your wits about you today, thanks to your master's beaver."

On the outskirts of the town we came on a band of revellers carrying may boughs and singing the old ditty –

"Robin Hood and Little John,
They both are gone to Fair O,

And we will to the merry wood,
To see what they do, O,
And for to chase O,
To chase the buck and doe,
With ha, lan, taw,
Jolly rumble O."

The streets were garlanded and beflagged, the air athrob with voices and the music of fife and drum. Between crowded pavements we rode to the Angel, whence, after stabling the horses, we hurried out to take our place in the line of couples drawn up near the Corn Exchange. A tall man in a scarlet hunting-coat and velvet cap, who carried a long silver stick, put us in the fourth place from the band.

"That is Loveday Rosewarne, isn't she lovely?" I heard a lady say behind us.

"And her partner?" asked the dark gentleman with her.

"I do not know from Adam."

At that moment the band struck up, and off we went. We danced in the street, we danced on the pavements, we danced along passages that led to lawns where fountains played and almond trees and camellias bloomed, we danced on the Bowling Green, we danced up Coinage Hall Street to the Corn Exchange where, after dancing Sir Roger de Coverley, we broke off amidst the cheering of the crowd gathered to see the finish.

As it was now two o'clock, I took Loveday to Master Penaluna's to dinner. There we expected to meet her father and mother, but no sign of them could I see at either of the two tables that ran the full length of the tent. I have been accused of not trying to see them; but that was not so, honour bright.

The meal ran me into three shillings, not including sixpence for the waiting-woman. It was a big sum to give for mere attendance, but then, as I said to myself, if you set yourself up for a squire you must expect to pay for it.

On leaving we made a round of the town, attracting attention wherever we went. I felt proud to be seen with such a well-known beauty, and I make bold to say she felt no shame at walking with "the pride of Lanyon".

It was on the stroke of six, and the air getting a bit chilly, when we rode down Coinage Hall Street on our way back along. We chose that road because Loveday wished to see the "Ghost"-Walk and the spot under the oaks where I had lain and watched the smugglers' boats. Better, ten thousand times better, if we had not! For there at the foot of the hill, on a splat of grass called Helston Lower Green, with her eyes on the passers-by, sat the Gipsy Queen. She was seated on the steps of the caravan as on the day I first saw her; and at sight of her I thought of a spider awaiting its prey. I hoped to pass unrecognised, but in vain.

"Are you going by without a word? Do not say you did not know me."

"I was not going to," I replied, pulling up my horse.

"Then why pass me by? Am I, Zillah, beneath your notice, because you are arrayed in your master's fineries?"

"That had nothing to do with it."

"Then tell me what had."

"I feared you would cast a shadow across the happiest day of my life."

"How foolish of you!" she replied, rising to her feet and coming forward all smiles. "Let me tell the beautiful lady her fortune."

"Not today, the air is cold, Loveday is lightly clad and might take a chill."

"That is not the true reason."

"It is not; but I have told you that already."

At this her eyes flashed and, raising her right hand, she said in threatening tones: "You refuse? you dare refuse? then you shall pay dearly for the slight put upon me," and with that she flounced round, and, with her gliding step, passed into the tent by the side of the caravan.

"She's like a wild beast," said Loveday, trembling. "Let us get right away. See, her evil eyes are glaring at us from beneath the curtains."

We set the horses to a canter and went on at a brisk pace along the track beneath the oaks, past the spot I had intended to point out, even to the cliff road and indeed a good mile beyond Porthleven, where at last we drew rein on Rinsey morrops.

"I feel better now," said Loveday, "but tell me, John, why you feared that woman's tongue."

"Because when she told my fortune, she prophesied nothing but evil, father's death and . . ."

"And what?"

"Shall I tell you?"

"Yes, why not?"

"Well, she said I should have a troubled courtship and that I should drink the cup of jealousy to the dregs."

"And has it come true?" asked Loveday, putting her horse to a gallop before I could answer.

When at last I overtook her – for Nubian was no match for Snowball – I said, "How could you put such a question? You must know what I have suffered on account of your attentions to Dickie."

"John, not a word against Dickie, please; he is as brave as a lion, and never once breathed a syllable against you. And do you think he has suffered no jealousy on your account?"

With that she was off again, and the dickens' own job I had to catch her. Law, me! she was like a Will o' the Wisp.

"Loveday," I said, as we drew near her gate, "I am going to ask you . . ."

"Do not ask now; come in six months."

"How am I to keep going all that time? Have you no pity?"

With that she raised her face for me to kiss, and the next moment she slipped off the horse, and ran indoors like one shamed.

"Women are rum creatures," I said to myself as I led the horses away; "danged if they don't puzzle me."

But that kiss worked wonders, it made a different being of me, and my ride home was through an enchanted country with joy bells chiming all the way.

CHAPTER XXIX

DISGRACE AND
DESPAIR

❧

F IVE MONTHS HAD PASSED since Flora Day; but one remained before
I should go to Loveday for her answer, when, like an evil fate, the
gipsy queen appeared, pitched the camp on our moor and wrecked
all my hopes.

I was in the barn picking over the seed corn when I heard the rumble of
the caravan; and the moment I saw whose it was, I drew back into the dark,
where I could see without being seen. Geordie was driving, the woman
looking out of the window with wild, restless eyes that searched the
mowhay, the barn and other outbuildings like those of a beast in search of
prey. When they had gone by I ran across to our rickyard to watch what
they would do. I expected they would draw up by the millpool, where gipsies often camp and where, as related at the outset, I once saw two gipsies
fight. But to my surprise and relief they kept on and on; the caravan disappeared over the hill, and I exclaimed, "Thank goodness, and may I never see
her face again."

But it was otherwise ordered, as I was soon to learn.

Next day when on the moor, I wondered to see smoke curling up from
the Funnel, as we call the deepest of the ancient tin workings. Yet I never
connected it with the gipsies. I put it down to an old antiquary fellow, who
haunted the moor and sometimes kindled a fire there, though never to my
knowing in that out-of-the-way spot. But that the sun was low I should have
gone to see, instead of hurrying on with my work fearful of the light failing
before it was done. And lucky it was that I did, for most of the cattle were
on the marshy waste beyond Hannibal's Coombe, their coats showing up
plainly in the lurid light.

The sun was down by the time I had accounted for the last head, but
bright blood-red streaks laced the clouds and a crimson afterglow suffused
the sky. On regaining the Galver I stood to gaze at the uncommon spectacle, and as I did so a voice behind said –

"A grand sky, is it not?"

"Zillah!" I exclaimed, as I turned, "whatever has brought you to this lonely, wild spot?"

"Lonely, wild spot? I love lonely, wild spots. As to what brings me here, cannot you guess?"

"I cannot, unless it be to fulfil your threat. But I do not mind what you say now, for I am to go to Loveday for her answer within a month, and my hope is that before the bilberry bells redden these slopes a second time, as the sun now reddens the sky, Loveday and I will be man and wife."

"I do not wonder you should think so: happier faces than yours and hers on Flora Day I have never seen, but . . ."

"Not another word," I exclaimed angrily.

"Do not fly into a passion," said she, dropping her voice: "I came not to cast a shadow on your happiness, but to tell you a pleasant secret. Yonder where the smoke rises is my camp. Come when your work is done; it is but a step to my tent, come and hear me sing what no Georgio's ears have heard, the love song of my tribe."

"Never," I replied, "I cannot do that."

"You are afraid; you think it would lead to trouble?"

"Yes, my character would be gone."

"Have no fear: there is no more virtuous, no purer people on this earth than the Romany."

"But people would talk, and I should be ruined."

"Then you will not come? Now listen, you shall come, because I will you to come."

"Do not be angry; I cannot bear to see a beautiful face disfigured by rage."

"Then you think me beautiful?"

"To be sure I do – very beautiful for a gipsy."

"For a gipsy! I see you take us for an inferior race, yet we raised temples and pyramids when your fathers lived in caves and set up these moorstones to their dead. Look at me!" said she, drawing herself to her full height, "do I appear to you to belong to a degenerate people?"

"No," I replied, awed by her dignified mien, "you look like a queen."

"Then you will come and let me sing to you?"

"I won't promise," I said.

Thereupon she took herself off, muttering angrily as if out of patience at the coldness with which I had met her advances. I had no wish to be rude, but how could I go without seeming false to Loveday? I regretted that I had not more flatly refused her invitation.

Next day at dinner mother said, "A gipsy woman came here just now for milk and cream, and to my astonishment she asked for you. Do you know anything about her?"

"Yes," I replied, "I came across her when on the round with master."

"I don't like the look of her," said mother, eyeing me narrowly; "she slinks along like a skulking vixen, and her eyes are full of evil. No good can come of her being on the moor; the sooner she is ordered off the better."

"That may be; at the same time I doubt whether master will do it. He had three head of cattle poisoned when he turned away the last lot."

"Well then, look to yourself, my son, or that woman will be your ruin."

"Oh! I will keep away."

"Is the man who drove the caravan on the moor with her?"

"I did not ask."

"Then you've spoken to her?"

"Yes, last night, on the Galver."

"You never told me. What did she say?"

"That trouble was in store for me about Loveday. At least, that is what she was going to say, when I stopped her."

"Most likely, and she the cause, if only you let her get round you. I had a feeling the moment I saw her in the caravan that she had come to torment us; now I am sure of it. My son, she is an evil spirit, tricked out with a beautiful face to lure men to their downfall. I beg and pray you to have nothing, nothing whatever to do with her."

"Never fear for me, mother. I shall take no notice of her."

"Do not be over confident, my son. I've seen stronger men than you led away."

Thus it was not unwarned that I faced the temptation.

On Monday night, just as I had done seeing to the horses, I heard the ting, ting of a lute, and the next minute a voice richer and fuller than any I had heard fell in with the accompaniment. The passion and the yearning the singer threw into her song were enough to stir a stone, and moved me as music had never done before. Fearing she would see the light, I blew out the candle, stole across the yard into the house and shut the door quietly behind me.

I said nothing to mother, but scarcely had I lit my pipe when she exclaimed, "Did you see a face at the window?"

"No, I saw nothing."

"Well, I thought I did, and what is more I thought it was the gipsy's, but there, it may have been fancy, for her face haunts me."

With that she pulled down the blind and – a thing she seldom did – bolted the door.

For a full week I saw neither the gipsy nor any smoke from her fire.

"She has taken herself off," I said to myself again and again, and one night after supper I went to the Funnel to make quite sure. She had not gone; and the moment I reached the edge of the pit she called up –

"So you have come at last, when my heart is weary with waiting for you."

"I came to see if you were still here, nothing more."

"And having come, you will hear me sing just one short song; you will not refuse me that?"

"Well, just a verse or two," I said, and made my way down to where she stood.

"Kindle the fire," said she, handing me flint and steel, "I'll be back in a twinkling."

When she returned the furze had blazed up, lighting the gold chain she had put around her swarthy neck and the gem stones in her raven-black hair. Seating herself beside me, she played and sang till I was like one bewitched and no longer master of my soul. I had been there perhaps half an hour, when a harsh, rasping voice called out –

"That's your game, is it, John Penrose, that's how you keep faith with Loveday Rosewarne? Ah! you low, two-faced villain, she shall hear of it."

I looked up, though I had recognised the voice. Felton's tall figure stood out black against the sky for a moment, and was withdrawn.

"Zillah," I exclaimed, jumping to my feet, "did you plot my ruin? Was this fire a signal to Felton to come and catch me?"

"John Penrose, I swear by this earth and by the sky above that I am guiltless of the treachery you suspect. I used my wiles to draw and keep you here, but I have never spoken to that man nor he to me."

"I believe you, I have only myself to blame."

I bid her goodnight and left her.

"John," she called out, "if you are in trouble, come back to me."

Her parting words sounded like the knell of my happiness. But mine was the fault, and on my way back it was myself I cursed, cursed for going to the Funnel, cursed for yielding when I got there.

I sat up late and wrote letter after letter only to tear them up; even by my own account I stood condemned. I thought of going to Loveday and telling her everything, but when morning came I shrank from the ordeal and decided to await the breaking of the storm. Oh, the agony of that week!

Then Johnny Curnow brought word that Andrew wanted to see me.

"Tell him," I replied, "that I will be at Forest Carn as soon as I can get away"; and by seven I was there. Andrew, who was pacing up and down as I entered, looked terribly agitated.

"You know why I have sent for you?" he began.

"Yes."

"Well now, tell me, is it true that thee'st got tangled up with that gipsy woman, and been goin' to her at night? As Loveday's grandfaither, I've been told to ask; and I've a right to know."

"Certainly you have; only this I beg, bear with me whilst I answer in my own way."

Whereupon I related all my dealings with the gipsy, from the time I met her on Tehidy Downs to the moment Felton surprised me sitting beside her.

"Well," he said, checking his steps, "I believe you; but it's an ugly story, even on your own tellin'. Just consider it: there you were in the Funnel Pit, nine o'clock at night, alone with this gipsy woman, and she tricked out in gimcracks and gewgaws singin' love songs to you. How do you think that Loveday, who you've pretended is the one and only girl in the world for you, can ever look at you again? What would you have thought had she gone to a gipsy man in like circumstances?"

"Don't, Andrew, don't," I cried out, "I own I was a weak fool, I admit that I should never have gone near; but believe me or not, no wrong came of it."

"I believe you, and in my letter to Honor I shall say so; but then, what could you have been thinkin' about to get into a position that is so hard to explain? And you would never have gone down and sat beside her had you thought Felton would see you .... You don't answer."

"No, I confess I should not."

"Ah, Jack, I fear that after all you are not the clean, fine fellow I have always taken you for."

There was no more to be said. I came away.

As I trod the road to Lanyon, there was not a more miserable man in Penwith. If ever a man's cup was full, mine was. Yet worse was to come. Jim the Pedlar brought the bad news a fortnight later.

"What's wrong," I asked as he hurried towards me, "that you must come here to me to Long Downs?"

"Pull up the horses and I'll tell you; though God knows I wish the errand had fallen to another's tongue."

"As quickly as you can, Jim."

"Well, yesterday on the road to Helston I dropped into the Falmouth Packet as I generally do, for a glass of beer; and there I found two Prussia Cove men engaged in a conversation that made me prick up my ears. Said the man on the far side of the fire, 'So she's going to marry Dickie Felton after all.'

"'That's what they're all saying, though where her eyes can be to take him before the fine upstanding chap that danced with her on Furry day is more than I can understand.'

"'That's the puzzle to my missus too, who has said all along she would take the curly-headed one and will have it she's marrying the boat-builder out of spite because the other has jilted her.'

"'I know nothing about that, only that the wedding is to be as soon as they can get called. Joan Oliver says the banns are to be put up on Sunday.'

"On hearing that, I tossed off my glass and came here straight away. Law, why take it like that? Don't give way. There's as good fish in the sea as ever came out of it."

"Jim," I replied, "take the horses in, see to them and tell mother not to wait supper."

CHAPTER XXX

TURNS POACHER

S A STRICKEN BEAST seeks the solitude, so in my trouble I betook myself to the Galver, where at my approach a buzzard rose and flew away, leaving me alone with the rocks. Yet not alone, inasmuch as I had for company the angry passions roused by the wrongs done me. I call them angry passions, but they were more like fiends, so dark and devilish was the revenge they counselled. They urged me to murder; that I should kill and do away with Felton; they pointed out the place where I could waylay and fire into him without risk of detection; they indicated the spot where I could hide the body and where nobody would dream of looking for it. They had nearly won me over when a voice whispered, "Remember that your enemy is Dickie's father, that his murder would haunt you to your grave."

Then the fiends were at me again; and when I turned on them and said, "I will not," they fell back, calling me fool and coward as they went. The fact was that I had sobered down. I reflected that Jim's story, though it fitted the situation, was, after all, public-house gossip – mere hearsay that might prove to be false. And if so, and if Felton's body was by that time sunk in the depths of the pond as the fiends had suggested, what then?

"No, no," I exclaimed, "nobody but a mad man would do away with him till satisfied that Jim's tale was true; I will at least wait till I know."

But he had poisoned Loveday against me, and must be made to suffer. I puzzled my brain as to how I could wound his feelings, and knowing that he valued the preserves as he valued his life, I decided to invade them, gun in hand, and work havoc with the pheasants he so dearly prized.

That night in the barn I set about my preparations: filled the powder-flask and shot-pouch, I tried the caps to make sure they fitted the nipple, I glued a white feather on the gun-barrel to help my aim; then, putting out the lantern and closing the shutters, I practised loading in the dark. There remained the charging of the blunderbuss, which I left to the last minute for fear of its going off.

My opportunity soon came; for on hearing next day, which was Wednesday, that the Squire's opening shoot was fixed for Thursday I

215

resolved, despite the storm that was raging, to go that very night.

Black clouds, driven by a nor'westerly gale, were scudding across the moon when I set out on my desperate errand. For fear that master might see me, I did not leave the yard by the gate, but stole under shelter of the mowhay wall to Barn Field and, crossing the road near the Quoit, made my way through the brake and up athirt Bosiliack Downs, so as to come in on the Forest Carn from the farther side. I did this because I knew the pheasants would be roosting there out of the eye of the wind.

The moment I reached the wood, I got to work examining pine after pine, where I could get them against the moon. At the fifth tree I sighted a pheasant, took aim and brought it down. This and three others which I soon secured, I put in my big inside pocket, removing the blunderbuss to make room for them.

Part of the wood had been wrecked by the equinoctial gales; and when I came to this I had no little difficulty in crossing the fallen timber, encumbered as I was with the gun in one hand and the blunderbuss in the other; but I managed it without mishap, and after laying the blunderbuss on the ground, was soon busy picking off the birds in the trees beyond. Here in the heart of the wood I met with wonderful good luck; but in the excitement I lost my bearings, and when it came to recovering the blunderbuss I could not find it anywhere. In a fever of anxiety I searched on hand and knees, and was about to despair when my fingers lighted on the cold brass barrel; the feel of which at once made me happy again.

This unpleasant experience decided me to discharge the weapon forthwith. I chose the spot where the Squire generally took his stand when shooting the wood, because from there the ride in the direction of Sunny Corner was almost in the form of a funnel and would allow free vent to the explosion. For it was part of my plan that the report should reach the ears of Felton and draw him away from the Sanctuary Wood, which was my main objective. To fire the blunderbuss with its heavy charge of powder, marbles and broken ox cues, from the shoulder, would be looking for trouble; so I laid it on the ground with the muzzle towards Sunny Corner, and to give it the proper tilt, propped up the barrel with fir-cones, then getting out flint and steel, I lighted the tinder, and from it a finger of touchwood, whose glowing tip I applied to the powder in the priming pan.

The noise of the discharge was enough to waken the dead; it shook the forest, and would have shaken Andrew, had he not been at the King's Arms.

The thought of the old man and of Loveday brought it forcibly home to me that I was an outcast committed to a course that might end in transportation. But what did it matter? I had begun: I would go on.

Picking up the blunderbuss, I went to Andrew's garden and concealed the weapon and pheasants in a rabbit sett, blocking the holes with turves from the rick to keep out the foxes. Then I crossed the road to the Carn where I hid amongst the rocks, waiting to see Felton go by before I ventured into Sanctuary Wood. The wind moaning about the Carn drowned, for the most part, all sound; but in a lull I heard the beat of the keeper's footsteps, and as if of their own accord my fingers gripped the gun. It was well for him that I did not know all, for I had got him against the sky, and had but to press the trigger to have my revenge, and no one the wiser. But I had resolved against such measures and let him pass.

When he had gone by I hurried down the slope and, leaving Boutz-an-Gaverne earth to my left, made across the hummocky ground to the Hollow Tree. I hoped to find birds in the scattered pines but saw nothing till, on searching the trees around the Upper Pond, I espied a bird near the tip of a long branch, all open to the sky, affording a most tempting shot. I shouldered the gun and pulled the trigger, but without any result; the bird never as much as raised its head. Then it dawned upon me that I was wasting powder and shot on a dummy, and it vexed me to think how Felton would chuckle on finding the decoy riddled.

I had but poor success in Sanctuary Wood, getting only three pheasants where I had hoped for half a score. But in my violent mood it was good to be there, with the great trees heaving and tossing like an angry sea, and the wind hissing like furies in the tops.

Now and again when the moon rode clear, it was a fine sight to catch the crowns of the pines and the naked limbs of oak and beech against the sky; grand to behold the play of light in the roughened surface of the pond, weird to witness the shadows come and go in the woodland rides.

Thus it happened that I was so taken up by the wild, almost tempestuous surroundings, that I gave scarcely a thought to Felton, until I had left the Lower Pond and leapt the hedge to the home plantation: then I kept a sharp look-out. At every shot I expected to see him come running up, but never a sign. This emboldened me to go right up to the Mansion, where I brought down a bird from the branch that stretched across the Terrace almost to the Squire's window. It was my last.

Scarcely had I picked it up when I tripped over a wire which fired an alarm-gun. The tremendous report had scarcely died before a bell clanged out, followed by shouts from the stable yard. As fast as I could lay foot to ground I made for the North Lodge, scrambled over a stone wall, and ran towards the Carn. I had got within a couple of hundred yards when I saw Felton coming like the wind – but not before he had seen me. Then began a race, he on the upper, I on the lower side of the strip of furze which separated us.

"Stop," he kept crying out, "I know you; stop, or it will be the worse for you."

He was a fool to waste his breath: as well might a huntsman have cried "Stop" to a fox. The pheasants hampered me; but it would take a few seconds to disencumber myself, and I had not a single second to spare. The moment I sighted the Carn – how huge it loomed! – I quickened my pace in an attempt to pass it ahead of my pursuer and be the first to gain the rocks beyond. There I hoped to elude him. Despite my utmost efforts, it was only by a few strides that I led along the foot of the Carn's precipitous face, only by a few strides that I reached the scattered boulders, in and out of which I wound at a frantic pace before plunging into a clump of furze, where I lay wondering whether I had thrown him off.

Presently I saw him come round an outlying rock and gaze all agog, like a greyhound that has lost sight of a hare.

Finding no sign of me, he concluded that I must be in the furze, which he approached in leisurely fashion as if he felt sure of his captive. While I watched him draw near, I swore to myself that, rather than be taken, I would fight to the death. I expected he would fire the furze; instead, he began trampling it out, driving me before him till only a few yards remained to the edge towards which he was working. I was in two minds whether to rise and confront him or to try and break back. I chose the latter, worming my way past him and missing his feet by inches.

On coming to the end, he snarled out, "The young scoundrel has beaten me again, but I'll see him transported yet."

Thereupon he withdrew to the Carn; and the moment he had passed from view I crawled away through a patch of fern, gained the ditch of a gurgoe, and so reached the rab-pit, where I intended to hide the game before making for home. I had only just entered the cave there when Felton, in his mad haste to reach Lanyon and apprehend me on my arrival, tore past at what – considering the gale in his teeth – was an astonishing pace. This decided me to dispose of the game forthwith: so fetching the birds from Andrew's garden, I made for the lonely cottage on Boswarthen Moor, where lived the receiver of poached game.

I found him seated by the fire with a nearly emptied bottle of brandy on the table beside him, yet able, fuddled though he was, to count the birds and the six florins which he handed me in exchange. He pressed me to drink and seemed vexed that I refused; but I did not want his brandy and, to tell the truth, I disliked taking his money. But there, once you set out on an evil course, the Devil alone knows where it will lead you.

On leaving the frowsy den, I made for Ding Dong, where I hid the money at the foot of a waste heap, and marked its position with two bits of spar, so as to know where to find it. Then I fetched round by Further North, and reached the cottage by the secret passage.

"There is somebody outside," whispered mother as I came through the trap; "twice there has been a knock at the door and just now the latch was lifted. There it is again."

"Hush, mother! 'Tes Felton!"

At that she dropped on her knees and buried her face in her hands.

"Don't be troubled, mother; I had to go poaching or go mad. I shall be better after this."

"Promise me you will not go out to him."

"I won't go out, I'll speak to him out of your window."

So I crept upstairs, flung off my cap and jacket, threw up the window and called out, "What do you want?"

Again he was dumbfounded and took himself off without a word. But this time his suspicion was aroused; for he was back next morning, spent a good hour searching the rickyard for a secret way to the cottage and, failing, went away baulked but unconvinced.

CHAPTER XXXI

IN A QUANDARY

❦

T HE EXCITEMENT of the poaching soon wore off, leaving me as reckless and as sullen as ever. For a time mother bore with me; but one
morning at breakfast, driven beyond endurance, she broke out.

"Why ever don't you say what it is, instead of sitting there glum, and
going about your work like a bear with a sore head? If only you would
confide in me, I might help you."

"You were at Andrew's last night?"

"I was."

"And he told you everything?"

"He told me that Felton went to Prussia Cove after he had found you
with the gipsy girl."

"Felton went there, did he?"

"The very next morning."

"And with his viper's tongue poisoned Loveday and her mother against
me, so as to get me thrust on one side, and make it easy for Dickie to marry
Loveday. Felton is at the bottom of all the trouble and of all the talk. Did Jim
tell you what he overheard in the Inn?"

"He did."

"And about the banns?"

"Yes, and a lot more prittle prattle; but you don't believe it, I hope?"

"I do."

"Then I understand why you have been going about like a wild man and
coming in at all hours. Ah, my son, if you had only let me know of your
trouble! and I'm myself to blame in not speaking before. But there, the
question is, what can be done now? Have you never thought of going to
Prussia Cove to clear the matter up with Loveday and her mother?"

"A thousand times."

"Then why haven't you gone?"

"Don't torment me, mother. Supposing for a minute I did go, and
Mrs. Rosewarne asked me, as she would, whether I was alone with the
gipsy, what could she think when I confessed? And how can I face
Loveday with a story like that? Why, she ran in like one shamed when

I gave her a single kiss, and that on her cheek! Could I look her in the eyes with this ugly thing in our minds? Would she ever look at me at all? The chances are that she would run upstairs or take to the cliffs till I had gone."

"Ah, my dear son, if only you understood woman, you would not talk like that. No woman throws a man over in his hour of trial if she loves him, as I am convinced Loveday loves you. She will rather go through fire and flood to save him."

"You would, mother; but Loveday is only a girl – and you see, I've vexed her past amends."

With that I left the table and went to field with the horses. On the road I met Andrew and pulled up, never doubting he would stop and at least pass the time of day. But he held on as though he had not seen me; and how I felt about it I can't put into words. Then, just when I was at my worst, an evil chance offered; and had the devil arranged it, it could not have come more pat to my black mood. I had perhaps gone the length of the field and back half a dozen times when Geordie and Zillah came driving along the road, pulled up at the hedge and beckoned to me. I held up my hand as a sign that I had seen them; and after tying the horses up to a furze bush walked towards them. As I crossed the upturned ground I felt like a bad spirit going to meet two others no better than itself.

"You shouldn't have kept us waiting," said Geordie rather sharply, "we've driven all the way from Hayle Kimbra on purpose to see you and are in a hurry to get back."

"I don't see how I was to know that, any more than I know why you've come."

"That is soon told, I want you to go with me on Saturday night."

"Where and what for?"

"Bless the lad! if you will give me time to get the words out, I'll tell you. I'm going to poach yon preserves, if you will join me. Will you come?"

"I will."

"Your hand on it."

"I knew you could depend on Jack," said Zillah, smiling as we shook hands.

"Be at the camp by eight o'clock; meanwhile mum's the word."

"I will be there."

With that he turned the pony's head and drove away in the direction he had come.

About half an hour later, rather less than more, who to my amazement should pass but mother and Miss Jenifer in the trap, with Andrew driving.

"Wherever can they be going?" I asked myself as I watched them out of sight.

"To Prussia Cove to try and smooth things over," came the answer. And I had no more doubt of it than that their going was the outcome of a sudden resolve formed since breakfast, probably as the result of a conference in the big house.

At dinner time I found a note left by mother on my platter –

"I shall be away till night, and if I'm not back in time, you are to go across to the big house to supper."

Over the meal, I pictured the kitchen at Prussia Cove with mother, Miss Jenifer and Andrew, all speaking up for me: mother calling Loveday downstairs, taking her into the garden or perhaps along the cliffs, and pleading with her in language no living soul could resist.

I found comfort in rehearsing these things: but when supper time came and mother had not returned, I hadn't the courage to go across, and even now I do not wonder at it. For how could I be expected to sit at the same table with master and missus and they knowing I had been caught on the moor with the gipsy? It is possible that one here and there might have done it but, at all events, I hadn't the face.

Between eight and nine I went up the road, where I laid ear to ground listening for the trap. For a long time I heard nothing but the faint patter of some creature's pads as it crossed from the brake to Nearer Pokess; then I caught the rumbling of wheels, the sharp beat of Snowball's hoofs, and soon the voices of the little party: mother taking the treble, Miss Jenifer the seconds, and Andrew the bass. For they were singing, and of all songs – "Shall Trelawny die?"

"They've made it all right," thought I, and then and there, between the Quoit and the Trucks, on a spot I could point out, I leapt for joy; for, as it seems to me looking back, that was one of the most thrilling moments of my life. They sang right up to the iron gate whither I had run to await them. I held Snowball's head whilst master, who had come out, helped mother and Miss Jenifer to alight.

"You see we've returned in the best of spirits, Jack," said Miss Jenifer.

"Mother will give you an account of the day's outing. But be sure and see to Snowball."

"That I will, Miss; 'tes a bravish journey to Prussia Cove and back."

"To where?"

"To Prussia Cove, Miss."

"Ah, Jack, you are sharper than I took you for; goodnight."

On going indoors, mother said, "Well, my dear, how did you get on without me?"

"Never mind that, mother, tell me how you got on?"

"Almost better than I expected. You remember what I said about a woman when she loves a man?"

"You said she would go through fire and flood if need be to save him."

"I did."

"Then Loveday stood by me?"

"It would not be fair to say what passed between her and me, but I am free to tell you that there wasn't a word of truth in what Jim overheard."

"You don't say so?"

"Nothing but idle gossip."

"Well, well! You've no message from Loveday?"

"No, there was no need; she is coming to Forest Carn for Feast Day."

"Do you mean it?"

"I do."

"Then it's all right, mother?"

"Yes, you great ninny, and now give me a kiss, and for the future come to me with your troubles."

So I kissed her, as I did again later before she went up to bed.

"One thing I have forgotten," she called down from the top of the stairs, "Andrew wished me to say he was sorry for having given you the go-by this morning."

"I am more than glad to hear that," I replied.

I sat up smoking and thinking over the events of the day. I was beside myself with joy at the turn things had taken, and but for having given my word to Geordie, I should have been the happiest of men. Now that I knew that Loveday stood by me, I was resolved at all costs to have nothing more to do with the gipsies except to let them know that I should not keep my promise.

Day after day I kept a look-out for their fire; and when Friday had gone by without a sign, I began to hope that something had caused them to change their plans. No such luck! Between four and five on Saturday afternoon when I was out fetching faggots, there was the smoke. Knowing that the longer I thought about going, the less I should like it, I dropped the pitch-fork I carried, and started off there and then on my unpleasant errand.

On reaching the pit, I found Geordie and Zillah seated on the ground mending a net. Between them and the fire lay the panther with, by my life! a small lantern strapped to his neck.

"Welcome, brother," said Geordie, "you're in time to lend a hand with the preparations."

"I've come to tell you I can't go."

"Can't go, eh? Is a heifer or the piggywidden took bad, or has a mabyer got the pip that you cry off at the last minute? Do you think I can work this" – here he held up the net – "single-handed?"

Then altering his tone, he said smilingly, "Jack, you're only playing with me; of all the men I know you are the last to go back on your word and leave a pal in the lurch."

"I mean what I say; I can't go with you."

"You don't say why."

"I can't tell you that."

"But I can," said Zillah, bitterly. "His girl has come. That was she we passed on Madron Hill with the old earth-stopper; and that is why he has broken his pledge. But never mind, Geordie, he shan't wreck your plans, for I will take his place." Then springing to her feet she hissed out, "Be gone, false one, be gone and smarten yourself for my rival!"

"You have no right to say that," I replied hotly.

"No right? when you came to my fire and listened to song after song; no right? when you praised my beauty and would have been my slave if Felton had not stung you to your senses."

"No, none," I replied, as I turned and left them.

Geordie said no more; but Zillah called after me, "John Penrose, I never forget or forgive."

CHAPTER XXXII

A GUILTY
CONSCIENCE

🔊

T HOUGH I WAS glad to be free shame made me shrink from meeting
Loveday. I dawdled over my work, and took so long in changing
that mother at last called up –

"Jack, the clock is on the stroke of eight; you are never too shame-faced
to go to Forest Carn, are you?" As I did not reply, she called up again, "Do
you hear what I say?"

"Yes, I hear, mother," adding as I came downstairs, "Yes, but I don't feel
I can face Loveday alone. Come with me, there's a dear."

At that she put on her bonnet and shawl, tucked the box of dominoes
under her arm, and said, "Come along, my innocent, I understand how
you feel."

On the road to Forest Carn I kept trying to throw off my shyness, so as
to appear before Loveday as my usual, natural self; but it would have been
better if I had not tried, as it only made me more self-conscious and
uncomfortable than before.

"You go in first," I whispered as we went up the garden path, "and for
pity's sake keep the conversation going, or we shall rue having come."

Loveday came forward, kissed mother affectionately, and shook hands
as heartily as ever with me. Andrew's welcome, "I'm glad to see 'ee both,"
was in his cheeriest voice, and if greetings could have made me feel at my
ease these would. But I was in such a state they were lost upon me. Oh! the
curse of a guilty conscience!

Whilst I was at my worst, however, mother was at her best. To see the
free and easy way she chatted with Loveday without once looking across at
Andrew and me, one would never have dreamt that an ugly incident was, as
I felt sure, uppermost in her mind. Loveday, too, seemed equally free from
its baleful influence. I say again that women are cleverer play-actors than
men; and any one who, like the magpie in the cage, could have been in that
kitchen to witness the difference between mother and Loveday on the one
hand, and Andrew and me on the other, would say so too.

225

Andrew, instead of talking freely as usual, sat with never a word, fitting a new plug to his tinder-box, seemingly engrossed in his occupation, which all the time was only an excuse for keeping his head down and hiding the shame he felt on my account; and while I sat watching him chip off a bit, now here, now there, I was haunted by a vision of myself seated close beside the bedizened gipsy, listening to her love songs. I suffered agonies of shame and remorse; and the moment the conversation between mother and Loveday began to flag, I wished that the earth would open and swallow me up. In the silence that fell, mother turned to Andrew and said, "What do you say to a game of dominoes?"

"The very thing, Mary, hand here the box."

Whereupon he put the knife in his pocket, brushed away the chips, emptied the dominoes on the table, turned face down those which were the wrong way up, shuffled, and by the time we had settled in our places, counted out nine each. "Anybody got double nine?" he asked, as soon as we had set them up on end. "Double eight?" Nobody making a sign, mother put out double seven with another to follow. Then the game proceeded, mother doing most of the drawing, though Andrew and I, in this respect, were not far behind her. There was only one domino left in the pool when Loveday, playing double blank, exclaimed, "I'm out!"

Just then the door opened and Dickie walked in, carrying a little boat which, with its supporting cradle, he put down in front of her. It was a wonderful bit of work, a model of the fishing-boat *Mystery*, then, as all West Cornwall knew, being fitted out at Newlyn for a voyage to Australia.

Whilst we were admiring it, Dickie turned to Loveday and said feelingly, "I made it for you, and beg your acceptance of it."

"It is most kind of you, Dickie, to have gone to all this trouble; but I do not think I ought to accept such a valuable gift."

"Why valuable?" he asked, in a voice that betrayed the disappointment he felt. "It cost me nothing but my spare time, and was a work of love if ever there was one."

"Granfer, what do you think?"

"Well, my dear, I hardly know what to say; but after the trouble Dickie has been to, it would seem ungracious to refuse it."

With that Loveday got up and said, "Dickie, I thank you very, very much. It is a beautiful present. I love boats and adventures; no gift would have given me greater pleasure."

It made me as jealous as fire to hear her speak with such warmth; but it pleased Dickie, whose face lighted up like a field when a cloud has passed over the sun.

"Sit yourself down," said Andrew, looking up at Dickie, "and tell me all about the *Mystery*; I'm as much interested in her as any Newlyn man."

"Well, Andrew, she measures thirty feet from stem to stern, and has a twelve-foot beam."

"That is to say, she's thirty foot long and twelve foot broad amidships?"

"Yes."

"A small craft to cross twelve thousand miles of ocean."

"True, but then she is well found."

"Tell me."

"She has been fresh caulked and tarred; she is sheathed in zinc as a protection against barnacles; she carries spare spars and sails and – to help her ride out the gales – a storm anchor."

"What if food and water give out?"

"In that case we shall look to the homeward-bound ships for supplies."

"How many hands?"

"Seven."

"And you are going as boat's carpenter?"

"I expect so: there is only one thing that would prevent me."

"You mean if somebody said, 'Don't go,' then you wouldn't?"

"Well, Andrew, excuse me if I fight shy of answering such a delicate question."

Here Loveday rushed across to the dresser, and was so long rearranging the cups and saucers that she was still there when Dickie said –

"I must be leaving now, Andrew, though not before I have given mother's message. She told me to say that she will be delighted to see you and Loveday to tea goodnight. She will expect you about four."

"I am sorry, Dickie, but we have promised to go to Mrs. Penrose."

"I am sorry too, very sorry; but our loss will be Mrs. Penrose's gain. Good night to you all."

With that he left, closing the door and the garden gate quietly behind him.

Then mother put on her bonnet, wrapped her shawl about her, and said,

"Come, Jack, it's past ten; we are keeping Andrew and Loveday up."

"Just one word before you go, Mary," said Andrew, rising from his chair; "I caan't keep it back. I want Jack to understand that the past is buried and done with – edn't it, Loveday?"

For answer she rushed into mother's arms, kissed her and ran upstairs.

"You see, Jack," said Andrew, "the trouble thee'st caused by goin' to that gipsy. Let it be a lesson to 'ee."

"No fear of that, Andrew. What I've suffered no tongue can tell."

From the gate he called after us, "We shall come in our stopping clothes tomorrow, Mary," and "highest spirits," mother answered back.

Then we were alone with the stars.

"Well, my dear, we managed to get through the evening."

"You managed it, mother – you and the dominoes. I couldn't have told you had anything on your mind."

"Perhaps not, though the trouble was present to me all the time. I'm thankful Andrew spoke as he did; it was painful, but it cleared the air. Now, as Mr. Tasker once advised you, let us raise our eyes and behold the splendour of the heavens."

Whereupon she pointed out the stars and constellations, and as we descended Paunshallow Hill quoted a verse of a favourite hymn: –

> "Soon as the evening shades prevail,
> The moon takes up the wondrous tale,
> And nightly to the listening earth
> Proclaims the story of her birth,
> Whilst all the stars that round her burn,
> And all the planets in their turn,
> Proclaim the tidings as they roll,
> And spread the truth from pole to pole."

She had scarcely finished when from the valley came shouts followed by two shots, then more shouts, then sounds of strife, that at last died away to silence.

"Poachers!" whispered mother, catching her breath.

"It's Geordie, the gipsy."

"How do you know?"

"I'd arranged to go with him, and should have gone if Loveday had not come."

"Then God be praised!"

We walked on without speaking till near the Quoit, when mother plucked my sleeve, and said, "Did you see somebody cross the road?"

"I did; it was the gipsy woman."

"And what's that light crossing it now?"

"A lantern on the neck of her panther!"

❦

CHAPTER XXXIII

A GHOST STORY
❧

F EAST NIGHT '48 WOULD STAND well out amongst Feast Nights in my
memory, because Andrew and Loveday spent it with us; even if
there had been no other incidents to make it memorable.

The evening opened pleasantly with our little party of four gathered
round the table, enjoying the good things which mother had provided.
Every one was in the best of spirits as the conversation showed; once only,
and then but momentarily, did the gipsy come into my mind. When tea was
over and we had smoked a pipe I asked Andrew to come with me on my
round of the houses.

"Delighted, Jack," he replied; "I dearly love seein' the animals enjoy their
food. Besides, the kitchen is no place for a man whilst the tea things are
bein' put away and the fire made up for the evenin'."

As we crossed the yard he came to a sudden stand and, looking up at the
sky, said, "What a grand night to be sure! I don't know when I've seen the
stars so bright."

"Nor me, Andrew. Just look at the Bear, the Twins, and the belt
of Orion."

"I caan't call them by name like you, Jack; but I know them by sight as
well as I know the faces in Penzance, perhaps better."

"No wonder, Andrew; they've meant much to you."

"Iss, Jack, a great deal more than to most people; think of the
winter nights they've lighted for me, and what they've been in the way
of company. I misdoubt whether I could have kept goin' all these years
without 'em."

In the shed he leant against the wall and watched the cows pull the hay
out of the racks, seeming to enjoy the sight ever as much as Bill used to
enjoy standing outside the stable, listening to the horses munch their corn.
From the cow-shed we went to the corral, where, on coming to the end stall,
I held up the lantern that he might see the robin that roosted above the head
of a white steer.

"Do it always perch theere?"

"Yes, ever since the bullocks were housed."

"What do 'ee think? Is it a case of comradeship?"

"I think so; leastways that's how I've got to look upon it."

When we went indoors we found mother and Loveday knitting before a cheerful fire; and as Andrew settled himself in the arm-chair that had been drawn up for him and started filling his pipe, I felt that we were going to spend an interesting evening. And it proved far and away more interesting than I expected, because of an incident that no one of us could have foreseen.

Between eight and nine o'clock Andrew was leaning forward to knock the ashes out of his pipe when there came the old rumbling noise, which we had not once heard since the time it had caused us so much anxiety.

"Hark!" exclaimed Andrew. "That's surely a badger moving about under the dairy."

"Bravo, Andrew! you've hit it straight off."

"Then thee dost knaw, Jack?"

"He does, Andrew," interrupted mother, "and I'm more than sorry now that we did not call you in at first. But in that I'm hardly to blame; it was master who from the beginning was against anything being said; and when we discovered that a badger was the cause of the trouble, enjoined silence lest Lanyon should get a bad name."

"But how could a badger give Lanyon a bad name?"

"You're right there, Andrew, I haven't explained myself properly; it wasn't the badger, but the finding of a secret passage that weighed with master."

"Secret passage or not, master needn't have been afeard of lettin' me know; I'm no leaky basket."

"Certainly not, Andrew; and if you care to hear the story, Jack will tell you."

"Care to hear, Mary? I'm daggin' to hear."

Whereupon I told everything; the hearing of the noise night after night, the consternation it caused, the badger in the Bartons, the finding of the secret passage and the cave to which it led.

"Well, well!" exclaimed Andrew, who had listened open-mouthed to the end, "that beats all I ever did hear; and the badger was a white one, white all over?"

"Yes, as white as the steer in the corral."

"Thee'rt certain sure?"

"Sure as that I am here sitting beside Loveday."

"Then I'll be bound that that was the wisht old thing that skeared me out of my seven senses one pitch dark night at Boundary Pool."

"At Boundary Pool?"

"Iss, Mary, bless your life, it was crossing the river, and if you please, by my steppin' stones." Then after a pause, "And to think theere's a drive all the way from the tatie garden to the cottage and me never know of it till now! That clears up a mystery which has puzzled longer heads than mine."

"What is that?"

"Why, the escape of Jack's granfer from the Press Gang. Surely Rechard must have told you how when the gang failed to find him upstairs and down, they got a ladder from the mowhay, set it against the house, and drove their cutlasses into the thatch in the full belief that he was hiding theere. You never heeard that?"

"No; Richard was very silent about his young days."

"Hark! theere's the badger again stretchin' his legs before goin' on his beat; though how he knaws it's time to be stirrin' is more nor I can tell. It's quiet again, or maybe the crittur is on the way out. I've most a mind to run down to the Bartons for a glimpse of 'un. But no, I've a long tramp before me, and I'm loth to leave the fire."

So he lighted his pipe again and went on, "The night Jack's granfer escaped, old Mr. Pearce, muster-master though he was, rang the alarm with his own hand; but as bad luck would have it, the wind drowned the bell, so that five Morvah men were taken in their beds. That was a tarble time, men hidin' in mines, adits, caves, whilst quite a number took to the fursse braakes. I carried food to three tin-streamers who hid in Quoit Croft till Sam Leggo – one of them – was seized with a bad cough; then they betook them to the cave of the fogou in Hannibal's Coombe, wheere Sam could cough without bein' overheard."

"Why weren't you pressed, granfer?"

"I've always supposed it was because I was reckoned more useful at home than beatin' about the seas or killin' Frenchmen."

"You mean as one of the Mount's Bay Yeomanry?"

"No, I don't; it wasn't because I was a yellow-hammer or a dishwasher as they nicknamed us 'because of our facin's; it was because the old Squire and his friends would have gone melancholy mad without me."

"I'm afraid I'm very stupid, granfer, but I don't understand now."

"You will when I tell you that a good run with hounds is the very salt of life to the aristocracy; and that a good run depends upon good stoppin'."

"I see now, the press gang got word from the old Squire not to press you; that was it, was it not?"

"Now thee'rt askin' a question, my dear; as well ask why thy own faither was not exchequered after the affair of Helford river, and when a price had been put on his head. All I can tell 'ee is, theere's wheels within wheels; and that people in exalted stations are hearkened to when a man low down would be kicked to doors."

"Supposing that he did beg you off, there is this to be said for the old Squire, he would have found it next to impossible to fill your place. It isn't every one who knows the earths in half a score parishes, or who has got the nerve to be abroad at night in all weathers over a haunted country-side."

"Thee'rt right there, Mary; one night with the hags and witches at Carn Kenidzhek, or a night at Bosprennis Splosh with the phantom hounds, above all a night along the Land's End cliffs with the drowned sailors hailin' one another would be more than enough for most people. Ah, Mary, an earthstopper's life is as tryin' a life as I knaw; and those who think slight of me for droppin' in eearly at kiddlewinks, little dream what I've been through the night before."

"No wonder your hair turned white so early."

"Iss, white as snow, Mary, before I was fifty."

"And very becoming it is, granfer; and now won't you tell us a ghost story, a real ghost story; it's Feast Night remember; and we've a right to call for one."

"Well, my dear, ten o'clock is rather early for a ghost story, but I'll do my best."

"Get a faggot or two handy, Jack," said mother, "something tells me we shall need them before Andrew has done."

"Maybe you'll be glad of a bit of a blaze by then, for I've somethin' I've been wantin' to get off my mind this long time, and unless told now, it may never be told at all."

After thinking a minute or two, he began: "My mate for many years, as you may have heeard, was Tom Hal, of the same havage as Billy that haunts the Bottoms. Well, Tom and me worked the country between us, he the east'ard side, I the west'ard; and never in company except when the Land's

End cliffs had to be stopped; then we went together."

"I've heard the Land's End cliffs are dangerous."

"Not partic'ler, Mary, not more so than the cliffs I'm stoppin' tonight; twadn't for that we welcomed company, 'twas because of the drownded sailors hailin' one another; their cries when the wind is in from over the saa bein' more than flesh and blood can stand. The night of my story, which was Christmas, years afore Loveday was born, we were stoppin' the Land's End cliffs, so I was to call for Tom. I left Forest Carn betimes to reach the cliffs by midnight, allowin' for haa'f an hour or so at Tom's for a pipe before startin' out. Churchtown was makin' merry when I went through, but I noticed that Jim hadn't lit the lanterns on the Tower, owin' no doubt to the gale that was blowin'. My way led past Nanteglos shute and the lodge gates to Boswednan Hill and Tremethick Cross, where Tom lived opposite the toll-house.

"On comin' in sight of the cottage, I wondered at there bein' no glim of a fire nor any light except in the upper window, but without thinkin' theere was aught amiss, till I lifted the latch and put my head in. Then I knew something was very wrong."

"How, granfer?"

"How, my dear? why Janie, Tom's wife, was sobbin' as if her heart would break.

"'Whatever is wrong?' I called up.

"An'rew, An'rew, my dear man is lyin' dead. He passed away an hour agone, mutterin' about you and the cliffs to the last.'

"'Never dead?'

"'Yes. He caught a chill on a chill, and was gone in no time. Come up, won't ' ee? I know he would like you to look upon him.'

"My old mate was white as alabaster; the hands that had stopped so many earths lay crossed on the sheet, the lids with their black lashes closed on the eyes that had been quick to ball a fox, spy a hare, mark a snipe or cock. My life seemed to go out of me as I gazed upon him, the sight shocked me so."

"What did you say to Janie, granfer?"

"'Twas little enough, and when I'd got through the few words of comfort I could lay my tongue to, I tiptoed out of the room, leavin' the poor woman kneelin' theere alone with the dead. Some have found fault with me for not stayin'; found fault did I say? Why, they could not have gone on

234

worse if I had been a hard, unfeelin' brute; which I trust I never have been. But then they overlooked one thing, one all-important thing, that the eearths had to be stopped.

"I crossed the river at Skimiel Bridge, passed Sancreed Church, and comin' to Lower Leah struck across the field for Buryan Churchtown. Theere too I found the people keepin' Christmas up, and not a soul to doors. I was most tempted to drop in at Nickey Berryman's; twice I sidled forth and back before the door, but in the end I did not go in, lest my face should betray the fear I felt, and word get round that my narve was no longer equal to my work. On the open road beyond the village the gale had me at its mercy; but I held on in the teeth of it, and in course of time reached Treen, wheere the folk were just as merry as in the Churchtowns. As these few housen weere almost the last human habitations on the beat, I felt more than ever inclined to knock at a door, but again I bethought me of my good name, and leavin' the hamlet behind me, held on across the three fields that lay between me and the cliffs.

"In the lewth of the laast hedge, I lit the lantern, called Vennie to heel, and then made over the cliff land for Treen Dinas. The saa lashed the win'ard side of the neck connectin' the headland with the mainland, the wind screeched about the great castle of rocks; but I did my work, recrossed the neck, and held along the cliff. On, on I went, past Porthcurnow Cove, past St. Levan Church to Porthgwarrah, where I turned aside and stopped the big sett under Roskestals.

"Then the stretch lay before me that Tom and I dreaded most: theere was not a 'preventive' cabin nor even the light of a lighthouse, nothing friendlier than the bell on the Rundle Stone. Between the gusts I could hear it tollin', and mingled with its dismal sound came the blood-curdlin' cries of the drownded sailors. Then the bitch started whinin' – a thing she hardly ever does – and the next minit I felt that Tom was by my side. To take my thoughts off him, I called to mind the things on which I loved to dwell: my meetin' with Martha at Corpus Christi Fair, our company keepin', our weddin' day and goin' home to Forest Carn. But 'twas no use: the feelin' that Tom was theere on the side he always walked was stronger than ever. Next I stopped to light my pipe, so as to give 'un a chance to go on ahead; but again 'twas no use. He waited; and when I moved on, theere he was keepin' step for step as he had done ever since he came back from the wars, till at laast when we were touchin' Bosistow eearths I felt he had gone.

"These Bosistow eearths are just an ordinary cliff sett, with nothin' peculiar about 'em except that at one place, on the side near the sea, the ground, from long underminin' by badgers, has caved in like the sand on the upper part of an hour-glass. Tom and me had christened it by the name of the Funnel, and the hole at the bottom the Funnel-hole. Now it chaanced that I left the Funnel-hole till laast; and haalf an hour might have passed from the time I started stoppin' the sett before I made for it, wonderin' as I went what had become of Tom. I was soon to know; for on reachin' the pit's edge and lookin' down – I saw him at the bottom with a lantern to light him, kneelin' to stop the eearth just as he had done in life."

Andrew had scarcely uttered the word "life," when he turned deadly pale and went off in a faint.

"Quick, Jack! run across for some brandy," cried mother, as she started beating the palm of his right hand; and off I ran.

By the time I returned, Andrew was coming to; and after he had swallowed the brandy I had brought, he said, "It's nawthin', only a little qualm; I shall be mysel' in a minit or two."

Presently he got up, looked at the clock and said, "Loveday, it's high time we started."

"You shall not go stopping this night," exclaimed mother, firmly, "'tis madness to speak of such a thing."

"No, granfer dear, you mustn't think of it: I know the ground, I'll go."

"Thee'd never manage the cliff eearths: more like than not thee'd drop into the boil of the sea and never be heeard of again; I must go."

"You shall not go, Andrew," I said, "and Loveday shall not go alone: if the earths must be stopped, I insist on going with her."

At this Loveday looked at mother as if asking whether she should accept my company; and so mother understood it, for she answered, "Yes, my dear, by all means, why ever not?"

"I know what is passing through Loveday's mind, mother: she's afraid she will have difficulty in getting me along."

Then, smiling, Loveday put on her hat and jacket, lit the lantern, kissed the old man, and said, "Come along, Vennie."

But the terrier, instead of going to her call, looked up at Andrew with head on one side and ear cocked.

" 'Iss, my beauty, 'tes all right, go along with them and do your work as if I were theere; thy maister is about done."

So she rose, shook herself; and followed us out.

CHAPTER XXXIV

A NIGHT ON
THE MOOR

ᴥᵴ

O UR WAY LED PAST the great reed-bed to Men Scryfa Downs where, as we crossed the Barrows, I caught sight of the glow of the gipsy's fire, but said never a word of it for fear of arousing painful memories. Ahead of us the Galver rose boldly against the sky, from whose blue depths the stars kept watch over the slumbering earth. The stillness was profound; the sense of mystery that lay about the moor so told upon us that we scarcely spoke, and then only in whispers.

"Let me carry the lantern," I said, as we drew near the Ragel, for which we were making.

"No, Jack, as you've got the stopping to do, I must hold the light."

When we reached the pile of loose rocks, Vennie went to ground, the patter of her pads striking faintly on the ear as she threaded the hollows between the boulders. She might have got half-way along when I heard the spit and fizz of some animal she had encountered, and presently the rustle of the fern caused by the creature in its flight.

"Where next?" I asked, when Vennie came out.

"Hannibal's Coombe."

"Then follow me; I know the ground by heart."

So I led in and out amongst the furze to Hannibal's Carn, getting a momentary scare from my own shadow upon the great wall of rock. Whether Loveday noticed me start at this hobgoblin of my own making, I do not know; but she said nothing.

On reaching the edge of the high ground overlooking the coombe, we stood awhile to listen to the chattering of a badger; then made our way down the zigzagging track to the tangled bottom where, close to a deserted adit, the earth lay. I stopped the five holes with the faggots lying to hand; then with a view to skearing the badgers who might undo our work, and let the foxes in, I stuck a paper flag on each of the beaten paths leading to the sett.

"The badgers are the plague of granfer's life," said Loveday, as she went round inspecting the stopping, "and nowhere more than here. He is always back by peep o' day to head the varmints off."

The next holt lay some distance along the coombe. It was neither an earth nor a ragel, but an underground place called a fogou, where the old people used to hide, and where, as Andrew told us, the tin-streamers had sought refuge from the press gang. The entrance was just big enough to admit a man, no more: and there without a word, Vennie went to ground, and was lost to sight and hearing quite a while before she came out of the far end, where we awaited her.

On, on we went, now over stretches of heath, now past brakes of furze and fern, now by rush-fringed pools that reflected the stars like a glass, and so in time reached the heart of the moor, where the boulders stood arrayed like tents on the dusky slopes.

"I feel like a spy, Loveday."

"I don't, I feel like one of the four men who stole out by night and found the Syrian Camp deserted."

"But they were lepers, we are lovers."

"Sh'! Sh'! Jack, you must not talk like that out here."

Soon we were picking our way past Bosprennis Mire, where the reeds stirred faintly, and from out the distance came the moan of the sea. Then we followed a trickling stream from which, with a cry of "'tchick, 'tchick!" a snipe rose, and at length we turned into the lane leading to Chykembra.

We had not got far along it when Loveday, suddenly looking back, clutched my sleeve and whispered, "There's somebody following; I thought so on the moor, I'm sure of it now."

"You must be mistaken: who would leave their bed to come after us? No, no, it is only fancy."

The homestead lay as still as death; and the only sounds in Zennor Churchtown, a mile farther on, were the stamping of some fowls on their perches and a noise which Loveday said was made by the rocking of a cradle. This was in the last house before we set foot on Tremeddu farm, which we crossed to Wicca Cliff, our farthest point eastward.

"Look out for a white-washed stone," whispered Loveday, as we held along the edge of the cliff, "it's here somewhere; that is the place where granfer goes down."

Soon we came on it. Two hundred feet below, the Atlantic lashed the rocks and raged in the caverns. The void before us, the noises beneath, were enough to unnerve the strongest: it was in fear and trembling that I let myself over the cliff. With one hand clinging to the tussocks, the other gripping the lantern, I made my way slowly down Andrew's path, my eyes watchful for the earth. Nearer and nearer I got to the seething foam without a sign of what I sought; and I was beginning to think I must have passed the earth, when I saw a narrow cave-like opening near the foot of the under-cliff. I took it to be an adit driven by the miners; closer inspection showed it to be of nature's fashioning, and beautiful beyond words. The roof and sides, as far as the light reached, were crusted with spar that projected like the teeth in a hound's mouth and glistened like precious stones; it was a dazzling sight till the dripping from the roof blurred the lantern's light and dimmed the sparkle of the crystals.

On hands and knees I forced my way to where I could see great pieces of quartz lying, and with these I built up a wall, as Andrew must have done a hundred times.

It had not been easy to squeeze my way in, I found it ever so much more difficult to back out, owing to the crystals which pressed against my sides and strove to hold me prisoner. But by twisting and wriggling, I managed at last to get out of the trap. Then I clambered up the cliff, punishing my knees in my haste to reach Loveday. I found her greatly agitated.

"I'm so glad you've come, Jack; somebody stole past whilst you were gone. What have you been doing all this time? I began to fear you were lost."

"And if I had been?"

For answer she gripped my free hand with both hers and dragged me over the brink into safety.

"She surely loves me a little bit," I said to myself as we made our way back to Tremeddu Cliff. There the descent was easy, wind-clipt scaw trees affording a secure hold most of the way to the earth, which, however, I had much difficulty in stopping, for the foothold was scanty and, to make matters worse, all the time a blow-hole, a few fathoms below, kept hissing like ten thousand snakes.

On leaving Tremeddu we went to Churchtown Cliff, where the white-washed stone was as rounded as a boulder from Gwenvor beach, and probably came from Bosigran foreshore. The precipice was in ledges, down which I managed to scramble without mishap till near the sea. There I missed my footing, and but for a projecting rock against which I dashed, should have fallen headlong into the surge. After a minute's pause, I pulled myself together, brushed the sweat and spray from my face, and forced the faggots into the holes, noticing as I did so that they were made of sticks of blackthorn, scaw and tamarisk, and bound round with withy from which the bark had worn.

On leaving the cliff – and I was glad to get away from it – we made for the Gurnard's Head, where lay the last earth on the beat. The long black foreland stretched out into the wild sea.

"There must have been heavy weather somewhere to raise such waves," Loveday whispered as we crossed the neck, "don't you see them?"

"Yes, I see their snowy manes and the welter of white water around the rocks. But tell me, where is the earth?"

"That's at the very point, a long, long way on yet."

In the silence that fell between us I heard strange cries, and was wondering what they could be when Loveday exclaimed, "Hark! do you hear them?"

Then I knew.

"Do you hear them?" she repeated.

"Yes, I hear them, 'tes the sea-mews screeching for the dawn."

"They are men's voices! Listen!"

"Not a bit of it; they are razorbills and guillemots on the Ebbal reef, not what your granfer would have us believe."

I said this to comfort her; but to this day I cannot tell whether they were not the cries of drowned sailors hailing their mates: I only know they sounded like it.

It was quite a long way to the point and the white stone below which the earth lay, but we reached it at last.

"I don't like leaving you alone with those old cries."

"But you must: the earth must be stopped, t'would be the death of granfer if the fox got to ground. If you are not long, I will bear with them."

So I left her again and began the descent. I found the way down here even more difficult than the others, and however an old man like Andrew managed to reach the earth is beyond me to explain; I call it earth, but earth there was none as earths go, nothing indeed more than a wide crevice near the foot of the cliff. Whilst I was in doubt whether this could be the hole I was to stop, I heard Vennie yapping inside; whereupon I put my mouth to the hole and called out, "Lu, Lu, good bitch, drive him out."

241

At this she must have closed, for putting my hand over my ears so as to shut off the roar of the sea, I heard the noise of a scuffle as if terrier and fox – for a fox it proved to be – had scruffed each other and were rolling over and over. Then the noise suddenly ceased; and I had only just withdrawn my head when a fox bolted out, knocked the lantern over, and disappeared in the dark with Vennie at his brush.

I was soon clambering up the cliff again, and the moment I reached the top, "Let us get away," said Loveday, "those cries are more than I can bear."

The thought passed through my mind that perhaps a kiss would comfort her; but I was desperately afraid of offending her and ventured no farther than to take her hand, which I held all the way to the mainland.

"I never thought," said she, "that I should be glad to get away from the sea, but I am tonight: your cliffs are more awesome than ours."

Presently we reached Trevean. How homely the townplace looked as we passed through! How friendly was the crow of a cock that greeted us just before we left the fields and struck across the moor for Lanyon!

"Night is giving way," said Loveday, as we threaded the boulder-strewn slopes.

"Yes, the stars are paling before the dawn."

Soon a tinge of colour showed in fern and furze and granite, and when at last the great orb rose it touched with gold the lichened crest of the Galver and lit up again all the familiar face of the country. But alas! it also showed the smoke from the gipsy's fire.

"What keeps that gipsy girl on the moor?"

"I can't say; I only know that she will be a trouble as long as she stays: and, by my life, there she is! See, she is trying to overtake us."

"She is white with rage, Jack."

"I see she is: you go on, I'll wait and hear what she has to say."

"The fair lady is too ashamed to face me after being out all night. Do not deny it. I saw you leave the cottage, I followed you all the way to the cliffs, and I would have pushed you over, both you and her, if I had not lost you in the darkness. But I will be revenged yet, and on both of you."

"Revenged? Whatever for?"

"Whatever for? You know well enough, but I will remind you. You for betraying Geordie, her for stealing you from me."

"You wicked woman: your foul lies poison the air."

"And shall soon poison the air of Churchtown, where I am going to let

242

it be known that you and that girl have been out all night together; I am on my way to tell Mr. Felton now."

"I warn you that the moment he or you dare utter one word against Loveday Rosewarne, the village will rise in protest, you and he will be tarred and feathered, and your effigies will be burnt on the green."

With that I left her speechless with rage.

"What did she say?" Loveday asked eagerly when I overtook her.

"That I betrayed Geordie to Felton."

"When all you did was to break your promise to him?"

"Nothing more."

And so we came to the cottage, to find that Andrew had returned to Forest Carn.

Mother pressed Loveday to stay to breakfast; but Loveday said she must be getting back, and left immediately. I went with her for fear she should be waylaid, but nothing happened till we reached Andrew's gate, where we found him looking towards the Carn. We followed the direction of his eyes – and there stood the gipsy woman talking to Felton, and gesticulating wildly.

Though I foresaw trouble in the gipsy's threat, I never dreamt of the trouble that was to come.

CHAPTER XXXV

GOODBYE TO DICKIE

~§

W
HAT THE GIPSY TOLD FELTON can only be guessed at; but this at least is certain, that two hours later Felton and Andrew were seen to enter Forest Carn together. This information I got from Johnny Curnow, who was clearing the culvert of the leat that supplies the mansion, and who not only saw them go in, but saw Felton leave, slamming the door violently and walking away in a rage. Felton went straight to Newlyn to forbid Dickie – so we have always understood – to go near Forest Carn again; if so, Dickie must have defied him, as whilst Johnny was eating his dinner, Dickie, dressed in his working clothes, passed hurriedly by him and entered the cottage.

Whilst Johnny, whose curiosity was now thoroughly aroused, was wondering what it could all mean, Dickie and Loveday appeared together, and, passing the turf-rick took the path between the pines leading to the Beacon. What happened in the plantation Johnny could not see; but there must have been a troubled scene, for when they returned Loveday was holding her handkerchief to her eyes, whilst Dickie, who came behind, looked – to use Johnny's own words – like a man who has received his death warrant. Andrew, who had come to the door, led Loveday in; and Dickie returned the way he came.

Nor was this the last scene of the drama enacted in Johnny's sight. In the early dusk he saw Andrew go along the track leading to Sunny Corner, and to Johnny's amazement he was carrying a little boat. It all seemed very strange; nor was Johnny able to make anything of it until he heard next morning that Dickie had definitely signed on as boat's carpenter to the *Mystery*. Then he understood all: that Loveday had refused him and, having refused him, had returned his gift.

When Andrew brought word of it to mother, she became greatly excited, and the moment she had heard him out, rushed across to tell Miss Jenifer. In a few minutes she was back again with a message from Miss Jenifer that Loveday was to be ready at two o'clock, when she would call for her and mother to go to Penzance. She took them to a performance of the Marionnettes in the Assembly Room, and afterwards to tea at the Union

Hotel, for no other reason I can give than to distract Loveday's mind from thought of Dickie, who was to sail the following afternoon.

On Tuesday morning master came to the barn door, and, holding up his hand as a sign to me to stop threshing, said –

"You can have the afternoon; I dare say you would like to see Dickie off."

"Thank you, master; I've been hoping you would let me go."

At dinner time I found a little silver pencil-case beside my platter. "What is this for, mother?" I asked.

"That is for you to give to Dickie as a keepsake."

I went straight away from the table, overtaking many, both men and women, bent on the same errand as myself.

Newlyn was belaurelled and beflagged; the quay, cliff, and shore were black with people. From the bridge over the river I could see the Mount's Bay fishing fleet moored in two lines that stretched from the pier-head away towards Penlee: the *Mystery*, with the Union Jack flying, floated proudly in the middle of the harbour.

But it was no easy matter to reach it. By elbowing my way through the crowd for what seemed like an hour, I got from the bridge to the steps near the light-house; and then no boat was to be had. I was thinking of having to swim for it when the gig which had brought me off the *Triton* came round the pier-head, and took me on board at once. It was but a few strokes of those long oars to the *Mystery*, yet in that brief space Matthey managed to put me many questions.

Dickie came to me the moment I set foot on the deck and, smiling as he spoke, said, "I have been looking out for you, and was beginning to fear you would not come in time."

"It's not my fault nor master's that I'm so late; there was no getting to you for the people."

"An immense crowd, is it not?"

"Enormous; the long voyage in a little boat is an adventure that has drawn everybody from far and near. And now, Dickie, before I forget, I ask you to accept this little pencil-case as a token of my lasting friendship."

"Thank you, Jack," he replied as he took it, "I shall prize it to my dying day."

Then, as the captain shouted, "All friends ashore," he gripped my hand and, with his clear eyes looking into mine, said –

"Goodbye, Jack; I wish you and Loveday every happiness."

"I believe you, Dickie; goodbye, and may God take care of you."

On that he turned to help cast off from the buoy, whilst I got aboard the gig, and was rowed ashore.

It was a thrilling moment when the brave little ship, with her mainsail hoisted, moved majestically towards the pier-head amidst the deafening acclamations of the onlookers, the crew standing bareheaded in acknowledgment of their enthusiastic send-off.

"Who's that young fellow next Captain Badcock?" I overheard a woman ask.

"That's Richard Felton, the boat's carpenter, and as fine a character as ever trod the streets of Newlyn," replied a tall, fair-bearded man beside her.

As soon as the *Mystery* passed between the lines of fishing-boats that were to escort her to the offing, the cannon began to speak; first from the Battery Rocks, then from St. Michael's Mount, then from Penlee, and last of all, when the fleet was well under weigh, from the two three-pounders at Acton Castle.

Resting on the harbour wall, I stood watching till the ship looked only half her size, then made for home. When near the look-out at Tolcarne I got one more sight of her, and watched till the escort had turned back, leaving the *Mystery* a mere speck upon the ocean.

My mind was full of Dickie; and I realised, as never before, the splendid character he was. He had never been known to tell a lie, to do a mean action, to talk or even listen to filth. I speak of him as I knew him at Daniel's; but what he was as a boy, he was as a man, only more matured in his high qualities.

When I crossed the village green and beheld the old school where we had spent so many happy hours, I made a covenant with myself that I would strive to live as nearly as I could at the level of my old schoolmate.

I was surprised to find Forest Carn in darkness, more surprised still when, on opening the door and calling, "Loveday," I got no reply.

"Wherever can she be?" I kept asking myself as I hurried home-along, and my first words on going indoors were, "Mother, do you know where Loveday is?"

"Yes, my dear, she is over at the big house; Miss Jenifer went and fetched her after dinner."

"Then I had better go across and see her."

"I don't think I would, Jack."

"Why ever, not?"

" Well, you see, she must be thinking of Dickie; it is not in human nature that she should not be. No, no, don't go near tonight."

It was perhaps as well I did not, for Miss Jenifer told mother that at the sound of the cannon Loveday turned pale, and for the rest of the afternoon was like one in a dream.

CHAPTER XXXVI

ROMEO AND JULIET

❧

O
N THURSDAY MASTER WAS UNEXPECTEDLY SUMMONED to Reskageage, and missus kept to the fireside by tooth-ache; so it fell to me to go to Penzance with the butter, eggs, and poultry, and to bring back the groceries and a score of odds and ends set down on paper by Miss Jenifer. On the way in I made up my mind to sell as dear and buy as cheap as I could, and this I did; but what with extolling my own goods and chaffering over my purchases, it was a quarter past two before I had got through my marketing and was free to have an hour or two to myself.

The first thing I did after depositing my bargains in the well of the trap was to make for Mr. Ackerley's cookshop, where I pacified my stomach with four threepenny pasties eaten standing at the end of the counter. From there I made for the labouring men's mustering-place, the Green Market, where I took my stand near the Three Tuns to look at the traffic and to learn what was going on. Amongst the company gathered there I recognised crofters from Brahan and Dowran, fisher-men from Sennen and Penberth, a Lamorna quarryman who told me he was out of work, Johnny Ladner, the Sancreed sexton, Tom Singleton, a light-keeper of the Longships, ashore on leave, and – as I knew by their Yankee beards and chains of bright yellow Californian gold – a sprinkling of miners returned from the diggings.

Carts and wagons from half a score parishes went by, now and again a farmer on horseback with his wife riding pillion, fisher-women with cowals on their backs and a ready answer on their tongues; Henry Quick, the Zennor poet, moved about selling his poetry, and, just before I left, the town crier came along, stood in front of us, rang his bell, and cried in a loud voice: "Lost, between Neddy Beddy's Lane and the Market Cross, a green silk purse containing five golden guineas, in the teens of shillings, and a brand new wedding ring: whoever shall return the same to the landlord of the Turk's Head will be handsomely rewarded."

When I had seen and heard enough, I went down New Road past mother's old school on the way to the Barbican, to bespeak some lime and to have a look at the sea in passing. On reaching the shore, I stood and looked out over the bay. A three-masted vessel lay at anchor near the Gear Pole, a shag rested on the Chimney Rock that was nearly awash with the tide, and a pilchard boat under her mizzen was making lazily for Newlyn, which looked wondrously peaceful with the smoke rising from its chimneys and veiling the upper part of Paul Hill.

As the arm of the quay caught my eye the scene of two days before flashed across my mind, stirring the imagination which conjured up the *Mystery* ploughing its lonely way over the waste of waters.

With the picture of the boat cleaving the waves, there came the picture of Dickie, as it had presented itself whenever I called him up, with a distant look in his clear eyes as of one lost in reflection. I tried to make myself believe that he was dreaming of the life that lay ahead but to no purpose; he was thinking of Forest Carn and of that last meeting with Loveday.

Then a brawling drunkard came along, shattering my thoughts, and I resumed my way to the lime-kiln.

At Sandy Bank I was again brought to a stand, this time not by a dream but by a travelling theatre, which had been pitched on a splat amongst the sand-hills. Whilst I wondered whether a play was going on, sounds of applause reached my ears and drew me to the bill pasted up against the woodwork. I read: –

"WHITE'S THEATRE,
under Royal Patronage.
Mrs. White's renowned company will play on
Thursday and Saturday the 13th & 15th
December, both afternoon and evening,
THE LAND'S END PLAY
entitled
DUFFY AND HUEY,
followed by the
LOVE SCENES FROM
ROMEO AND JULIET,
that famous drama of the immortal William Shakespeare, whose
popularity extends to the banks of the Nile, the Ganges, the
Amazon and St. Lawrence, where people of all colours unite
in adoring his memory on this side of idolatry, as that of the
greatest dramatic genius the world has ever produced."

249

"This famous love drama is the very thing for me and Loveday," I thought, "provided the language is fitted for Loveday's ears and the tickets are not beyond my means."

So to ascertain the price, which was not stated on the bill, I mounted the steps to the platform, and inquired of the Funny Joey seated on the edge of the drum there, smoking a pipe.

"Front seats sixpence; pit and gallery threepence," he replied in a low voice.

"And is the love drama fit for a young girl to hear?"

"What! Romeo and Juliet fit for a young girl? – well, I never! But there, for threepence you can buy a copy of both plays, and see for yourself."

"I will take a copy to once; and I shall require four sixpenny seats on Saturday if on reading it, the drama proves to be as clean as you say."

"Sh'! Sh'! you'll interrupt Romeo: you had better take the tickets now."

"I can't do that, sir, without using master's money, which I won't do."

"Very good," he said, handing me the plays in exchange for a three-penny-bit, which, however, he tried between his teeth before letting go his hold of the little book.

"Be in good time," he added, as I turned to go; "early doors threepence extra."

"What did you say about doors?"

"Early doors threepence extra," he replied, making a trumpet of his hands.

Puzzled though I still was, I dare not ask again; so I left, cudgelling my brains to find a meaning as I went down the steps.

A tremendous burst of applause, which drove the thought of early doors out of my head, made me more eager than ever to run my eyes over the play and see whether it was fit for Loveday's ears.

I hurried off to the lime-kiln, where I hoped to borrow a lantern, but finding the gates locked, I went on up Quay Street. Here there was a ship-chandler's shop, and by the light of a lamp in the window I started to read the play. The more I read, the more I wanted to read, and when I came to the end I was lost in admiration and delight.

It was about two lovers, another such two as me and Loveday, that is if Loveday loved me as I loved her; only Romeo and Juliet were of noble havage. But the trouble was that the families were at such enmity that the attachment had to be kept a dead secret. So whilst keeping company they, like father and mother, had to meet by stealth; and when they wedded, the ceremony had to be performed in the privacy of a Friar's Cell. To my thinking the play has one great defect – I mean the ending. Why, in the name of all that's good, did not William Shakespeare bring things right in the end, instead of finishing these two young people off with poison? Great as he was, it seems to me he made a mistake there.

The chandler, who came to his door just as I had finished, returned a good night to mine as I passed, going straight to the Western Hotel, where I helped the ostler to put Hector in the trap, and paid for stabling. Then I drove up Clarence Street on my way home.

On reaching Forest Carn I pulled up and ran indoors.

"I brought this for you to read," I said, handing Loveday the play: "I want you and Andrew to go with mother and me, and see it performed on Saturday afternoon. I'm going to stand treat; will you both come?"

"I shall be delighted," replied Loveday.

"And I too," exclaimed Andrew. "'Tis years since I saw a play acted; I should dearly like to see one more."

"Very good. Be ready by two o'clock, and excuse my running away now; I've got Hector outside, and a terrible restless horse he is."

"Anything wrong with Snowball?"

"No, Andrew, nothing wrong; master went off on him first thing this morning."

"Where to?"

"To Reskageage."

"What called 'un away?"

"I don't know. Good night."

Mother fully approved of the step I had taken, and was surprised when, on asking me how much money I should require, I replied, "Not a penny; I've enough and to spare."

"Enough and to spare? Wherever did you get it from?"

"Never mind where, mother: I can only tell you I had to work hard for it."

That quieted her.

On Saturday morning I was up at four; and when I had threshed, set out with lantern for Ding Dong burrows to fetch the six florins I had hidden there. I had trouble to find them, as a fox or a badger had disturbed one of the bits of spar and destroyed the bearings; but after a search, I came on my devil's money, as Maddern people call the proceeds of poaching. The coins were discoloured, but on getting back I rubbed them with quicklime, and soon had them bright as when mint-new. Then I put my back into my work so as to make things as light as I could for master in my absence.

At last the time came for tittivating ourselves for the play. Mother put her best dress on, and she was afterwards glad she did, for Loveday had done the same, whilst Andrew was not only in his Sunday clothes like me, but had actually gone to the expense of a brand new billycock for the occasion.

Loveday and I walked together; but our conversation, instead of being brisk and lively as became a young couple bent on pleasure, was poor and marked by dragging silences. Yet for all its seeming strangeness, this was natural in the circumstances. For ever since the sailing of the *Mystery* I had been thinking of asking Loveday to be my wife, and that morning on the way back from the mill I had made up my mind to do so after the theatre. And I shall always believe that Loveday knew my resolve.

We got very good seats: they were in the third row from the curtain, and such a curtain! I mean the painting on it. It pictured the pines standing in the sunshine on a hillside like Sancreed Beacon, with a homestead at its foot: mowhay, barn, maids milking, and in the very forefront, near a pool, a barndoor cock, stretched to its full height, in the act of crowing. We soon discovered there was a reason why the bird was so conspicuous – every now and again a man on the other side of the curtain cock-a-doodle-dooed so like reality that you would have thought the cock in the picture had crowed, if only it had flapped its wings.

At each crow we all roared with laughter; and in the interval sat waiting so quietly that now and then we could hear the sound of the waves on the beach below.

"Do you hear them?" I said, softly, in Loveday's little ear.

"Yes, Jack," she whispered in reply, "their music is very sweet to me."

"Are you happy?"

For reply she looked up at me with the lovelight sparkling in her eyes. And I was like one in a dream till two women behind me began whispering about our little party, and brought me back to reality.

"That's Mary Penrose just in front."

"Which one?"

"Why, she near to the old man."

"Law! so it is; but, dear me, how grey she's got; she must have had a pile of trouble. And who's the old man?"

"Why, Andrew Stevens, to be sure – he who traapses the country at night with a lantern; and the maid he's leaning forward to spake to is his daughter's cheeld."

"What! Honor's cheeld – the one the men are so mad after?"

"The same: caan't 'ee see what beautiful hair she's got, and how hand-some her neck is set upon her shoulders?"

"I was thinking so before you spoke: I'd give anything to see her face. Who's the young chap making up to her?"

"Why, that's Mary's boy – an anointed limb if ever there was one, and the plague, so they tell me, of Felton's life."

"Elizabeth Ann, thee'st mentioned Felton: wasn't Felton's boy Dickie once tokened to this same maid?"

"I don't know about tokened; report says she refused 'un, and that that was why he sailed in the *Mystery*."

"By all accounts he was a worthy young fellow."

"He was."

"And yet she refused 'un?"

"She did, I suppose: you see he wasn't such a fine upstanding man as the limb in front, nor so full of life and devilry; and you know what girls are – they'd rather have a madcap than an angel any day. See how he's making up to 'er, law look at 'un, did you ever see the like? in a public place too!"

"I'm watching; I caan't keep me eyes off. 'Tes better than any play, 'tis life itself."

I was on tenterhooks as to what they would say next, when up went the curtain, silencing my tormentors, and showing a kitchen in Trove Manor House, with Duffy seated before the fire, and Huey Lenine, an old sweet-heart, coming in at the door.

HUEY: What cheer, Duffy, my dear? Thee custna say now the lanes are longer'n the love, when I've come to see 'ee in this strame of rain.

DUFFY: Joy of my heart and apple of my eye, come by the fire and dry thyself.

[Huey sits at the far end of the chimney stool, and for quite a while not a

word is exchanged.]

DUFFY: How doesn't thee spake to me then, Huey?

HUEY: What shall I say?

DUFFY: Say? Why that thee dost love me, to be sure.

HUEY: So I do.

DUFFY: That's a dear. Bra purty weskit thee'st got up.

HUEY: I put it on to please 'ee, cost purty money too!

DUFFY: What did it cost 'ee?

HUEY: Gold buttons and all, two and thirty pence!

DUFFY: Take care of 'un then.

HUEY: So I will, for thy sake.

DUFFY: That's a dear.

[Another long silence.]

HUEY: I'm thenkan we'll get married next turfy season, ef thee'rt willin'.

DUFFY: How doesn't thee set a lil nearer then, 'stead of fouchin' off like that?

HUEY: Near 'nough, I reckon.

DUFFY: Nigher the fire, I mean. Well, I'll be married to 'ee any day tho' thee'rt no beauty, to be sure.

HUEY: Beauty or no, I'm very fond of 'ee.

DUFFY: Are 'ee?

HUEY: Iss fay, I'm always thinkin' of 'ee.

[Here he kisses her.]

DUFFY: Thy face is as rough as Morvah Downs, that was ploughed and niver harved. But I'll have thee for all that, and putty up the cracks, and paint them over, and make 'ee as purty as a noo wheelbarra!

[Here the Squire is heard calling his hounds: Duffy starts up in a fright, seizes a furze-prong and says]:

DUFFY: Maister will be here in a twinklin'. Look alive! Jump into the 'ood carner and I'll cover thee over with the furze.

[Huey hesitates.]

DUFFY: Then clemb into the oven, a little more bakin' will do thee no harm.

[Huey gets into the great oven as the Squire comes in.]

SQUIRE: Joan, I'm hungry as a hound!

DUFFY: Joan is gone to bed, maister, so I've stayed up to get supper for thee.

SQUIRE: Why I heard thee talking when I came to the door. Who was here then?

DUFFY: Nobody, only a git owl, maister dear, that had tumbled down the chimbly and perched upon the stool, glazin' upon me like a git blinkin' fool, till as you lifted the latch, he cried, "whoo! whoo!" and flew off by the way he came.

[The squire is satisfied, then stretching before the fire, he says]:

SQUIRE: Duffy, my dear, these stockings of your knitting are the very best I ever had; I've been out all day in the worst of weather, yet my legs are as dry as bones.

DUFFY: I may as well tell 'ee, maister, I shan't spin or knit for thee much longer, for Huey Lenine and me have been courtin' a painful long time, and are thinking to get married between the harvests.

SQUIRE: What! A young skit like thee thinking of getting married! Now listen to me.

[Then the squire, by promising her satins and silks and sparkling jewels, gets her to accept him, with the sad result that all Duffy has to say to Huey when she lets him out of the oven is]:

DUFFY: Now betake thyself off, outside the door,
    Nor show thy black face here any more:
    Don't think I'll mate with a poor pitiack like thee,
    When I may wed a squire of high degree.

When the curtain fell I got out of my pocket two paper bags of nicies, one of pear drops, the other of pine-apple, which I had bought at Mrs. Hampton's on the way down Chapel Street. Loveday fancied the pine-apple drops, which she and mother shared. The pear drops I handed to the mischief-mongers behind, and so kept their tongues quiet.

In my eagerness for the love drama, the time of waiting seemed endless; but the curtain rose at last, revealing a lovely moonlight scene: a mansion, an orchard, and Romeo jumping down from the wall. The moment he says, "He jests at scars that never felt a wound," Juliet appears at the open window over the doorway. The scene brought to mind Forest Carn on the night of the handbell-ringing and Loveday at the casement, but I dared not say so for fear of interrupting Juliet.

JULIET: By whose direction found'st thou out this place?

ROMEO: By love, who first did prompt me to enquire;
    He lent me counsel, and I lent him eyes.

I am no pilot, yet, wert thou as far
As that vast shore washt with the farthest sea,
I would adventure for such merchandise.

JULIET: Dost thou love me? I know thou wilt say "Aye,"
And I will take thy word.

Here I squeezed Loveday's hand, and by my life Loveday squeezed back, though ever so gently.

Farther on, after the ceremony in the Friar's Cell, we had the orchard scene again, and Romeo climbing a silk ladder to Juliet's chamber.

Then followed the saddest scene of all – the parting before the husband goes into banishment.

JULIET: Wilt thou be gone? it is not yet near day:
It was the nightingale and not the lark,
That pierc'd the fearful hollow of thine ear.

ROMEO: It was the lark, the herald of the morn,
No nightingale: look, love, what envious streaks
Do lace the severing clouds in yonder east:
Night's candles are burnt out, and jocund day
Stands tiptoe on the misty mountain tops.

Andrew was so touched by these words that he leant forward and looked at me. He seemed to be thinking: "Shakespeare must have been abroad many a time at peep of day. It's like that –and I never knew it till now."

[Soon the nurse appears, and addressing Juliet, says]:

NURSE: Your lady mother is coming to your chamber:
The day is broke; be wary, look about.

JULIET: Then, window, let day in, and let life out.

ROMEO: Farewell, farewell! one kiss and I'll descend.

[Then he goes down, but ere he leaves, Juliet utters words prophetic of their fate.]

JULIET: Oh God! I have an ill-divining soul:
Methinks I see thee, now thou art so low,
As one dead in the bottom of a tomb:
Either my eyesight fails, or thou look'st pale.

ROMEO: And trust me, love, in my eye so do you:
Dry sorrow drinks our blood. Adieu, adieu!

A terrible time for Juliet follows as her father and mother insist on her marrying Count Paris. To thwart their purpose, she takes a potion that causes apparent death and her body is laid in the family vault. There Romeo finds her and, believing she is dead, drinks poison, kisses Juliet, and falls down dead.

Then – oh, the cruelty of it! – Juliet comes back to life and finds her dead lover holding the cup from which he had drained the poison.

JULIET: O churl! drunk all, and left no friendly drop
      To help me after! I will kiss thy lips.
[Then, hearing the watch coming, she snatches Romeo's dagger, stabs herself, and dies.]

The sky was jewelled with stars when we came out and made up along for tea. And a good tea Mrs. Hampton provided: bread and butter, sponge cake and raspberry-jam puffs. Mother and Andrew ate heartily, I but little, for thinking what lay in front of me, and Loveday almost nothing.

After tea, Loveday and I strolled ahead of the others down the Mennaye fields, on our way to the Lareggan sand-hills. It might almost have been midsummer; the air was soft, the waves languid, and the moonlight asleep upon the sandbanks.

I think Loveday knew what was coming; she was so quiet.

All of a tremble I took her by the hand and said, "Loveday, I love you as I love my life, will you take me for your man?"

"If I say yes, will you not think me too quickly won?"

"Quickly won! what, after all this time?"

"And are you sure you will not weary of me?"

"As soon expect the sea to weary of the sands."

"It forsakes them twice a day."

"But only to return more caressing than ever, as I shall do in coming home from work."

"You give me your word?"

"I'll pledge my life if you will hold it."

"Then I am yours, my dear Jack, till death us do part."

Whereupon I clasped her to me and kissed her lips again and again.

"You love me?"

"I've loved you all along, you dear anointed limb."

Then arm-in-arm we went back to tell mother and Andrew, the wry old face in the moon smiling at us as we went.

"Mother," I said, "we're tokened; take her to thee."

And mother took her.

There was a bit of a crack in the old man's voice when, gripping my hand, he said, "I can die happy now, my dearest wish is fulfilled."

CHAPTER XXXVII

THE FIGHT

❧

THE NEWS THAT LOVEDAY AND I WERE TOKENED was known far and near in a day or two. Tongues had been set loose by our walking through Churchtown arm-in-arm, but the thing which proclaimed the tidings to the country-side was the ringing of the joy bells on the Tuesday; not just a round or two, but a full peal, as when the Squire's heir was born, and on the memorable occasion when Queen Victoria honoured Mount's Bay with her presence.

Felton, who happened to be in Churchtown, dropped into the belfry to learn the cause of the jubilation, and when informed, swearing a dreadful oath, went away in a rage. On his way home he declared to somebody who made it his business to tell Andrew, that the wedding would never take place, that he would have my life first; and Andrew, knowing Felton's wicked nature, came straight to Lanyon to put me on my guard. He found me in the barn. As I write I can see his grave face and hear the serious tone in which he delivered his message.

"Bless your life," I replied, "his words are mere froth; he means nothing."

"I wish I could think so, but I caan't; Felton is not the man to waste his breath in idle threats."

"You really think then that he will make an attempt on my life?"

"Do you think I should have come three miles on purpose to warn you, if I did not?"

"But why? what have I done that he should wreak his vengeance on me?"

"Evidently on account of Dickie."

"On account of Dickie! Did I cause him to sign on?"

"In a way you did; it was being crossed in love that made him do it."

"But because a man has been crossed in love, is that any reason why his father should threaten to murder his rival? Tell me, Andrew, did Dickie propose to Loveday?"

"He did, and Loveday refused him, and from Forest Carn he went to Sunny Corner, had a tremendous row with his father, and told him to his face that he would never return."

"Why a row with his father?"

"Why, because his father, after seeing me and learning that Loveday had really been out all night with you, went to Newlyn and forbade Dickie – if what I hear is true – ever to see Loveday again."

"And Dickie defied him, and within an hour or two was refused by Loveday? Well, Andrew, I am bound to say that I feel honestly sorry for Dickie; but why his father, who forbad him to see Loveday again, should threaten my life and prevent me and Loveday becoming man and wife, is more than I can understand."

"Or me either, but then there is no accounting for the actions of a black-hearted scoundrel like Felton. My advice is, take the threat seriously and look to yourself." And with that he was gone.

Andrew had given me so much to think about, that presently I dropped the threshel and started pacing up and down the barn to reflect on it. Before many minutes had passed, I had come round to Andrew's view and, in anticipation of a fight, was measuring myself against my enemy.

It would mean a stand-up fight, I imagined.

Well, in weight, height, and reach, there was not a great deal to choose between us; Felton's advantage lay in skill, in the force of his hammer-blows and in his power of lasting; against all which, I had nothing but greater quickness on my pins and smartness in dodging. He was of course much older, but he was a practised fighter; he had beaten in fair fight the famous Noy brothers, whilst all I could boast of was a bout in the belfry, in which I floored my fellow-ringers, and spoiled a bell practice. They were four stiffish chaps, I allow, but nothing beside the Noys, who were afterwards champion fighters in the Navy. Still I was prepared to go through with it; I would meet him.

But soon I found that things could not go as simply as that. On Thursday night Andrew warned me again, calling me into the garden to listen to the cry of a bird, as he said, but really to be out of Loveday's hearing.

"Jack, I've got more bad news; the man who came to me before, met me this afternoon to say he had reason to believe that the attack was about to be made, but how and where he could not tell me. My dear Jack, keep a sharp look-out, not only for your own sake, but for the sweet cheeld indoors. God help us! she's singin'! listen!"

"And as she went along the high road,
The weather being hot and dry;
She sat her down upon a greenbank,
And her true love came riding by.
She started up with a colour so red,
Catching hold of his bridle rein;
One penny, one penny, kind sir, she said,
Will ease me of much pain."

"Ah! she's worth facing any danger for, but the maddening thing is, there's no being even with a cunning, desperate man like Felton; he may wait for me behind a hedge, he may waylay me on the road tonight – and he's a dead shot. What can I do? What measures can I take? Can you tell me?"

"For one thing, I wouldn't move without a loaded gun; I wouldn't go to field nor pass, from mowhay to corral, or from corral to cowshed without one; for another I wouldn't follow your ordinary beats. Now let us go in, but with a smile on our faces, for the sweet cheeld is quick to note anything amiss, and wouldn't rest day or night if she thought thy life in danger."

"You've been a long time listening to the strange bird, granfer?"

"Only a minute or two, my dear, and part of that we were all ears to my own little nightingale; but what am I sayin'? Are not minits of separation like long hours to those in love? I won't call Jack away again."

Then we sat round the fire, Loveday in the midst plying her needles, whilst Andrew and I smoked. After a while Loveday said –

"You are very quiet tonight, granfer, and you, too, Jack; whatever is the matter with you? Have you something on your minds? If so, why are you keeping it from me?"

"My dear Loveday, an old man caan't be always talkin', and Jack, no doubt, is tired from his day's work; you must make allowances."

"Then I must talk as well as knit; I can't bear being in the doldrums."

Then she spoke of our great day at the Flora, of Prussia Cove, of the boats, the sea, the cliffs and the flowers that deck them in the spring time, and the birds that build on them. Last thing before I left, she sang a little love song called, "The Oak and the Ash."

At the gate she said, "Jack, you have been very cold tonight; are you tiring of me already?"

For reply I kissed her passionately, then tore myself away and made for home – not, however, along the road but, as a precaution, over the Crofts.

Friday broke gloomily, angry storm clouds obscuring the sun, which hardly showed throughout the day. Come afternoon I started off to see the moorland cattle, taking my gun with me. Instead of going by Trucks Lane as usual, I took across North Field and Further North, on my way to the Galver, which I reached without encountering Felton, or getting as much as a glimpse of the gipsy. There a woodcock rose almost under my feet, affording a tempting shot, but though I raised the gun, and a pull of the trigger would have made the bird mine, I refrained from firing. My restraint was due to a foreboding of coming ill that had taken possession of me soon after setting foot on the moor; a vague feeling that Felton was waylaying me, and that the charge in the barrel would be needed to save my life. Two or three times since coming through the gap in the hedge, I had turned in affright, expecting to find Felton's gun aimed at me, but saw nothing more than the heath, the furze, and the ferns.

I soon gained the ridge, from which I looked down on the coombe and had a view of the moor for miles. But where were the cattle, which, with the sou'west wind that was blowing, should have been in the sheltered ground below the ridge? Whilst I stood wondering, the sun broke through the clouds, lighting up the heart of the moor with its deserted mine and showing near it a white yearling. This gave the needed clue to the whereabouts of the herd. "Whatever are you doing on the Barrens?" I asked aloud, without finding an answer.

Strangely enough, I never thought they must have been driven to this poor feeding ground, but the dread which possessed me deepened as I journeyed thither. I covered perhaps half the distance without seeing any sign of life; then a raven flew croaking hoarsely over-head, and farther along a bittern rose from the reeds of a black, dismal pool.

"What next?" said I; "it's a wisht spot." The wind had scarcely borne my words away when Felton issued from the ruin and, with a heavy stick in his hand, came striding towards me. He was in his shirt sleeves, his head bare, his face terrible to behold.

"Stop," he shouted, brandishing the club. "I have business with you. I am here to settle the account between us. You have robbed my son of the girl that should have been his wife; you have driven him across the seas; you have desolated my home. I mean to have your life."

With that he flung the stick behind him and, tightening his belt, came towards me.

I dropped the gun, whipped off my coat and waist-coat, doubled my shirt-sleeves back and, as two of the holes of my belt had run together, tied my handkerchief tightly about my waist.

Whilst making the knot I shot a glance at my adversary. He stripped well; his chest was enormous, his forearms big with muscle; but what I recall best were his steely cold eyes that spoke of the revengeful heart within. To lash myself up to fighting pitch I thought of what I had suffered, and to show him that my spirit was not cowed, I stepped to within a couple of paces, and charged him with the wrongs he had inflicted.

"You say I have wronged you. What about me? You murdered my little dog. You set the man-trap whose marks I shall carry to my grave, you have done your best to get me transported, and – meanest of all – you have tried, you and the gipsy woman, to destroy the character of an innocent girl. Vile wretch, do your worst!"

He heard me out, then rushed at me like one demented. Stepping to one side I caught him a smashing blow on the right cheek, and stood ready for him when he came on again. But he dodged and landed a blow that made me reel. Then closing, he tried to get my head in chancery but failed, and in breaking away I tore the shirt off his back. We stood up again; and in pounding me about the body he exposed his face. Before he could raise his arms in defence I got in a blow which cut the skin above his left eye, and blinded him with blood. Then was my chance to go in and finish him off; but it seemed to me like taking an unfair advantage, and – fool that I was – I let him bind his handkerchief about his brow, and lost my opportunity.

"Haven't you had enough?" I gasped out, for the work had been fast and furious. For answer he came at me seemingly as fresh as ever, and at the end of the third round had beaten me to my knees. It was touch and go. If he once got me down he would strangle me and cast my body into the mine shaft.

The thought of losing my life roused every bit of strength left in me. Nearly done though I was, I felt I had so much to live for. Live for? I should think so! God in heaven! Loveday and I had agreed to wed in February month! I rose and met his furious onset with a resistance that must have surprised him. How long the round lasted I cannot tell; I only know that we fought till we could fight no longer, and stood with bodies half doubled and hands on knees, gasping like stranded trout.

He must have despaired of killing me with his hands alone, or surely he would not have had recourse to other means. On getting his wind, he staggered to the bush where he had thrown his club, seized it, and came at me as fast as his strength allowed. Meantime, seeing his purpose, I had grabbed my gun.

"Drop that club," I shouted, "or take the consequences."

But to do as I bid him was to acknowledge defeat.

Twice I avoided his vicious onslaughts; either blow would have laid me out.

"Have done," I screamed, "there's nobody looking on."

But no, he only gathered himself to come on again; nothing less than my life would satisfy him. Grasping the end of the barrel, I awaited my chance, and, as he raised his club to fell and finish me off, I struck him a heavy blow full on the temple and brought him to the ground, where he lay without a quiver.

Kneeling beside him, I cried aloud, "Mr. Felton, Mr. Felton, for God's sake speak!" but he made no sign, and all the time the bright blood, spurted from his forehead, saturated his handkerchief, till it was sodden through and through in one crimson mass.

I stayed by him for a few minutes, then ran to tell master.

At sight of me he looked horror-struck and exclaimed, "What has happened to you? You're smothered with blood."

"We've had it out: his body is lying on the Barrens."

"Felton's?"

"Yes, master, Felton's."

"Thee'st never been and killed him!"

"I believe I have: 'twas his life or mine."

"Then heaven help us!"

For a while he leaned against the gate of the pound like one dazed; then, coming to his senses, said, "Living or dead, we must bring him in." Without another word, we set forth with a stout hurdle and two trusses of straw. No need was there to point out where the body lay, for the cattle had gathered bellowing round, and the gipsy woman was there bending over him.

"My God!" exclaimed master, at sight of Felton's face.

"Is he dead?" I asked.

"Why ask, after the blow you gave?"

"Don't argue with her," said master; "get your jacket on."

We laid the body on the hurdle, with the straw under it, and started back with our burden; the cattle and the woman falling in behind and following to the edge of the moor. How long the cattle stayed there I cannot say; I only know that we heard their bellowing even when we reached the townplace. As soon as we had got the body into the house – for master would not hear of its being placed in the cart-shed – I was ordered to go and fetch the doctor.

Whilst putting the bridle on Snowball, I heard mother singing, and as I rode away she called out, "Where are you off to? Shall I milk your cows?" I was too much excited to speak, but raised my hand, which the dusk prevented her, however, from seeing, and luckily, for it was swollen and bloody. I galloped all the way to Penzance, where, as good fortune would have it, I met Dr. Giddy near Chapel St. Clare.

When I told him that he was wanted at Lanyon for an urgent case, he said, "You look as if you needed attending to yourself; been fighting, have you?"

"Yes, doctor," I replied, "I have;" and with that I turned the horse's head round and galloped away to Forest Carn. On reaching the gate I jumped off, left Snowball to find his way home, and ran indoors.

"Bless me! what a state thee'rt in," exclaimed Andrew looking up from his tea. "Been throwed, have 'ee?"

"Mercy on me!" cried Loveday, coming out of the back kitchen, "whatever is the meaning of it? Oh! my patience!"

Then I told them everything from the moment I sighted the yearlings on the Galver. They listened as though turned to stone, till I had done; then Loveday buried her face in her hands and wept aloud, whilst Andrew started out of his chair and paced up and down, like a man beside himself.

"Surely thee'st never killed 'un, Jack?" said he, stopping suddenly and looking hard at me.

"'Tis too true, I fear."

"Then God help thee, lad! help us all for that!"

"But, granfer," said Loveday, raising her tear-stained face; "Felton brought it upon himself: surely Jack was justified in taking his life to save his own?"

"Yes, my dear, that's good law, I believe, but theere's that gipsy woman to be reckoned with, and then theere's the Squire and his friends who will move heaven and eearth – I don't say to send Jack to the gallows, God forbid! – but what's almost as bad, to rot at Botany Bay. 'Tis a tarble business: theere will be a warrant for your arrest before the night is out."

"I'll not be arrested if I can help it."

"Sober, Jack, 'twould tell against 'ee to take to the country."

"Tell against me or not, Andrew, that's what I'm going to do. I'll never be led through Churchtown, if I can help it, like Black Jim."

"Couldn't father smuggle Jack across to France, granfer?"

"Time enow for that, my dear; it's the present I'm thinkin' of. If Jack is goin' off, he'll want victuals; so go and put what thee'st got in the big pocket of my oiler and a bundle of brimstone matches; he'll be glad of all three. And whilst Loveday is doin' that, you wash the blood off your face and hands, and listen to what I've got to say; for I shall be the one to bring thee food, as the ravens did to Elijah. Are you listenin'?"

"Yes."

"Very well; on Monday night meet me by the bridge in Lamorna Cove: Thursday at Carn Kenidzhek. Keep a look-out for the lantern any time round mid-night. Now, lad, 'tes time to be on the move; if thee'rt really goin' off; for the minute the murder is noised abroad, they'll come to take thee."

"I'm going, Andrew."

"Then, keep a brave heart, and remember that what-ever betide, Loveday and me will stand by thee."

"To the death, granfer."

I thought Loveday's heart would break when I kissed her good-bye.

"I can't bear to think of you being hunted like vermin, and every man's hand against you," she sobbed out.

"Bear up, my dearest love; sure as there is a God of Justice, all will come right. Comfort mother all you can; I fear 'twill be the death of her."

CHAPTER XXXVIII

OUTLAWED

❧

URRYING PAST THE CARN I reached the Sanctuary before I dared stop to think out where I should go. As Madron would be ransacked in search of me the moment hue and cry was raised, I dismissed the idea of hiding near home and turned my mind to the wild hills and cliff fastnesses, choosing for my refuge a cave near Lamorna that Dickie and I had discovered during one of the Saturday outings. Besides its secret situation and dangerous approach this cave offered the advantages of water and fuel; the water being drippings from the roof, the fuel flotsam which storms had washed into its recesses.

I had done well to fix on a destination: it gave energy to my movements as well as direction to my feet. I held athirt the Great Downs to Ventonvean Moor, and, passing the mill where I had seen the boy asleep and the ash-grove where I had eaten the barley bread, I came to Skimiel bridge, which I crossed. I was now in Sancreed. On reaching the church I sat down on the steps to consider which I should take of the three ways open to me: the road by Drift, which to this day some folk will have it that I followed; that by Catchall; or whether I should keep along the stream that rises under Bartinney and empties itself in Lamorna Cove. I chose to do the last; it was the longest distance to cover, and I felt I could battle with my troubles better afoot than cooped up in a cave.

So I made westward across the fields, leaving Tregonebris townplace behind and crossing the Land's End road to Boscawenoon Croft, where I struck the stream between the Giant's Foot and the Nine Maidens. Without a glimmer from a farmhouse to cheer me or a star for company, I felt so lonely that on reaching the Buryan road my heart leapt at the beat of hoofs. I was about to hail the horseman when I remembered I was an outlaw; and I kept close for fear of being seen or perhaps recognised.

After he had gone by I crossed the road, passed Vellandruchar mill and entered a sort of wilderness where, but for the guiding voice of the stream, I might have lost my way. However, I came without mishap to Trevider fowling-pool. Here master in his younger days had made great

267

play with the blunderbuss. It had been better for me if I had not known it; for the recollection called up the vision of him talking the tragedy over with missus and Miss Jenifer, and then – what was ten times more painful – of mother, stricken and crushed, kneeling at my bed.

"The very places conspire to torment me," I said aloud on passing Trove Manor House which, as the scene of the play, recalled the happy time in the theatre and the golden hour on the sand-hills, memories that flashed across my mind like lightning across a storm-sky, and left me a victim to the blackest despair. At Lamorna Gate I caught the roar of the sea, a sound more in keeping with my mood than the noise of merriment from the cottages past which I was stealing like a thief.

On reaching the Cove I made for Carn Dhu, and then for the place on the cliff from which Dickie and I had made our way down the face of the precipice to the cave. The descent was dangerous in broad daylight. It was ten times more so now; but by grasping the rocks and furze-stems, and holding on with my hand till I had found a sure place for my feet, at length I got down to the mouth of the cave. Here I crawled along a sort of ledge all but awash with the tide, and so gained the sandy floor beyond the run of the waves.

I lit one of the matches, stuck it in a crevice in the wall, collected arms-full of the drifted wood which I piled on the sand, and after a great deal of trouble succeeded in setting fire to it. The blaze, which lighted up every nook and cranny of my refuge, cheered me as nothing else could and, dreading the darkness when it died down, I kept feeding it till I tired. Then I scooped a hole near the embers, lay down on my side and tried to fall asleep.

But sleep would not come. I counted the sheep passing through the gate of Long Downs, I counted the yellow-hammers as I had often seen them at sunset sitting close-packed on the ridge of the barn, I counted the starlings roosting on the reeds; and then at last, before I had counted them all, I dropped off. I had feared that I might dream of Felton on the Barrens, but I need not have done so: I did not dream of Felton, I dreamt of my trial. The Guildhall was crowded. In the well of the court were master, Miss Jenifer, Andrew, Mr. Rosewarne, and Mr. Tasker, and opposite to them the gipsy queen, bedizened as on the night in the Funnel pit. Sir Rose, who had a seat on the Bench, kept looking at her, and so too did the Judge, in whom, despite the wig and the scarlet gown, I recognised my companion of the seal cave. Then the gipsy woman got up, entered the witness-box and began giving evidence. For a time she went on quietly, but presently she began to gesticulate and, turning so as to face the dock where I stood, shrieked, "I saw him do it." At that I awoke.

I must have slept for hours before I dreamt, as I had not been long awake when the dawn came stealing in; soon I was able to make out shag after shag flying very low over the sea which, but for a line of dull red glow, would hardly have been distinguishable from the sky. The lurid sunrise foretold the rain that towards noon fell in slanting sheets making a loud patter on the sea and blotting out a smack that had come into view. The wretched weather was in keeping with my feelings; and to a miserable day succeeded a miserable night in which I got scarcely a wink of sleep.

Next morning, as I was pacing the cave to try and get warmth into my limbs, the bells of Buryan rang out, calling up memories of Churchtown, of Forest Carn and of home. In that hour I seemed to drain the cup of misery to the dregs, and how I got through the day I hardly know. Monday proved fine, the sun shining into the cave and causing a network of reflected light to dance on the roof as I had many a time seen it dance under the hollowed bank at Boundary Pool. I gazed at the shimmering meshwork for hours, yet not with half the eagerness with which I watched the shadows of the cliff lengthen on the approach of night. For in the night Andrew was due; and long before the appointed time I climbed the cliff and kept a sharp look-out for his lantern.

It must have been close on midnight when at last I saw it following the zigzag of the great hillside. In my excitement I walked towards him.

"That you, Jack?"

"Yes, Andrew."

Thereupon he blew out the light, took my arm, and led to the edge of the cliff, where he said, "Speak low, I'm followed."

"Is Felton dead?"

"No, he's still hoverin' between life and death."

"How's mother?"

"Very bad, she's taken to her bed, but sent word that you're not to fret: Miss Jenifer and Loveday are with her night and day."

"And how is Loveday?"

"She's bearin' up brave; she sends her love."

"Any news, Andrew?"

"Mr. Pearce and Miss Jenifer have been to the mansion twice, but the Squire won't see them: there's a warrant out for your arrest; thee'rt posted on the church doors."

"Is Lanyon watched?"

"Iss, night and day, and Forest Carn too."

"Anything else?"

"That viper on the moor is musterin' the gipsies to search the country: not a Maddern man is out, nobody so far as I know except the constables."

"Ah! and is that all?"

"No; somehow the authorities seem to suspect that thee'rt hidin' in these cliffs; you had better shift your quarters and to once. Now take this," he added, handing me a parcel, "it's food to keep you goin', and a few broadfigs and oranges besides. Do 'ee know that yester-day was Christmas Day?"

"I'd clean forgotten it."

"Perhaps it was as well; anyway meet me Thursday at Carn Kenidzhek. Hark! they're comin' this way, look to yourself, lad," and with that he let go my hand which he had gripped, and was gone.

When Andrew and his shadowers had had time to get clean away, I went straight across country to Buryan, all curiosity to read the warrant. The village was in darkness, there was no sign of any living soul; and so I entered the church gates, walked up the path to the porch, and there, by the light of a match, read the warrant pasted on the door:

"WANTED for a murderous assault on Jethro Felton, of Trengwainton, Madron, John Penrose, of Mary's Cottage, Lanyon, for whose arrest, or information leading thereto, the sum of £50 is hereby offered.

"*Description.*

"Age twenty, but looks older; height six feet, well proportioned, stands erect, steps quickly; yellow curly hair, slight moustache, keen blue eyes ; winner of ploughing matches at St. Levan, Towednack, and St. Erth: well known as a bellringer.

"And be it known that any person or persons harbouring the absconder will be liable to the penalties which the law prescribes.

"Given under my hand this twenty-fourth day of December, 1848,

"JOHN CARMINOWE, SHERIFF."

Twice I read it down, then made for Bartinney, on which I had decided for my next hiding-place. On the almost bare summit I groped about until I found the pit from which Dickie and I had once started a fox, and there with the wind whistling overhead I curled up under the furze and fell asleep.

I awoke in time to leave my bolt and stretch my legs before the darkness had greyed enough to betray me to any one on the plain, and then returning to it watched the world about me take shape; the great hill itself, Caer Bran, Chapel Carn Brea, the croft lands and farms right to the cliffs, and last of all the vast expanse of ocean with the Lizard stretching out into it below a sky athrob with the coming of the sun.

At earliest dawn a badger had shuffled by on its way to the sett on the northern slope; with sunrise a hare came loping up the hill and on reaching the crest showed me a bit of wild life which delighted me even in the midst of my trouble. She laid trails now this way, now that, kept criss-crossing them till she had woven a maze that no fox or fitcher or indeed pack of fitchers could unravel; and then, to crown all, took a huge bound that landed her on a gurgoe, where her great upraised ears showed pink against the sun till she squatted amidst the withered grasses.

During the afternoon not fox nor fitch, but five evil-looking gipsies, came and searched the furze on the lower slope, beat out the scattered clumps fringing the summit, and, after running their eyes over it, crossed to the southern slope. They passed within a few feet of the hare, but the creature kept as close to her seat as I did to my pit and, like me, escaped with only a fright. But the thought that the murderous crew might return kept me in such a fever of apprehension that I welcomed the closing in of day when the fires died out of the low western sky where the Scillies had looked black as ink against the blood-red afterglow. The lantern had long been lit in the Longships before I forsook my retreat, stole down the hill, and made aimlessly across the waste land.

I wandered for hours uncertain where to conceal myself, until the passing of the night compelled a decision: when I made for Durval fox brake. On my way I almost stumbled upon another party of gipsies. Three of the four lay asleep, but the fourth challenged me. As I took to my heels he jumped on to the hedge that hid them, and started shouting, "Look out, mates; here he is!" Answering shouts came from the hills around, and for a moment I was so bewildered as hardly to know where to turn. But I soon recovered myself, swung off to the left to avoid the four gipsies whom I could hear tearing after me, and made for Botrea plantation. There I climbed the tallest of the pines, ensconcing myself amongst the spread of branches in the crown.

When the day broke I saw that Durval cover was surrounded by gipsies who, at a signal, moved towards the middle, beating the furze as they went. They did their work so thoroughly as to prevent any possibility of escape had I been there; and great was their disappointment to find a blank. To disappointment succeeded angry recriminations which threatened a free fight, averted, however, by the arrival of the gipsy queen – and on our little roan mare. She had, I take it, been summoned to witness my capture; but after a conference with the gipsies rode off again, and the band dispersed. One lot passed through the plantation, and, seeming to me, the very trees looked affronted by their intrusion.

I did not quit my hiding-place till long after dark, but I had already fixed on my next refuge. I had resolved to throw myself on the mercy of the Balieswhidden miners. When I reached the mine I crept up to the pumping-house and peeped through the window. The engine-driver, who was busy oiling the machinery, had a kindly face. That meant everything to me: I overcame my hesitation, went to the door, lifted the latch and walked in. The man, who was whistling "Cheer, boys, cheer," at first kept on with his oiling; but the moment he laid down the can and looked me in the face, he exclaimed –

"Why, thee'rt John Penrose!"

"I am, and have come to you for shelter."

"And you shall have it. I'm downright sorry for thee and thy mawther: heerd how ill she is?"

Without waiting for an answer he went on, "The gipsies are scouring the country, but we can hide 'ee where a whole tribe of 'em cussn't find 'ee."

"I shall be glad of a day's shelter."

"As long or as short as you like, but make your mind easy."

I went underground with the morning shift, and spent the day with three miners, who were driving an end at the bottom of the mine, interested to watch them bore, tamp and blast, which they did by the light of the candle stuck on the brim of their hats. These men shared their food with me, and were more like brothers than strangers. Their names were: Henry Maddern, John Rowe, and Ben Angwin, and I am glad to have been able to show my gratitude to them since. When night came I climbed the ladders to the surface, and, after thanking the engine-man, left by way of Bostraze to meet Andrew at Kenidzhek Carn.

Again it was near midnight before I espied the lantern, and then, to my surprise, not on Chun downs, but at the foot of the Carn. This so aroused my suspicions that I lay close, where I could get the bearer of the lantern against the stars as he passed.

"Good lor', Mr. Tasker! You ist it, sir?"

"Yes, Jack, I've come because Andrew is shadowed; and, what is worse, I bring bad news. Jack, lad, your mother is ill, very ill; she keeps asking for you, and you must go to her at once."

"I'll go, sir; but first tell me how Mr. Felton is."

"I can't say; I only know that he has been moved to Sunny Corner."

"The cottage is still watched?"

"Yes; but Mr. Pearce has got the men across at the big house, so you'll run no risk. Loveday will be on the look-out for you."

Loveday was at the door. As soon as she could speak for sobs she said, "You must see her at once," and led the way up. On the landing she turned and whispered, "Be prepared to find her much changed," and then, looking into the bedroom, "Mother, dear, Jack has come to see you."

"Where is he?"

I stepped up to the bed, took her in my arms and kissed her shrunken face.

" I am very ill, dear. Tell me, was it your fault or Felton's?"

"Felton's, mother."

"Thank God: kiss me, dear; I can die easy now."

Presently the lips moved, and I caught the words "Leaving you . . ." then "Father," and then after a pause, "Angels and Archangels," and with that her spirit fled.

Whilst Loveday watched at the open window, I dropped on my knees and prayed to be forgiven. I had not been long there when Loveday exclaimed, "That's the gate! they're returning; you must be gone."

So we hurried down the stairs, and as I tore myself from Loveday's arms, she said, "It will kill me too if it lasts much longer."

From the cottage I went to Sunny Corner, where a light burned in the parlour. Opening the gate quietly, and keeping to the turf I gained the open window and peeped in. There on a low bed lay Felton with face as pale as death. I thought he too had gone; but whilst I looked he turned a little, moved his left hand from under the clothes, and let it rest on what I saw was the model of the Mystery.

"Mr. Felton," I said, in a low voice, "you have killed mother; you are killing Loveday; why not confess?"

He made no sign.

"Jethro, why not confess?"

Turning completely round he looked towards the window. As I was about to appeal to him again, Mrs. Felton entered the room and, fearing what she might do, I withdrew.

I had run risks enough for one night, so whilst it was yet dark I made for Bosullow hill, where I hid amongst the ruined huts. Never before had I been so really unhappy. There had always been some little leaven of comfort, but now everything seemed lost; for me the dawn was hopeless.

As soon as there was light enough to see by, I opened a letter that Loveday had handed me; it was from mother.

I read: –

"MY DEAR SON,

"I cannot leave you without a word or two of explanation. I am the elder daughter of Mr. William Pender, of Rosigran, dead these many years. He disowned me for marrying your father. Whether he was justified, God will judge, but I have never regretted my choice. Your father was one of Nature's gentlemen; never once by word or by deed did he wound my feelings. And as you know, he was a good kind father. He worked early and late to keep you at school, went without his glass of beer, and even his smoke, in the hungry year, and all without a murmur. Hold his memory in honour. I am glad to be going to him, but distressed at leaving you. You will never know what you have meant to me; there was not a prouder woman in England the afternoon you read your composition before the Squire, and many's the time I've lived that hour over again. Ah, those happy school days! Your homecoming then, and indeed at all times, has been a never-failing delight; not once have I heard your step, no, not even in the dead of night, without a thrill. I die loving you as tenderly as when you were a child in my arms. My dear, give up dark ways and keep the little home together. The bits of furniture and china that have been my pride, the savings and the few things out of doors; all are yours. The trouble will surely pass, leaving you free to marry Loveday and live father's life over again. God bless you!

"Your loving Mother."

Mother's funeral was of the simplest; Mr. and Mrs. Pearce, Andrew and Loveday, Miss Jenifer and the old schoolmistress were the only mourners. From my hiding-place beside the road I watched the little procession go by, and when the bell ceased tolling, unable to resist the impulse which urged me, I hurried to the churchyard. My appearance, as was only to be expected, caused real alarm. Parson Veale seemed like one stunned. Mrs. Pearce clutched master's arm, Andrew stared at me in terror, Loveday alone remained calm as she came and stood beside me at the foot of the grave. Her composure had such a steadying effect that Parson Veale resumed his reading, and was nearly himself at the end of the service.

An excited consultation about myself followed, in which Miss Jenifer and Loveday stood firm for my return to Lanyon till overborne by master and Andrew; then they yielded, though reluctantly, as anybody could see. So I stayed behind with Jim Beare, who insisted on my going into church whilst he filled the grave. There presently he came to me and, sitting by my side, told me of father and mother's courtship and wedding, as I have related at the beginning of my story. The kind old fellow remained till it was dusk, and when he left I stayed on alone.

In the dead of night I went out, knelt at the grave, as I had already done at the altar rail where mother had been married, and begged and prayed for forgiveness for the trouble and anguish I had caused her. Presently the silence was broken by the creaking of the gate, and thinking the gipsies had found me, I jumped to my feet ready to resist. But there was no need; the intruder was no gipsy; it was Loveday!

"My dear, whatever brings you here this time o' night?"

"To find you and take you home! Felton has confessed! You are free!" she exclaimed excitedly, throwing her arms about my neck and crying like a child. But this time her tears were tears of joy, and soon we were hurrying back to Forest Carn along the road she had come. Half a score candles burned in Miss Jenifer's window as we passed, but ah me! how dark and dreary the cottage looked.

"Where is Andrew?" I asked, as we drew near Forest Carn.

"He and the Squire and half Churchtown are out looking for you."

"Pity we can't let them know I'm found."

"I'll see to that whilst you are making yourself clean and tidy."

I had hardly washed and changed, when through the back kitchen window I beheld great flames shooting up into the sky; Loveday had fired the beacon!

CHAPTER XXXIX

JOY-BELLS

❧

THOUGH I HAD BEEN CLEARED OF THE CRIME, I was still haunted by fear of the gipsies. I dreamt of them where I lay through the night in Andrew's chair, and next morning on the way to Lanyon I felt as if they were after me.

"Whatever makes 'ee keep lookin' over your shoulder," said Andrew, as we were descending Paunshallow hill, "thee'st nawthin' to fear now?"

"True," I replied, "but I can't help it. The gipsies are never out of my thoughts for long; though there's a worse trouble really."

"What's that?"

"Why, the empty cottage; I haven't the courage to go indoors."

"Theere's no need; thee'rt to live over across, at least for the time bein'."

"I'm glad of that; glad to be going to work again too."

"You'll call at the big house first?"

"Yes." And on reaching it I walked in.

At sight of me master broke down.

"Be a man, Henry," said Miss Jenifer who, like missus, was crying herself.

"I can't help it, Jenifer, for the life of me I cannot. See how the lad's troubles have told upon him; he's looking years older."

"I see he is," was all she could say in reply; though she tried to speak again and again, her emotion choked her.

It was a painful scene, too painful for me, remembering that I was the cause of it; so I said, "Master, I'm going to field."

"Very good; Fraland is as you left it."

I at once crossed over to the stables, put the gear on Hector and Madam, led them up the road to Fraland and started ploughing where I had stopped. It was good to be behind a pair of horses again with the smell of the freshly upturned earth in my nostrils. Yet even then I kept looking nervously about me.

After perhaps two hours of this I saw an oddly-dressed man hurrying along the road and behaving in a manner that aroused my suspicions. For despite his haste he stopped at every field to peep over the hedge, and every now and again, after resuming his way, leapt a foot or so off the ground as if to get a wider view and assure himself that he had not overlooked what he was seeking. Little wonder that my apprehensions were excited. But I laughed, yes, laughed the first time for many days, when I saw he was none other than Mr. Timothy Tripcony, the squire's butler, who presently dashed through the gate and rushed towards me, his long coat-tails flying in the wind.

"Wo, boys," I called to the horses as he came up.

"I'm glad to see you at work again," said he, grasping my hand; "night after night I have laid awake wondering what had become of you. I said all along you were innocent, but Sir Rose wouldn't listen. This morning I could hear him in the small hours pacing the corridor, and now he's like a man beside himself. His temper is something awful. 'Take this to John Penrose,' said he savagely, when he gave me this note; 'and don't let me see your face till you have delivered it into his hand, and got his answer.' That to me who had served him faithfully these five-and-thirty years!"

I read aloud, "Sir Rose Tresillian will be pleased to see John Penrose at the Mansion at 3 o'clock."

"For goodness' sake," exclaimed Tim, "don't say you can't come. I'd as soon take to the country as go back to Sir Rose with that answer."

"Tell the Squire, with my respects, that I will be at the Mansion at 3 o'clock if master can spare me."

"Let's have no 'ifs'. I can't face Sir Rose with an 'if' on my tongue; I can't, I really can't. Don't you think I had better see Mr. Pearce myself?"

" No, I think it will be all right."

"No thinking; are you sure?"

"Yes, quite sure."

"Then you will be at the Mansion without fail at 3 o'clock?"

"I will."

With that Mr. Tim took off over the furrows in his cloth boots, holding his tall hat as he ran.

At dinner I handed the note to the master, who said, after reading it, "Go by all means," to which Miss Jenifer added, "Yes, go and meet courtesy with courtesy; don't you agree, Andrew?"

"I do, miss; the Squire has been very unreasonable, and played us a nasty trick; but if he's sorry about it, why, he's taken the first step and should be met half way."

At half-past two I led the horse and trap round to the iron gate, and the next moment, to my astonishment, Andrew appeared at the door with the glass case containing the gamecock.

"Jump up in front, Jack," cried master, who came out behind him; "you, Andrew, get up behind and hold the case on your knees, glass outwards; I would not have it broken for a ten pound note."

Master took the reins and, after a wave of his hand to Miss Jenifer, drove slowly off. Not a word fell from him till we were ascending Paunshallow, when he turned to me and said –

"Be sure and speak civilly to Sir Rose: he was misled by your going off into thinking you guilty; who would not be? If he is going to admit the wrong he did you, return courtesy by courtesy, as Miss Jenifer said; and as a token of the feeling of Lanyon beg the Squire's acceptance of the stuffed gamecock."

"I'm still a bit sore, master, but I'll do my best."

The stable clock struck three as we pulled up at the mansion.

"One word, master, before I jump down; I've been running things over, and I think Andrew should wait in the hall till the Squire has had his say; otherwise the sight of the gamecock may put it all out of his head."

"Excellent, Jack, and don't forget what I said."

Tim must have been on the look-out, for he opened the door before I could bring down the knocker, admitted us as respectfully as though we had been people of quality, took us to the library, announced "John Penrose," and closed the door behind me.

Sir Rose and Lady Tresillian – for she also was there – came forward at once and shook me by the hand, her ladyship saying sympathetically, "Poor lad, you have suffered much; I can see it in your face."

Before I could get out a word, Sir Rose, who looked pale and troubled, began, "John Penrose, I wish to acknowledge the wrong I did you in getting the warrant for your arrest. I believed that you waylaid Felton to murder him; I know now that it was he who waylaid you and, I fear, for that very purpose. I repeat, I have done you a great wrong which I am anxious to undo so far as reparation can undo it. Now, my man, tell me what you would like."

"I don't look for anything, Squire."

"But you must, you cannot be so inconsiderate as not to allow me to make some amends."

Then Lady Tresillian said, "I understand that you are betrothed to the earthstopper's grand-daughter?"

"That is so, my lady."

She turned to Sir Rose, "I was going to suggest that you may see your way to place John on one of your farms when he marries."

"Clarice, I shall be glad to let him have the first farm that falls vacant; what is more, I am willing to stock it. For my own peace of mind, I feel that I cannot do less."

"No, no, Squire, you are very good but we shall be quite content with our little cottage."

"You had intended getting married in February, I think," said Lady Tresillian.

"That was our intention, my lady; but I don't know now."

"Then there is nothing I can do for the time being?"

"There is one thing, Squire, though I hardly know how to put it."

"You have only to ask."

"Well, Squire, it is this – you might show a better feeling towards master. Since that fox was found in Trucks Lane, you have avoided him at the meet, you have given him the go-by in Penzance. Sir Rose, you have wronged my master perhaps more than you have wronged me. All he asks is that you should pass the time of day when you draw his covers, and recognise him when you meet in the street. To show his wish in this matter he begs your acceptance of the only thing that he has that you are likely to value."

Here I opened the door for Andrew, who came in, holding the case.

"Well, I'm damned, it's old Spartacus; wherever did you resurrect him?"

Whereupon I told the story of the Towans. When I had finished, her ladyship exclaimed –

"Do you mean to tell us that you routed the whole assemblage of squires?"

"I did, my lady, but it wasn't me, 'twas the shiny hat and the swallow-tails that did it."

Her ladyship was greatly amused, while Sir Rose, who took it all in good part, looked more like his natural self. His voice, too, was less strained when he said –

"Thank your master for his gift, and say that for the future we meet as friends."

Then Andrew and I left, but had hardly got through the library door when her ladyship followed.

"Andrew," she said, "when the wedding is fixed, be sure to let me know the day."

"Thank you, my lady; I won't fail, my lady," he replied.

Master wanted to hear every word of the interview and by the time he drew up at Forest Carn to set Andrew and me down, I had told him twice over all that had passed.

"You have done me a good service, lad; I am delighted to know that the Squire is reconciled," and off he drove in the highest spirits.

Loveday was not a whit less eager than master, and kept putting question after question till I mentioned that Lady Tresillian had asked to be told the wedding day: then she fell to thinking, and for the time I found nothing to say.

It was a week before I mentioned the wedding again. "The cottage and everything in it is going to rack and ruin, and I'm miserable without you: can't you make up your mind?"

"Jack, you forget."

"I don't. Mother knew how lonely I should be, and was all for our marrying at once."

"She was, I know; but whatever her wishes, we must show respect for her memory."

January was half through before she would name the day; and then the fourteenth of February was her choice. Forthwith the banns were put up; we were in church and heard them read. The rejoicing was general, and the excitement great when it became known that Lady Tresillian was giving the wedding breakfast.

St. Valentine's Day was as fine a February day as ever broke: the sun shone brightly as master drove me to church along the road that had witnessed my troubles and my joys. At Loveday's wish I was wearing my corduroys, with a white satin rosette she had made for a buttonhole. Oliver Gendall was best man, and I was glad of his company at the altar rail whilst awaiting Loveday's arrival.

The hush that fell on the crowded church told me when she had come; and I can still hear the patter of her little shoes as she came up the aisle and took her stand by my side. She was in white with a spray of faded flowers pinned at the neck of her dress: and she carried a bunch of snowdrops I had picked early that morning. Her father gave her away; Parson Veale joined us together.

When we walked down the aisle, the band in the gallery struck up the wedding march, and the moment we were clear of the porch the bells rang out a peal of joy and triumph that was in our ears all the way to the mansion, where the breakfast was set in the servants' hall.

"If only mother had lived to witness this day," Loveday whispered to me as we sat at the head of the long table, filled with our friends.

Everybody was at his best: wherever you looked your eyes lighted on joyful faces. Loveday cut the wedding cake; and Mr. Tripcony carried the pieces to the guests. He had scarcely made the round of the table when Sir Rose and Lady Tresillian came in, offered their congratulations to Loveday and me, greeted all they knew, and then came and stood behind Loveday.

Whilst I wondered what was going to happen, Sir Rose said, "Friends and neighbours, fill your glasses. I am going to propose the health of the bride. This bright, joyous scene is the sunshine following the storm that threatened to wreck two young lives. That is my only reflection on the past. As to the future, we trust – I speak for Lady Tresillian as well as for myself – that the life of John and his beautiful bride will be one of continuous happiness; and on behalf of one and all, I offer Mrs. Penrose a hearty welcome to the parish."

At that the company rose and drank, Loveday acknowledging their good wishes with her sweetest smiles.

Whilst this was going on, Mr. Tasker came and whispered in my ear, "You must return thanks."

"But, sir, I don't know how."

"You must."

So, after collecting my thoughts as best I could, I got up and said, "Squire, I thank you and your gracious lady for the honour done to Loveday and me. We shall never forget it as long as we live. I am the happiest of men to be able to call Loveday my wife, but oh, the trouble I had to win her! She laughs at this, and points to the faded flowers as proof of her love from the very outset. They are the forget-me-nots which I picked by the millpool years ago. I can tell you exactly when: it was the Sunday next after I left my rod in the Squire's pond. (Loud laughter.)

"Sir Rose and Lady Tresillian, your kindness lays me under an obligation beyond my power to repay. But, Squire, I promise never to go poaching again in your preserves, either with rod or gun, so long as you live, and may that be for many and many a year, both you and your lady."

Shortly afterwards Loveday and I left, the company coming to the door to see us drive off. When we approached Churchtown, the bells broke out again, and so great was the ovation we received as we passed up-along that master had all he could do to hold Snowball. At length we left the village behind and came to our quiet high country: to the crofts and Quoit and Fraland. At Lanyon, the smoke was rising from the cottage chimney: and in the townplace Loveday and I got down and walked across the yard to our home.

THE END

GLOSSARY

A

abeer to bear or endure.

Abernethy biscuit a caraway-flavoured biscuit

adit an almost horizontal mineshaft used for drainage or access

airymice bats

anist, anyst nearby or close to

apple-bees wasps

arish stubble

athirt across

B

belving blubbering, crying out loud

blowth blossom

bra very

brake thicket

brandis an iron tripod which stands in the fire amongst the embers of turf or furze; used to support a kettle or crock

brembles brambles

broadfigs raisins

buccaboos scarecrows

bussa a large preserving pot

C

carn a pile of stones; crag

cayer a sieve

cheeld child

cheens the loins or small of the back

clayers boys' marbles made of brown clay

clome earthenware

cowal a basket used for carrying fish to market on the backs of fisherwomen - the basket was supported by a brow-band

craw a crow (bird) or a hut or hovel (as in "pig's craw", a pigsty)

crittur creature

croust refreshment of cakes and cider at harvest time; refreshment generally

crying the neck an ancient Cornish custom (now revived and institutionalised within the calendar of Old Cornwall Society events) when at the harvest's end, the reapers having cut their last handful, waved their hands and shouted to each other:

First harvester: "I have'n. I have'n. I have'n."

Second harvester: "What have ee? What have ee? What have ee?

First harvester: "The neck! The neck! The neck!"

All: "Hooray!"

cundard a conduit for water; a water course

cusn't, cussn't cannot

custna can't you?

D

daggin' draggling (as in "daggin' in the mud"); also longing or anxious to do something; or weighted down

downses moors, downs

dumbledores cockchafers

E

earthstopper the man who blocked up the fox's lair or earth in advance of the fox hunt

edna isn't it?

edn't is not

emmet an incomer

F

facin's spots or small infections

fairing a ginger biscuit

fay faith

ferny-cock a small brown beetle used as bait for trout

fitcher a polecat

flushet fully fledged

fogou a cave or underground chamber

forthy officious, forward

fouchin' poking around, being in the way
fowling-pool cess pit
frele small basket

G

git great
glassen also glazen, staring (as in "glazen lyk a stat", staring like a stoat)
gleany a guinea fowl
glim glimmer
grammer sows woodlice
granfer grandfather
groat silver coin
growan granite or granite-like ground
guise dance a kind of carnival at Christmas
guldice harvest supper
gurgoe a long narrow lane

H

hambros horse collar made of rope
handmow hayrick

I

I haben I haven't, I have not
iss, ess yes

J

jennyquick an Italian iron

K

kiddlewinks a beer shop
kidneys potatoes
killick small anchor
knaws know (as in "tha knaws", you know)

L

leat an artificial channel or trench for bringing water to a watermill
lewth a sheltered place
linhay a shed, open in front

M

mabyer a young chicken
mawther mother
mayhorn a large tin horn traditionally blown by boys on Mayday
morrops waste land on the edge of cliffs
mowhay a rickyard, an enclosure of ricks of hay or corn

N

narve nerve
nawthin' nothing
nicies sweetmeats
nigher nearer

O

'ood carner wood corner

P

peetha a well
piggywidden the smallest pig of a litter
piliack a poor fellow
planchen a board; a wooden floor
Powhll, the a well-known fishing ground west of the Scillies
prents prints
prinked out finely dressed or well turned-out
pulrose deep pit beneath the mill-wheel
purgy short, stumpy
purty pretty

Q

quillets three-leaved grass, clover
quoit a large thin, table-stone or rock

R

rab-pit pit of granite subsoil
ragel or radjel a pile of loose rocks
reapy infinitive version of the verb, to reap (as in "get tha zwy ta reapy the corn")
rubbing-post a post in the centre of a field for cattle to rub against

S

saa sea
scawtree elder tree
scratted scratched
shute a water channel made of iron or wood
skeared scared
sley sleigh, sledge
spence cupboard under the stairs
stares starlings
strothing hurrying

T

tarble terrible
taties potatoes
taws toes
tealing to till or set
thenkan thinking
tokened to betrothed, engaged to be married
towans sand dunes
townplace the farmyard
twick a sharp pull or tug; to snatch

V

varmin, varmint vermin
vears a sucking pig

W

weskit waistcoat
wether a castrated ram
whitneck a stoat
win'ard windward
winnards redwings
winnowy infinitive of the verb "to winnow"
wisht sad, low in spirits, pale in the face